BORN TO RULE

Cover Designer: Amber Thoma

Editing: Erynn Snel

Interior Formatting: KB. Formatting

PRONUNCIATION GUIDE

Mira – Meer-uh
Eurok – Yer-rok
Atreus – Aye-tree-us
Aethier – Aye-theer
Eiresh – Air-esh
Erezos – Air-a-zoh-s
Senuae – Sen-u-aye
Diablere – Die-ab-ler-ee

TRIGGER WARNINGS

Graphic Violence
Profanity
Alcohol Use
References to Child Abuse
References to Alcohol Abuse
References to Forced Abortion
On-page Consensual Sexual Acts

GLOSSARY

Aeithier – Light God.

Altar – A witch who has taken on an apprentice.

Druid – The prominent race of Vylandria. Ruled over by the Druid High Council and split into four clans. The Rider Clan, The Border Clan, The Dark Clan, and The Mountain Clan.

Erezos – God of mana and darkness.

Mana – The life force the Earth provides, wieldable by those who possess a mana core.

Seer – An individual with an innate extra sense beyond a natural wielder's abilities; ranging from emotional sensitivities to the ability to speak to the Gods.

Soothsayer/Shaman – A Seer who speaks directly to the Gods.

The Shaft – A shaft built into the back of the royal prison emptying into the Ebbonharrow River. Rumored to be used for the disposal of imprisoned wielders.

Variant – Also known as realm. Represents the various planes of existence on Earth.

Vylandrians – Residents of the province of Vylandria.

Witch – The female constituents of the Druid race who separated themselves to form the four covens led by four appointed High-Witches.

Calrund - The central province of Westryelle and home to most humans including the royal city of Bronne.

Decanting - The ability to transfer a being's soul or mana from one's body into a vessel or towards the veil.

To the ones who find strength in purpose and
solace in found family,
this is for you.

PROLOGUE

ANNORAH

A dust cloud bloomed on the horizon as the druid rider grew closer, racing to deliver the news of how my brother planned to kill me. A southern wind blew, tugging at my hair, carrying the faint scent of a distant fire—an ominous warning. One that caused the fine hairs on the nape of my neck to stand on end.

Three forest fires set waste to my people's land along the borders between Calrund and Vylandria, driving all beings and creatures away from the river. Druid forces were sent to drown out the fires, but I feared spreading them too thin would be a mistake. Druids were Vylandria's warriors. If my brother, Atreus, sought to attack with our father's army, there wouldn't be enough of them to defend the people. Vylandrians would fall to the humans without ever making a stand.

For hours, I stood here at the base of the Diablerie tree, where mana first blessed the land, waiting and praying for the gods' guidance. The Diablerie's blackened bark twisted into high-stretched leafless branches with tangled roots that grew in mounds over the ground. Here, the veil between variants of this world felt thinnest, allowing stronger communication with the gods and more control over my power.

Today, though, that control wavered. My heightened emotions invoked a chaotic storm cloud overhead as my mana roiled like an irritated serpent within my veins, waiting to take over when my restraint faltered.

I pressed my lips into a firm line, and dropped my head, doing my best to force the cloud to disperse. How had I been so foolish to have missed Atreus' hatred burrow so deep? These last three days, I spent examining every conversation we had, deciphering any clues as to what his plans were for this civil war he waged. Nothing made sense.

My power's shadowy thorns crept to the surface again, and I fought to reinforce my hold. It was no secret I struggled with control those first years after my blooming, but I never dreamed of using it against him. Still, could my mana be the reason for his sudden resentment, his fear?

Atreus and I were born with a sole purpose; to foster peace between the wielding races and humans, and rule Westryelle together. But two days ago, while I tended demands within the northern province of Vylandria, where most mana-wielders resided, Father fell ill. I made for the castle as soon as the raven delivered the message. In my absence, Atreus announced his regency over the kingdom and ordered the removal of all wielders from the royal city—including me.

The thundering of hooves rattled the earth beneath my feet, and I lifted my head as the rider clan's first in command slowed to a stop.

Vinz lowered himself from the horse and gave a gentle dip of his chin. "Princess Annorah, I have news from the borders."

My fists clenched between the folds of my gown. "Go on, Vinz."

"Before I report, Your Highness, I fear there is another pressing matter."

"What is it?" Trepidation bled into my voice. That he believed this to be more pressing than my potential death at the hands of my brother sent a flood of ice through my veins.

"The forests along the southwestern border are scorched, reduced to ash."

My stomach sank at the confirmation of my earlier suspicion—the warning carried on the bitter wind. A tingling sensation numbed my fingers, as it did whenever potent emotions washed through me. Beneath my skin, my power surged like a caged animal. I reined it in, though the corners of my mouth dipped with my agitation.

"Survivors?" I asked.

"I didn't stop, Your Highness. I came straight here."

"You were right to do so, Vinz. Thank you. Will you show me?"

The warrior nodded, and I stepped aside.

Thoughts of my impending death were forced down as I raised my hand and allowed that tingle in my fingertips to consume and spread, focusing on the space ahead. Veiling was a gift I worked tirelessly on mastering, and before long, a fissure formed, hovering and flickering just above the ground.

"After you," I said, waving Vinz on.

Something akin to curiosity and awe crossed his features. Druids didn't possess this facet of power. They, like most mana-wielding beings, were confined to nature's laws, with the few exceptions of soothsayers and silencers. Veil walking was not within those boundaries.

With a brave face, he climbed onto his horse and rode into the fissure. I followed after.

Entering the veil was similar to stepping into a shadowed space after basking in the sun. For the briefest moments, darkness consumed everything. When exiting, things eased into view, much like one's eyes adjust to light.

On the other side, charred earth crunched beneath our feet. The acrid stench of ash and burnt wood thickened the air, and I coughed at the sudden dry heft singeing my throat. My eyes stung and watered as I took in the scene, grief rattling my bones

3

to the marrow. Flames still licked and spat, devouring a portion of the forest in the distance. We moved toward it, scanning the land for any signs of life.

A small mound caught my eye as if something was buried under the debris. I bent down to dust a bit of the charred wood aside. Beneath, were the blackened remains of a Kerrigan fairy. Flames had destroyed its wings, leaving nothing but blistered cartilage where they'd once been. So much devastation, and for what? My legs went numb, then buckled, and I dropped. Blackened ash billowed around me, flecked with tiny orange embers as I hugged the fairy to my chest.

Kerrigan fairies were peaceful creatures. They tended to the forest's extensive interconnected system of mushrooms and vegetation, monitoring its health. They posed no threat to anyone. Yet they suffered the initial casualties of this senseless conflict.

From behind, the druid cleared his throat, drawing my attention. He nodded toward a distant rise beyond the thin haze of smoke, where a large white wolf watched from the hill's crest.

"Vinz." Heat and emotion distorted my voice. "Please see that these creatures are buried respectfully." I pushed to my feet and lifted the fairy into his arms.

The wolf regarded me as I approached, its sapphire eyes assessing the scene.

"Are you really going to make me walk all the way, Sidelle?" I called, trudging up the incline.

Its ears pressed back, and its head bowed before a whirlwind ensued around its frame, lifting black ash and bits of charred wood with it. With muffled thuds, they dropped to the ground. When the wind came to an abrupt halt, where the snowy white wolf once stood was a beautiful lilac-skinned female druid, or witch, as they now preferred to be called.

4

"My apologies, Your Majesty. The devastation has me a bit shocked," she said, starting toward me. "This is the worst one yet."

"Atreus." A quiet sigh chased the name. "It seems he wants to prove a point."

Within reach, she wrapped me in a gentle hug, and I returned the embrace. Composure and decorum didn't matter to Sidelle. I could be myself with her, and for that, I was grateful.

"How are you?" she asked, holding me at arm's length.

"It's hard to say exactly. I feel this could be resolved if only he would speak to me. But when I see this—" I shook my head at the ravaged decimation. "I just don't know how we got here."

Her dark eyes, contrary to her wolf's icy-blue, were glossy with unshed tears, conveying her pained understanding. She said nothing. There were no words to ease our heartache.

When Sidelle spoke, every sentiment held meaning and intention. It was in her nature to be precise. She rarely did anything without good reason. Soon after we met, I considered her a trusted advisor and teacher. As a powerful soothsayer and loyal friend, she would be a tremendous asset if this conflict with my brother escalated. *By the mountain.* The mere notion of considering such things was beyond belief.

"Come with me. Vinz has news of my brother's plans. I'd like for you to join us." I turned, and we walked down the hill together.

Vinz nodded in acknowledgment of Sidelle as we approached. The relationship between druids and witches was turbulent ever since the witch's cessation from the males, but Sidelle's tireless efforts resulted in a level of synergy between the two factions that steadily improved conditions over the last ninety years. Many respected the witch for her accomplishments, and because of this, she became a prominent figure in Vylandria.

"Vinz, if I may, have you heard any news of King Carlisle's condition?" Sidelle asked.

"Only that it has worsened. Many fear he may take his final breaths before this situation is resolved." His soft gaze found mine. "I'm sorry, Your Highness."

My mana shuddered, and my throat grew tight. If only my brother weren't keeping the healers from him. His stubbornness and sudden, unabashed hatred for Vylandrians was killing our father. I wondered if I'd even get the chance to say goodbye.

I didn't share the king's blood, but he was my family in every way that mattered. As was my brother, until he betrayed me. Now, Father lay dying in that castle, just barely visible on the horizon across the border of Vylandria and Calrund.

A curse flared in my thoughts. No matter how hard I tried, I wasn't able to veil into the castle as I'd veiled us here. Long distances and heavily populated areas were exceedingly difficult, but I thought, just maybe, I could make it. Wielding was about intention, after all. Sidelle taught me that. *I should have trained harder.*

There was no telling what poison Atreus filled Father's head with. Was he telling him I kept the healers from saving him, or that I abandoned them? The world swayed as I fought against the bile creeping up my throat.

"Why do you think Atreus had the forest burned?" Sidelle asked. "The places he's chosen just seem so... random."

"It's a message. He's showing us what he will do if this comes to war." I stopped myself from clenching my hands at my sides again. "His numbers far outweigh ours. He can more than afford to spread his forces between destroying the Vylandrian people and the land, obliterating everything we hold dear here."

Sidelle folded her arms around herself at the prospect. "But it's his land too."

"Vinz," I said. "Please tell us what you've learned."

The druid dismounted his horse and retrieved something from his saddlebag—a map.

In one fluid gesture of my hand, I lifted two fissures. With a burst of power, a large boulder at the river's edge rolled into the fissure beside it. A moment later, it emerged from the second fissure nearby. The druid unrolled the map of Westryelle and placed it on the makeshift table, using small stones to pin the corners.

"Four of the seven ships that sailed out of South Port have returned." Vinz pointed to Breckenridge, the southernmost province just beyond the Calrund border, then slid his finger across the map's surface. "Currently, they're moored at the royal city's docks."

"How long was their voyage?" I asked, hoping to gather information. If it took over three weeks, then the ships likely vacated the kingdom altogether before returning.

"We don't know the exact day they arrived, only that it's been within the past three days. Our sources confirmed they left South Port nearly sixteen weeks ago."

That long? I glanced at Sidelle, whose eyes already told me she understood. Atreus had been planning this for months.

"But what is the connection between those ships and Atreus' betrayal? Do we know what cargo they carried when they set sail?" I asked.

"Unfortunately, we do not." He leaned over the map, bracing his arms on the large rock. "Our scouts weren't successful in gaining access to the ship's inventory before they departed. But we found out what they *returned* with," he said, lifting his gaze to me. "Two scouts snuck onto a couple of ships while the fleet transitioned from the tributaries into the Ebbonharrow. They carried barrel-loads of fine ash."

Another tree succumbed to the smoldering embers, clattering to the ground in a cloud of hot flecks. We exchanged dejected looks.

"What sort of ash?" Sidelle asked.

Vinz gave a slight shake of his head. "We aren't sure exactly."

I straightened and crossed my arms. "Did they discover what he plans to do with it?"

"No—but we have a good idea what it's capable of." A level of caution sharpened his features. "While attempting to gather some for examination, one of our scouts came in direct contact with it, and... well, it left him entirely unable to call on his mana for a time."

Tense silence fell over our trio. "What sort of ash would have such power?" Sidelle asked.

I sympathized with the unease that painted her features.

Vinz only shook his head, unable to offer any words of explanation.

I lowered my eyes and leaned over the map again, scanning the waterways that spread throughout the kingdom. "Has his mana returned yet?"

"It has. The effects wore off quickly once the ash was washed from his skin."

Sidelle pressed close to speak privately in my ear. "What if he means to weaponize it? With such an advantage, in addition to the sheer size of his army, he could wipe out the entire population of Vylandria. Without their mana, even our best druid warriors would be nothing against his forces."

She was right. I swallowed against the thickness swelling in my throat. My stare fixated on the map as if answers to the endless questions plaguing my mind were etched within its lines. What Sidelle suggested was entirely possible—as were any number of things. The only certainty was that my brother intended to destroy everything and everyone I lived for. Our father.

Our people. These lands. He knew nothing of the devastating consequences that would ensue if he succeeded.

"Sidelle," I said, finding the most strength I'd spoken with in the last two days. When she looked up at me, I could have sworn she winced at the intensity she read in my eyes. "I need your help."

SIDELLE

"This is crazy! You can't sacrifice yourself." I half-chased Annorah as she paced at the top of the hill where we met earlier.

"I have to protect our people." She waved me off.

My patience withered quickly. "It would change nothing."

"It's the only way."

A charred stick snagged her black dress, and she stumbled. With the opening, I grasped her by the arm and pulled her to face me. "It isn't, though. If anything, you are leaving us more vulnerable. If that ash does what we believe, he could just as easily annihilate us once you're dead.

She spun away and put a couple of paces between us. "That is why I need *you*. Once I'm gone, you will take my body to Atreus and convince him you killed me for the good of your people—that you swear loyalty to him. If he believes the druids will serve him and he can benefit from their power, he will spare them."

"This is madness." I scoffed, cautioning her with a slow shake of my head. "And what of the druids? They won't serve Atreus once King Carlisle has passed. Not after this."

I couldn't allow Annorah to throw her life away like this. This feud had barely even begun. Vylandrians, humans, her kingdom—needed *her*. My lungs burned with the urge to yell, to make her see reason.

"Convince the druid council of this plan. If anyone can do it, it's you."

I was already shaking my head before she finished the sentence. "No."

"Sidelle," she paused, waiting for me to meet her stare, "there's no other way."

I wasn't giving up. My thoughts raced, scouring my mind for anything else. "You can veil. We can convince him you're dead. Rule from beyond the metaphorical grave until we have more information. A solid plan, allies, *something*." My voice pitched higher, conveying my desperation. "Annorah, please."

She closed the distance between us, nodding her head as I spoke, cupping my jaw in her slender, warm hands. "Yes. Yes, we need all of that. A plan, allies, numbers. This buys time for *all* of it. Don't you see?"

Her eyes burned with determination while my anguish consumed me. I gave a tentative nod, and she released my face.

"We can fake your death, Annorah." I couldn't let this go.

"Without a body, he'll never believe it," she said. "He needs to be convinced you killed me for the good of your people and that you mean to serve him."

"And what then?"

I sent out a surreptitious tendril of power, and a wave of nausea slammed into my gut. My attempt to sway her struck the invisible defenses that served as her protection against manipulation.

Annorah smirked sweetly. "That won't work, Sidelle. I will not be soothed out of this decision."

A quick burst of wind blew a cloud of ash. The small black funnel swirled over the ground, then dissipated in the air. *Time.* She meant to buy us time—and there would be no talking her out of it.

My resistance ebbed, and my loyalty took precedence over my instinct to keep her safe. If she required me for this plan to succeed, then I would do whatever she needed. *By the mountain.*

"What of Erezos?" I asked.

"Do you trust me?" A bit of her dark auburn hair floated across her face as she held my gaze.

My eyes fluttered shut as I drew a deep breath into my lungs. "I trust you," I said, then waited for her to tell me how she planned to handle the gods' stipulations on her and Atreus' existence.

My foresight was in direct correlation with the gods. I saw what they wished to reveal, only when they wished to reveal it. Two days ago, Erezos, the god of mana and darkness, ripped me from my consciousness, thrusting into the deepest corners of my mind.

Erezos was not solely a malevolent god by nature, but on the day he revealed Atreus' desire to kill Annorah, he promised his intentions to obliterate the kingdom as recompense for the destruction of his gift. Once released from his hold on my mind, I rushed to Annorah to warn her of her brother's deceit, but by that time, she already found out.

"What if we don't destroy my power?" she began. "What if we only destroy my body?"

At that, my eyes snapped open. My stomach twisted as footsteps signaled someone approaching from the base of the hill. Still, I could not pry my stare off the princess. "My gods," I whispered. "You want to decant your soul."

CHAPTER ONE

MIRA

923 Years Later

I rolled over and wished they'd all just shut the hell up. The birds chipping from atop the narrow alley walls and the merchant's carts creaking along the cobblestone streets were tolerable. But the baker's whistling? I stifled my groan, ignoring the ache in my hips and the ground's cold sting.

The warm scent of fresh-baked bread drifted beneath the door I slept against, taunting me until my mouth watered. I squeezed my eyes shut, forcing my thoughts elsewhere and my contemptuous stomach into submission. There was still time for rest. The sun hadn't crested the city's ivory stone walls, but when it did, it would bring with it that godsforsaken heat Bronne was known for. *Aethier's ass. I can't wait to leave this fucking city.*

Last night, this secluded back alley seemed the perfect location to rest. It was far enough from the riverfront market to avoid the steel-happy guards, but not deep toward the city's center where the slums waited, saturated in the filth of humanity. Though, the filth of humanity *was* my job.

The royal city hugged the northern border of Calrund, Westryelle's human province. Here, the wealthy lived their lavish, ignorant lives, gazing upon that ostentatious ivory castle,

13

all while pretending the rest of us didn't exist. Who could blame them, though?

From the outer districts, one could spend their entire existence and never see the depths of their city's depravity. The dark places cast in shadow and soot, where flesh and blood were as abundant as the rats. That was where I was headed today.

If I wanted my share of the highest-paying bounties in Westryelle, I had to endure these monthly trips. Luckily, I kept the only friend I ever truly had tucked into a sheath at my side. Early on, I promised myself I would only kill as a means of protection. But the truth was, I was always in danger, so I was always killing.

I never would've ventured within the city's center if not for the naivety of my youth—back when I knew nothing of the dangers that awaited me. In the slums, men had zero qualms about assaulting vulnerable women in the ruddy streets. On the first night after leaving home, I saw it happen. On the second, one of them came for me.

I'd never forget the bite of cold steel in my palm, mixed with the warmth of their life source pouring from the wound I caused. Up until that point, I'd never felt powerful in my life, never felt like I had a fighting chance in this world that had taught me nothing but pain, hunger, and heartache. Survival was all I'd known. But as I watched the light leave my attacker's eyes, and the rancid stain of his breath on my face faded, I felt relief. I saved myself.

In that brief moment of relief, an idea, fervent and unyielding, took root. I could do *more* than survive.

It was days later when I scored my first bounty, sealing my fate forever. I scraped by on the streets for months, learning to hunt the monsters among men. Taking them out meant safety, food, and, if I could become skilled enough, comfort. That was all I ever really wanted from life.

Now, eight years later, having worked my ass off to master the tools at my disposal, both of flesh and steel, I made a name for myself as the only female bounty hunter in the kingdom. I was eager to take on jobs with higher rewards. Doing so would enable me to establish a secure and comfortable life. And perhaps, someday, have a home of my own.

I was a new face to the greaseball who ran the bounty clerk's office. Still, he heard my name enough to recognize me the first time I darkened his doorstep. Despite my reputation, it required some convincing for him to give me his largest bounty on the books. In the end, though, what did he care if I got myself killed?

I craved a world where tyrants who called themselves 'gentlemen' couldn't prey on those weaker than themselves. Once I claimed this bounty I carried, there'd be no questioning my abilities. This would be the one to change things forever.

It was my most difficult mission to date, sure. Once I got in, however, it only took me fifteen minutes before I was on my way to Bronne with the poor bastard's head bobbing around in my sack. My plan was the same as always; get in, get the cash, restock supplies, then get out.

Footsteps from inside the bakery startled me from my lucid rest. Before I had time to react, the door at my back swung open, replaced by the angry baker's foot, kicking me from my resting place.

"Get outta here, you filthy little shit!"

The sweaty man clenched his fist and shook it at me, his face looking more like a plump blueberry every second. I feared it might pop if he kept yelling.

I gathered my things and stormed down the alley toward the cobblestone street. He spun a web of unnecessary expletives that followed my every step and grated on my nerves. I snatched a browning apple from my bag and chucked it at his head. He spewed another long line of insults and ducked. Despite my impressive aim, the fruit hit the doorframe with a low thud. Still muttering to himself, he waved me off with both hands, then rushed inside, slamming the door shut. *Cranky fuck.*

I readjusted my bag on my shoulder and ventured deeper into the city. The tempting scents of the riverfront market faded, replaced by the slum's filthy, vermin-filled streets. The bounty house sat in this dilapidated area of town between a bloodletting clinic and a dingy pub that I wouldn't have eaten at, even on my hungriest of days. In these parts, the buildings were decrepit and battered and the people looked much the same.

A worn sign hung from a rusty nail, pinned to a narrow wooden door with chipped, blue paint. When I pushed it open and walked inside, the expression on Goodrum's face shifted from hopeful to indifferent.

"I have no more bounties to give you, girl. I'm all tapped out."

"Somehow I don't believe you, Goodrum, but that's not why I'm here." I dropped the bloodstained sack on his desk with a sickening thud.

"What the fuck, kid! Get that off my desk. I run a respectable business here."

"Oh, please. The only thing you clean is your damn plate. A little blood is probably the least nasty thing in this office." I plopped into the chair across the desk from the paunchy man and crossed my legs.

"So who'd you bring me?" he asked, daring to lift the bag open a bit.

I let out a mischievous laugh when he gagged and snapped it shut again. "Yeah, it's been a couple of days. It was a long trip from Hanover."

"Hanover, you say?" His thick salt-and-pepper eyebrows raised high. "So that's where this ol' son-of-a-bitch's been hiding out?"

I nodded. "Caught him just outside town, squatting in a barn on some abandoned farmland. The place was guarded pretty well, though. Took me three days before I found an opening."

"I tried to warn you it wasn't gonna be easy."

"Did you know he'd have Vylandrian guards?"

Goodrum's ears perked, but otherwise, he seemed uninterested. "Nope. You know, most people just bring me a piece of armor, a patch of skin with a tattoo on it..." He poked the bag with the end of the fountain pen. "But no, not you. You bring me the whole godsdamn head."

"I don't want any confusion," I said, bouncing my foot.

"Hmm." He opened a drawer, then slapped the dead man's file onto the desk. "One, Mr. Greggor Hood, let's see." His face pinched. "Says here, the king wants this fellow himself." He flipped to another page. "Looks like you'll need to take this chap 'cross the river to get the lent you're owed."

I snatched the folder and reread the information. An inked decree scrawled at the bottom of the page declared whoever gained the whereabouts or proof of Mr. Greggor Hood's death was to report to the King's Guard.

"What does it mean?" I pressed the folder shut, then nudged it across the desk.

"Means this guy's wanted for something pretty bad. Probably more than the murder charge they have listed." He scratched at his chin, frowning. "I wondered why his bounty was so high."

"You never thought to look?" I asked through gritted teeth.

"Didn't care." He shrugged. "Doesn't make much sense if you ask me."

Agreed. In my eight years of hunting, I never encountered a king's bounty placed on someone for a single murder. My shoulders slumped with my sigh. I sensed the display of defeat on my face, but I didn't care. I intended to spend as little time as possible in this city. A trip to the castle was just about the least enticing thing I could think of. Maybe I could drop the head in an alley—grab another bounty elsewhere. But I *needed* the lent. Those days of scouting had cost me dearly. A roiling growl sounded from my stomach as if to echo that sentiment.

I pulled the bloodied sack from the desk. It dropped and swung like a morbid pendulum in my hand, leaving behind a grotesque smear.

Goodrum grimaced at the stain as he handed me the file. "Here, take this with you. They should cash you in up there."

"Should?" I asked, not dampening my skepticism.

"Come on, kid. I dunno. Never had one like this before." He held his hands up in mock surrender under my glare. "How about you stop back in here when you're done, huh? Let me know how it goes in case I see something like this again."

I rolled my eyes. "Yeah, sure."

I'll be back to shove your head in a sack next if this is a piss-poor attempt at a joke.

My shoulder rammed into the old stubborn door, then I stepped out onto the dingy street. Crumbling brick and sandstone walls headlined the stagnant environment—a compliment compared to the reek of working men and emptied chamber pots.

I jammed the bloody sack into my bag and pulled out a small strip of fabric from the outer pocket. My hair's thickness and raven-black hue was a curse in the godsdamned heat that midday would bring, and the morning air would've been comfortable if it weren't for the smells it stirred up. After gathering the strands, I braided them away from my face and headed for the market.

Here, the air sweetened with aromas of delicious pastries, curing meats, fruits, and foreign spices from all over the kingdom. Their scents drifted on the breeze as if cast out, tasked with luring hungry customers. I rounded the corner and beelined for a cart that sold my favorite roasted nuts—when I caught a glimpse of the castle across the river. *For fuck's sake.*

I was so hungry that I'd almost forgotten. I peered at my filthy clothes, stifling a grimace. Perhaps I should clean up first? My black, form-fitting hunting garb made it easy to sneak in and out of places unnoticed, but it'd been some time since I bathed. Blood and grime muddied my hair, and I reeked of travel.

Unfortunately, until I received my payout, I was dirt-broke—the last thing I wanted was to spend the day stealing an entire outfit.

As I passed, I looked into one of the dress shops that lined the streets. The doors were open, and the scent of roses and vanilla floated from within. The contrast between the heavenly essence and my stench stabbed at my confidence, but then I caught sight of the middle-aged woman behind the counter. Her upper lip curled like she found something nasty stuck to the bottom of her fancy shoe. I sneered back, then picked up my pace. I didn't want any of those gaudy floral monstrosities, anyway.

Difficult circumstances aside, I was no stranger to what it felt like to wear fine clothes, feast on rich dishes, and live among the elite. Though, thinking about those days left a sour taste on my tongue. Yet another reason I hated this city. Memories always clawed to the surface, no matter how deeply I buried them.

I turned to appraise myself in a storefront window, studying the lean lines of my limbs. My fair skin seemed to glow in contrast to the darkness of my hair and clothes. The glare made it impossible to see my burgundy eyes, but I knew they were ringed with heavy purple splotches due to my lack of decent sleep.

My attention lingered as I backed away. I spun on my heel to move on, immediately colliding with a passerby.

"Oh, my apologies." The man grabbed my elbow to steady me.

A string of curses sat on the edge of my tongue, but I cut them off when I met his gaze, then offered a smile instead. "My fault."

His tailored royal-blue overcoat felt clean and well-made beneath my grimy hand. His straight-backed stature and handsome, groomed appearance reeked of prestige.

Once settled on my feet, I took a step back and dipped my head in submission. "Thank you."

With a quick nod, he continued on his way.

I turned the small leather pouch over in my hand. After testing its weight, a wry smirk tugged the corners of my lips. I had plenty to suit my needs. I stuffed the man's lent in my pocket and started for the cart with roasted nuts.

Once I ate, bathed, and finished shopping with the lifted lent, I made my way to the castle. At the main gate, I handed the bounty file to the guard, and he hurried off with a barked order to stay put. When he returned, he appeared a bit more sweaty and red than before.

"The king would like to offer you a short wait in the gardens. We will retrieve you for an audience with His Majesty shortly."

"What? Why?" I demanded. "Just give me my payment so I can leave."

The guard's expression didn't change. He stood aside, then gestured with an outstretched arm for me to enter. With a sharp scowl, I passed through the large iron gates, unable to ignore the gnawing skepticism in the back of my mind. Why would the king request to meet the hunter of a bounty? The drive to bolt itched at my limbs, but I reminded myself, again, that I needed this money.

Three thousand lent—that's what I stood to gain. That would set me up for months. I could find a horse, stock up on supplies, and make it to Westryelle's southern province before autumn set in. Breckenridge, known for its sandy coasts and comfortable climate, was a good place to ride out the winter months. I just had to get out of this hellhole first.

When the guards left me outside the garden's entrance, taking the head with them, I lingered a short while before my curiosity got the better of me and I meandered toward the flowers. The romantic perfume of roses and the calming layer of lavender created a pleasant ambiance as my fingers danced along the delicate bells that grew in rows on the lavender's stem. A bumblebee hovered inches away from my hand, its fuzzy body caked in small bundles of pollen. I smiled as it dipped into another waiting flower.

I'd love to have a lush garden brimming with lavender and roses someday. My long days would crawl by while I watched bumblebees and hummingbirds zip in and out. I'd sip tea and read in the sunshine. Just like my mother used to do.

The thought pulled me into childhood memories of overflowing planters that hung from balcony railings. Their gentle scents wafted through our family home. Those were simpler times—back when my father was still the royal foreman. And my mother was still alive.

I followed the path of trimmed and polished stone, seeking a place to sit. When I rounded a bend of puffy hydrangeas, the expanse opened into a clearing. A large marble bench sat facing an elaborate fountain at the plaza's heart. As I found my seat, I rubbed at the tight muscles in my shoulders, studying the craftsmanship. The fountain's center depicted the god of light, Aethier, as a tall man with a falcon's head. The water fell in a glossy sheet at his back, creating the illusion of a tower of light. At the base were etchings and engravings of humans, all kneeling in worship.

I swung around and kicked up my feet, positioning myself to take in the array of flowers instead. I never paid much mind to the gods or their stories. That'd been more my mother's thing. Besides, prayer never proved as effective as quick wit or a steel dagger.

As I waited, anxiety simmered in the pit of my stomach. What had the sorry bastard done to warrant not only his death, but required me to answer for it, too? I scraped at the underside of my nails with the point of a small throwing blade, considering a multitude of scenarios. Had I killed a man who never murdered anyone? I overheard talk of illegal assassin work disguised as bounties, but never put much merit in those rumors. My frown tightened at the notion. If that were true, taking his life would contradict everything I stood for, violating the promise I made to myself.

There was nothing to be done about it now. For fuck's sake, I was still picking the remnants of the man's blood from under my nails. I earned this bounty—I might as well get my pay.

The symphony of clacking metal drew my attention as two guards approached. The glare of sunlight off their bronze armor had me squinting to make out the emblazoned seal on their chest. These were the King's Guard.

"Come with us," one said, though I couldn't tell which spoke. Their head-to-toe armor concealed any distinguishing features.

They escorted me to a side entrance, then down the castle halls to a set of polished wooden doors laden with decorative iron filigree. Floral fragrances permeated the air as I passed between two beautiful arrangements cascading from pearled vases. My nose crinkled as I fought the urge to sneeze. *Chrysanthemums.*

The hall's glass ceilings were steep and dramatic. Framed and focused as the centerpiece was a throne, ceremoniously raised upon a dais. Pillars painted in ostentatious design depicted victorious battle scenes. They stood tall and sturdy, supporting a shadowed balcony that oversaw the space.

One such pillar portrayed an armor-clad druid warrior and a human soldier caught side by side in the throes of battle against a drak. As the pillar curved, the scene revealed how the druid used his magic to ensnare the flying demon in a web of tangled roots, and the human's sword sank through the beast's chest. Its skeletal head was thrown back, epitomizing a guttural scream.

My mother often told me stories of when humans and druids fought against the drak. And how, following their victory, the former king built this castle at the center of the kingdom to encourage peace between the northern races of Vylandria and the southern human strongholds. One of her most precious possessions was a shield passed down through her family line, said to be used during the war. It'd been the only thing of hers I stowed in our carriage the night we fled the royal city following her death. I cherished it until the day my father stole it from my room, then sold it to buy more ale. *Bastard.*

The metallic creak of a door hinge echoed off the stone walls as King Atreus entered. He moved with the smooth, commanding confidence of a lion. All the while, the heat of his predatory stare made me feel like a potential meal.

When he came to a stop beside his throne, I sucked in a deep, steadying breath, then approached the dais. At the base of the stairs, I sank into as perfect a curtsy as I could manage in my leather and lace corset, and fought the urge to meet his eyes.

"So you are the bounty hunter who has brought me Hood's head."

The guard behind me moved forward and dropped the sack at my feet.

I searched my memory for the last remaining bit of tact I possessed. "Yes, Your Majesty." My voice was steady—a small mercy.

I finally lifted my gaze. His face was professional, soft at first, but something indiscernible crossed his umber eyes and his expression narrowed with suspicion. An icy chill prickled across my scalp.

"What do you call yourself?" he asked.

"Mira, Your Majesty."

"Mira?" He strung the question out, seeking my surname—one I refused to give ever again.

"Just Mira."

"And how old are you, *just Mira?*"

"Twenty-three."

He said nothing for a long moment. The depth of his gaze made me want to crawl inside myself and disappear. This was an excessive amount of attention to handle in one day, but I stood resolute, my eyes fixed ahead, longing for it to be over.

"Am I to believe that this," he nodded toward the sack at my feet, "is your doing?"

"If you're asking if I killed him, then yes."

The king's eye nearly twitched at my tone, but my patience was wearing thin.

"That's a big job for such a small girl."

My eyes narrowed at the patronizing comment, but I did my best to feign indifference. "I came here with the understanding that I would receive my payment and be on my way, Your Majesty. Unless there's anything else, I would like to do so."

"Who helped you?" he asked, ignoring my statement.

"No one."

"Who taught you?"

"No one."

"I find that hard to believe."

His grip on the back of the throne grew increasingly strained, and I almost expected to hear the wood crack beneath his white-knuckled fist.

"I'm sorry to disappoint you."

The unenthusiastic bite in my tone was not lost on him. He pressed his lips and stood there, glaring as if I were a vexing puzzle to be solved. My heart threatened to pound out of my chest as I surreptitiously gauged every exit, the number of guards, and how many weapons I had on my person.

My weapons.

If they meant me harm, wouldn't they have searched me? Surely they knew a hunter would be armed to the teeth. This agitation buzzing beneath my skin had to be paranoia—nothing more.

The king drew in a slow, deep breath before saying, "I'd invite you to stay, if you would, Mira. I have someone I would like for you to meet."

"I'm not sure I—"

"It won't take long, I assure you."

I wasn't eager to indulge the king's request. Every nerve screamed a warning, but I pushed those instincts aside and gave a single quick nod.

"Good."

With a nearly imperceptible gesture of his head, the guards seized my arms, their gauntlets bruising my skin. Another approached and searched for my weapons. I struggled against them, straining to shove them off. I banged my shin on a guard's greaves in an attempt to kick him off. Pain drew a hiss past my lips as they shoved me to my knees. My effort to stand again was overpowered as they finished their search.

"Why are you doing this?" Panic stained my furious tone.

Without a word, King Atreus left the way he'd come. The guards jerked me to my feet and dragged me from the great hall like a feral animal. I kicked, thrashed, and screamed until they tossed me into the dank dungeon in the belly of the castle.

CHAPTER TWO

SIDELLE

I hated walking these castle halls. The cold, gray stone echoed each footstep like a mocking, petulant child. The dank stench felt as if fresh air never graced the spaces within.

Without delay, I headed straight for the great hall, hoping to resolve whatever matter this summons held. It was crucial that I return to Vylandria, where I was needed, as soon as possible. My sisters were beginning preparations for the Honing, a sacred ceremony in which a high witch would be selected, and a new sister would join our ranks as coven leaders.

Death among the High Witches of Vylandria was a rare occurrence due to the extended lives we druids lived. This would only be the second Honing since our cessation over a millennia ago. That I was being called away from it only fueled my resentment.

The tight fabric of my lavender dress rode up around my hips, and I tugged it into place. My riding garb would've been more comfortable. Though, these gowns proved to possess their own influence—influence I strategically employed while working as the king's liaison to the Vylandrian province.

King Carlisle passed shortly after I laid Princess Annorah's body at her brother's feet all those years ago. Atreus became the official immortal King of Westryelle and after a few short generations, Annorah's name was all but lost to human memory.

While most regarded her story as legend or myth, I was never so foolish.

At the great hall's obnoxiously large doors, I paused, allowing my mana to enter before I did—carefully, as to not alert Atreus of my presence. Unless it was at his request, he didn't sanction the use of mana within the castle. The tendrils were invisible, but I could sense them clearly. Like smoke given intention, they acted as extensions of myself, sweeping over the room.

An uncomfortable amount of negative emotion saturated the energy, and my mana shuddered from it. Heated anger, like the leftover embers of a fire. Fear—and something *else*. A foreign chill nestled in my lungs, at odds with the day's tepid warmth.

I shoved the way open, and when I found it empty, unease settled beneath my skin. Stepping inside, I made the connection of what I sensed. A young woman, maybe in her twenties. She had to be the reason he summoned me.

I headed for the large council chamber where Atreus spent most of his time. Just before I could knock, the way swung open, and his severe features filled the doorway. Not an unpleasant face to look at, as much as I hated to admit it. Despite his current scowl, he usually wore a grin fit for the devil. His tall, broad stature was a huge factor in his initial appeal to the human population. His charisma was something to behold as well.

King Atreus fostered a relationship with his people. In turn, they respected him and his leadership. However, instead of using this trust to encourage humans to mend relations with wielders—or mags, as they called us—he allowed fear and distrust of mana to fester and spread.

Atreus' eyes slid over me like a snake sizing up its prey, and I steeled my spine against my instinct to recoil.

"Sidelle, I'm glad to see you."

"With all due respect, Your Majesty, I am eager to learn what was so important that required my immediate attention. I was making preparations for–"

"Yes, well, this takes precedence."

Cutting me off. Off to a great start.

He stepped around me. "Cade!" His boisterous voice ricocheted off the stone walls, bringing on the first pangs of a headache. "Have two men escort Sidelle to the dungeons. I'd like for her to meet our guest."

I pressed my eyes shut so he wouldn't see them roll. *You've got to be kidding me.* "The dungeons?" I asked. "What was this guest's crime?"

"No crime to speak of yet," he said, ducking inside the chamber. The scent of boot polish and tobacco lingered in his wake. "If my suspicions are correct, then we might both have reason to be worried."

"You already have me worried." I ventured a few tenuous steps toward him. In truth, it was that woman's energy that concerned me—that rich fear and anger she left behind. What had he done to her?

"I want you to feel this girl out. Tell me what you think."

"You won't give more detail than that?"

"No."

It took a lot of effort not to glower at the man. "Is she dangerous?"

"She's a bounty hunter. We've taken her weapons, but I wouldn't put it past her if she killed you the first opening she got." His face held a stoic mask of indifference.

In his eyes, my demise would be a minor drawback. He would miss the sight of my body, the convenience of knowing a seer, and the false impression that he had influence over the druids. *His ego will be the death of him.*

What he didn't realize—I was the only thing that stood between him, his people, and an entire army of druid warriors.

He reopened the borders many centuries ago, but there'd been a recent uptick in poaching, exploitation, and cruelty toward Vylandrians—all of which he turned a blind eye. His arrangement with me was the only thing holding that horse at bay. Though, thanks to Brodrick, one of the newest members of the Druid High Council, my hold on those reins weakened every year.

The guards to be my escorts approached, and I nodded to Atreus. He slammed the door without a second glance.

We descended into the bowels of the castle on a series of spiraling stone staircases, all attached by zigzagging hallways. The air felt cold and damp, as if it could penetrate my bones and settle in. The reek of mildew and dirt choked every inhale. Something about this woman clearly riled him, but what?

At the bottom level, the din of shifting gravel and dripping water echoed throughout. We stopped at a nondescript wooden door while the guard lifted the ring of iron keys into the torchlight. He selected one with a wavy pattern etched onto its surface, and I couldn't help but ponder the symbol's significance.

He struggled with the stubborn lock for a moment before the bolt slid free. When he tugged the way open, I cleared my throat.

"I'd like to speak with her alone."

They shared an apprehensive glance before the guard with the keys spoke. "I'm not sure that's a good idea."

"I didn't ask your opinion. Wait out here." There was more confidence in my tone than I felt. Regardless, I stepped past them, then shoved the way shut behind me. They made no move to object.

Iron bars ran the length of the chamber on either side. With shoulders squared, I canvassed the room. I sensed her, though

I saw nothing. The far wall sported a door with that same wavy symbol etched onto the keystone above the frame. *Interesting.* At the door, I raised onto my toes to peer through the small window near the top, hoping to satisfy my curiosity. Beyond the bars was pitch black, a hollow darkness. A distant, steady roar sounded from far below, and a chill spider-walked down my spine.

The river.

I spun around at the feather-light sound of shifting feet. *She's here.*

A strange chill filled my lungs, the same sensation I struggled to place earlier–

Something lurched out from behind, snaring my neck in a firm hold. I froze. My mana instinctively rose to the surface, but I kept it subdued. I sensed no intention to kill, only her need to defend herself.

"What the fuck do you want, witch?" Her voice was smooth and smoky, her tone hard. She *was* young, maybe just beyond her teens.

"I'm here to assess the danger you pose to the king," I answered.

"Danger? I wouldn't be here if the *king* hadn't set those degenerate fucks on me." She gave a firm tug as she spoke, a warning not to move, then raised her voice so the guards could hear. "And I want my shit back!"

Her words echoed off the damp walls, ringing in my ears. I'd definitely have a headache later.

"The king lacks finesse. An attribute I'm inclined to say the two of you share."

"*What* do you *want?*" she snarled.

"As I said, to assess the danger you pose to the king." The hostility in the air pulled my nerves taut. "I mean you no harm, and if you can prove the same, I will do my best to secure your freedom."

"Why did he send *you?*" she asked.

"He and I have a—special relationship." The words were acid on my tongue.

She released her hold, but retreated to the shadows before I managed to get a look at her.

"What does that mean?" A hint of dry amusement sharpened her tone. "Are you his magical whore or something?"

The thought of bedding that vile man... I shuddered, then feigned a gag. "Absolutely not."

She made a soft sound, as if considering, then stepped into the torchlight's weak glow.

"I'm going to use mana, magic, to brighten the room." I formed my words with caution, holding my hands up in a placating gesture. "Don't be alarmed."

She said nothing.

With a faint twist of my wrist, I summoned all static energy nearby to flow toward me. It condensed in my palm, forming a small orb. Delicate light lit the space just enough to reduce the shadows she could retreat into or attack from. While I nestled it on the crate beside the door, her gaze tracked me, assessing, so I took care to avoid any unanticipated movements.

When my eyes found hers for the first time, I inhaled a sharp breath and paused, unable to speak. Nine hundred and twenty-three years had passed since I last saw that face. The king's behavior made sense now, why he imprisoned her when she committed no crime. She bore the exact image of his sister, Princess Annorah, save for her black hair and the frigid, hardened distrust in her gaze.

She rocked back on her heel, arms crossed firm to her chest. "Why am I here? And why the fuck are you looking at me like that?"

I shook my head, unable to comprehend this—impossibility. "What is your name?" I asked.

"Mira," she said, her tone razor-sharp. "Listen, this is exactly how the king's interrogation started before he had me tied up like some godsdamned animal and dumped down here. So how about we cut the introductions and you answer my questions instead?"

Annorah's face, but all similarities ended there. Everything from her thin, hungry figure to the sharp edge of her glare told me this girl lived a very different life from Annorah. But her energy was what truly caused me to take pause. It was akin to being locked in a room amidst an unrelenting blizzard—intense, viciously cold, and yet, so familiar.

That raw, icy essence spread to my chest, blooming outward as I stepped closer, peering into those eyes. She possessed none of the warmth that Annorah once had. Still, the longer I searched for a trace of dissimilarity, the more my certainty took root. It truly was Annorah. That truth flickered like a small flame behind a wall of ice.

There was more—it bore a striking resemblance to the dungeon's bleak expanse. Still cold, yes, but *empty*.

I closed my eyes, ignoring the girl's impatient glare, and focused. Something echoed from within her, as if calling out to whatever it sought. When I narrowed in, trying to make sense of it, the essence *surged*. I pulled away, nearly overwhelmed by the sheer force of it.

My heightened apprehension shook my limbs, and I perched atop the crate to compose myself enough to formulate a plan. I needed to get this girl out of these dungeons—and fast. I'd have to think on my feet.

A pregnant silence hung between us before Mira took a few careful steps closer, her eyes darting between me and the ball of light as if worried it might go out. It wouldn't, of course. Mana didn't work like that. It was all about... Realization hit me like a forceful wave. That emptiness, why it felt as though it were calling out—it was her mana core. Shock widened my eyes as I inwardly reached for my own, that inner sanctum in which all wielding races' power resided. A mana core—inside a *human*. Just like Annorah.

As an empath, I was sensitive to the temperaments of others' mana. Annorah's felt like basking in the presence of an active volcano. Contained, it was a marvel of nature. Magnificent, but dangerous.

I readied myself and focused on Mira's core again. It was equally capable of bearing such power, but it was barren. It echoed its desolation like an eerie, melancholic song.

A flood of questions drowned my thoughts, but despite my desire to spew each one at her, now wasn't the time. I needed to put as much distance between her and Atreus as possible.

"So?"

Her voice startled me from my cascading thoughts.

"You gonna speak? Or just stare like the king did before he threw me in this shithole?"

I steadied my nerves, willing myself to maintain composure, and spoke with every bit of conviction I could muster. "There's not enough time to disclose my knowledge. Nor for you to answer my questions—and there are *many*." Her features scrunched, but I pressed on. "I'm your only way out of here, but in order to help you, I'll need your trust."

Repugnance flashed across her face. "You? A witch who willingly works for the king responsible for her people's hardship?"

"What would you know of *my* people?" I avoided coming off as aggressive, despite how deep her words cut. I needed her to see me as her salvation, not her enemy.

34

"It's no news your people suffer." She shrugged. "I don't take sides. I only call them as I see them. And right now, I see a traitor. So why would I trust you?"

"That's an interesting stance coming from a human who kills humans." I arched an eyebrow in challenge. "Sometimes we do the wrong thing for the right reason. For instance, kill to survive."

By her scowl, it was obvious she hadn't missed the jab. "If you know I'm a bounty hunter, then you know I can kill you."

A faint smirk conveyed my mirth. Her arrogance was intriguing. *She must be a damn good hunter with confidence like that.* "That shows me just how little you understand of mana, my people—and of me."

"As you said, I *am* human."

A human that possesses Annorah's face, a mana core, and one hell of an attitude.

I pushed out a deep sigh. This was going nowhere. "Tell me, if you refuse my aid, then what's your plan?"

Her mouth snapped shut.

"That's what I thought. How about we set aside our preconceived judgments, and you let me handle getting you out of here?" I stood and walked toward the girl, doing my best to ignore the uncomfortable cold that nipped at my senses.

The hem of my dress dragged like a sodden dish towel over the grimy stone floor as I stepped closer to ensure the guards wouldn't overhear. "I will answer all of your questions if, and only if, you agree to leave Calrund with me."

Her mouth opened, but before she could speak, I lifted a finger to silence her.

"Before you answer, let me remind you how very few options you have. I promise you this, King Atreus will not let you out of this dungeon alive—not without my help."

The intensity in her gaze and firm set of her jaw conveyed her inclination to tell me to fuck off. Then, like a trapped predator, she paced in tight circles, picking at her lips with her nails. A few heavy sighs later, she stopped and looked around as if weighing her petty few options.

When she spoke, her tone was softer than I expected. "I know what this place is."

"I'm afraid I don't follow," I said.

Her frown deepened, then she dipped her chin at the marking above the door on the far wall. "You heard it, right? The water?"

I nodded.

"Hang around enough pubs in these cities, and you're bound to cross a guard or two. Their tongues loosen like any other drunken bastard." A hint of disgust pinched her words. "They call it the shaft. Rumor has it any mag that comes to the castle is dumped down here. And they don't leave."

I stood there rubbing the soft fabric of my dress between my fingers, a nervous twitch, trying to puzzle out what she made of her circumstances—a human imprisoned in a cell meant for Vylandrians. The awkward silence stretched as I gave her the time she needed to form a definitive answer.

"Fine." She huffed a defeated sigh. "Get me the hell out of here, and I'll go with you."

I nodded, then placed my palm over our ball of light. At the brush of my hand, it dispersed into a burst of illuminated dust, the specks flicking out one by one. I didn't miss the spark of awe in those hardened burgundy eyes. *Annorah's eyes.*

When I left the cell, I stood tall and lifted my chin. "Release this prisoner."

Again, the guards looked at one another, and my foot tapped, conveying my impatience.

The guard with the keys spoke first. "High Witch, we would prefer to hear it from the king himself. We recall no mention of–"

"What I recall is his order for you to escort me and do as I wish." I pitched my words higher, selling my feigned frustration. "Now, which of you would like to suffer his ire when he's forced to repeat himself for your benefit?"

While he took a moment to ponder my integrity, I pushed my mana at their resolve, bending their judgment where my confidence hadn't. Using my power as much as I had today was a risk, but I was done playing it safe.

The second guard shifted his weight, his armor clinking together, then nodded to his comrade to do as I asked.

"Good," I said. "Now you may escort us to King Atreus."

I left Mira with the guards in the great hall, then let myself into the king's council chamber. He peered up from his work with an expectant, knowing look, and I spun on my heel to set a sound-shield spell over the entryway. A rippling sheen signified it worked, blocking any noise from leaving the room.

"How did you come by this girl, Atreus?" I asked, my back still to him.

The soft click of his quill returning to the inkpot filled the silence before he responded. "She claimed to have brought down a rather difficult bounty I posted."

I faced him with bated breath. "Who was it?"

He rose, crossing his arms over his broad chest, then stood before the large stone table at the center of the room like a monolith. "Greggor Hood."

My jaw clenched. A pulse of power strong enough to concuss the man surged beneath my skin, but I fought it back. Greggor Hood was dead. *Tomorrow's problem.* I forced my shoulders to relax and voided all expression from my face. "And you question if she took him out?"

"Not necessarily." He released the clasp at his neck and removed his long robes, tossing them over the back of his chair. After unbuttoning the cuffs of his tunic, he shoved the sleeves up over his muscled forearms. All the while he assessed me, waiting for me to speak the words that confirmed the suspicion he hadn't yet voiced.

"After meeting the girl, I will say her temperament is similar to that of an angry wasp rather than a well-mannered young woman. I have no doubt she is capable of what she says."

"Did she say anything?" The tension in his stature conveyed he was moments away from demanding I tell him everything I knew.

"Your unjustified detainment seems to have caused her to be a bit—resistant to my questioning," I said with a bite.

His brow furrowed, and he braced his hands on the table. His slow and decisive movements were meant to be an intimidation tactic. One he often used when I challenged him. I walked on treacherous ground, but the day's events weighed heavily on my resolve. I had no more patience for games.

"Unjustified?" Darkness settled over his features. "Sidelle, do you mean to tell me you don't see it? I'd think that you, of all people, would find my actions entirely justified. She looks exactly like—"

"Like Annorah, I know. And you wish to discover if she poses a threat."

Even under the heavy cloud of anxiety and anticipation, his eyes followed my hips as I moved across the room to the windows lining the wall.

"Are you saying she doesn't?" His tone took on an incredulous edge. Though he didn't say as much, it was obvious he wouldn't be swayed to release her easily.

My shoulder lifted in a half-hearted shrug. "Perhaps."

He dropped into his chair and leaned back, pinching the bridge of his nose. "Speak plainly, Sidelle. If this girl is connected to Annorah—if she is a threat to my kingdom in any way—"

"There is no connection to Annorah. Though she seems to possess a certain amount of talent for such a young age." I chose my words with care. "Perhaps you will consider keeping her close."

"Is it magic you sense?" he asked.

The disgust in his tone was beyond irritating. I let out a breath, ready to sell another lie. "No, I don't believe so." I took a few demure steps in his direction. "There's no reason to jump to conclusions, Atreus."

Though his shoulders relaxed some, anxious energy exuded from him, regardless. "I brought you here seeking answers, but all you're giving me are more questions." He flicked his wrist in a gesture of impatience. "Would it not save trouble to stifle the potential threat before it has a chance to grow beyond our control? Why bother keeping her close?"

A shiver rocked through my bones at the callousness of his statement. "You would end her life so easily? Even without concrete evidence?"

Tension darkened his earth-colored eyes. "If it means protecting my kingdom, I would do anything."

Kingdom, I inwardly scoffed, *more like power*. "I don't believe it needs to come to that."

39

"What would you have me do?" he asked, voice clipped. "Let her run free in my city and just hope that nothing bites me in the ass?"

The harshness of his tone set me on edge, and I stole a moment to allow the heat pouring through the windows at my back to calm my nerves. *Damn his spiteful, prejudiced ass.*

I often walked this precarious tightrope with the King of Westryelle. He teetered between the level-headed ruler—who had all the answers to the inner-workings of governing a human population—and this bitter, fear-ridden man whose suspicion of wielders and their mana made him unreasonable, unpredictable even. I couldn't decide which was worse, his ignorance, or his paranoia.

This conversation needed to get back on track. With a deep breath, I urged my mana to test the atmosphere. The tendrils discreetly uncoiled from my core like vines. They wound around him, tasting his energy while I monitored for any sign that he sensed their power.

They returned, confirming the worst of my fears. He had no intention of releasing Mira. He'd rather have her killed out of spite, just for looking like Annorah, than allow her to live in peace. Why had he bothered to send for me in the first place?

I paused at the thought. *Thank the gods he did, though.*

"Let the girl come with me to Raven Ridge," I said. His features soured, but having expected as much, I went on, "If she is as clever and talented as I suspect, then I feel it would be wise to familiarize her with the Vylandrian races."

He pushed from his seat in a disgruntled burst, making to leave.

"Atreus, please listen to me." I was on his heels. "If we do this correctly, then you will have an assassin like none other in the kingdom, someone with experience and training amongst the

Vylandrian races. If she ever *does* reveal some connection to Annorah, we will have seen every move she makes."

"Seen by who?" he asked.

"Me, Atreus. Someone you can trust."

His eyes narrowed in contemplation. I could only hope my confidence would do the trick to sell the lie I spun. I peered up at him from below my lashes, effectively sugar-coating every loathsome thought I had for this man who saw me as nothing more than a prized puppet.

He ran his hands through his short brown hair, weighing the options. All the while, I envisioned a flash of my storm-like power frying the bastard alive. *Oh, the relief it would bring me.* So many times I wanted to. It wasn't cowardice that stayed my hand. It was patience, perseverance, and hope. Hope that Annorah knew of what she spoke in the days before her death, and that when Erezos' gifted queen returned, we'd be ready.

CHAPTER THREE

SIDELLE

Time stretched on as I sat in that room, methodically responding to his barrage of questions. Many of my answers were outright lies, others were riddled with embellished or omitted details. I did what I had to do, said what I had to say; always, adamantly, denying the girl possessed any connection to Annorah or mana of any kind, and promised that if anything were to change regarding either, I'd report to him immediately.

Lying to him was easy, always had been, but I never employed so much deceit at once. I could only pray that nine centuries of service had earned me enough trust that he wouldn't question my motives.

However, once his concern over the girl ebbed, the conversation took a dark turn. We spoke of the advantages he stood to gain by employing an assassin familiar with 'magical' cultures of Vylandria. As much as it sickened me, I had to convince him he'd acquire those advantages to ensure the girl's security. I made the girl valuable and, therefore, safe.

One of Atreus' many stipulations was that Mira receive combat training from the absolute best Vylandrians had to offer. Eurok Dramagan, the druid army's newly appointed captain. The request was a test of my loyalty. Druids seldom welcomed outsiders, let alone trained them in their combat techniques.

Atreus knew this. Which was why his gaze brightened at the prospect—like a blazing midnight flame.

The girl sat across from me, curled tight in the carriage's corner, safe on Vylandrian soil. She was free.

My elaborate web of lies won me two years to convince Mira of who she was, then teach her how to access and use her mana before the king came asking questions and learned of my deceit. It wasn't much, but I'd make it count.

I settled against the plush headrest and closed my eyes. We traveled through the night and I was exhausted. While the girl slept, I spent hours pounding on the walls of my mind, demanding answers from the gods. More specifically, Erezos. What plans did he have for her, and why was I just now learning of her existence? The next two years might prove more successful if I had a clearer understanding of what to prepare her for.

I could push for insight until I collapsed, though. Erezos would only speak to me when ready. Even *I* didn't possess the power to make demands of the gods.

I fell asleep at some point and woke to find Mira still curled in the corner. She was so young, and yet she killed Greggor. The man who had more guards surrounding him at any given moment than the king. Such was the way when one dealt in illegal smuggling. His loss was regrettable, but taking him out spoke of the girl's skill set.

I adjusted myself in my seat and folded my hands in my lap, considering how to go about breaking the silence that dominated the carriage since leaving Bronne. I came close to speaking a few different times but never settled on the right words. Mira made it clear she saw me as nothing more than the king's traitorous magical pet, and as much as it pained me, I wasn't yet sure how to convince her otherwise.

It didn't help that I left the shackles on her wrists and ankles, either. Until I knew she posed no risk to the residents of Raven Ridge, and wouldn't bolt the first opportunity she got, this seemed the safest route. To transfigure into my wolf form and give chase through the woods would not be conducive to building her trust.

It was difficult to tell if she was still sleeping. She tucked herself tight to the plush cushions with her long raven-black hair hanging like a heavy curtain over her face. Her dark, short-sleeved tunic beneath her leather and lace vest exposed her light, blush-colored skin. Flecks and streaks of silver along her arms conveyed the many wounds she suffered throughout her brief life. Had she acquired the scars before or after she decided to hunt men for a living?

Knowing so little about the young woman who would soon share my home made the situation quite daunting. My mana tugged like an eager canine at the end of a leash, wanting to explore her energy. It was still unclear if the girl could sense such things. Had her core always been empty? Did she feel its presence? Did she know *anything?* The onslaught of questions raided my mind like a swarm of pestering insects. I batted them away as such. *One thing at a time.*

My impatience driving, I loudly cleared my throat to see if she'd stir at the sound. Not even a twitch. As I smoothed the wrinkled fabric over my lap in long swipes, I couldn't help but regret not changing into my riding pants before we left. This dress was as good as being naked.

Outside the large carriage window, I caught a momentary break in the treeline. Soft shades of pumpkin and periwinkle painted the sky as the sun stretched its light from behind the mountains on the horizon. Sunrise. We'd reach Raven Ridge by sundown.

I coughed—again trying to stir her. Nothing. *It's gonna be a long day.*

MIRA

The creak of wheels rolling along the packed dirt road set my teeth on edge. The incessant jostled squeaking and crunching was a steady, maddening roar. I would've slept better in the dungeon.

I ignored the witch's attempts to get my attention and only stirred when the carriage hit a hole, jarring me enough that I bit down on my tongue. *Fuck, that hurt.*

Unfurling myself from the corner, I stretched my tight muscles, only to have the motion hindered by my restraints. The cold iron clanked, and my wrists howled in pain where the skin wore raw. I clenched my jaw so hard my teeth protested, sick of being treated like an animal. In a fit of frustration, I grabbed a large handful of the metal links and shook them. They clattered and clanged, scraping against the carriage floor, until I dropped them in a heap and sat back, casting Sidelle a bleak, frigid stare.

The witch deadpanned, then returned her attention to her window. *Bitch.*

I peeked outside to see where we were. Dense Vylandrian woodlands took on a bruise-colored haze with the early morning light. I fought the urge to ask, like a whining child, how much longer it would take. I hadn't spoken since we left. Even though Sidelle secured my freedom, I wasn't convinced she was an ally. She seemed pretty disinclined to free me from these shackles thus far. My stomach tightened with my unease. Had I traded one prison for another?

Sick of the tense silence, I blurted, "Are these really necessary? We're in the middle of nowhere. Can't you take them off?"

"That depends." Her voice was like thick honey.

"On?"

She waited a few heartbeats before answering. "If you plan on running."

"If I do, will I be killed?" I raised a single brow.

"Not by me." She dipped her chin toward the dark trees along the path. "Though I can't speak for the forest—or the king."

My shoulders slumped as I slouched lower in my seat. "He set me free."

"Only because of the promise I made on your behalf." Her schooled expression of absolute certainty gave nothing away.

My eyes narrowed. "What promise?"

"It doesn't matter."

"The hell it doesn't!" I fired back. The overwhelming urge to punch the witch right in the face itched along my fist. Perhaps it was a good thing she left the shackles. "So I'm still a prisoner."

"You are not a prisoner, Mira."

"What the fuck do you call this?" I demanded, flashing my restraints.

She cast them a quick glance before locking her dark doe-like eyes on me. When she shifted in her seat and leaned close, I recoiled just to spite her.

"I need you to understand something," she said. "It doesn't matter what I promised King Atreus, because I have no intention of fulfilling that promise. Believe it or not, I hold no loyalty to him."

The sound that came out of my throat was somewhere between a scoff and a snort. I didn't buy a word of it.

"In fact," she continued, "I've grown rather tired of answering his every beck and call. He treats me no better than a common whore, a toy for him to summon and gawk at." Tangible spite sharpened her words. "In my centuries of service, not once has he offered me a position on his council, nor has he made me feel like a true voice for my people. No notable respect of any kind. My mana is a plaything to him. So no, there's no loyalty there."

She leaned in closer, placing a gentle hand on mine.

"You *are* safe with me."

I didn't buy a word of it. "Bullshit." I pulled my hand away. "Why keep the shackles on, then?"

"It's not bullshit, and I'll explain what I can in time," Sidelle said, still resonating calm. Her patience was impressive. "My life isn't the only one I'm worried about. Your restraints remain because, if you run, retrieving you before you get yourself killed would be no simple task." She settled back in her seat, giving me a once-over. "There's also the fact that you took down Greggor Hood—that alone speaks of what you're capable of. It doesn't help that you've been nothing but aggressive since the moment we met. Bottom line, those shackles ensure you won't hurt yourself—or anyone else."

A bitter twinge of guilt sank low in my stomach as I regarded her every word, weighing her sincerity. When reading people, listening to my gut hardly steered me wrong, but this was a gods-knew-how-old druid witch. My instincts were unreliable here.

"I thought you weren't afraid of me," I said, with less bite than before.

"I am bringing you back to my village, Mira, opening my home to you. My people's safety is paramount."

"So let me go," I pleaded. "Don't get me wrong, I'm grateful you got me out of that hellhole, but I have no idea why I was there in the first place. Just—remove these and I'll be on my way."

"It's not that simple."

"I can take care of myself."

"I believe that, I do." She clasped her hands in front of her. "Truth of it is, you are in grave danger, more than you realize. Please, let me help you."

I'd never seen such dark, obsidian eyes. Yet they were soft—softer than I expected. Unsure whether it was magic at work or the genuine look in her features—it was oddly easy to believe her desire to protect me. And though my pride writhed against the idea of needing protection, I sensed Sidelle had good intentions. Still, a burning question sat at the forefront of my thoughts. *Why* did she want to help?

"Do you plan on giving me a chance, or am I doomed to be shackled forever?" I found it difficult to remove *all* the acid from my tone. I wanted these fucking things off.

Her wary gaze met mine, and for a brief moment, I questioned whether she would truly keep the irons in place. Yet, her brows furrowed with sincere worry when she noticed the fresh blood seeping from the wounds on my wrists.

She loosed an uneasy breath. "Don't make me regret this."

I gave a tight nod, and she reached across the carriage, waving a delicate hand over the shackles. One moment, the cold, painful metal rested against my skin, and in the next, the cuffs on my wrists and ankles dissipated into fine metallic dust.

I started, struck by the potency of her power. How could something so limiting for humans hardly be a whisper of effort for her? I was at more of a disadvantage than I thought.

"Thank you," I said, quiet but honest, rubbing my tender wrists.

"Do you want me to..." She gestured at the small bit of crimson staining my skin.

"No. I'm fine."

The witch nodded and leaned back again, crossing her legs. The high slit running up her skirt slipped to the side, revealing her long, lean-muscled thigh. Her complexion was an elegant, unmarred violet, the color of summer storm clouds, and I found it hard not to stare. She was *beautiful.*

She tugged the fabric over herself, almost self-consciously, then opened the leather sack beside her. "Are you hungry?"

I was in no condition to refuse food. My stomach had been nauseatingly empty for hours. I accepted the pastry, apple, and small waterskin filled with sweet drink. The soft bread melted in my mouth like a glazed slice of heaven, and the juice soothed my parched throat.

"So," I said between bites, "who was the bounty? Why did the king want him?"

"Greggor served as a king's officer. He was a skilled warrior, but didn't harbor the same hatred for Vylandrians as many humans do. Eventually, he left the guard and started smuggling refugees into the kingdom. He was a—a mag smuggler." The witch winced at the words like they tasted foul on her tongue. "He snuck refugees from less fortunate kingdoms into the Vylandrian borders, where they would be safer under druid protection."

"Druid protection," I echoed. "And the king wanted him dead?"

"Clearly," Sidelle said.

Her cool mask fell a fraction as if, for a moment, her emotions were too heavy to bear. Then it was gone.

"And I killed him," I whispered, not hiding the guilt that gnawed on my conscience.

She gave a fervent shake of her head. "His death is not your fault."

I nodded, turning the red apple over in my hands. My bitter taste for the man on the throne grew more distinct in the back of my throat. He lied, used me, imprisoned me, then bartered my life as if it was his to give. And according to the witch, I still wasn't safe from him.

"Why am I in danger? What did I do to piss him off so much?"

Sidelle looked around, as if trying to decide where to begin. Sweeping a stray moonlight-silver hair out of her eyes, she released a slow sigh. "To put it simply, he believed you to be connected to his sister."

"King Atreus has a sister?" My teeth sank into the apple, its crisp crunch filled the carriage. I never heard of him having any family—aside from the long-dead king legend claimed he was gifted to.

Sidelle nodded. "Her name was Annorah."

I took a few more bites, waiting for further elaboration. Juices slipped down my chin, and I wiped them with the back of my hand, then tossed the core out the window.

When she offered nothing more, I asked, "Why would he think I was connected to her?"

"Because," she pressed her lips, seeming almost *sad*, "you look exactly like her."

The food in my stomach churned.

"Save for your black hair," she added. "Annorah's was auburn. But your face, those burgundy irises—identical."

I grew quiet, trying to process. My eyes had always been a mystery. Father'd been convinced they were some clue to my mother's betrayal. But to be mistaken for a princess? It sounded like something from storybooks. Still, if King Atreus threw me in the dungeons simply for *looking* like his sister, it begged to wonder what Annorah did for him to harbor such hatred.

"Where is she?" I asked.

"Dead."

"Did he kill her?"

Sidelle's eyes held secrets under lock and key, but I understood well enough. The king's sister was dead, just as I would've been had the witch not saved me. It was as if I'd been thrust from my reality, catapulted into someone else's life entirely. So many questions raced through my mind—I could hardly finish a single thought. Only one truly mattered, the same that repeated over and over since we passed through Bronne's gates.

"Sidelle?" I'd never given voice to her name before. She was no more than a stranger—a stranger who held my fate in her delicate hands. "What is it you want from me when we reach Raven Ridge?"

She offered a small, contrite smile. "I'm still trying to figure that out."

***

Hours passed, and the witch failed to provide a concrete answer. Under different circumstances, I would've fled the first chance I got, regardless of her intentions. I'd stick to my plan of riding out the winter in Breckenridge, then venture off to somewhere nobody knew this face.

But, after some level-headed appraisal of the situation, Raven Ridge didn't seem that bad. Fleeing meant navigating miles of unfamiliar forests, risking run-ins with any number of strange inhabitants. Seeing these forests for the first time reminded me of a book I owned as a child, *The Beasts of Westryelle*. In which I learned most creatures resided right here in Vylandria.

My interests had always been a stark contrast to other girls. While they liked romantic, heroic adventures, I loved to read about wolves as big as bears with dagger-sharp fur around their necks, and tricky wood spirits called nymphs that confused the minds of travelers, luring them to their deaths.

And night-mares.

Those were my favorite—a black horse with a fleshless skull for a head. Protruding from the space between their empty eye-sockets was a spiraled golden horn meant for impaling its enemies. Larger males bore fleshy wings, akin to a wyvern, and were said to be aggressive and extremely territorial.

I always wondered if they were real, or just embellished stories to scare us into staying far away from Vylandria. But if creatures like that truly existed, I wasn't ready to meet them. Thanks to the king, I never received my lent for the bounty—and the bastards never returned my weapons.

If Vylandria's beasts weren't dangerous enough to keep me from fleeing, the extensive trek would be. I'd need to cross the entirety of Calrund before reaching Breckenridge, though the journey itself wasn't what worried me. If the king found out I fled, he'd likely throw a bounty on my head. Unfortunately, I knew plenty of hunters who would be happy to oblige. Men I crossed, rejected, or out-killed—who still held a pathetic grudge against me. A king's bounty would be like ringing a dinner bell.

I'd have to be two teeth short of a smile to refuse the witch's aid. And though I was a lot of things—stubborn, impulsive, hot-tempered—I wasn't stupid.

I reclined against the carriage wall, observing the land transform outside. The forest dwindled into vast rolling plains. Streams cut along the road, peppered with late summer blooms and thick moss. My only certainty regarding this province was its immense size. I didn't know how far we had left to travel, but if we kept heading north, I'd need to acquire warmer clothes. The chill was already more than I preferred.

Last winter, I had a good thing going with the innkeeper's son in New Haven, near Calrund's eastern border. He ensured I had a bed to sleep in, provided he could warm it from time to time. And warm it, he did.

I never told him so, but I was grateful to him. Rhymes never tried to make us into anything we weren't. I'd been upfront with what I was, my lifestyle—and he never balked. Not even when I returned in the dead of night with blood staining my shirt, or when I kept my bounties' heads beneath the bed as he fucked me. He never complained, never asked questions. He was just—Rhymes.

I glanced at the witch, who'd been sitting in silence for hours. Her large, dark eyes darted behind closed lids, as if searching for something. I held my tongue this whole time, but it gave me the creeps.

"What are you doing?" I asked. A fraction of annoyance slipped into my tone.

Her eyes flew open at the sudden loss of quiet. "I'm seeing. Or at least trying to."

"Seeing?" I let out a small laugh. "Like a fortune teller?"

Sidelle's lips pursed. "Humans jest about soothsayer gifts as if they're nothing more than a party trick. We are highly revered among the druids."

I went silent and chewed my cheek, folding my hands in my lap. "So how much longer 'til we get to your village?"

The witch, trying to return to her strange meditative state, said, "It's a two days' ride from the castle. We should arrive at Raven Ridge by nightfall."

I nodded, mostly to myself, since her eyes were closed again. "So... what are you seeing?"

Sidelle answered with a frustrated sigh. "Nothing. The lines of communication are irritatingly one-sided." She dropped her hands onto the cushioned bench with a thump.

"Do the gods talk to you often?"

"Usually it's Erezos I speak with, but he's been silent for a couple of decades now."

My nose scrunched. "Who?"

She shifted, getting comfortable, then crossed her legs as if to settle in for a conversation. "Erezos, the god of mana and darkness."

"That sounds... ominous."

"Yes, I suppose it does." A soft chuckle escaped from Sidelle's lips, adding a touch of levity to the moment. "Not all darkness is malicious, just as not all light is good. But where light and life can never exist, darkness thrives," she said, pushing that same troublesome strand of hair out of her face.

I propped my feet up on the bench. "So why do you think your gods aren't talking to you?"

Her lips formed a tight line, and gave a dejected shrug.

A heavy blanket of shadow fell over the carriage, drawing our attention. We turned to the windows to see the sun's rays crowded from the sky by dark clouds. I hurried forward and pressed my face against the window, hoping to get a view of the sky above. The cool glass bit at my warm cheek as my eyes widened at the sight.

Overhead, clouds churned like thick, inky swirls bolstered by heavy winds. The immense, slow, thunderous roll that escaped them made the land shudder. A shape in the distance caught my eye. Amidst the overgrown, sun-kissed grass that danced in the wind were gray formations. They strewed about the ground in all directions, varying in shape and size.

A flash of lightning streaked the sky, illuminating the fields below, and I narrowed my eyes to make out what they were. Broken stone men. There were so many of them.

"What is this place?"

"The stone forest." A hint of sorrow dusted her words. She leaned forward to get her own view of the massive stones.

"Who carved them?"

"They weren't carved. They, at one time, lived."

My ears perked, and my gaze snapped to hers. "What happened to them?"

Instead of answering, Sidelle pulled a long wooden staff from behind the drapery, then used it to knock on the far wall, alerting the coachman. The staff bore beautiful intricate carvings all along the sand-colored wood. However, what really caught my attention was the decorative rough-hewn stone affixed to the top. Iridescent even in the muted light, and larger than my fist.

A moonstone—one that would fetch a small fortune in the dark markets. Aside from its beauty, there was something strange about it. This allure—a dull tugging within my chest that I couldn't explain. An invisible tether pulled taut.

Sidelle noticed my lingering gaze, and I forced my eyes away, doing my best to seem unphased.

"Let's take a walk to stretch our legs."

"Now?" I asked. "It's gonna storm."

She laughed. "The sky's been this way for centuries."

When I emerged from the carriage, wind slammed against my body with the weight of crashing waves. It stopped, only to gust again, catching me off guard. A sudden throbbing ache pounded in my skull, and I pressed my palms to my forehead. It had to be all this magic, mana—whatever. The air was utterly saturated with it. Like the thick yellow pollen of springtime, it bombarded my sinuses, building pressure behind my eyes.

The dwarven coachman cleared his throat, his bushy features conveying his irritation. "It'll be dark soon, m'lady," his gruff voice warned.

Sidelle paid him no mind and led me up a small hill east of the carriage. The wind blew in furious gusts, rousing the grasses into rippling waves that nipped and stung my bare arms like tiny snake bites. I trudged behind her to the crest, where she stared out over the plains.

It was worse than I could've imagined—a necropolis of stone bodies.

I moved to one of the nearby statues and ran my fingers over its rough, grainy surface. The sculpture was on his side, but where the face should've been was a blank space of crumbled, deteriorating rock. Further out, I spotted a stone face half-buried and twisted into an agonizing display of gritted teeth with eyes squeezed shut. I'd seen the same expression on many men's faces as I drove a blade between their ribs. When I turned my gaze toward the statue beneath my palm, it was evident the two pieces were once whole.

The witch appeared at my side. "It's awful, isn't it?" she said with solemn sincerity. I could only nod. "Annorah created them."

I frowned. "She had magic?" I spoke so low I worried the wind carried my words away unheard.

But she gave a slow nod. "You know the story of Atreus, how the god of man and light gifted him to the former king."

I nodded, though it wasn't a question. All humans knew this tale. King Atreus, bequeathed by the light god, Aethier, to be the one true king of Westryelle.

"A king promised to rule forever." Sidelle gave a soft scoff at her own words and shook her head. "What humans don't remember is that there was another child presented that day."

"Annorah, I presume?"

"She was gifted to King Carlisle first, actually, from Erezos."

I was still processing the fact that I looked like a long-dead princess. Now I'm to find that she was a gift from mana and darkness? My stomach churned with the sky overhead. Sidelle sighed and shifted her staff to the hand closest to me. That strange tugging sensation returned, accompanied by the growing discomfort in my head.

"The same day Erezos blessed King Carlisle with Annorah, Aethier granted him Atreus. King Carlisle raised them with the intention that the two would rule together. 'A symbol of equality of the races,' he said." Her shoulders pulled back with indignation. "But human life is so fleeting, and Atreus took advantage of that. He betrayed Annorah, cast her and all Vylandrians from the royal city, and was set on killing her to protect what he claimed as his alone." A pained expression painted Sidelle's beautiful features.

"Did you know Annorah well?" I asked.

She nodded. "She was like a sister to me. I was heartbroken when she died."

My gaze settled on the horizon as lightning streaked the sky. "I've felt loss like that, too. That kind of pain sticks with you forever." *And when you live forever...* I met Sidelle's soft eyes, then quickly looked away, clearing my throat. "So what happened then, after Annorah died?"

"Atreus scrubbed the city clean of Annorah's image, then the record books of her accomplishments." Something burned in her words, as if her anger still thrived after all these years. "It only took a few generations for humans to forget all about her, and how our races were meant to be equals—not enemies."

The sky growled, low and rumbling, growing louder like a great approaching beast. It hit its apex and sent trembles through the ground beneath our feet, then dissipated over the landscape.

"So, what does all that have to do with this place?" I asked.

"Annorah was young when her mana first surfaced, twelve or so. She practiced her control by creating these stone golems." She gestured with the staff toward the bust beside us with an appreciative smile riding her lips. "It was impressive mana. Creating life, however simple it was, is something no druid had ever accomplished. And here was this young, human girl with such power.

"For whatever reason, each golem she created migrated here." She nodded to the rolling hills. "No one, even Annorah, knew why. Eventually, it became known as the stone forest."

"Who destroyed them?" I asked, rubbing the cold from my arms. My curiosity piqued, but my head pounded in a steady rhythm, and I longed to return to the soft carriage seats.

"They sacrificed themselves the night Annorah died. The mana that resided within them was used in the ritual that took her life."

My brows pinched. "Hold on—a ritual? I assumed King Atreus killed her."

"Oh, he absolutely wanted her dead. Make no mistake about that. But, leading up to his betrayal, Erezos came to me with a warning. One we couldn't ignore."

A shiver seemed to rock through the witch, making my stomach twist into a ball of knots.

She squared herself on me, a silent request for her undivided attention. "Annorah sacrificed herself. The High Witches of the Vylandrian Covens, myself included, freed her soul from her body while allowing her mana to reside in this variant."

Variant? "Why though?"

Her eyes burned with the memory seeming to play out behind them. "Erezos had granted Annorah access to his power. She possessed a fraction of the boundless mana of our god, and Atreus sought to destroy it. Erezos, in return, promised to bring destruction to Westryelle if we let that happen. His power was to remain safe."

I could tell she was expecting some sort of reaction from me, but I wasn't sure how to respond—or if I even believed any of it.

This heaviness pushed down on me as if someone piled crates on my shoulders. Perhaps I might still find a way to Breckenridge after all. Maybe once I got my wits about me, I could steal a horse, start for the coast, catch a ship. Risks be damned.

My head gave a violent pound of agreement. Whatever this was, whatever part the witch or the king thought I played in this, was a mistake. I didn't belong here. Less than twenty-four hours ago, I'd been riding high on a fresh bounty to fill my pockets with the outlook of sun and sandy coasts in my future. Now I was trapped in a foreign country with the same face as a dead martyr.

As if she sensed my spiraling thoughts, Sidelle said, "I know this is a lot to take in." Her voice was soft, gentle. "We don't have to continue, but I hope, when you're ready, I can share more with you."

"Of course there's more."

My sarcasm must have been lost on the witch because she came closer, placing a steady hand on my shoulder. It was likely meant to be a comfort, but all I could focus on was the proximity of that moonstone. My skull threatened to burst, and I struggled against the sensation in my chest. Like a winch, it yanked me closer and closer—as if pulling my heart from my body.

Somewhere far off, as if I'd been shoved underwater, Sidelle spoke, her words fading in and out, "I want you... a home in Raven Ridge... hope someday... trust... *friend–*"

The witch's mouth moved, and I tried with feverish effort to focus, but the roar in my head drowned everything out. The hiss of grass blades against stone whistled with the howl of the wind in a hollow, ghostly moan. But the stones echoed a voice of their own, a low baritone, a hum. It radiated inside me—I could *feel* what they wanted.

I tried to shove it away and told myself that it was the magic confusing my senses. It reverberated in the depths of my mind, a rhythmic mantra urging me to—to rebuild them. With the last bit of mental strength I could collect, I thrust the voices from my head, but my efforts were as futile as shoving against a wave of water.

Something must have alerted the witch to my discomfort, because I could faintly hear her honey-sweet voice repeating my name. Then the pain made a final, violent surge.

It was like being torn apart, trapped inside an echoing room with thousands of voices all speaking, shouting, calling to me at once. A blinding, bright light flooded my senses, so strong my eyes clenched shut, and my knees gave out.

Sidelle called my name again, but I couldn't answer.

Then—as quick as a blink—the pain was gone. Relief sagged my shoulders forward as a heavy sense of fatigue sank into my bones. It took everything in me to remain upright and conscious. When a feather-light essence of cool mist fanned my skin like a dense fog, I tried and failed to open my eyes. I could faintly make out the weightless sensation of being lifted from the ground and carried away.

Then I drifted into a deep, easy sleep.

CHAPTER FOUR

SIDELLE

A comfortable breeze cooled my clammy forehead, and I halted my haphazard pacing. From this vantage point on my balcony in the high witch quarters, I had a complete view of Raven Ridge. The immense, fortified gates on the horizon were opening to allow a requesting party through. It was impossible to see for certain, though I was confident I knew who.

The gates closed again, and I estimated about fifteen minutes until Eurok Dramagan arrived on my doorstep. The very male I was most eager to see. Sending for him had been the easy part. Eurok was a friend, one of the few I kept in the last few centuries. It'd been over two years since we last saw one another, though, and the subject matter of our meeting today was far from a happy one.

I choked back the thick sense of guilt climbing up my throat as I contemplated the best approach to steer this potentially unpleasant conversation. I despised asking this of Eurok. But I saw no other way to coerce Mira's mana into blooming before our time together ended.

I retrieved my teacup from the railing and went for another sip. Empty. Eager for a refill, I padded through the glass-arched doorway, casting a wary glance up the stairs where Mira still slept off my spell to ease her pain. I placed the china on the counter, then headed to the washroom. There, I poured some fresh water from the wooden pitcher into the basin. After a glimpse in the mirror, I set the pitcher aside and leaned closer, tugging at the edges of my eyes. My soft features seemed more haggard than they had prior to my trip to the royal city, like a gloomy haze cast over my complexion.

Yesterday's events replayed in my mind, and I analyzed each detail. I scoured for any holes, any doubts that warranted attention. Every timeless fiber of my being was convinced—Mira was Annorah's reincarnation. Another gift from Erezos, though a temperamental one. The way mana swarmed her like a moth to the flame—I thought she'd bloom right there in the stone forest. It still vexed me, though, how instead of flowing into her as it should have, it acted as though it were blocked, like she was protected behind a pane of glass.

All strangeness aside, the mana *had* recognized her and reacted, as if trying to return home. That was all the proof I needed. I sensed her sleeping strength and cunning with which she observed the world. Trust didn't come easily to her. It would take time for her to lower her guard.

If my top priority was to convince her to embrace and harness her power, I would need Eurok's help. The new captain had plenty enough reasons to deny me. If the council discovered who Mira was before we had definitive proof, they'd strip him of every title he's ever earned. He'd be deemed a traitor, if not executed altogether. Even so, he was the only person I entrusted to protect the secret of the girl's existence.

I returned to the balcony and leaned against the iron railing, tracking the crunch of hooves across loose gravel. Riding atop his dapple gray mare, cedar skin gleaming in the sunlight, was Eurok Dramagan. He caught sight of me and flashed a brilliant, confident smile that reached his liquid-gold eyes. I beamed and hurried inside to meet him.

The green wooden door creaked open, and I beheld the male leaning against the archway, an enticed expression already gracing his features. My intentions for this meeting had me feeling more predator than friend. Buried in my apprehension, I'd forgotten Eurok would have his own ambitions where I was concerned. His eyes slid over me, toeing that precarious line I drew to keep things professional between us.

Despite the way his mesmerizing stare warmed my skin, I managed a composed smile.

He'd been a trainee when we met. Even then, I had a weakness for that maddening confidence of his. The way he somehow sensed my presence and stopped, even mid-scrimmage, to watch me as I passed, that hungry look in his eye. He had always pursued me. And secretly—I hoped he'd never stop.

"Eurok, come in."

A whispered scent of sun-kissed skin and summer days accompanied him, and after a chaste kiss on the cheek, he sauntered into the sitting room.

"How were your travels?" I asked, my face tingling from the warmth of his lips.

"Ah, well, you know. Beats the trek you just made." His tenor was low, soothing, like hoofbeats on cobblestone or the rhythmic pulse of a drum. He dropped into an overstuffed chair near the hearth. "So what did the royal cunt want this time?"

There was the caveat to that voice. He used it to say every thought that crossed his mind—no matter how crass. He never failed to make sure people understood exactly where they stood with him. It won him a lot of allies and plenty of enemies.

My head jerked in subtle surprise. "Wait. How did you know where I was?" Only the high witches knew of my whereabouts.

"Saura met me at the gate. She's heading back to Oakrend tomorrow, and asked me to bring you this." He retrieved a jar of valerian root from his pack and set it on the end table. "She also mentioned it was a shame that your duty to the king prevented your presence at the Honing."

The Honing. I completely forgot. I'd need to find time to visit Black Sand Calms to congratulate Vitany in person.

"So?" Eurok asked, crossing an ankle over his knee. "What was so important?"

I took a long eyeful of the druid—just as handsome as when I last saw him. The harness strapped to his chest contained a vast array of blades, foregoing the ax that normally hung from his hip. His soft cream-colored tunic showed signs of travel, and light flecks of mud speckled the black trousers tucked into his riding boots. A warrior in every right, he looked out of place, sitting on the cozy, stuffed furniture of the sitting room. The sight drew a faint laugh, which triggered him to raise a curious brow.

"It's nothing," I said, responding to his silent question.

When our eyes locked, I swore that crooked grin made a button on my shirt come undone. He leaned forward, resting his elbows on his knees—a cat ready to pounce.

"It's good to see you again, Sidelle."

I stood there, fingers toying with the top button of my blouse as I fought the urge to cross my legs beneath me. *By the mountain, this male will be the death of me.*

I broke the spell and started toward the beverage cart, letting the moment roll off my shoulders. "I'm glad to see you, too," I said. "There's much I'd like to discuss. Tea?" I poured some steaming water over the sieve in the cup.

As I hoped, he allowed that sinful tension between us to dissipate and resumed his previous casual demeanor.

"Got anything stronger?"

I brought him a glass containing a double of my best bourbon. I kept it here for guests, anyway. When he accepted the beverage, his fingers grazed mine—warm and gentle. He took a sip, rolled his lips, then eyed the drink appreciatively before setting it aside.

He appraised me for a moment, then said, "Do you intend to answer my question?"

"Hmm?" I asked, sipping my tea. "Oh, the king? I'll explain all that later." I waved him off. "Tell me more about what's happening in the southeast. Are reconnaissance missions underway?"

The recent increase in poaching was a responsibility Eurok took on as captain. Perhaps I was a coward, but it felt too soon to bring up Mira, too eager.

He threw back the remaining swig of bourbon, then rested his elbows on his knees again. This time, the gesture seemed more dispirited. The fine sun-hewn lines that graced the edges of his eyes when he smiled disappeared. "Not yet."

"What is it?" I set my teacup aside, giving him my full attention.

"Broderick." He sighed and ran a hand through his dark brown hair. "He believes Saura would be better suited to handle the high witches' duties in regard to the poaching."

"My mother?" I asked, stunned. "She's never handled a situation of this magnitude before. Not like I–"

"Like you have, I know." He cut me off, not disrespectfully, but in a show of support.

In truth, Eurok had my back from the day we met. Maybe I'd been overthinking things, doubting him *too* much.

My belly filled with fire at the notion of the council displacing me from the position I established and held the past thousand years. Our people feared being plucked from their homes by these poachers. The last thing they needed was controversy among the ranks of their leaders.

"This is because of my work with the king, isn't it?" I glowered, returning to the conversation. "He feeds the council poison against me. He's the only one who doubts my loyalty."

"Hey," in a swift motion, he knelt before me, "don't worry yourself, love."

A mesmerizing warmth consumed his sunlight eyes as he unlaced my knee-high boots. I watched with tentative scrutiny, butterflies replacing the angry heat in my belly. When he removed my boots and rubbed slow, attentive circles into the pads of my feet, my troubles faded. *What is he doing?*

He'd always been bold, but he behaved as if we hadn't just spent nearly two years apart. It caught me off guard, though not entirely in a bad way.

"I told them if I'm to be captain, I'll work with no one else. While Saura is a talented, respectable witch, she's not right for the job."

His hands moved with such focused intention, I couldn't help but imagine them all over my body. "And if they had relieved you of that title, Captain?"

He smirked. "They know I'm the best, just like they know you're the best. Once I made it clear where I stood, they dropped the subject."

"And here I thought I was doing them a favor."

"You *are.*"

His gaze lingered on my skin, and when those hands moved further up my leg, it was obvious he wanted more. I'd have to put a stop to it before long. *Just a little longer, though.*

"We need the witches' support in this. While you might be the council's least favorite individual as of late, you're damn-well the most influential."

He reached that predetermined line near my knee, and I pulled away, tucking my legs beneath me. Unbothered by my movement, he pushed to his feet to pour himself another round.

"They'd be damned fools to replace you, and they know it."

It was true. Despite how difficult it was to be the bigger person, I did my best to ensure the Vylandrian communities that witches and druids stood firmly together when it came to their safety and wellbeing. *How dare Broderick try to shut me out!*

"Thank you," I said gently.

"Ah," he purred, brow raised as he gestured toward me with his drink, "if you think *that* was good, you should see what I can do elsewhere."

Heat bloomed low in my belly at the thought, and I smirked at his mirth. "You know exactly what I mean."

With an easy laugh, he strolled out onto the balcony.

I was grateful for him speaking on my behalf, but it made the stagnant guilt in my gut writhe again. I watched him through the window, amazed by his strength and composure. He had no idea of the hardships I was about to impose on his life. I fought back the urge to vomit and stood. *It's now or never.*

I leaned against the railing beside him, scouring my mind for where to start. He truly held all the cards. If he chose not to help, I'd need to find another avenue to draw out Mira's power. I had to choose my words wisely.

"Eurok?" I could already hear pleading in my voice. I reined it in. "There's something I wish to speak with you about."

When he faced me, I started from the beginning, with Annorah. I spent the next hour explaining every detail, from Erezos' warning to Annorah's sacrifice, ending with Mira asleep upstairs. Periodically, his gaze drifted toward the village, then back to me, but he never interrupted.

Though he remained quiet, something in him shifted and became more serious the moment I mentioned my promise to Annorah, the reason I suffered the king all these years, and again when I told him how desperately I needed his help. "Now you know everything," I finished. *Every last shred of it.*

With everything laid bare, all I could do was wait.

His silence was unnerving. A sense of dejection robbed my hope, but I kept quiet, allowing him to process. I spent the time considering every possible outcome, preparing myself for each one.

Then, with grave concern hardening the gilded hue of his eyes, he spoke. "Who knows about this?"

"You're the only one I've shared this information with."

"Do you plan to tell anyone else?"

"No."

"Good. Don't." With his elbows propped on the railing, he dropped his head, running his fingers through his dark, earthen hair. "Damn it, Sidelle. Why haven't you told me?"

My nerves twisted, knotting the words in my throat. "I only just found her. I told you as soon—"

"Not that." His brow furrowed, pulling his features into a tortured expression. "Why didn't you tell me what you've been doing all these years—what you're *still* doing—to protect, not just your own people, but his too?"

"I made a promise." It was all I could think to say. If I said any more, I worried the tightness in my throat would betray me.

He pushed off the railing, stepping close. "You've carried this burden all this time—alone."

He took my hand in his, and I marveled at the contrast of my soft lilac skin clasped in his rich cedar. My eyes flitted up to his. They read of sorrow intermingled with relief.

"I'm here now, love. You don't have to do it alone," he said. "Not anymore. We'll save this kingdom together."

His palm pressed against that delicate space below my jaw, and that molten gaze entranced me, drawing me in like a dancing flame. Tears sheened my eyes as I stared up at him, unable to speak.

I never made the decision, never asked my body to move, but I felt myself lean into him. We were so close—storm clouds and sunshine sharing the same air. When our eyes fluttered shut, I braced for the moment our lips would meet, but something in my chest heaved.

That line.

That line of great importance I'd drawn for both our sakes made itself known, and before our lips touched, I dipped my chin.

Eurok let out a long, slow breath, and the honeyed sweetness of it tickled my cheek. I settled my forehead against his chest, fighting every urge in my body.

His hand found the nape of my neck, and he pressed his lips against my hair.

"I'm sorry," I whispered.

At my words, his hold on me tightened. "Yeah. Me too."

CHAPTER FIVE

MIRA

In an instant, I jolted upright and reached for the knife by my side, only to find it missing. *Fuck.*

I hugged my arms around my knees and buried my face, trying to recall what happened. The blinding throb in my head was gone, as were the stone giants' chanting voices. I tried to hide my pain from the witch, but in the end, it surged like an active volcano. The last thing I remembered were those cool, airy hands lifting me from the ground.

Birdsong and the distant roar of water drifted through an open window, but I couldn't bring myself to look around yet. I wasn't ready to take in the unfamiliar setting.

A gentle whisper caressed the side of my arm, and I lifted my head. An airy gossamer curtain floated, caught on the morning breeze. The soft scent of hyacinth and freesia beckoned me toward the window, and I uncurled myself. As I followed their lure, I tripped on something. A sharp ache radiated through my toes, and a hiss cut through my teeth. I hopped on one foot, seeing my boots set neatly beside the bed. *She removed my shoes?*

At the round, wooden-framed window, I took my first look at Raven Ridge. From the top floor of this home, meticulously hewn into a massive sandalwood tree, the view stretched out like a scene from a storybook.

Far below, flowers poured from carved planters along the sprawling cobblestone streets. Little homes and shops bore beautiful ash-wood trimming littered with intricate designs that gave the structures an elegant but whimsical touch. The town itself was charming, but the backdrop had me captivated enough to still my breath.

The village was nestled within a natural fortress of immense waterfalls. Their thunderous roar echoed across the expanse, while a sturdy wooden wall safeguarded the exposed side, its gate displaying the same elegant carvings. Misty spray billowed from each cascade—it should've been enough to drench everything nearby, but I felt none. The air was dry, comfortable. I took a deep breath, savoring the freshness of it.

An aurora of pink, yellow, and green rippled above, quick as lightning, drawing my attention to what must've been the spell that blocked the mist. It was the only explanation. Raven Ridge was quaint, but in the most incredible way.

I pushed off the sill, then appraised the bed I slept in. The white sheets were mussed and dirtied from my outfit—filthy from my time in the dungeons. On the chest of drawers sat a neat pile of freshly folded clothes, a pair of boots, and a note. My fingers traced the black-on-black paisley embroidered along the length of the knee-high boots. They were finely made and absolutely perfect. I picked up the delicate stationery, my cheeks pulling tight, and read Sidelle's note.

Mira,
I hope you find the room to your liking. Down the hall to your right is your private bathing chamber. Once you feel up to it, I'd love for us to have a talk. I'll be downstairs when you're ready.
Genuinely,
Sidelle

I grabbed the clothes and laid them out on the bed. A lacy tunic paired with a silk vest and fitted pants. All black, and the correct sizes. *She went shopping for me too?*

I fingered the tunic's sleeve while two vastly conflicting instincts warred in my mind. One of wary caution, and the other, a foreign instinct that told me the witch's kindness was genuine. The clothes, this room—not to mention she saved me from the king's ill-placed rage. I hadn't expected any of it, and yet Sidelle extended these generosities. No one had ever made such an effort for me before. And why would they—why would she?

After I canvassed the space for anything suspicious, I searched outside my window for an escape route should I need one. Apart from scaling this enormous tree, though, there was no way down. The reflex to keep my guard up coiled itself in my thoughts like a defensive cobra, reminding me to remain vigilant until I found out exactly why I was here. I spun to face the bed where I laid out the new outfit. *I'm still going to wear those boots, though.*

The clothes hugged my body perfectly, and as I passed the washroom's mirror, I stopped to peer at myself properly for the first time in a long while.

Nothing would have prepared me for the image that stared back. I'd always known I was attractive. It'd been a leg up on my competition as a bounty hunter. Men's egos were often their greatest weakness, making them rarely suspicious of a beautiful woman who showed them interest. But regardless of how many times I used my looks to gain an advantage on a hunt, I never saw myself look so *healthy*.

It must have been the tangerine-scented oil I found and added to my bath. Perhaps it contained some magical ingredient? My skin had lost its sallowness, and the dark circles under my eyes brightened into a plump, vibrant appearance. My hair, though wet, cascaded down my back in a sleek sheet. And my scars—my scars were gone. Something between astonishment and elation swelled in my chest.

After towel-drying my hair, I secured it in a high ponytail with a clasp I found in the drawer. Then, with one more appreciative glance at my reflection, I ventured out to meet Sidelle.

A spiral staircase at the end of the hall led to the first floor. Hushed voices, sizzling bacon, and rich breakfast scents drifted from below. My palm slid against the wooden banister as I descended the steep curves, its raw texture grainy beneath my fingers.

The home was less elaborate than I assumed, judging by the room and bathing chamber, but it had a cozy ambiance. Natural light poured in from the many arched windows, all overlooking the landscape from different points of view. *A reader's dream.* Though I was neither a reader nor a dreamer.

The voices came from a room just out of sight. Sidelle's soft, honey-like tone was easily distinguishable, but the other was deep. A man. *Male.*

I paused, trying to listen, but couldn't make anything out, so I rounded the corner to cross the threshold.

The familiar hiss of metal cutting through the air snared my attention. In a blink, I dropped into a crouch, out of the impact zone. The dagger sank into the wall, embedded deep, right where my head had been.

Chest tight and senses heightened, I snapped my eyes up and locked onto the male, an intrigued sneer gracing his lips. A single glance was enough to realize this was a being honed for war. His every muscle, sculpted to perfection, exuded his capability to take down enemies. And though I had no way of knowing how old he was, something told me that a presence like that could only be shaped by centuries of experience.

Against all self-preservation, I returned his smirk with a red-hot glare. On the defensive, I studied the blade protruding from the wall. It still vibrated from the impact as I grabbed hold of the jeweled handle.

"That's *mine!*" I hissed through my gritted teeth, yanking it free, then squared myself on my enemy.

Sidelle pinned him with a scowl. "Eurok, what the *hell* are you doing?"

"What?" He shrugged. "You said her skills were impressive. Wanted to see for myself."

"You could have killed her." Her fists clenched tight at her sides.

"If she couldn't dodge that, then she'd never survive my training." He took a carefree swig from his glass.

My temper was venomous. I angled my knife at him, though directed my glare at Sidelle. "What *training?* And why did he have my fucking blade?"

"She's a feisty one too? This should be fun." He turned away, then winked at me over his shoulder.

My rage ignited like grease on a fire. I slung the dagger, and it whizzed toward the exact point on the druid's back at which I aimed.

I was prepared to hear the slick sound of metal penetrating flesh—when he sidestepped out of its path. He caught the blade in mid-air, so fast my mind barely grasped what happened. My jaw dropped with my sharp gasp.

The witch walked toward me, shooting a look at Eurok like it served him right, but the druid only gave a bored half-shrug and plopped in a chair near the hearth.

"What was he doing with my blade?"

"I'm afraid that's my fault," Sidelle said. "I meant to return them to you once we had the chance to talk, though I wasn't expecting Eurok," she shot him another incredulous leer, "to pick one up and start hurling them at you."

Eurok only winked again, then sipped his drink. His arrogance wasn't helping anyone's irritable state.

"If he winks at me one more time, I'm going to make it permanent." I'd pluck out one of those pretty eyeballs and wear it as a necklace.

Sidelle pursed her lips. "He won't. He means no harm."

With a huff of disbelief, I crossed my arms and kicked out my hip. "Really?"

After a moment spent exchanging a silent look with Sidelle, he pushed to his feet, then offered his hand. "Eurok Dramagan, Captain of the Druid Army."

I refused the gesture, letting my disdain show.

Sidelle spoke again, "Mira, Eurok is here because I requested his help."

"With what?"

"Would you like to sit with us?" she asked. "There's a lot to discuss, and I think it's time we were all on the same page."

I nodded and let the witch lead me into the sitting room. I surveyed the spacious area and glanced at the table beside the druid captain. Next to his empty glass were the rest of my daggers and my holster. I walked over and kept a challenging eye on him. He held my stare with an air of indifference.

Confident? Arrogant? I couldn't decide.

"Captain, huh?" I asked, securing my holster around my hips. "Guess that explains it."

"Explains what?" he drawled, tone bored and flat.

I smirked, allowing my taunting appraisal to linger over the warrior sitting on the floral-stuffed chair. I slid my blades into place and glanced at Sidelle. A humorous, knowing smile wavered on her lips.

"All—of this." I made a show of waggling my fingers down the length of the druid's armor-clad physique.

Sidelle's composure slipped in a small snort of laughter.

The druid cast a look of annoyance between the two of us, shaking his head, then stepped around me to refill his glass.

After securing each familiar blade in their respective holsters, I found the seat directly across from his. To my surprise, he returned with a drink for me as well.

"Here, you'll need this."

I accepted the offer and swirled the amber liquid. I hadn't tasted bourbon in ages, and the intoxicating aroma of this particular one was a pleasant bonus. After a sip, savoring the smooth burn, I set the drink on the table beside me.

Eurok sat with his ankle crossed over his knee. He intrigued me. It was obvious he was highly skilled. I never witnessed anyone move so fast as when he caught my dagger. From what I gathered, he'd been *playing* with me when he threw it—testing me, as he said.

I found myself wondering how I'd fare against the warrior in a real one-on-one. Something told me not very well.

I studied his hand wrapped around his glass, the same one he caught my knife with. My brows pulled together with my shock—it was completely unharmed.

"Your hand!"

Eurok set his drink aside, giving the appendage an unconcerned once-over.

"There's no way that blade didn't slice you."

"Oh, it did." He removed a dagger from his baldric and, without so much as a thought, split his palm.

Sidelle loosed a sharp hiss from across the room. "Eurok, is that necessary?"

Crimson spurted and welled in a pool around the knife. But almost as soon as he pulled it away, the gash sewed itself together, leaving no trace of there ever being a mark.

"Healing mana," he said.

My head swiveled between the two. "Can you all do that?"

"Not all, but it's one of the more common gifts among our kind," Sidelle answered.

"Makes us pretty hard to kill." He slid his blade back into place and winked again.

Now I know he's doing it to fuck with me.

I narrowed my eyes, but sensing this antagonistic behavior might just come naturally to the haughty bastard, I ignored it. "Gifts?"

"Gifts. Talents," Sidelle said. "There are four common ones—healing, shifting, earthing, and decanting. But there will be plenty of time to talk about all of that, I promise. Instead, Mira, I want to discuss where we go from here. How are you feeling, by the way?"

I shrugged one shoulder. "Fine. Though, it would've been nice if you warned me the magic would affect me like that."

"So you *did* sense mana in the stone forest. You recognized it?" The witch's eyes lit up like moonlight on a dark pond.

A mixture of caution and irritation slowed my response. "Yeah."

"Have you possessed mana before?" Sidelle stirred her tea in gentle strokes as if she hadn't just asked such an absurd question.

I scoffed. "Of course not, I'm human."

She paused a heartbeat before saying, "I think it would be beneficial if we started experimenting together. I'd like to see if you can learn to wield mana to some degree." She eyed me over the edge of her teacup as she sipped, seeming to be thoughtfully choosing her words.

"To what end?" A heavy dose of skepticism laced my tone. I didn't take the idea of being anyone's guinea pig lightly. What good would come of teaching me about magic? I was just an ordinary human, and not once in my entire miserable life had there been any indication of anything different.

I reined in my frustration and reminded myself that I decided to treat the witch with kindness. Aside from sensing her cautious choice of words, I didn't feel as if there were any ill intentions behind her strange suggestion. So I sat, like a marble statue, and waited for her to elaborate. Eurok, brooding over his bourbon, said nothing.

"That's another matter we need to discuss." She leaned forward, set her tea aside, and met my intentional stare.

Foreboding crept in and clamored up my spine, but I was determined to hide my vulnerability. Though we all knew I irrevocably *was*. I had no lent, no bounty, and a mad king at my back who would sooner see me dead than let me roam free. My choices were whatever the witch offered, or—death.

So I waited for these two powerful beings to reveal what was to come of my life. *Just say it already.*

"I suppose the simplest way to explain this is to start from the beginning," she said, "I believe it's import–"

"No."

Her jaw snapped shut at my interruption, and she cocked her head. "No, what?"

"No, beginnings." My tone was adamant, and it was clear both druids noticed the shift. I hadn't meant for it to sound so harsh, but I was through with waiting. "No more stories. I want answers. Why are you doing all of this?" I waved a hand around me, then down my length, gesturing at the new attire. "Why am I here?"

"And why is that?" Sidelle asked. "Why is it you prefer only answers and not have any of the details? This is such an unfamiliar situation. I would think you'd want to gain as much insight as you can."

"That's assuming I care." I was through schooling my tone.

"On the contrary," she said. "It seems to me that you're trying to *avoid* caring."

I raised an unimpressed brow.

"Is it possible," she continued, "that you are not inclined to learn anything that might cause your heart to impede your decision-making?"

"My heart has never had much pull in my decision-making." How dare the witch pretend to know me? She only just met me. She knew nothing of what I was capable of and knew nothing of my heart. "My patience wears thin, witch."

Eurok's eyes narrowed, and his lip curled in warning. I ignored him. *Arrogant.*

Sidelle crossed her legs, smoothed nonexistent wrinkles from her lap, then leaned to one side of her chair, perching an elbow on the armrest. She was a picture of cool patience—and it was getting on my nerves.

"How about a deal?" she finally asked. "I'll give you three yes-or-no questions of your choosing, and in turn, you agree to listen to what I wish to share with you."

I relaxed my shoulders a bit and weighed the offer.

Three yes-or-no questions. She was smart for making that stipulation. The more people talk, the more they give away. It was a tactic I used while hunting for my targets. But conversing with drunken men in a bar was quite different from being limited to three questions to ask an ancient witch. I'd have to be smart and only ask what I believed to be most important, rather than what snared my curiosity.

"Any three questions?"

Sidelle nodded.

"And you'll answer them truthfully?"

She nodded again.

I gritted my teeth, contemplating. "Deal."

She gestured with an open hand. "Whenever you're ready."

I did my best to keep my expression neutral, thinking over the past few days and what the witch had said to me. She assured she had no intention of fulfilling her promise to the king, and claimed to hold no loyalty to him. Asking what that promise entailed didn't seem like a priority if she wasn't going to fulfill it.

If that were true, though, then why answer his every beck and call? Was it simply because he was the king—a requirement of her job? Or was there more to it than that? What did she stand to gain in all of this? Or was she just a prisoner with a very long leash?

"Do you plan to use me to end this," I wasn't sure what to call it, "arrangement you have with the king?"

Sidelle's face fell ever so slightly. Apparently, she hadn't expected that to be my first question. But a soft smile slowly spread across her features—almost as if she was *proud* of me.

"Yes." Her answer was unapologetic.

Surprised at the witch's reaction, I had to rally my rationale to find my next question. My initial assumption was that she was using me for her own benefit. But I sat with it for a moment, dissecting her response. It was her expression that left me conflicted. A spark ignited in her eyes like she was happy that I was putting the pieces together.

When I formed my second question, I asked it with a wrenching ache in my gut. "Does anyone else stand to benefit from my participation in whatever *this* is?"

"Yes." Her response was immediate. "Many, in fact."

The king throwing me in a dungeon meant for wielders, the recognition on Sidelle's face the first time we met, and that stroll through the mana-drenched stone forest. And now she wants to train me in magic? *They think I'm her.*

The room leaned, and I gripped the arms of my chair tight 'til my fingers ached. They suspected I was some godsdamned mag princess. *How the fuck will I get out of this?*

Finally getting answers, I tried to compartmentalize the information from the emotions that threatened to spew from me like a geyser. All I really wanted to do was run. But run where?

Between Eurok's bated breath and Sidelle's expectant eyes, I felt like a candle threatening to go out. Whatever the witch had planned for me was clearly important enough for her to go through all this trouble. What did she want me to do that *many* would benefit from? *Kill the king.*

It didn't matter. None of it. Because I was not who they thought I was. I was just an insignificant human, nothing compared to them. I wanted to believe so badly that some good would come of this that I let my better judgment slip, and now I careened face-first down a slippery slope. *They have the* wrong *person.*

With my mind made up, the final question was more or less a waste, but I decided to ask the only other thing I needed to know. "If I decline to help you, am I free to leave?"

For the second time, this didn't seem to be what she expected. Her brows furrowed, and her lips pulled into a tight frown. "Yes."

Eurok opened his mouth as if he wanted to challenge her words, but he didn't speak.

Sidelle went on, "If you feel like that is the best decision by the time I've finished saying what I have to say, then yes. You are not a prisoner, Mira, as I've said. But leaving poses substantial risk."

The hint of disappointment in her voice nicked at my heart, but I nodded. *Screw the risk.* As long as I didn't have anyone but myself to worry about. *A princess,* I inwardly scoffed. *She'd be better off asking Captain Gold Eyes here to be her princess.*

I'd let the witch tell her story, but as soon as she was done, I'd thank her for her kindness and be on my way. Eager to put this behind me, I started making silent plans. I'd acquire a horse and some food later, find a way to make enough money to get my ass on a ship, then disappear for good.

Sidelle suggested we move to the rooftop balcony for the next part of our conversation, and once again, it had taken me a moment to recover from the view. She had a magnificent spread of foods brought up from the village. I filled two plates, planning to work through them as I listened. *I might as well fill up while I can.*

We sat around a circular table that looked as though it were a rippling pool of water. I ran my fingers along its solid surface. An illusion.

Sidelle spooned fresh fruit onto her plate, then offered some for me. When I nodded, she served me, then spoke. "I do not take you for a fool, Mira. I suspect you've figured out why I am asking you to stay." Her cool words told me she was gauging how I was handling everything thus far.

"I'm not sure what I know," I said flatly.

Eurok slammed his cup down, rattling the table and its contents. After a feigned apologetic shrug, he shoveled another forkful of food into his mouth, chewing a bit more aggressive than necessary. He'd been acting strange ever since I asked about my freedom to leave. Something told me he liked the idea of forcing me to stay a hell of a lot better.

Sidelle looked as though she wanted to roll her eyes at him, but faced me instead. "It's not my intention to hide anything from you. I only wish not to overwhelm you."

I finished chewing with an unhurried demeanor, then wiped my mouth on my napkin. "Not to overwhelm? Or is it to keep control?"

Another slam sent tremors across the tabletop. Sidelle jumped, and our glasses shuddered in response. Eurok's hand lingered on the cup, and those amber eyes hardened on me.

I raised an eyebrow and cocked my head. "Is something the matter?"

"Tell me, Mira, did you feel disrespected when you proposed your questions?" he asked, each word clipped.

I set my jaw and lifted my chin. "No."

My pride writhed, feeling like a chastised child, but I saw the point he was trying to make.

"Well, then maybe you wouldn't mind showing her the same respect."

There was a rumble beneath the table, and I glanced at my water to see it rippling. I nodded once, and the rumbling stopped. *Confident.*

CHAPTER SIX
SIDELLE

923 Years Earlier

In a matter of seconds, the storm intensified from a gentle drizzle to a torrential downpour, as if the gods themselves mourned this day. I braced my bare feet on the sopping wet ground and joined hands with the other high witches. All of whom agreed to help kill the would-be queen we all loved and adored.

Annorah found a way to save everyone—everyone except herself. Some small part of me knew the gods would reward her selfless act, though I couldn't be certain. I heard nothing from Erezos since his warning.

Together, we prepared to decant Annorah's mana into the medium-sized stone chest. Constructed with quartz from The Aupex Mountain, our efforts to commission the vessel had been hasty and discreet. Now, with hands clasped, encircling Annorah, a golden shield radiated intense heat. The force of it burned my face as it spread across the princess.

Channeled energy from her stone giants took form in wisps of flowing light. It swept past us in all directions, arching over our circle, converging into a single beam focused at the center. The giants' monolithic bodies not only acted as conduits for the spell but as capable guardians, ready to defend against any threat.

For a moment, I thought the storm switched directions, then I noticed the shield, hovering inches above Annorah, emitted a phantom wind. It whipped around, a wrathful beast, snaring the breath from my lungs. I fought to stay upright and kept chanting.

Some witches squeezed their eyes shut, while others stared, unblinking, despite the spell's intense golden light. With the potency of a falling star, the shield slammed to the ground, surrounding Annorah. It dispersed into a million shimmering pieces, and my grip on my mother's hand tightened. The blast hit us with such force we flew apart like leaves in a gust of wind.

Ribs aching from the blow, I sat up. Breathless but unharmed, I looked around at the others. We locked eyes and, as if sensing one another's desperate thoughts, we scrambled to reconnect the circle. We could not leave this spell half-done for long. If the soul caught onto what we were up to and resisted, it could unravel everything.

As soon as our hands met, Annorah's ruby eyes shot open. Her features twisted into a grimace of pure torment as she lurched in a violent gasp for air. My heart stuttered, and just as quickly, she stilled. A gurgled sob wrenched past my lips. Despite the pain that wracked my bones, this was no time for grief.

Wind surged, whipping rain against my back in merciless lashes. Then, as a translucent purple cloud rose from Annorah's body, entirely unbothered by the surrounding torrent, all sound, all traces of the raging storm dissipated. It was as if we stood within a glass dome.

We watched, still focused on performing the spell, but astonished by the display before us. The stone giants' power poured in from the crest, a stark contrast to that strange violet cloud leaving our lost princess.

I looked a bit closer at that deep lavender hue. It was undoubtedly Annorah's—her essence was unmistakable. Though, as it lifted from her, entwined like a whispered shadow, was a soft layer of green. The two floating energies resembled the Borealis lights that graced the northern mountains.

Realization sank like a stone in my gut. We cast our spell to draw out her mana, but somehow, her essence entangled itself around it. It grasped on with its own ethereal might instead of freeing itself, retreating to the veil.

"Focus, ladies," I called. "We must separate the mana from her soul before it enters the vessel."

Our eyes closed, and we murmured the words in unison. We shifted the intention of the spell to separate the two layers, ensuring Annorah's mana remained while her spirit ascended to find peace. As we did, the purple cloud receded into the stone chest as planned. The subtle green hue lifted toward the sky just as it did when the druids ushered a creature's soul to the veil.

We worked at the continuous feed as it flowed, on and on, from Annorah's body. Our spell pulled at the tendrils of mist, separating them like undoing yarn from a spindle. Things seemed to be going smoothly, and we settled into an acceptable rhythm.

Then the chest vibrated, emitting a low hum. It grew louder, more violent until it shook so uncontrollably that it shrieked like cleaving marble. The piercing resonance threatened to shatter our eardrums, causing all of us to clasp our hands over our ears. Through narrowed eyes, I peered at the chest to find the bright, purple-hued light of Annorah's mana spilling over its edges. *It's full.*

"It's full!" I lifted my voice over the relentless howl, but only those close by heard me. "It's full! We need another vessel!"

My head snapped in every direction, failure clawing at my heart, desperate to find anything we could use. This was an unknown territory of mana that I never expected. We would have to split Annorah's power in half to contain it within this realm, but I was nowhere near sure if it was possible or what the ramifications would be.

"Your staff, Sidelle!" Saura, the Oakrend coven high witch and my adoptive mother, shouted over the clamor. With her arms pressed close to her head, body curled, agony distorted her features.

I glanced up at the stone giants, their faces mirroring our torture. Some fell to their knees, desperately fighting through their pain.

With the last of my resolve, I pried my palms from my ears and reached forward, slamming the chest shut. The intolerable, deafening screams cut short.

Anguish battled within as I dropped to my knees and grasped Annorah's limp hand in mine. Her skin had already begun to take on the placid coolness of death. Bile and grief rose in my throat, but I had to move fast. I retrieved the small dagger strapped to my thigh, sliced Annorah's ivory skin at the wrist, and squeezed what thickening blood I could onto the chest, praying there was enough soul still present to seal it, ensuring that this half of her magic was safe within.

There was a hiss of stone locking onto itself. It was done. I tossed my staff into the center of the spell and stood to clasp hands once more with my sisters. We stood in solemn solidarity, determined to hold true to our vow and fulfill our princess', our friend's, dying wish.

Shifting our focus again, we coaxed out the last of Annorah's mana set on separating it from her spirit. But the soul, tired of our meddling, had grown suspicious. It clung to what remained of her mana.

"Keep going!" I urged them on.

The stone giants poured their energy into the spell, supplementing our depleted power. We wrestled tirelessly to free the two energies. Though when the soul lost its grasp, it didn't release into the veil. It lingered, surrounding us in a thick green mist, obstructing our vision.

Just as the last smoky tendrils of energy separated from her body, an explosion erupted. The ground rocked beneath our feet and the translucent dome shattered. The concussive blast slammed into my chest, and everything went dark.

I woke to a dull ache in my head and the pained, worried voices of my sisters. When I pushed myself upright, the world swayed. I pressed my forehead to my knees until it settled enough for me to take in my surroundings.

The others appeared disheveled, some minor cuts and bruises, though altogether unharmed. Annorah's body lay utterly still. I moved closer to retrieve my staff. The water-logged grass soaked into my knees as I knelt beside her. Biting my tongue against the building sob, I collected the last drops of blood on her delicate wrist, smearing the crimson onto my staff's moonstone. It flashed a brilliant glimmer of light, an ethereal glow, signaling the mana was safe within. I breathed a heavy sigh of relief.

I gripped the staff with new meaning. My fingers traced the wooden grooves, then I stood, taking in the vast field. Devastation plunged through me. Annorah's stone giants were obliterated. I dropped to my knees, eyes locked in grief on the crumbled bodies cast in all directions. Footsteps approached from behind, and Saura settled her palm on my shoulder.

"Sidelle, honey. We need to talk," she whispered.

I blinked away the haze of tears and clasped onto her wrist, peering up at her. "What is it?" I asked, voice trembling and unsteady. I didn't think I could bear another shred of bad news. "Are the witches alright?"

"Yes, dear. We're fine." Her tone was calm, but earnest. "It's the chest."

I stood, frantic. It was gone.

"Where is it!?"

Saura urged me to meet her eyes. She pressed my hand to her heart while my frenzied gaze scoured the surrounding hills. "Sidelle! Sidelle, look at me!"

A hollow breath snagged my throat, and I forced myself to obey.

"It's gone!" she said. "It's gone, honey."

I tugged out of her hold. Wet hair slicked to my cheeks as I twisted, searching. "What do you mean? It can't be *gone!*"

Saura followed me, tight on my heels. "Her soul, the other half of Annorah's soul–"

When I spun around in a fury, she came to an abrupt halt. Her wet curls framed her stricken face. Again, she grasped my shaky hands in hers.

"Annorah's soul," she shook her head as if trying to make sense of it, "it stole the chest and escaped through the veil."

CHAPTER SEVEN
MIRA

"Why do I need to know all this?" I asked.

A stain of disappointment marked Sidelle's features, as if I entirely missed the point she'd been trying to make all day.

Dusk's fading light bathed everything in gold as the witch concluded her tale. We sat around the roaring fireplace now, cider in hand, bellies full from yet another spectacular meal, but I couldn't shake the feeling I'd been tricked. Her stall tactics were both pathetic and incredibly obvious.

She paused her story on multiple occasions. When lunch rolled around, she didn't bring up the subject at all while we ate. Then, when an unhurried visitor knocked on her door offering fresh flower arrangements, she entertained them for far too long. Even Eurok seemed mentally drained. That or the endless glasses of bourbon he'd been drinking all day were finally getting to him. *Do druids not get drunk?*

I stole a glance out the window, seeing the tall gates in the distance. The day's stress had them feeling more like the walls of a prison.

"The point is, Mira," Sidelle said, "it's not pure happenstance that you look exactly like Annorah, and suffered a vast reaction in the stone forest. That swirling storm of static energy *was* Annorah's mana. The chest only contained a fraction of her power. We vastly underestimated how much she possessed, and the residual mana lingering there recognized your soul."

My lack of enthusiasm sat plain on my face. The toll of the day was evident in her tired eyes and slumped posture. The patience I once believed to be endless was waning.

After a long sigh, she continued, "I believe your souls are one and the same, and just as Annorah could possess mana, we," she gestured between Eurok and herself, "think you can too."

I zoned out, paying more attention to the pattern of the woodgrain floors than the words coming out of her mouth. Their heavy stares were pinpricks on my skin. Perhaps it was a combination of overwhelm and shock, but I couldn't deny my presence had been reduced to mind-numbing fatigue and emotional detachment.

Instead, I went over my plan to leave again. Follow the river, find a town, obtain a horse. I'd travel to South Port, board a ship, then get the hell out of this kingdom. *I should've done it years ago.*

A sour pinch of guilt picked at my insides, pondering how long Sidelle had been fighting for this cause and the hope Annorah represented for her. She just wanted what's best for her people, and though some small piece of me sympathized, it still changed nothing for *me*. I was human. I couldn't wield magic, and I wasn't some dead princess reborn. My resolve rising, I grabbed my bourbon and tossed it back in one large swig.

"Listen, I mean no disrespect, but I can't wrap my head around how this is possible." I made a conscious effort to control my tone, though politeness wasn't a practiced skill set. If that didn't emphasize how far from a princess I was, I didn't know what would. "Thank you for your hospitality, but I would like to leave now." I stood.

Eurok raised an eyebrow in an expression that said, 'Oh shit.' then took another sip from his glass. Sidelle, though, looked at me with those endless dark eyes. For a fraction of a second, the years I learned about today stared back at me—years of diligent service, years working toward a future she staked her entire life on. With a single sentence, I just fractured some large part of that nine hundred years of hope.

Something shifted in her expression, an emotion I hadn't seen yet. Anger? Desperation? It faded before I placed it.

She braced her elbows on her knees and clasped her hands. Her brow pinched, as if she didn't want to deliver her next words. "This truth will follow you beyond every border, across every ocean. And someday your powers will emerge. It pains me to say this, but you don't have a choice in that."

My eyes narrowed, and she straightened.

"I am not your enemy," she said. "I only wish for you to see me as the ally I can be—that I *want* to be."

Red clouded my mind, fueling my irritation. "I don't need allies."

Eurok stood from his place by the fire. "Sidelle, love, let's give her a moment. It's been a long day."

I didn't want a moment. I wanted to leave.

Sidelle ignored him anyway. Her brows furrowed in a stern mixture of frustration and determination, and perhaps a bit of pity, too. "You think you have something to prove? Good." She nodded. "That determination has, no doubt, aided you all your life. But wherever it is you plan on running to," she jerked her chin, gesturing beyond the village gates, "will not be where you prove it."

"What makes you so sure?" I asked, my stubbornness driving.

"She speaks directly to the gods, girl," Eurok said, as if it were obvious.

"She told me they've been silent."

His eyes flicked to Sidelle.

But I wasn't done. I dropped into my chair again and sat back, crossing my legs and folding my arms. "Besides, I don't believe in the gods. If I am of such high importance, where the hell were they when my mother died? Or when my father forced ale down my throat until I blacked out?"

Eurok's sharp jaw clenched. Whether at the edge of my tone or the uncomfortable story from my childhood, I wasn't sure.

"Where were the gods when I stole to survive? When I killed to save myself from being raped in the streets?" Sidelle stiffened. "If you truly speak to the gods, do me a favor, will you?" I jerked my chin. "Tell them to fuck off."

A heavy, suffocating silence ensued, prompting me to stand and head for the door. As I did so, the druids exchanged yet another anxious glance.

"You put no faith in the gods? Fine. I can understand why you feel that way."

Her whispered words slowed my retreat, and I stopped. She rubbed her brow as if warding off a headache.

"Still, you stand here today stronger than you otherwise would've been. We don't choose our monsters, Mira. They choose us," she said. "I don't have all the answers, though I wish I did. What I'm offering you is a home, food, clothing, whatever you like. It is at your disposal."

"This sounds a lot like bribery."

"Perhaps. But what have you got to lose?"

Had my eyes been a blade, they would have sliced her. "What have I got to lose? Are you fucking kidding me?"

I had lost everything *because* of these people. Yes, it may have started with the king, but she could have set me free immediately after leaving the castle. Not hire a carriage to transport me hundreds of miles in the wrong direction.

"I could've boarded a ship in Breckenridge by now." My shoulders squared. "I had the chance at a fresh start somewhere no one has seen this *godsdamned* face. But because of *you* and that vile son-of-a-bitch on the throne fucking it up for me, I lost *everything*."

Somehow my dagger made it into my fist, though using it never crossed my mind. I wasn't stupid enough to think I could kill either of them, especially after witnessing their power. Despite my disadvantage, I was not about to let them treat me as if my miserable life somehow meant less than any number of lifetimes they've lived. These ancient druids lived tenfold beyond any human lifespan. They couldn't comprehend what it was like to have *one*. Just when I thought my life was becoming my own, something I could finally cherish, they ripped it from me.

Eurok pinned me with a glare, a warning not to do anything stupid. From the moment I raised my voice, his hands never left his daggers. My fingers traced the familiar grooves etched into the hilt. As hard as I could, I swung the blade downward. With a loud, infuriated yell of effort, I stabbed the cedar table, then stormed upstairs to my room—cell.

Sidelle called after me, my name dusted with regret, but I heard enough. I sat there all day listening to the story of her precious princess and how she sacrificed herself for her people. But that was just it—I had no people. I took care of myself, and I was fucking good at it.

In the room, I kicked off the boots and dropped onto the bed. I stared up at the vaulted ceiling, following its arched wooden beams to the spectacular stag-antler chandelier. If I wasn't so caught up in my temper, I might have appreciated the intricate copper inlays and bleached-bone, but my blood was *boiling*.

Like a cobra flushing a rodent from its den, any tenderness I held for the witch fled my body. I'd been so stupid. I buried my head underneath the thick down pillow. Hidden from the last glimpse of dusk, I willed sleep to drag today's nightmares from my mind. She said I was free to go—and I expected her to hold true to that promise. At first light, I'd demand a horse. It was the least she could do.

Rest took over, effectively fogging out my furious thoughts, and I woke to a low knock on the door. I leaned across the plush mattress and lit the lantern on the bedside table. As I did, a series of sconces along the bedroom walls ignited as well. I shook my head. I'd never get *used* to mana, let alone wield it.

"Mira?" a gruff voice called.

I half-expected someone to come to talk to me, but truth be told, I didn't think it'd be the captain.

I sat up with a sigh, threw back the soft, white comforter, and slid off the bed, landing on the jute area rug. The space had a light, airy essence to it. The strange, rounded walls served as a constant reminder that the home was woven into a tree. Every soft surface was white, from the long gossamer curtains that blew in a comfortable breeze to the cushioned lounge chairs tucked into a small reading nook. A simple blend of comfort and nature.

I padded to the door and cracked it open.

Eurok's severe face was lit by the light behind me. "Can we talk?"

His expression was difficult to read, but he seemed less angry than when I stormed out of the conversation. I stepped away, leaving the way ajar so he could let himself in.

"Uh, perhaps you might join me outside—or in another room?"

The answering glower I gave him over my shoulder was all he needed. He cleared his throat, then followed me inside, gently closing the door behind him. I moved to the large circular window overlooking the village, and Eurok took up the space beside me. For a moment, we stood there, our eyes fixed on the view.

Outside, the moon bathed the waterfalls in gentle silver light, and they glittered back in spectacular thanks. Lanterns lining the empty cobblestone streets flickered. All was calm and silent. It was so peaceful, so beautiful, it almost wasn't fair. While the heat of my anger lingered, the sharp edges softened, my ire dissipating.

"Are you okay?" Eurok finally asked.

"I'll be fine." I almost didn't recognize the melancholy in my voice.

"Sidelle didn't mean for it to come out like that, you know?"

Maybe not, but my frustration wasn't that simple, and we both knew it. At least he tried.

"I owe Sidelle. I know that I do. But I think she makes the mistake of believing that, just because I lived on the streets prior to all of this, that I didn't have a life—that I wasn't working my ass off for something that mattered to me. Sure, I was a pathetic street rat, but I had dreams of my own." The edge in my tone sharpened with my words, but I had enough yelling for one night. After a slow, steadying breath, I managed a whisper. "And now all of it's gone."

"It would've been gone anyway had she not saved you from that dungeon."

"I know that!" I snipped. My gaze dropped, and I picked at a loose bit of paint on the windowsill. "Just because I have Sidelle to thank for saving me, doesn't mean I *owe* her my life. Does it?"

He paused a few heartbeats before answering. "She has no desire to control you. She wants to encourage you."

"To be something I'm not." With a huff, I pushed away from the window. When I plopped on the bed, the springs squeaked in protest. "I'm no princess. I can't wield magic. And I don't belong here."

"Humans," he shook his head as he faced me, "you're all the same."

"How so?"

"You're all so self-absorbed."

I crossed my arms over my chest and quirked a brow.

"Hold on now." He chuckled, sensing my disapproval. "You spend your lives seeking happiness, do you not?"

My eyes rolled. This was getting too philosophical for my liking. "Is that not the point?"

"Not in the way *humans* think it is."

"Well, don't keep me in suspense," I drawled.

He loosed a hearty laugh this time and scratched the dark brown scruff on his chin. "You see, humans seek individual contentment. You all assume to have achieved happiness *despite* the world, *despite* your challenges, yields a successful life." He leaned his weight against the windowsill. "But you have it all wrong. It's within like-minded communities where true pleasure lies—serving others and contributing to each other's prosperity."

My face conveyed my doubt. I refused to accept that anyone, human or not, wouldn't be driven by the pursuit of happiness. I still wanted *my h*appy ending—even now, when it seemed impossible. He might as well have been speaking another language, for all the good it did to convince me. It was a pipe dream.

"If that were true," I said, "and you've witnessed firsthand what life's like across that border, then you'd know it would never be enough, nothing is ever enough. You'd recognize just how far gone we really are."

"Do you believe that about all humans?" he asked, his gaze as pensive as a sunrise—with the colors to match.

"Maybe not *all.*"

"And what about yourself? Are you too far gone?"

At that, I fixed my attention on anything but him. "Maybe." A tightness swelled in my throat, and I swallowed against it. "Or I just never belonged there, either."

"Where do you belong, then?" He settled on the edge of the bed, and the mattress dipped with his weight.

The truth? I had no idea. Though, admitting that out loud seemed counterintuitive to the point I was making—that I didn't belong *here.*

But he read the silent answer on my face, anyway. "Sidelle believes you belong here."

"Sidelle believes I'm a princess with magical powers," I scoffed. "What do you believe?"

"That doesn't matter."

"That only makes me more curious."

I doubted his view would change anything for me, but I was interested to hear it from someone other than the witch, and something told me Eurok would give it to me straight. He carried himself with poise and certainty, a being who knew exactly where he belonged, the surety of a true leader.

He drew in a long, slow breath before answering. "I don't possess the same skill set as Sidelle. I've never spoken to the gods. To be honest, I'm not sure they're listening anymore. But—if she claimed I was destined for something, I'd be willing to listen."

"Even if it goes against everything you know about yourself?"

"I've lived for hundreds of years. If there is one thing I've figured out, it's that we are always learning about ourselves. If she revealed my life was intended for something as extraordinary as what she believes yours is—then yes. I'd listen."

Confident.

Realization dawned on me then, and I couldn't keep from smiling. Pieces slid together like a mosaic made to be admired from a distance. He'd been entirely at ease, witty even, when my anger was directed at him. But the moment my ire shifted to Sidelle, he tensed, readying himself to defend. That alone would suggest nothing more than his willingness to protect her. But I recalled the way his intense stare consumed her, and how all day they seemed to move with one another as if a tether bound them. Having never felt it myself, it was strange how easily I read it on his face.

"You love her, don't you?" I expected him to deny it. But he didn't.

"More than my own life."

"Are you," I wasn't sure what the term was for them, "partners?"

"No. Though it's not for a lack of trying on my part." A sly smile crept across his lips.

"Does Sidelle not return your affections?"

With a soft laugh, his attention returned to the window. "She denies her feelings because she feels she needs to."

My eyes narrowed, both with curiosity and skepticism. "Why?"

"Because, ironically, Sidelle is working toward a future where all can find happiness. And she believes, though I doubt she'd ever admit it, that if she were to give in to her feelings, it would distract her from what she has been pursuing her entire life."

"That's very," I fought the urge to say naïve, "insightful of you."

"No, it's not. Nearly three hundred years, and I've only *just* learned the scope of what she's capable of, what she's fighting for."

"And what would that be?" I asked.

"The same thing Annorah gave her life for. A world where everyone belongs."

SIDELLE

My guilt surged, threatening to invoke a rising storm for what I said to Mira. I spent the last hour pacing at the base of the stairs, waiting for Eurok to return from speaking with her. My heels ached from how heavily I pounded against the pine planks. When I finally gave it a rest, I ventured into the den to steep in my turmoil near the fire.

Gods, how could I have been so ignorant? Less than forty-eight hours passed since she lost everything. Of course, she'd be furious with me. Nine hundred years of navigating diplomatic relations between the royal court and the druid council, and here I was struggling to surmise what a twenty-three-year-old girl wanted.

I swallowed against my own shame. I didn't ask, never stopped to *think*. My focus dwelled on closing the deal, securing her agreement to help. I never considered what she was going through. I'd been no better than a spider, luring her into my web with my promises of food and comfort.

Upstairs, the door creaked open, and I stood. Mira descended the stairs, her long, dark hair swaying with each step. Eurok followed close behind.

"Mira, I'm so sorry."

Her energy still escaped my ability to read it clearly, so I checked her features for some clue as to how she felt. With a desperate heart, I searched for any hint of forgiveness written there.

"It's okay. Eurok explained where you were coming from and," she paused a breath as if to gather her words, "I've... I've decided that I'm going to stay. I'll *try* to do as you ask."

Doubt still resonated in her tone, but it was a start.

Eurok's eyes were alight with satisfaction, and I could have kissed him.

"I'm so glad to hear that. But Mira, I never meant to be so insensitive. I just—"

"I know," she said through a sigh. "So we're clear, I don't *believe* I am who you say I am, but," she paused again and pressed her lips, "I'll try."

I blinked, stunned that this was the same young woman who stabbed my end table hours ago.

Eurok nudged me in the arm as he walked past. "Nearly a century old, and we still haven't figured out how to keep from putting our foot in our mouths, have we?"

I rolled my eyes, then faced Mira. A small, strained smile wavered on her cheeks.

"Well, I'm tired." She shrugged, jerking a thumb over her shoulder. "I'm gonna head to bed." She dipped her chin at Eurok. "See you in the morning?"

He nodded, and she shuffled back upstairs.

When her door clicked shut, I turned to Eurok with a wide smile. His countenance lit up in response, and I leapt into his arms. He lifted me off the ground as if I weighed little more than a sack of feathers.

"I don't know how to thank you."

His eyes darkened as he flashed a suggestive grin. "Oh, I have a couple of ideas," he said, setting me down. The devil in him replacing the angel that'd just been my saving grace.

"Eurok, please." A giggle escaped through the words. I pushed a bit of hair behind my ear, casually stepping away.

His rough, calloused hand wrapped around my wrist, pulling me to him again. With gentle fingers, he gripped my chin, holding my gaze. I thought he would press his mouth to mine—but he didn't.

My body was a charged volt under the molten swell of his eyes. They poured over me. I worked to steady my heart. *Erezos, save me.* He was so beautiful.

I settled my palm against his cheek, my mana seeking his energy, but it came up empty. Disappointment gnawed on my soul, though I had no right to feel that way. Eurok kept his energy close, as many males did. Still, a small part of me always hoped he'd let me in.

In the early years of our friendship, that sly smile and clever wit weakened my knees despite my insistence to maintain clear professional lines. One night, I even dreamt of how it might feel if he offered me his arm in a senuae. The customary gesture of interest stole my breath, even in my sleep. With arms and auras open, we presented our literal and spiritual selves to the other. His light fingertips grazed mine, our auras intermingled in a beautiful, intimate display, the two of us becoming one—becoming mates.

Though, in the waking world, Eurok understood where my true commitment resided. With my people. While time and distance did little to quell his interest, I spent years denying the depth of my own. But today, it was as if something had changed. I sensed it in how he found any excuse to touch me, to be near me, the way his eyes tracked my every move. It was growing more and more difficult to ignore how much I *craved* it—craved him.

"Why do you keep your energy under lock and key?" I asked. A soft burn warmed my cheeks. I'd spoken to seize my only chance to avoid succumbing to that stare—I hadn't expected the words to come out so forward.

One edge of his mouth twitched upward in a devastating smirk. "Because if you read what you do to me, love, I doubt you'd allow me in the same room with you again."

CHAPTER EIGHT

MIRA

The situation was temporary. I was curious to see where this would lead—nothing beyond that. I knew myself well enough that if I made it to Breckenridge and onto a ship, the 'what ifs' would fester and plague me like a cancerous tumor across oceans. So, I stayed.

When I made it downstairs, Sidelle sat perched in the same chair as last night, her feet neatly tucked beneath her, a tea cup wrapped in her delicate hand. With the other, she combed through a rather large book in her lap. There was a distinct pinch in her brow, hinting at her dissatisfaction or frustration with what she had come across, or perhaps what she hadn't. She must have been deep in thought because when I spoke, she started.

"Morning." I waved as I started for the door.

"Good morning." Her smile brightened, showing her enthusiasm. "Where are you off to?"

"Eurok promised we'd start training today. I was gonna go find him."

She closed the book and set it on the table, seeming pleased by my excitement. As she stood and headed to the kitchen counter, I read the tome's spine. *Vylandrian Legends of the Twelve.*

"I believe he said he'd be at the stables. Here." She tossed me an apple.

I caught it and took a large bite, then spoke around my mouthful. "Thanks."

I stepped out onto the arched stoop, then wandered down the incline to the gravel path that led into the village. Hoofprints from what I assumed were Eurok's horse pressed into the dirt. I followed them until small, picturesque buildings bordered the cobblestone road. Wooden signs hung over shop doors, and quaint dinette sets or benches were placed out front for lounging. Homes with second-story balconies overlooked the quiet street. Everything felt simple and peaceful, like an oasis between the cascading falls.

A peek through a window showed the clothing store Sidelle stocked my wardrobe with. The witch had my style pinned. I ran my hand over my stomach, admiring the soft satin of the long-sleeved blouse I wore today. Black, of course.

The round window of the next shop snared my notice. Dingy cobwebs caked with dust hung from the panes. Inside, hundreds of vials lined the shelves from floor to ceiling. Four witches waited to be served at the counter. Two of them seemed to be of a higher status, similar to Sidelle, while the others were meek handmaids, wearing servants' apron dresses. A rickety, green sign hanging from metal hooks above the door creaked and swung in the gentle breeze.

Agatha's Mortar and Pestle
'Charms, Curses, and Potions'
Custom orders inquire within.

Unable to resist the temptation, I slipped inside behind an elderly, tan-skinned witch who smelled of rosemary and wood smoke. I lingered near the outskirts to avoid unwanted attention and browsed. An unimaginable array of potions for various ailments filled the shelves. Some were labeled as simple remedies for things like rashes, pain, and warts. There were sleeping tonics, invigorating brews, and items charmed to increase sexual arousal or luck. Others were designated for specific interests—a tincture to induce inspiration, and an elixir to change eye color.

I fingered the small bottles, not looking for anything in particular, when a familiar vial snagged my notice. The tangerine-scented oil I added to my bath. I pushed my sleeve up and traced my forearm, where a good bit of scarring used to be. A faint reappearance marked the heavier scars, though still lighter than before. I plucked it off the shelf to examine the label.

Topical Diminishing Potion
Scent: Tangerine

I turned the bottle over, trying to find some clue of its contents, what made it work. Did it consist of simple ingredients, things I could gather and make myself, or was there true magic inside? Abandoning my previous plan to remain invisible, I stood in line, making sure I was the last one in the store before I stepped up to the counter.

The shopkeeper was petite and plainly pretty. Her straight brown hair hung down in a sheet to her hips, and her sage eyes were bright beneath long, dark lashes. My errant thoughts had me wondering how old she was. Sidelle's youthful appearance didn't look a day over thirty. This girl—witch—could be centuries old.

"Hello." She cocked her head in silent scrutiny.

I chewed my cheek, unsure how often humans visited Raven Ridge, then shrugged off my unease and held up the oil. "I have a question about this."

Somehow, without letting her smile drop, her brow furrowed, as if confused. Had I missed some customary greeting? I produced my best attempt at a polite grin that might've looked more like a twitch and set the vial on the counter.

She barely glanced at it, then said, "I don't believe I've seen you around here before." Her voice was sickeningly sweet.

"Nope, just got here. So, does this have magic in it?"

"I'm sorry?"

"Magic, uh, I mean mana. A spell?" Gods, I looked like a damned fool. I had no idea how to phrase my question or what terminology they used for their powers. Had Sidelle been using 'magic' interchangeably for my sake, so my simple human brain could follow? I plucked it from the countertop and gave it a little shake. "What's in this stuff?"

Her face lit up with realization, and she secured the vial between her finger and thumb, letting the faint light from the windows filter through the blue glass. After a soft, delightful laugh, she nodded. "Some of our inventory contains mana. Others are tinctures or potions passed through generations of teachings and contain none at all. This particular one is made using my altar's mana, though."

"Your what?"

"My altar, Agatha. This is her shop." Still smiling, she set the vial aside and placed her palm against her chest. "I'm her apprentice. She's helping me hone my healing gift, so I might have a shop of my own someday. Would you like a free sample of my very own menstruation brew?" Pride poured off her as she retrieved a small box from beneath the counter. Inside were a dozen neatly folded tea bags packaged and prepped for sale.

I raised my brows and nodded, trying to give her some sort of satisfaction. "Oh, okay. Um, no thanks."

I backed up a step, making to leave. There was zero chance I'd get any answers without getting sucked into a full-length conversation with this exhaustingly cheerful witch. Before I reached the exit, a boisterous voice boomed from the back room, slowing my retreat.

"Belle!"

A burly witch, whose face resembled the wrinkly morel mushrooms I used to forage from the forest, hobbled out between two flimsy swinging doors. Her long, skinny legs poked out beneath the skirt of her dingy orange dress, which hung off her round body like a drape. She waddled from side to side toward the counter, then shooed Belle off with her cane.

"Quit your blabberin' and get that deadnettle I asked for."

A sudden tickle overwhelmed me, and I sneezed, drawing their attention. "Excuse me."

Belle nodded submissively, that sweet smile never leaving her face, then hurried out the door, still wearing her apron.

The old witch turned her eyes on me, a pipe hanging from her dried lips. "You're Sidelle's girl, aren't ya."

It wasn't a question. I sniffed, attempting to ward off another sneeze. Were there chrysanthemums nearby?

She leaned against the counter and gestured to her surroundings. "Welp, she told me if you made your way here to let you have your pick—to put it on her tab."

"Sidelle said that?" Another sneeze.

The hag smacked her lips as she took a drag from the pipe, her expression marred with boredom. "Mmhmm. So, is this all you're after?" she asked, pointing at the potion.

"Actually, I was just wondering what was in it."

She arched a weathered brow. "You want me to give you my recipe?"

I sneezed again. "I was curious if the ingredients were things I could forage—make myself when I leave here." This was far too much for a simple question. I regretted bothering to ask.

Agatha leaned over the counter, looking at me through narrow, watery eyes, smoke rolling out her nose like a cantankerous dragon. "You ain't spent much time 'round witches, have you, girl?"

"Name's Mira. And no, I haven't."

"Well, first rule—don't just *ask* for a witch's recipes. It's ceremonious for a witch to pass on her spells. But seein' you're Sidelle's apprentice..." she trailed off, hobbling away.

"I'm not her apprentice," I called, chasing my words with another sneeze. *Fuck these allergies.*

Agatha waved me off and disappeared behind the swinging doors. I scanned the shop in her absence, shifting my weight from foot to foot, unsure if she'd return.

A moment later, she teetered into view, holding a dark green tome. "Here, girl. Take this to your *not-a*ltar." The mockery in her tone wasn't lost on me as she dropped the book on the countertop beside the potion.

"What is it?" With a single finger, I lifted the cover. The verdant leather was supple and worn. *This must be as ancient as she is.*

Agatha slammed it shut, smacking my hand away. My nose wrinkled at the cranky witch.

"Girl, if you ain't got a lot to learn." Her dry chuckle morphed into a cough. "Don't be screwin' 'round with that now. You take it to Sidelle. It's my grimoire—has all my spells in it. Some require mana, but a few don't. Tell 'er to start with those, though I can't imagine why she'd be tryin' to altar a human anyhow. Seems like a waste of time to me."

Agreed. "Then why give this to me?"

"Because what Sidelle wants, Sidelle gets, and you best listen to her if you know what's good for ya. Few witches rival that one's power. If she thinks you're worth trainin', well, let's see what ya got, kid."

I sneezed again. "Are there chrysanthemums somewhere in here?" My annoyance laced the question.

Agatha peered down her nose as if giving another thought to her last words, then straightened and smacked the thick oak countertop with a clack of her many rings. "Welp, good luck."

Then she hobbled away, leaving me with her grimoire and the potion.

By the time I finished retracing my steps to deliver the tome, the afternoon sun reached its zenith. I was running way behind. When I made it to the stables, I found Eurok sitting atop his dapple gray, holding the reins of a beautiful buckskin mare.

"What's this?" I asked, trailing my hand along the animal's sleek neck.

"Thought we might go on a hunt for your first day of training."

My stomach knotted at the mischievous glint in his eye, but I climbed in the saddle. "What are we hunting?"

He must have noted my apprehension, because he chuckled, then handed me the reins. "You'll see."

The massive wooden gates opened, and the guards atop the wall gave a casual salute to Eurok as we rode through. Instead of following the road, he cut to the left. After breaking through the brambles hedging the treeline, our horses trudged along the mossy forest floor. The horses were familiar with this terrain. They hopped over gnarled roots and snaked around broad trunks.

We rode in silence for a while, listening to the symphony of birds and insects. The forest's scent was thick with the sweet rot of leaves and wood. Something about it felt so different from any forest I'd been in. I thought back on those books I read as a child, recalling which creatures might prowl these woodlands.

Aside from the baldric of daggers Eurok wore yesterday, and the ax strapped to the saddle, I spied no other weapons. *I'll be pissed if he dragged me out here to track a damn deer.*

If that were the case, then why not just say so? I doubted it was something so common. Maybe a paragon wolf? My books described the latter as skilled hunters—they'd be a challenge to take down. Our close-range weapons would put us within reach of their dagger-like fur around their throats. Though, if I remembered correctly, those beasts were considered rare nowadays. Surely a druid wouldn't be interested in hunting a creature whose presence in the forest was so sparse.

A high-pitched whistle broke the silence. I snapped my head to the right, searching for the source.

"Ignore it," Eurok called over his shoulder.

"What is it?"

"If I tell you, then that wouldn't be ignoring it," he said flatly.

My lips sank into a firm line as I canvassed the thick canopy and misty undergrowth, searching for any sign of movement. It was eerie. The deep shadows and distant trees emitted an ominous, overbearing essence.

A twig snapped to my left. The sound echoed off the trunks, ricocheting in all directions. Save for the steady hoofbeats and Eurok's exasperated sigh, I detected nothing else. This time, tiny child-like giggles rattled off behind me.

I whipped around in the saddle. "What was that?"

I'd never admit it, but that sing-song laughter made my skin crawl. An unsettling chill lifted the fine hairs on the nape of my neck, and my horse's ears pressed flat against her head. Whether she sensed my anxiety or something else, I wasn't sure.

"Mira, settle yourself!" Eurok whispered, harsh and irritated.

"But–"

He turned in his saddle. "I said–"

From an overhanging branch, something dropped, landing right behind me. I spun, a shriek sitting on the edge of my tongue. A spindly figure, no larger than a common house cat, stared up at me with black, bulbous eyes. With a strange, mischievous grin, it lifted a tiny green hand and smacked my horse's rump with a sharp crack. Then it was gone.

Agitated and now scared, the horse reared and bucked my ass out of the saddle. My back hit the forest floor with a muffled thud, all air knocked free from my lungs in a violent huff.

I lay there, staring up at the canopy. A chorus of laughter erupted from all sides—tiny little chiding voices.

Nymphs.

Eurok's unimpressed face appeared, hovering over my own. "I told you to ignore it."

"Oh, shut up," I snarled.

I shoved myself upright, brushing off clumps of moss and debris. A flood of embarrassment and fury coursed through my veins. I should have known it was a nymph. Those tricky little bastards were known for their ruthless sense of humor.

Eurok lowered himself from the saddle and stalked toward me, his footsteps hardly audible on the dense forest floor. He offered his hand to help me to my feet. I accepted, but when I tried to let go, Eurok did not.

His severe gaze narrowed on my face, features pinched with disapproval. "Do you enjoy learning things the hard way?" he asked. "Or do you just naturally do the opposite of what you're told?"

I tugged, attempting to free myself from his hold. "I don't know. Maybe no one has ever said anything worth listening to."

Eurok let go, and I stormed toward my horse.

"Mira, stop."

I didn't. Bitter embarrassment roared in my ears, clouding any shred of obedience.

"I said, *stop!*"

A burst of air hurled into me, rocking the trees and tossing my face in the dirt. Impulse took over, and I snagged my dagger from its sheath, flipping onto my back. My fingers flexed around the hilt, prepared to defend. If he decided I was too much trouble to deal with, if he was tired of my attitude and wanted me dead, I didn't care how strong he was—I wouldn't go down without a fight.

Indignation coated his expression, and for a moment, I thought he might climb onto his horse and leave me here. He stomped past me instead, kneeling a few paces from my head, inspecting something.

I shook off the fact I'd been knocked to the ground, not once, but twice in a matter of minutes, and pushed myself up with a groan.

"What is it?" I asked.

Eurok rose from his crouch and turned on me. "When we train, you are in my charge. That means you check that *fucking* ego at the door."

His words cut at my pride like daggers raining over my skin. That rumble of power I felt on the balcony yesterday trembled along the dirt beneath my feet.

"If you are unwilling to listen, then you're unwilling to learn," he said. "You will die in these woods. Do you understand?"

Few things have caused me to take pause like I did as the forest surged in response to his energy, as if every living thing swelled, reaching toward the power that poured from this druid. I'd seen nothing like it, *felt* nothing like it.

Those easy, molten eyes from last night, that glowed when he spoke of Sidelle, were no more. They were hardened into solid topaz. My back straightened with the force of his glare. This was not the same Eurok who I shared a casual conversation with, nor the cocky jokester who enjoyed antagonizing me when we met. This was the captain of the druid army, and to him, I was an unrestrained subordinate in need of his training. I swallowed my pride and gave a tight nod.

Eurok nodded too, and his shoulders relaxed as he settled back into his crouch. "This is what we're here for."

I knelt beside him, examining the mossy bit of ground he inspected. Even this close, I couldn't see anything but a single string of a spider's web stretched across two fronds.

"This?" I reached for the thin webbing.

"Stop."

This time, I listened.

"Don't touch it." He pointed toward the canopy. "Look."

Directly overhead, nestled between the trees, was an immense webbed net. It was difficult to see, but I tracked the string it hung by. It curved upwards around a thick branch, then down the trunk until it jutted across the space ahead. The thin strands seemed so precarious, so fragile.

"If that dropped on you, you'd be constricted to death."

"Constricted?" My mouth fell open.

Eurok straightened, then grabbed our horses' reins, guiding them over. I stood, still gawking at the web above. What sort of creature could create something so horrifying?

"It's triggered by the flow of your blood—your pulse. It constricts with every beat of your heart until there isn't one. Then all the adraknid needs to do is come slurp up what's left."

"We're here to hunt something capable of both spinning a web that size," I pointed up with raised brows, "*and* setting a complex trap?"

"Isn't that what all spiders do? Set traps and slurp guts?"

He chuckled to himself while all I managed was a choked gag.

"It made its nest too close to the village," he said. "It needs to be taken care of."

We mounted our horses, and I followed closely behind, giving the trap a wide berth. Silence hung in the air for a short time while I scanned the treetops for more webs, and even more so for the thing that spun them. I did my best not to sulk, but that bitter taste of embarrassment settled in my chest, boiling like acid.

But Eurok was right. Just because the idea of me being some street rat remake of their princess was a load of shit didn't mean everything here was a joke. Had he let me storm away like a petulant child, that thing would have fallen on me, and I'd be dead. Every moment of the last eight years was spent trusting my instincts, honing skills, and doing what I thought was best to keep myself alive—none of it mattered here.

What *did* matter was that one of the most powerful druids in the kingdom wanted to train me to remove *real* monsters from the world. If I meant to see that for the opportunity it was, I needed to accept that I knew nothing. This place was full of dangers I never conceived. To survive here meant letting go of my pride and learning to listen. If not, it was likely I'd end up in the belly of one of these foreign beasts.

"What did you call it? The thing we're hunting?" I asked, still scanning the treeline ahead.

"An adraknid."

I revisited the encyclopedia in my mind, recalling every creature I read about as a child, but came up empty. Though, having 'drak' in its name made me take pause. "Drak? As in drak demons?"

He pulled on the reins and waited for me to reach his side before moving on. "What do you know about the drak?"

"Only that they somehow got into our world and couldn't be reasoned with, so humans and druids of Westryelle worked together to defeat them." I recited the condensed version of the history I'd been taught.

"And for humans, that's all there was to it."

I ducked under a thin branch. "That's not what happened?"

Eurok pulled out his waterskin and took a sip. "That's not how it ended."

"So, how did it end?"

"It didn't. Not entirely, at least."

"Are you saying drak are still here? In Westryelle?" I restrained the flood of apprehension from bleeding into my voice.

"In a sense." He replaced the top on his water skin and stowed it away. "When drak first arrived, their presence went unnoticed for a time. It was before the four clans had been established. There weren't as many of us back then, so Vylandria wasn't patrolled as heavily as it is now."

I tried again to wrap my head around how vast and ancient this country really was. "Were you there when the clans split?" I asked.

"Fuck no. That was way before my time." He smirked. "I'm about four hundred, give or take."

"You don't know how old you are?" I raised a brow.

"It stops mattering after the first couple hundred years."

He closed his eyes and listened for what I assumed my ears would never hear.

He looked no older than his late twenties, hardly a wrinkle on his ruddy, handsome face. But he carried himself like a force, one that felt ancient and unconstrained. It was hard to imagine him young and untrained, a mere subordinate to his superior.

"How were they discovered?" I asked.

"After the first few made it through the fissure, they wreaked havoc on our ecosystem. They mated with our native species, and the resulting creatures were horrendous abominations. Nightmares."

The warrior rolled his shoulders. His leather spaulder flexed over his sculpted muscles, and I couldn't help but wonder how many abominations he executed over the centuries.

"And adraknids are one of them?"

He nodded. "Most of the hybrid species have been wiped out completely, but adraknids and a few others have unfortunately flourished. The one we're after has taken up residence in an old mausoleum." He peered my way. "And you're going to clear it out."

My lips clamped shut, fearing my voice would give me away, but he read my trepidation all over my face.

"You'll be fine," he assured me, "as long as you're willing to listen." Then he kicked his horse to move ahead, avoiding my searing scowl.

Traps were scattered throughout the forest, growing denser as we neared the creature's hideout. We dismounted and hitched our horses to a branch, then skirted between trees that were safe to walk beneath, our footsteps hardly a whisper over the damp undergrowth.

Soon, the mausoleum came into view. Made from crumbling moss-covered stone, the deteriorating old structure barely stood out from its surroundings. There were no signs of life here. No birds, no insects, no scurrying creatures. The silence was pregnant with warning, and my spine chilled in response as we knelt down beside a tree at the edge of the clearing.

"It'll be easier to fight it in the open instead of going in after it. They're nocturnal, so it's best to wait here for it to come out."

He didn't so much as whisper, appearing as casual as if we were hunting rabbits.

Was I overestimating this creature? Or was he just so powerful that a demon hybrid spider was a trivial concern?

The sun touched the horizon, casting the forest in bruised shadows, when a guttural scream ripped me from my thoughts. Our heads snapped the direction we'd come as a terrified whinnying echoed out. My heart skidded to a halt.

The horses.

Eurok stood and, without hesitation, grabbed me around the wrist and flung me onto his back. I gripped his neck and was forced to bury my head in his shoulder as he ran. He dodged trees with the ease of a whip-poor-will, and in seconds, we were at the horses. Gut-wrenching screams pierced out from overhead. I lowered myself from him, staring into the canopy, worried this commotion might stir the vile creature before we regained our advantage.

The last amber light of day illuminated the horrific scene. My horse hung by a net of webs. Vast disbelief slackened my jaw as its screams were strangled from its body.

Eurok threw himself at the tree, scrambling up with ease. Balanced near the branch the poor creature dangled from, I thought he might cut it free somehow. Instead, he placed a hand against the enormous trunk, and the bark beneath his palm took on a warm golden glow. His expression was pleading, as if urging the forest to respond.

The branches, to my astonishment, lowered, bolstering my horse's weight to the lichen-covered earth. Entangled and suffering in a mess of webs, I moved to free the whimpering animal. Before I reached it, a shuddering snap reverberated through the air as the horse bones, the size of carriage axles, folded in half. My stomach heaved as I struggled to retain my composure—then it stopped.

I froze, gaping and dumbfounded, unable to move. Eurok dropped with a muffled thud, and for a moment, we stood in silence, our faces pressed in dejected remorse. He stepped up to the animal's mutilated form, muttering some sort of prayer. I might've appreciated the rhythmic, deep sound had I not been too busy trying not to hurl, faint, or scream.

"I'm going to usher the animal's soul to the veil now." Eurok dipped his chin. "While I do this spell, I won't be able to fight. Do you understand?"

I snapped out of my trance and met his eye, gauging how serious he was. Me—protect *him*—from the creature that just did *that?* I worked my ass off for years to become a confident killer of men, but this was way outside my realm of experience. Still, the confidence in his words steeled me. I swallowed my apprehension and nodded. I angled myself toward the mausoleum, only now realizing I never asked Eurok what the hell an adraknid looked like.

"What am I—"

On glancing over my shoulder, a bright swirling mist engulfed Eurok and the horse. He sat as still as stone, his eyes closed, with his hands on the horse's side. It was painfully beautiful, yet eerie. I forced my mouth shut and tore my gaze from the spectacle to keep watch. But it was dark.

So *dark*.

Only the faint glow of Eurok's spell emitted any light. Once again, I couldn't quite believe the mess I'd gotten myself into. How was I, a completely normal human, supposed to be helpful in a fucking place like this?

I thought back to how Eurok closed his eyes to listen to the forest. My sight would be of no help, so I gave it a try. I took a deep breath and willed my body to stop trembling, my heart to slow. A low rustling moved in the trees above, swift and easy like the breeze itself. My eyes flew open to complete, hollow darkness, the spell's light gone.

Sound was truly my only defense now, so I forced my heaving breaths to soften. The profound stillness was blood-curdling. Another rustle of leaves, though different somehow, more predictable than a moment ago. *There.* Closer this time. *My gods, what is taking him so long?*

I fixed my grip on my dagger. My throwing knives would be no help if I couldn't see.

"Mira," Eurok whispered in the lightest breath. "We have to get out of here. We can't fight it in the trees. Give me your hand."

I reached toward his voice, swiping the air where I thought his arm should be, but came up empty.

"Where are—"

A force, as if struck by a bucking horse, sent me flying.

I slammed into a tree, pain lacing through my left side. The sharp ache radiated through my torso as I braced myself to hit the ground, but I didn't. I was pinned to the rough bark, a stringy wet substance fanned over my body. Panic flared in my chest. *The beast's web.* I held my breath, expecting the sticky strands to press in, waiting for my life to be wrung from me like water from a dishrag.

Nothing moved.

I hung there in the dark. No sign of Eurok or the monster that slung this vile contraption.

I wriggled my arm, trying to slide it between the web and my torso, grasping for my dagger. The stuff was *strong*. It pressed into my skin like fine strands of hair, as if it might slice me open if pulled any tighter. Despite my efforts, it was no use. I couldn't move. I was trapped under the web's sticky grip, no less significant than a housefly waiting to be devoured.

Desperate for a glimpse, a sign, a whisper of the captain, my wide eyes scanned the darkness.

A blast of overwhelming heat and light struck the forest floor, paces away. I squinted against the stinging pain and forced myself to find the source.

Crouched, fist still pressed to the fractured ground, Eurok looked every bit the powerful warrior I expected. That thunderous blast, that blinding light and searing heat—it was him. It poured from fissures that spiderwebbed beneath his fist. Power pulsated around us like an echo in a cave.

"Eurok!"

He didn't seem to hear me.

Again, I struggled for my dagger, only to skim the hilt with my fingertips. When I thrashed against the web, my features scrunched into a wince. A tormenting ache seized my ribcage, but I shoved harder. Pain sliced through my forearm and my lips pulled back, teeth bared. *Fight through the pain.* My fingers wrapped in place around the blade.

Then I saw it.

Hurling itself toward the light emitted from the fractured earth where Eurok stood was a creature whose grotesque existence didn't seem possible. The thing was *massive*. Flesh-colored skin spread tight over its eight long, bony legs. The sickening, wet sound it made as it propelled forward would be branded in my mind and my nightmares forever.

Eurok rose, facing the nightmare head-on as I frantically sawed at the web wrapped around my middle. The creature reared, its front legs swiping in chaotic thrashes, as if to block out the blazing light.

I kept sawing, even as my feeble attempts seemed useless. I had to help. When the first band snapped free, my ribs throbbed like a galloping horse.

Eurok swung his ax. The hiss of metal squelched into flesh, slicing through a front leg. Using the force of his backswing, he rolled over the beast's back, landing on its other side. Another leg hit the dirt, twitching in horrid spasms. I might've gasped if my lungs had the capacity. With a final blow, he severed the monster's oblong, gnashing head clean off.

It fell with a sickening thud and rolled to a stop in front of me, its pinchers still clicking in its grotesque mouth.

CHAPTER NINE

SIDELLE

My head lulled to the side, jolting me awake. I'd fallen asleep reading again. Calming my startled heart, I rested against my chair's tall cushioned back and peered through the circular floor-to-ceiling window to my left, wondering how long until the sun crested the falls. I pushed out a pulse of energy to sense if anyone was home, but it returned as flat as pond water.

Eurok and Mira hadn't come back yet.

I shifted my gaze downward to the massive book I had dozed off on—a newly distributed compendium detailing the diverse forms of mana harnessed worldwide, still open to the page I studied. When I plucked it off my shelf earlier, I hoped to find information from various kingdoms and cultures that might've helped, but...

A disappointed flick of my hand flipped it shut. The cover's heavy dull thud punctuated my frustration.

I spent a whole day searching through my extensive personal library and found nothing. Not a single clue as to how I could hasten Mira's blooming. I had two years. The time felt like a relief days ago. Now? It was a low-hanging cloud, torturing me with its threatening presence. The workload was daunting, especially with so many questions left unanswered.

I made my way to the kitchen to refill my teacup, creating a mental timeline of my progress, estimating how much longer I needed to scour the remaining sections of my library. That was when I caught sight of Agatha's tattered grimoire, like a dingy beacon of leather-bound hope, sitting on the dining room table. *When did you get here?*

The remaining dregs of my fatigue melted away, and I threw the cover open. Enclosed within was knowledge from a time when gods walked among us instead of offering guidance from afar. If there were a spell to draw out Mira's power, it would be in this book.

I leaned over the crisp, browning pages, tracking the contents with care. One contained an incantation to carve through mountains, a single testament of the power druids once held. This tome comprised hundreds just like it. A reminder that we druids helped the gods shape the balance of nature.

Erezos' continued silence was a stark contrast to the god's involvement in the old world. Sour resentment bled into my thoughts. What was the point of blessing me with this gift if he wouldn't use it when we needed him most?

As I raised my head, the stillness of the space stole my attention, leaving me to ponder the reason behind Eurok and Mira's prolonged absence.

He hadn't mentioned what his plans were for their first training session. Whatever it was, I hoped Mira enjoyed herself. Things would run much smoother if she opened up and learned to trust a little. She, no doubt, had a difficult life, and the path ahead promised to be more treacherous. At least she didn't have to be alone in the world anymore.

Here I go again, assuming I know what she wants.

After glancing at my teacup, I made a mental note to get a refill of my calming brew, then continued flipping through the grimoire. A sketch in the top corner of a stained page caught my eye. A keyhole shape, outlined by a series of small patterns. No. Runes.

Beside the sketch, scrawled in intricate handwriting, was a name I recognized.

Vitalis.

As in Vitany Vitalis, the new High Witch of the Black Sand Calms coven. I flicked my eyes down the page to the text. It was a half-completed lunar-communing spell of some kind. I eyed the sketch again. *This could be helpful.*

I pressed the cover shut, then scooped Agatha's grimoire into my arms. Completely forgetting about my tea, I returned to the den.

The front door creaked open, then closed with a jarring slam. Mira and Eurok shuffled inside, their hushed voices filling the room. I changed course to meet them. By the time I rounded the corner to the foyer, she was halfway up the stairs.

"Is everything okay? How did it go?" I called after her.

"Yeah, everything's fine. I'm tired."

She didn't pause, didn't glance back. Her bedroom door pressed shut with a finalizing click. Seconds later, the sound of running water carried down from the bathing chamber.

Eurok plopped into the chair beside the fireplace. His clothes were filthy, and the rich aura of the forest mingled with his familiar scent. As he dropped his head against the cushions, exhaustion seeped over his handsome features.

I frowned. "What happened?"

His expression shifted as I approached, and he gave a light chuckle through a wince of fatigue. "She wore me the hell out, that's what happened."

"You look like you got your ass kicked."

"Well, what can I say? This girl's putting us both through the wringer."

With a wink and jerk of his chin, he gestured for me to come closer. Tentatively, I took his outstretched hand, allowing him to pull me to stand between his sprawled legs. The golden hue of his soft, expectant gaze stared up at me. Everything in me wanted to lean down and kiss him, to welcome him home, and let him fold me in those waiting arms.

But I couldn't bring myself to do it. I was already asking so much of him. There was no way to give him what he wanted without drawing a spotlight. At such a tenuous time for our people, a relationship between the captain and the high witch who works for the king would open us up to scrutiny—open him up to scrutiny. We couldn't afford the council to question either of us.

I swallowed hard and forced myself to speak. "What really happened?"

His face fell, the movement so slight it was hardly noticeable, but my gut wretched at having disappointed him once again. My mana searched for his energy, but as always, he kept it close, wound tight like a fortress wall.

"She has some issues with authority."

A small laugh escaped. "You're surprised by this?"

"Not a bit."

When he straightened to rest his elbows on his knees, I retreated to the neighboring chair.

"She will need to trust us if she means to learn anything," he said.

"I agree. Unfortunately, we don't have time to coddle her." I hoped that didn't sound as cold as it felt.

"I can't push her to the limits of her strength if she doesn't believe me when I say she'll be okay on the other side." He frowned, flicking his eyes between the floor and his hands. "There was a moment in the forest today—she stormed off. I had to knock her down to stop her from getting herself hurt."

He paused, scratching his jaw as if searching for how to phrase his next words. When he met my gaze, a strange blend of distress and concern marred his expression.

"I could see it in her eyes," he said. "She thought I was going to kill her."

With a sigh, I wrapped my sweater tightly around myself. "We knew this would be difficult. I sense so much of Annorah in her, so much good, but there's a coldness there too." My voice trailed off to a whisper, remembering her hardness in that dungeon, that hollow chill that echoed from within her.

His mouth formed a tight frown as he nodded. "That cold reflects what the world has done to her. It's going to take a force of nature to shake this mistrust from her."

He stood and approached me with slow confidence. My heart quickened to a deafening roar I was sure he could hear. His soft fingers traced my cheek before he tucked that troublesome strand of hair behind my ear.

"Just do me a favor, okay?" he said, low and subdued, holding my chin in his tender grasp. "Remember, some of that good in her *is her*—not Annorah."

I gave a gentle nod. He let go and stepped around me to the bar cart.

I spun, tracking his retreat. "Wait, what do you mean by a force of nature?"

The ice in his glass tinked as he took a long sip, punctuating the silence as I waited for his elaboration.

"There is only one force strong enough to bring down walls as thick as hers."

He fell into step, finding a seat on the rough-cut wooden stool near the bar table. He patted the round, carved seat next to him for me to join. It was then that I noticed the cup of tea beside his bourbon. Steam billowed into the air like a stoked fire. Piping hot, just how I liked it. While my heart leapt at the sweet gesture, my worry remained.

"What are you proposing?" I asked, settling in.

He grinned, and I pursed my lips at his mirthful indifference to my concern.

"Eurok?"

He sipped his bourbon in silent challenge, that maddeningly handsome smirk on his face. I flicked a bolt of static, zapping his lips against the glass. He jumped, the amber liquid splashing onto his shirt. The unamused look he gave me had me giggling into my tea, then he returned to the bar to refill his drink.

I turned around on the stool and spoke to his back. "We need to be on the same page here, Eurok. We have to keep her safe."

He filled his glass and used the crystal decanter lid to point upstairs. "I'm not sure 'safe' is gonna get us anywhere with that one."

The lid returned to its place with a clang, then he examined the wet stain left on his shirt. I was powerless to look away as he pulled off his baldric of daggers and hung it on the bar cart. Then he gripped the hem of his tunic and drew it over his head.

Those perfect mounds of hard muscle flexed down his back, across his broad shoulders as he moved. When he faced me, drink in hand, he used the fabric to wipe the wetness from his chest. I never craved bourbon so much in my life.

As he flipped the shirt over his shoulder, he returned, leaning against the bar. "We need to find a way for Mira to let her guard down. She needs to *want* to open up. That being said, I can't be here to train with her every day."

"I understand." I sipped my tea, noting that it tasted as perfect as if I made it myself.

"Good. Then let's hope you're understanding of my solution, as well." A wry grin graced those tempting, mischievous lips.

CHAPTER TEN

MIRA

A *peculiar building constructed with symmetrical red bricks blocked out the sun's glare. The entrance was made of clear glass windows housed within a black metal frame. A woman, carrying armfuls of brown paper bags, pushed a series of buttons on a pad beside the door. There was a snapping sort of sound, then she entered before the door swung shut behind her.*

Curious, I decided to follow before a wailing scream cut the thought short—like a hundred howling banshees. My hands clamped over my ears as I whirled, seeking the source. It was an immense red metallic beast, bright lights flashing from every direction as it sped toward me.

As it passed, I noticed two humans sitting inside, guiding it somehow. A horseless carriage of some kind. More magic?

My chest heaved with my rising apprehension as I gathered my wits. Where the fuck am I? *Voices from behind snagged my attention. A group of humans stepped onto the stone walking path, passing by without a second glance. They looked no older than me, all strangely dressed in blue pants and bright-colored tunics decorated with bizarre images and writing.*

"That's the last time we let you pick the restaurant, JJ," a petite woman said.

She faced away from me, but something about her voice had me taking a tentative step closer.

"It's not my fault our waiter sucked." The tall, dark-haired guy punched the code into the pad.

The other man, blond, threw his head back and laughed. "It wasn't just the waiter, bro."

They seemed harmless—and I needed to know where the hell I was. "Hey!" I called out, rushing over.

With furrowed brows, the men looked my way, but the dark-haired girl did not.

I froze. An odd, insufferable sensation rooted me in place, snaring my breath. I was dreaming. No matter how much I willed myself to move, to speak, my body refused to respond. Gods, I must've seemed like a lunatic. A vacant-eyed, slack-jawed stranger. An odd tug yanked on my chest—this desperate longing for the girl to turn around.

A thin girl with curly-red hair came stumbling out of the door they'd opened and tripped, sending an armful of heavy books flying at their feet. Their attention turned from me, trying to help the girl collect her things—

I jolted awake and sat up with a groan. *What the hell?* I was no stranger to unusual dreams, though never as vivid as this. The stagnant metallic heat of that foreign city hung in my lungs as if I'd really been there. The buildings, carriages, the people—none of them held any familiarity—except for the dark-haired girl. Though she'd been a regular occurrence in my nightly head-trips throughout the years, I had no idea who she was. As dreams often do, the images were already slipping through the cracks of my memory.

I rubbed my eyes with the backs of my hands, then shoved the blankets aside. When my feet hit the floor, that gnawing ache in my stomach returned full force. The thought of going back on my word after one day of training was shameful and embarrassing. My pride bucked like an agitated horse just thinking about it. But it only proved my point—I didn't belong here. I was leaving Raven Ridge today, with or without the witch's help.

I dressed in my old clothes and placed the ones Sidelle bought on the dresser beside those beautiful, godsdamned boots. It pained me to do it, but taking them felt wrong.

My feet dragged as I ventured to the window to say my goodbyes to that impeccable view, burning the scene into my memory so I might someday tell someone about it. But who? My mind wandered to the innkeeper's son, Rhymes. I don't know why I never loved him. In my life, love was a foreign concept, absent, both in giving and receiving. Except perhaps my mother. My memories of her were so distant. It was hard to distinguish between what was real and what my young imagination concocted about her.

Once I was done with all this nonsense, tucked away in another kingdom, I might find someone who'd fill my days with laughter and my nights with warmth. I'd tell them all about my years as a bounty hunter, how I was imprisoned by the king because he mistook me for some long-lost magical fucking princess. Gods, would anyone even believe such a story?

A welcomed breeze soothed the heat in my cheeks and I closed my eyes, listening to the waterfall's distant roar. It's funny how quickly the sound grew on me. I'd miss this.

After a few more steadying breaths, I worked up enough nerve to leave. I eased the door shut, then descended the spiral staircase. Eurok and Sidelle's voices floated up the stairs. She was laughing at something he said, and I thought back again to what Eurok told me that first night. It almost seemed cruel to deny herself love for the good of her people. Especially with someone as handsome and devoted to her as Eurok was.

My intention was to tell them my plans to leave right away, but my courage wavered at the sound of their laughter, then disappeared entirely when I rounded the corner to the sitting room. Sidelle separated from Eurok in a hurry, as if I interrupted something intimate. But where she took a few paces, Eurok moved with her, his hand low on her back, unwilling to hide anything.

I flashed a spry grin his way. "You're here early."

A wave of color spread across Sidelle's cheeks.

He leaned against the wall, propping up a foot. The glint consuming his features as he eyed Sidelle was entirely unapologetic. "I slept on the couch."

I wandered to the breakfast cart filled with fresh fruit and hot oats, picking a bright green apple. "Don't hold out on my account." I smirked at the witch, then took a bite. "A horse like that deserves to be ridden."

Eurok loosed a loud, boisterous laugh, and the sheer shock on her face had me joining in. I couldn't believe how timid the topic of fucking the druid made her.

When I first met her, I assumed she was more provocative. But thinking about it, I only made that assumption because of the dress she had on. She wore nothing like it since that day. Was that another reason for her bitterness toward the king? Did he make her wear those things? As if she needed any more reasons to hate him.

"Are you two finished?" she asked, shaking off her embarrassment.

She started toward the writing desk in the far corner, the long draping of her elegant coral tunic trailing her steps. The color against her flawless, smoky lavender skin made her look like a living sunset. She settled in the seat where an open ink bottle and half-finished letter rested atop the desk's surface.

I gave Eurok a once-over. He wore the same clothes from last night, a little disheveled, but nothing of obvious concern. "Are you alright?" I asked, unsure if I even had the right to ask that of someone so powerful in comparison.

He nodded, his smile reassuring. "You?"

I shrugged. "Fine."

"You did good," he said. "You—"

"Don't."

His face took on a puzzled expression at the sudden shift in my tone. The knot I suppressed in my stomach all morning writhed like a keyed-up snake.

"Don't patronize me. There's no reason to." I hadn't meant to sound so harsh. I only meant that his reassurance and praise would do no good. No more kindness needed to be wasted on me.

"Mira, I'm not patronizing you. I'm proud of you."

"Proud of me?"

Sidelle turned in her seat. Her shoulders tensed as she surveyed us, but she didn't speak. Had he told her what happened? How he asked for my help, then ended up saving my ass instead?

He'd been so calm in the forest while we waited for the adraknid to emerge, confident, like it was nothing more than removing a minor pest problem. But when things went wrong, and he needed *my* help, I'd been as useless as a dull blade.

"Yes, proud of you."

He pushed off the wall and started toward me, but I took a step back, conveying my resistance. He paused, noting my apprehension. Anything he had to say would only be a wasted effort to soothe my embarrassment and shame. I didn't want it—didn't deserve it.

I stared at the apple, probably the last thing I'd eat for a while. My stomach soured at the thought of taking another bite. I tossed it into the fire and watched it burn, trying to compose myself enough to tell them. The plan had been to deliver the news gently. I owed them that much after how hostile I'd been. Guess I fucked that up, too.

"I want to leave." The almost whisper that came out of my mouth sounded unsure, but I wasn't.

Sidelle spoke first. "Why?"

Her gaze fluttered to Eurok as if he might answer her question, but the druid's face was as pained as mine.

"I'm not the person you think I am." My apologetic tone felt so unfamiliar. "I know I said I'd try, but I almost got myself and Eurok killed yesterday. I just—can't."

The captain shifted. "I wouldn't go that far."

"Fine, I almost got *myself* killed." I rolled my eyes. "My point is, I'm just a human. I don't belong here."

Sidelle placed the delicate white quill that dangled between her fingers into the inkwell, then stood. She stood and strode over to me. The light sighing in through the window behind her gave her bright silver hair an incandescent glow that made the determined look she wore daunting. She didn't believe me—or wouldn't accept it. *No surprise there.*

She stopped a breath away, close enough that her clove, citrus scent enveloped me. Could she hear the thudding of my heart as easily as I felt it in my chest? Would she interpret it as fear? I hoped not. It wasn't fear that made my pulse quicken. It was my conviction to stand my ground against whatever ammunition the witch was readying to convince me to stay.

I wouldn't.

"Being human has nothing to do with whether you belong here."

The gentle assurance rolling off her was a punch to the gut. My steadfast expression wavered.

"What do you want, Mira?" she asked.

My ears perked at the question, though confusion knotted my tongue.

"I regret not asking earlier, but I truly desire to understand," she said. "Does even some *small* part of you wish to be here with us?"

I frowned and shook my head. "What I want is irrelevant. I won't waste everyone's time pretending to be someone I'm not."

That's all it would be if I stayed. No matter how much my future-self might wonder what would've been, I refused to be the reason they failed to accomplish their goals. My mind was made up. Let my life be my burden, not theirs.

"It is not a waste of time."

"It is," I shot back.

She set her jaw, and I could have sworn a fine crackle of purple lightning crawled across her exposed skin, her shell of composure breaching ever so slightly before she reined it in.

"Sidelle," Eurok said, tone pitched low in warning.

I didn't understand it, but the witch glanced his way, and her tense demeanor eased. Her features were still ablaze with sure determination, but I would not back down. We were locked eye to eye, will to will.

I leveraged every bit of rationale I had, despite feeling like a geyser ready to go off. Forcing cool confidence into my voice, "If you believe for one second that I will miraculously wake up with powers, that I'll be capable of *half* the things I've seen you two do in the last forty-eight hours—then yeah, it is absolutely a big *fucking* waste of time."

Sidelle winced but stood firm.

My fingers curled into fists at my sides as I turned on the stone-faced warrior between me and the door. His features were set in smooth, emotionless scrutiny, but I saw wheels turning in those topaz eyes. "Eurok, thank you for trying yesterday. And thank you for saving me." I meant the words, but they tasted like spoiled milk leaving my mouth. I never wanted to feel that helpless again.

Sidelle pursed her lips and raised a brow—another exchange I didn't fully understand, but I ignored it and walked past him. I said my final apology over my shoulder, then stepped outside.

Halfway down the gravel path, Eurok called after me. I stopped, tipping my dejected glare toward the sky instead of facing him.

He slowed to a stop beside me. "Mira, will you please come back and just talk to us? Please."

"It won't do any good."

"At least let Sidelle feed you before you go, then."

I crossed my arms. "I can find food for myself." Why was it always Eurok chasing me down for the witch?

My traitorous stomach growled, and he raised his brows in one last lighthearted plea. He smiled at my exasperated sigh, then wasted no time placing a hand on my shoulder to steer me back.

Inside, Sidelle emerged from a door under the stairs that I wasn't sure I noticed before, wearing a simple pair of brown riding pants and a forest green vest over a long-sleeved cream tunic. She looked the part of a druid huntress, were it not for the staff she carried in place of a bow.

"I wondered if you might join me outside. If you truly plan on leaving, I have something I'd like to give you first."

"I don't need any more gifts."

"I'm afraid I won't take no for an answer."

Of course.

Frustrated, I sighed and shook my head, my defeat evident in the gesture. A quiet smile painted her lips, and she motioned for me to follow.

On a lower level, she led me through a back door. My jaw fell slack. Two of the most *beautiful* horses I'd ever seen waited just outside.

"I had them brought up from my personal stable."

Unsure what to say, I wandered closer to the gorgeous animals.

Sidelle smiled and gestured to the solid black horse. Braided golden wire and wooden beads decorated its long mane. "This is Eiresh. He hails from the most esteemed Vylandrian stock and has undergone rigorous training with the rider clan druids of Star Hewn Valley."

Cautiously, I pressed my palm against his sturdy neck. Solid velvet muscle, sleek beneath my touch, shifted as he turned, watching me with stunning ebony eyes.

"Horses trained by the riding clan are special," Sidelle went on.

"I can see that." Delight pitched my tone higher. He sniffed at my hand in heavy, warm huffs, then I scratched along the bridge of his nose. "Hello, Eiresh," I cooed as if the massive beast were a small infant.

He nudged my palm, shaking his enormous head. Sidelle and I giggled.

"Well, beauty and personality aside, Arestellian stallions are fiercely loyal."

I stroked his muzzle, and my eyes caught Sidelle's. It was hard not to notice their similarities. Along with their dark, long-lashed irises, they shared the same gentle spirit.

"I'd like for you to have him," she said, placing a light hand on his flank.

A jolt of astonishment flowed through me. I'd never received anything so generous in my life. But the chill of skepticism reared its ugly head, bitter and venomous as it bled into my thoughts. Could this be a manipulation tactic, a trick to keep me from leaving? Would she truly let me take the stallion with me?

Something stronger told me, yes, she would.

"Thank you," I whispered, then cleared my throat. "I just have one question, though."

With a curious tilt of her head, she waited.

"Do I have to keep the name Eiresh?"

Sidelle laughed—not a tight, polite, composed sound, but a real, voluminous laugh that filled the air with its honey-sweet cadence. I joined in, feeling my eyes crinkle and my face ache by the time it ebbed.

"Will you have lunch with me in the plaza? If you are determined to leave, I'd like to give you a proper send-off."

I considered this a moment, stroking Eiresh's mane in long sweeps. Finally, I sighed, "Okay."

Music and the soft chatter of pleasant conversation blossomed into a pleasant din. We settled in at a tall two-person table near the eatery's edge. A series of peculiar carts carried a wide array of foods and dishes, pushed along on a phantom wind between the open-air tables. Everyone served themselves from the various platters of fruit, meat, and cheeses with no regard to portion or cost.

"There's no currency for food here," Sidelle said, noticing what pulled my attention.

No currency for food. My brain could barely perceive it. I spent a significant portion of my life in a constant state of hunger, resorting to theft for sustenance or enduring such long periods without eating that I feared vomiting when I finally did. But here? A family of druids sat at the far end. The mother nursed an infant at her breast while she ate her salad—starving was hardly even a possibility.

"We're a community," she said. "We all contribute, so we all eat."

I surveyed my surroundings. The shops and homes nestled along the river and amidst the trees seamlessly blended with the plaza, becoming an integral part of the surroundings. Most beings within Raven Ridge were druids, but there were others. I spotted a few short stocky dwarves, who I assumed came from the sharp western edge of the country where most of the mining took place. There was also the occasional spindly frame of the lesser fairies, whose delicate wings sent an iridescent spray of dust into the air when they fluttered by.

But no humans.

"Your energy seems very conflicted today," Sidelle said. Her expression softened as she rested her chin on her fist.

I shifted in my seat. "That's the first time I've heard you mention *my* energy."

"I've been avoiding yours. It takes a lot out of me. But I think being in such close proximity the last few days has made it a little easier."

My nose wrinkled. "Why would it be so overwhelming?"

A cart rolled to a stop beside our table, and when I peered at Sidelle, she nodded and reached for her plate. I hastily began filling mine with mounds of fruit and pulled three large rolls off the stack in the middle of the cart. She had a daintier approach to serving herself, though she also took an extra portion of bread.

"To be entirely honest, I'm not sure what makes your energy so difficult. Annorah's was similar, though. I suspect it has something to do with that."

I, inwardly, rolled my eyes.

"Unfortunately," she said, tone light, "if you plan on leaving, I'll never get the chance to figure it out."

I caught on to the sly twinkle in her expression. When I didn't smile, she let the look fall.

After a moment, she folded her hands in her lap and straightened. "Mira, I owe you so many apologies, most of all, for not acknowledging how much you've lost in such a short amount of time. My mind was consumed with thoughts of our future, safeguarding our actions from the king, and earning your trust. I should have made the effort to find out your true feelings or if you even wanted to be involved in this. I hope that as time goes by, you will discover your true potential and, one day, you'll want to help us save our people."

"*Your* people," I said. "You want me to help you save your people. There's no one here for me."

"*I* am here for you." A flicker of light reflected in her large, dark eyes, punctuating the meaning behind her words. There was no denying the intense desire she had for me to be here.

"And when I can't use magic—mana? What then?"

I was determined not to deceive them into thinking I was someone else. This province and these people deserved better than that.

"Just hear me out," I said, cutting off her answer. "You could be searching for some other solution to your problem, maybe even find Annorah's real reincarnation."

Sidelle's eyes fluttered around as if to make sure no one was listening.

"All this time and effort it would take Eurok to train me—it will be for nothing."

"Don't you want to train?"

"Of course I do," I scoffed. "But how does it benefit you, either of you, if I'm not who you think I am?" My lips pressed tight, forcing myself to calm the storm building beneath my skin. I preferred not to disturb anyone nearby, or alert them to something Sidelle didn't want disclosed. I dropped my voice to a subtle whisper. "Why do you want Eurok training me, anyway? Was Annorah a fighter, too?"

The witch shook her head, her long snowfall-white hair swaying with the motion. "No. Annorah spent little time with warriors," she said. "Eurok is training you because physical exhaustion can be a great conduit for a pre-blooming Vylandrian. When your body is pushed past its normal capabilities, your mana will instinctively want to take over. He is the only one I trust to push you to that point and help me guide you through your blooming."

"Guide me?" I asked.

A striking druid gave us a curious, interested, once-over as he passed. I let my eyes follow him, an errant thought dancing through my mind. Sidelle cleared her throat, tracking my gaze. I snapped my attention back, seeing her playful, scolding smile.

After a breath, a serious demeanor settled over her features. "There's more. That promise I made to the king?"

A nervous edge twisted through my stomach.

She swallowed, as if hating the words. "I swore to have Eurok train you in preparation to become the king's personal assassin. He gave me two years."

Well, fuck.

She folded her arms and leaned on the table. "I have every intention of welcoming you into my home, Mira, training you in our casting and wielding arts, and I plan to encourage you to continue your sessions with Eurok. However, if it turns out to be something you don't want. I would still be honored if you would accept the official position as my assistant and stay here with me."

My jaw fell slack. "Why would you do that?"

"Why wouldn't I?"

Every rebuttal I planned in my head fizzled out. I wanted to welcome her offer, but that distrustful serpent in the dregs of my mind, driven by experience and pain, coiled around my heart and held firm.

"I need to think about this," I said, nudging away my unfinished plate.

"Are you gonna eat that?" a familiar voice called from behind.

I turned to see Eurok approaching. When he caught my eye, he flashed a wide smile. He braced his elbows against the iron gate beside us, eyeing Sidelle's food. With a playful sigh, she pushed her plate closer. His grin brightened as he picked off an olive and popped it in his mouth.

"So, did you ladies get to talk?"

"We did," Sidelle offered.

"And?" He snatched another olive.

Sidelle shrugged as if to say my decision was unclear.

Still chewing, Eurok laid a hand on my shoulder and gestured with his head for me to join him, his mahogany hair falling to the side. I walked around the table and through the black iron gate. He fell into step beside me, leading me toward the plaza's arched wooden bridge. The structure consisted of twisted tree roots that spanned over the river that wove through the village.

"Why are you fooling yourself?" he asked outright.

I was so fucking tired of trying to convince them I didn't want to be here—not if it meant messing things up for them. If I stayed, I still only had two years until the king would expect a full-fledged assassin to be in his employ. While royal wages were a tempting idea, he was a deceitful bastard. I'd never feel right about serving him, especially if he'd have me hunting Vylandrian sympathizers like Greggor.

If I didn't go now, I'd have to eventually. Why would I do that to myself? Why would I wait until I've fallen in love with this place—with these people? All around me were the laughing, blissful faces of the patrons, the whimsical tranquility of the village, and could already feel a piece of that shell I built around my heart cracking. *I have to leave now.*

"Let's say I stay and my powers bloom. The king will hear of it and want me dead, and he'll know exactly where to find me. If I don't bloom, then he will want me for his own personal gain. I'm not fooling myself. No matter which way you look at it, I'm here on borrowed time." I expected Eurok to argue, but he didn't. "I can't wield magic, and I won't kill for him. Not again. Not after Greggor–"

"Wait. *You* killed Greggor?"

I swore I sensed a ripple of his power, though when I looked at him, his features were unreadable, emotionless.

"I thought you knew."

"No."

A few quiet moments later, he spoke up again. "Listen, Mira, as hard as it might be for you to admit it, I know you want to be here. I won't pretend to understand what your life was like. What I can say is that being here is something you *should* want. Despite whatever you tell yourself, you *deserve* this place."

Deserve?

That's the last thing that I deserve. "Why?" I asked. "You've hardly seen me wield a blade."

"I saw all I needed to," he said. "You didn't move when you heard the adraknid, didn't hesitate. You *wanted* to help, despite, as you put it, being *just* a human."

I chewed my cheek at his use of my earlier words against me.

"You could have run—hidden. It would have been safer, but you knew that, didn't you?"

I had, but I didn't say as much.

"You were ready to fight, to protect *me*." His gaze broke from mine, returning to the river below. "I'm leaving today. My duties to the druid army cannot fall lax to our mission here, but I'll return soon. I hope to find you here when I do."

Then he turned and left, leaving me to stare at my rippling reflection in the water below.

CHAPTER ELEVEN
MIRA

O nce we returned to Sidelle's place, I retreated upstairs, claiming I needed some time alone to reflect on everything. Really, I wanted to grab the boots. I thought about snagging that tangerine bath oil too, but decided against it. From now on, bathing would become a rare luxury.

Before I left, I threw together a poorly written letter, apologizing for how things had to be. Then I slipped out the back exit while Sidelle and Eurok spoke on the balcony.

I hated the thought of leaving like this, but no matter what I said, no matter what *they* said, nothing changed the fact that the king would come calling soon enough, asking for exactly what Sidelle promised to deliver. I didn't blame her for promising something so outrageous, especially considering it was the reason he let me out of those dungeons in the first place. Even so, I refused to become that bastard's murderous lackey. I killed on my own terms. No promise, even a lifesaving one, would change that.

As I rode through the Vylandrian forest, the trees serenaded me with their unique symphony. I stuck to the main road. It was risky, especially if Eurok or Sidelle came after me. But if I were being truthful, I preferred that outcome over getting lost and becoming some exotic beast's lunch

I needed to play it smart, at least while I was still within Vylandrian borders. After I crossed the Ebbonharrow River into

Calrund, I'd veer off the main roads. The countryside would cover my trail until I reached Breckenridge, where I'd board the first ship leaving this godsdamned kingdom.

Silence lapsed for hours as I fought to divert my thoughts from the druids. I didn't want to envision the shock and disappointment on their faces when they realized I left. Still, the image plagued me like a pestering mosquito that refused to give up.

I leaned forward and stroked Eiresh's smooth, sturdy neck. I never owned a horse before. The beast that belonged to my father was an aggressive son-of-a-bitch, and I avoided him at all costs. Though looking back on it, I couldn't blame the stallion. In fact, we shared more in common than I realized, both having been raised under the violent hand of my father.

Eiresh nickered at my touch as if to show appreciation, pulling my attention to the present. I smiled.

"Good boy," I said, happy for the company. *I can't believe he's mine—at least for now.*

A tightness in my throat grew at the thought of leaving him behind once I reached my destination. If I could stow us both away on a ship, I would, but it seemed next to impossible. He was one of the largest horses I'd ever seen. Fuck, it was ridiculous how soft I'd gotten in only a few short days. Then again, I always had a weakness for animals. Even when hunger gnawed at my desperation, it never made sense to kill a creature just to keep my bitter ass alive. They were innocent.

Not like me.

I justified my lifestyle by telling myself I killed monsters and protected innocent lives. But Greggor's glossy sea-blue eyes flashed to the forefront of my mind, and I blinked against the stinging in my own. *A few days' travel, then I'll be free of this place.*

The wrenching in my chest disagreed with the thought, but I kept riding.

A soft melody floated along the spring breeze, the tune soothing and slow. I pulled on Eiresh's reins, urging him to a stop to listen. Who'd be playing guitar in the middle of the forest? A merchant? Perhaps a traveling bard? I entertained the idea of retracing my steps, finding a more secluded path, and looked back. The sky had darkened with the threat of rain. *Forward it is.*

I convinced myself everything was fine, then rounded the corner, anticipating the musician. He sat at the base of a large tree, guitar in hand—undoubtedly the most handsome man I'd ever seen. I rode closer, trying not to stare. And failing.

His inhuman perfection had me swallowing past the anxious lump in my throat. This was no man—but a *druid*. Thunder cracked through the sky as I started past.

His eyes, an astonishing green, locked onto me. The heat of his gaze charged my skin like the electrified clouds at my back.

His warm walnut-colored features settled into a perfect display of intrigue as the melody stopped, and he set the instrument aside, pushing himself to his feet. The corner of his mouth lifted in a rugged smirk. "Well. Ain't that a sight to see?"

My eyes narrowed as a rush of caution flooded my veins.

He gestured between me and my horse. "A human on an Arestellian stallion. You're gonna get yourself fucking killed out here."

"Excuse me?" I pulled Eiresh to a halt.

As if discussing the weather, he leaned against the tree and jerked his chin. "Your horse, it's rider clan trained. Hope you're not taking that thing anywhere near the border."

"That's none of your business."

"You have any idea how much a beast like that goes for? You'll be dead on the side of the road within the week."

I glared in response. "What do you care?"

Something mischievous churned behind those brilliant eyes as he dragged them down my body. "Seems like an awful waste."

"Are you talking about me? Or the horse?" I mused.

He shoved himself off the tree with a wide, clever smile. "The horse."

The tension in my shoulders relaxed, and I smirked.

"Balis Gailstrong." He introduced himself and sauntered closer, casually reaching to pat Eiresh's head.

"Mira."

"Oh, I know exactly who you are."

His hand wrapped around Eiresh's reins, and a cold shudder raked down my spine.

"Who sent you?"

"Eurok."

Of course he did. A strange sense of relief fell over me, but I masked it with a blanket of defiance. I was not going back.

"Let go of my horse," I demanded.

To my surprise, he did.

My legs squeezed Eiresh's sides, and he burst into a gallop. I glanced behind, checking if the stranger followed. He didn't. He stood there, arms crossed. Unconcerned amusement graced his face before he slung his guitar over his shoulder.

I maintained the fast pace until I worried about pushing Eiresh too hard, then slowed to a trot.

Sidelle promised to let me leave if I wished, but Eurok hadn't. He must've meant for the druid to either bring me back or kill me for what I'd done to Greggor. So why did he let me get away so easily?

Thick clouds cracked open with a roar of heavy, soaking raindrops—a warm late-summer downpour. Petrichor danced through the air in a welcome rush, and I tipped my face skyward, allowing myself a few unbothered moments. Now soaked to the bone, I'd have to find shelter before nightfall.

"Not disappointed by this view one bit," a smooth, low voice cut over the torrent.

Balis. Damnit, I forgot how fast these druids are.

I spotted him just head, perched against a thin pine half his own girth. His gaze traveled up my body, lingering on each curve and contour. Realization sank in, and I peered down at myself. My tunic's airy fabric stuck to me like a second skin, and the faint chill left me prickled with goosebumps, my nipples on full display. That look in his eye had me setting my jaw in stark defiance.

"Enjoy it while you can. This is as close as you're gonna get."

"Hmm, a welcomed challenge."

His voice, like tempting smoke, entwined my senses.

With unwavering determination, I squared my shoulders. "You can tell Eurok thanks for sending his retriever dog, but I've made up my mind."

Balis took a few strides backward, a lopsided, roguish grin decorating his cheeks. "There's an inn an hour south of here. I'll meet you there." He disappeared between the trees without another word.

Like hell.

The storm grew more violent the further I rode, a deluge that sent the animals of the forest scattering to higher ground. By the time I made it to the inn Balis mentioned, I had no choice but to stop.

I tucked Eiresh away in the last available stall, then ventured inside. A torrent of boisterous drunken Vylandrians belted upbeat lyrics to the halfling bard's tune. The room's energy was almost as palpable as the humidity thickening the air. It didn't take long before I found him. Near the far wall, those jade irises sent a wave of cautionary intrigue sweeping through my body.

Don't fuck the druid. Tempting as it may be, something about the power I sensed lurking behind those calm, relaxed muscles told me it would be a risky endeavor.

"You made it," he said, an unsurprised lilt to the words.

He sat sideways in his chair, his back against the wall with a frothy ale in hand. There was no trace of the downpour on his clothes nor exhaustion of travel on his rugged face. While I, in contrast, dripped puddles on the wooden planks.

"The storm left me little choice." I plopped in the seat across from him, then snagged his tankard, taking a long drink.

He raised an eyebrow, then gestured to the waitress for another. "I booked the last room they had. We will make the journey to Raven Ridge in the morning."

It wasn't a question.

"Don't presume my being stuck here means I'm not committed to leaving. I'm not going back."

"Listen, princess—"

"Do not call me that," I snapped.

Would I ever have the pleasure of meeting a druid that wasn't insufferably arrogant—or was the demeanor just as likely as their staggering good looks?

"Is that not what you are?"

I sensed he was fucking with me, but I couldn't be sure. "I'm not a princess, and if you keep making such asinine presumptions, then you can kindly fuck off."

The waitress brought another ale, then hurried away. My next sip conveyed how little interest I had in returning the one I took from him.

He shifted in his seat to face me properly, elbows braced on the table. "You're not easily intimidated, are you?"

"Not a word often used to describe me, no."

"Well, not-a-princess," sarcasm dripped from his words, "I'm not that easy to get rid of. Raven Ridge or not, you are stuck with me."

Fear of getting kicked out of the only shelter nearby stopped me from decking him in the face. But I sure-as-fuck wanted to. "So what, you'll stalk me?"

A glimmer of excitement burned across his emerald gaze—in that moment, I felt like prey.

"Don't tempt me, princess. I prefer to play with my food."

My traitorous heart skipped a beat, but I held his haughty stare, unwilling to back down. How could I shake this guy by morning?

Morning.

"Wait—you booked the *last* room?"

His mirth fractured a bit, reading the apprehension on my face. "Don't worry, I'll sleep on the floor."

He most likely meant for that to be received as a kindness, but my annoyance flared. Not that I was opposed to sharing a bed with the druid. I was no stranger to one-night stands. Given that I was unsure of his intentions and needed to slip out undetected, the safe route would be to play it off as an appalling idea. Though climbing *that* tree was anything but.

"Absolutely not. I'm not sharing a room with you."

"Excuse me?" He almost choked on a gulp of ale. "Have you seen it outside? You don't seriously expect me to sleep in that storm, do you?"

"Frankly, I don't give a shit. But it won't be in the same room as me," I said.

His eyes narrowed like he was questioning how genuine my aversion was. "Am I to believe you're a virtuous woman?"

"Also not a word used to describe me," I said, "but I hardly know you. You could knock me out, drag me back against my will."

I schooled my features to be cold and uncaring, even as the hard edge of guilt pressed in on me. Behind him, a particularly violent bolt of lightning lit up the sky, rattling the rickety windows.

His jaw ticked, but he let out a slow sigh. "Fine," he said. "Have it your way."

Was it really that easy? I gave a tight nod and took a sip of ale. Balis didn't meet my eye. His dejected stare lingered on the rain pounding against the glass panes. The waitress returned with two steaming bowls of stew and biscuits, refilled our tankards, then walked away without a word.

"What's this?" I asked.

"I thought maybe you'd be hungry after your long day of traveling."

"How'd you know I'd show?"

As if in answer, the sky released another roar of thunder.

"I was pretty sure."

I swallowed back the shame rising like bile in the back of my throat and took in a spoonful of the hot stew. *So good.*

"So," he began, "since I was sorely misinformed about you, where do you come from, and how did you end up here?"

"What did Eurok tell you exactly?" I asked, dragging my wooden spoon through the thick broth.

"Only that the high witch believes you're a princess, one of great importance. He said you're in danger if left on your own, and it's imperative that I bring you home."

"Raven Ridge isn't my home."

He took a large gulp of ale, the muscles in his neck and jaw waving as it went down, and I wondered if he had the same immense tolerance as Eurok did.

"I figured that out the moment I saw you were human," he said.

"Speaking of which, how'd you know I was the one you were looking for?"

He tipped his chin as if it were obvious. "No one else would be so blatantly unaware of how dangerous it is for a human to ride an Arestellian stallion toward the border."

My cheeks flushed, and I stared at the diced potatoes and carrots floating in my stew. "I was a bounty hunter. When I got to the castle for my payout, the king threw me into the dungeon. He intended to have me killed, so Sidelle brought me here."

"And you don't like it here?"

Unwilling to meet his gaze, my shoulder lifted in a half-hearted shrug.

"You don't like Sidelle?" he asked.

"No, that's not it."

"Do you have family back there?" He seemed genuinely curious.

"No."

"What then?"

Irritation crawled like spiders beneath my skin. "Why do you care?"

"I don't know. You just seem like you need someone to."

That got my attention. When I looked up, he studied me with those lush, vibrant green eyes, all previous tension gone.

"Is that what this is?" I used the spoon to gesture to our surroundings. "The room, the food? Pity?"

"No. It's called common decency."

Unsure of what to say, I averted my gaze from his and stirred my food into a messy, mushy concoction. "What will Eurok do when you return without me?"

"I don't plan on returning without you." He shoveled in a few bites, his attention fixated on me.

I felt like an insect under a magnifying glass, waiting for someone to rip off my legs.

"I won't go back," I said.

"Consider me a companion on your travels, then. Because I'm not going anywhere."

I glowered. His undeterred chuckle did nothing to improve my foul mood.

After finishing the stew and ale, I stood, ready to find the room he secured. Rain splattered the panes, relentless and drenching, while streaks of lightning cut and webbed across the clouds.

"You gonna be okay out there?" I asked.

"Regretting your decision?"

"Just being polite."

"It would be *polite* to let me crash on the floor."

"No."

"Guess we'll wait and see, then."

"Don't you have mana? Can't you make yourself a shelter Or something?"

He dug into a small leather pouch and placed a tip for the waitress beside his empty tankard. "I have my ways of weathering the storm.

When he stood, I got my first proper glimpse of him. A black tattoo of braided vines snaked up his left arm over layers of mounded muscle. The design peaked from his tunic's neckline and flowed up the side of his neck.

He had this air of calm about him—like an oak tree's shade on a hot day.

"Sleep tight, princess."

His eyes danced like hearth flames along my curves. I warmed in response but turned and climbed the staircase, fighting the smile wavering on my lips.

CHAPTER TWELVE
MIRA

T he room did not differ from any inn I occupied in Calrund. There was an average-sized bed with a boring floral-pattern duvet, a bare wardrobe in the corner, and a desk that sat beneath the window. I warmed myself near the hearth, where the beginnings of a small fire crackled and spit.

When my soaked clothes felt more tolerable, I wandered over to peer out at the surrounding forest, but night had fallen. My disheveled reflection stared back at me, marred with the droplets of rain sliding down the glass. I pulled the ribbon out of my braid and ran my fingers through, smoothing the tangles as best I could.

The storm was still in full force. Thunder groaned, strong enough that its reverberations shook the walls. Lightning brandished the lush woods in light. My hands froze mid-stroke, and I straightened, a strange shape catching my attention. *Was that a—*

I shook my head, hoping to rid myself of the image I thought I saw amidst the trees. I leaned closer, squinting to distinguish the forest's contrasting shadows. Lightning flashed again, and there it was. An immense black cat perched on a limb outside my window.

Darkness returned, and I glued my gaze on the single droplet of rain marking the place I was sure I'd seen it. Seconds later, when another flash struck, it was gone. I waited, focusing.

Another flash.

Nothing.

I loosed a long breath and backed away. Balis was out there with that beast. I turned toward the door, prepared to warn him, but that familiar voice of self-preservation halted me. If he got eaten by that creature, he couldn't take me back.

My dinner spoiled in my gut at the thought, though. He was out there in the pouring rain with a prowling beast because of me—because he was respecting *my* space. I paced a tight circle, studying the wood grain floorboards, warring with my better judgment. To be torn apart was a horrid way to die—no one deserved that. I rounded on the door once more, only to stop again.

"Why do I care?" I hissed.

As if in answer, a log in the hearth snapped, spraying flecks of embers.

I owed him nothing. He was an obstacle, a hurdle that I needed to overcome. If he died, it would be Eurok's fault for sending him after me.

No matter how hard I tried to convince myself it was safer to leave the druid to whatever fate the forest may decide, something inside me blustered with disagreement as forceful as the storm roaring against the rattling windowpanes. *I can't do it.*

What the fuck is wrong with me?

With a forceful push, I shoved through the doorway and descended the stairs, berating myself for entertaining such a foolish idea.

As I passed the bar, I nabbed a glass beside a drunken patron, filled to the brim with dark liquor, then tossed it back without slowing my pace. I yanked open the inn's old weathered door, revealing the pitch-blackness of the night's howling storm. After pausing a beat to steel my nerves, I marched into it.

I cupped my hands to my mouth. "Balis!"

He hadn't said where he planned to sleep. The stables were a safe bet. I started toward them.

"Mira?" he called from behind.

Soaked through, his shirt clung to every carved muscle, igniting a warmth low in my belly despite the cool rain. I had no business being this attracted to a stranger. A druid warrior—a lethal druid warrior. *What the fuck am I doing out here?* I swallowed hard and forced my eyes to his face, which did little to ebb the heat in my cheeks.

"Everything alright?" he asked with concern of his own.

"I–"

My words caught, and a harsh dose of reality tugged at my senses. It was ridiculous. Me, an insignificant human, worried about a *druid*, a mana-wielding force of nature.

He took a half-step toward me, his head cocked and brow pinched, waiting for me to give him some sort of explanation, or at least a whole sentence. "What is it?" he asked.

"I changed my mind," I blurted.

"What?"

Exactly. What?

"I—changed my mind. You can sleep on the floor."

My nails dug into my palms. I was sealing my fate and relinquishing any chance I had at sneaking away. But my stupid mouth already said it.

"Why?"

His confusion did nothing to relieve my wariness. *Why?*

My teeth clacked together as I fought off a shiver, unsure of what to say. My growing frustration blurred my thoughts, and the sight of that tattoo peeking through the wet fabric of his fucking shirt was *not* helping.

"Because you were willing to sleep out here."

His eyes narrowed on me, asking more questions than I had answers to give.

"Look," I hugged my arms across my middle, "just get inside the fucking inn."

He ran a hand through his short, dark hair, sending sprays of rainwater in all directions, then gestured toward the building. "Alright, then. After you."

I grabbed him by the wrist and pulled him inside, immediately relishing the warmth from the dining room's roaring hearth. Passing that same man nodding off against the bar, I snatched the fresh shot beside him and downed it. This time, the bartender noticed and gave me an incredulous look.

I waved him off and continued up the stairs. "Put it on my tab," I called over my shoulder.

"Do you have a tab?" Balis asked, following tight behind me.

"No."

I pulled him into the room and pressed the door shut. He walked over to the hearth just as I had earlier, drinking in its warmth.

"I was worried it hadn't worked from out there," he said.

I plopped on the bed and peeled off my boots, wiping the muck off as best I could. "What hadn't?"

"The fire." He pointed at the flourishing flames. "I've never been much of a flame wielder." When he faced me, his bright emerald eyes were undamped by the dim light. "Can't be great at everything."

I pressed my lips in a tight line, fighting a smile. "So what kind of wielder are you?" I stood, then pulled my rain-soaked shirt away from my body to let it fall and cling to my skin again. "Not air, by any chance?"

"As a matter of fact," his long strides ate up the distance between us, "I'm more adept at earth forms, but air doesn't give me much trouble."

When his hand settled on the small of my waist, I froze. It could've been our rain-soaked skin, but the crisp scent of the forest flooded my senses—cedar with a hint of cinnamon.

"Hold your breath," he said.

I did, and when a whirlwind ensued around us, my eyes fluttered shut. Behind closed lids, shadows deepened and flickered as the flames guttered in the hearth. The drapes flailed on their flimsy rods, snapping against the windowpane.

The gust hurled into me, rocking my balance, and I grasped his strong forearms to steady myself against the force. As the winds peaked, my clothes, from the airy fabric of my shirt to the wool of my socks, dried, becoming lighter over my body. My hair whipped, tendrils lashing my cheeks, and when I loosed my breath, the fast current carried it away. My hold on him tightened—then everything stopped.

"Much better," he said.

I peeked through clenched eyes, seeing his amused smile.

"Can't say I didn't prefer the sight of you dripping wet, but at least you won't ruin the rugs."

My nose crinkled, and he chuckled, releasing me as my hold on him fell. The carefree, confident stride he took as he walked away invoked a thirst I hadn't quenched in quite some time. My throat dried—it was no longer a need I felt like suppressing.

What the hell. "If I didn't know any better, I'd say you're flirting with me, Balis Gailstrong." A wisp of gravel slipped into my voice.

His witty grin curved the corner of his lip. "Oh good. I was worried I was being too subtle."

"Subtle? I have a feeling *that* isn't a word often used to describe you," I said, turning my earlier words over on him. With my arms crossed, I leaned against the thick wooden bedpost at my back.

He strode closer, and my heart took off like a runaway horse. He braced his hand against the post above my head, then pushed strands of dark hair away from my eyes.

"Something tells me it's not a word used to describe you either, princess."

I did my best not to let him see how his proximity affected me, and kept a sardonic smirk glued to my face. "Subtlety rarely gets things done quickly." I straightened, closing what little space remained between the druid and me. "And I tend to be very efficient."

The flare of his green eyes inferred he intended to test that statement—I could've sworn he even flinched to do so, but the moment passed. Instead, he dropped his hand and retreated a step.

"Too bad." He shrugged. "Captain Dramagan gave me explicit orders not to fuck you."

An indignant scowl twisted my features. "Because *that's* not weird."

"Best not to complicate things, I guess." He gripped my chin, tipping my face. "Or maybe he knew I'd fall for this *winning* personality."

I jerked from his hold, embarrassment souring my mood. He backed up another step, eyes trained on me.

"Doesn't seem to matter much when you'll never see me again after tonight," I said.

"Oh, if I believed that, princess, I'd already have you coming." His smile was saccharine as he sank into the green-stuffed chair.

Unwilling to let him win this battle of wit we seemed to be having, I strolled closer, then braced my weight on the arms of his seat, and stood between his strong, thick thighs. "Fuck me, or don't fuck me," I whispered. "Either way, I *am* leaving tomorrow. And if you try to stop me, you'll learn a word that *is* often used to describe me."

"And what's that?"

He dragged a confident, mocking hand up my thigh—but stopped when he felt my answer in the fine point of my dagger at his ribs.

"Lethal."

His eyes danced with piqued interest, and he gave me a mirthful shove. I straightened, then sheathed my blade.

A few moments passed as I tidied the bed when he asked, "So daggers are your weapon of choice?"

"They kinda chose me."

I removed the spare blanket and tossed it his way. He wasted no time draping it over himself.

"How so?" he asked.

I pulled out my blade. "I was nine when I stole this from a man my father worked for."

"Why'd you steal it?"

The subtle concern in his features told me he knew the temperature of the answer he'd receive.

"So I could protect myself and my–" I stopped myself. "Just so I'd have something." I set it on the nightstand and pulled my baldric over my head to hang on the bedpost.

His intense scrutiny tracked every pensive draw of my brows. "Protect yourself from who?"

"Everyone."

His face fell a bit, but he nodded as if he understood. Maybe he did. I didn't know a thing about him. Even so, there was an ease to the druid's presence, like if he hadn't been here to drag me back to his captain, I might have actually enjoyed his company.

"So, what about you?" I asked, pulling my pants off. His eyes fell over my body, but I pretended not to notice and climbed between the covers. "What is *your* weapon of choice?"

"Most of us in the mountain clan use an ax for close combat and a bow for long range. Between the two," he scratched at his jaw, as if contemplating, "I prefer the ax."

An image flashed through my mind—an armor-clad Balis wielding an ax with the same ease and skill I witnessed from Eurok. I gripped the bedsheets at my sides.

"Get some rest," he said, gesturing with his chin for me to lie down.

I shimmied myself beneath the covers and yawned. The storm still raged, its endless downpour beating against the small window, and I closed my eyes, savoring the gentle crackle of the fire. Hopefully, that black creature I spotted in the trees would be long gone by the time I left in the morning.

"Can I ask you a question?" the druid asked, interrupting the thought.

Exhaustion slowed my response. "Mmhmm."

"Why did you really change your mind?"

My eyes snapped open, and I lay there for a moment, questioning how honest I should be. "You were willing to sleep out there, if that's what I wished."

I pulled the blankets up, tucking them beneath my chin, and waited for his response. "Goodnight, princess," he whispered.

"Goodnight," I whispered back, surreptitiously retrieving my dagger from the bedside table and sliding it under my pillow. *Just in case.*

I sat up, noting the eerie silence. A soft silver glow flooded in from the window, and roosters crowed somewhere nearby.

Early, but still later than I intended to wake. My eyes locked on the empty chair, the spare blanket neatly folded and draped over its back. *He's gone.*

After all that bullshit he spun about not being easy to get rid of, he let me go? I released a sharp exhale and fought off the slight, entirely irrational sting of rejection. *Fuck him. His loss.*

After I readied Eiresh at the stables, I glanced around to ensure I was alone, then climbed in the saddle and urged the horse into a gallop. The air still held the dank smell of last night's storm, and the rough roads leading away from the inn made it difficult to maintain a fast pace. I tugged the reins 'til he slowed.

A moment passed and his ears pressed flat. Something unsettled him beyond the forest's edge. I scanned the undergrowth for any sign of danger but could neither see nor hear anything aside from a small rustling beyond the treeline, which could have been any number of things.

"Easy, boy." I tried to soothe him with a comforting pat on his sturdy shoulder, but the horse remained alert.

By the time the sun neared its apex, we reached a crossroads splitting in six directions. I chewed on my lip. The wooden signs listed several cities I never heard of, with no mention of Calrund or the Ebbonharrow River. With no fucking clue which direction to go, I decided south was still my best chance. I was bound to run into the river at some point. Since it served as a natural border between the human and magical provinces, I could follow it until I found a safe space to cross.

I directed Eiresh toward the southernmost road and squeezed him into motion.

There was a sudden snap of a twig and something darted from the trees, sending the horse lurching to the left. My heart threatened to burst from my ribcage. Eiresh pranced, then took off as I struggled to gain purchase in the saddle.

I dared a glance over my shoulder as we sped off, desperate to see what caused his panic. The black cat from last night stood dead center of that road I intended to follow. My stomach tightened.

Eiresh continued fleeing, water spraying around us as he tread through deep puddles. My eyes remained locked on the beast behind us.

It wasn't chasing.

Once we were well enough away, I pulled back on Eiresh's reins to slow him, and though he may not have agreed, he slowed to a walk.

I couldn't recall the name listed on the sign, and there was no telling what direction this new road would take me. There was no chance I was turning back—getting stalked by an enormous predator was the last thing I needed.

Lost.

The word didn't raise panic yet, but I felt it building. *Stay focused. What do I know?*

I knew I was somewhere south of Raven Ridge. Villages seemed to be fewer here, and there'd been no legible distances listed on those signs. The thick forest left no room to glimpse the northern mountain range and the sun, directly overhead, offered no clues either. A brief wait, however, would give me a definitive answer which direction to head, but to stop would mean giving that beast a chance to catch up.

I was a fucking idiot for refusing the druid's offer to escort me to the border—foolish for thinking I could navigate such vast, unfamiliar territory.

With little choice, I halted Eiresh and watched for my shadow to appear, listening to the surrounding forest. There were no birds, no scurrying of small creatures. It was unnervingly silent. I zeroed in on the ground.

A twig snapped. *Wait.*

A deep growl, like the lightest of purrs, sounded from somewhere amongst the trees. It was out there. Eiresh stomped, jerking his head. *Just a little longer.* To the right—a low chuff and rustle of leaves. *Wait.*

I slowed my breath. Another hushed, prowling purr—*there.* My shadow emerged.

I yanked the reins, angling Eiresh south, then kicked him into motion. He erupted full speed into the treeline, away from the road.

What do I know?

A main trade route ran straight through the center of this enormous province from east to west, the same one my father worked on before he met my mother. I hadn't crossed it yet. If I found it, I could hopefully shake the beast on my tail and gain my bearings.

I clenched my jaw, gripped the reins, and leaned forward, willing the horse to move as fast as he safely could. He seemed to do just that, as if he sensed my request.

I didn't need to look back to know the cat was there, but I did anyway, finding those deep green, predatory eyes watching me evade him a second time. Tall ferns and undergrowth whipped and sliced my skin as we blew through the forest, but my attention was fixated on that creature.

Something didn't sit right with me—how it hadn't given chase, and seemed *unbothered.* A gnawing, cautionary notion consumed my thoughts. We weren't fleeing a mere hungry animal.

I steeled my reeling mind and focused on our dash through the woods. That beast wasn't my only concern. This province was as good as a hall of illusions. There was no telling what lurked behind any corner. That feline maw was just another danger to add to the growing list of reasons I had no business being here. *I'm a damn fool.*

CHAPTER THIRTEEN

MIRA

After a while, I lost the sun to the dense canopy and had no idea which direction the closest sign of civilization would be. The clamor of panic was setting in, and I focused on breathing slow, steady breaths. *Focus on what I know.*

What did I know? What had I learned from all those years surviving the streets? No, not the streets, the *roads*. I traveled through forests before. Maybe not as severe as this, but if I could live years like that, I could survive one day here.

A snap in the canopy had me whirling in my seat, squinting against the ever-changing shapes that danced to the breeze far above. But the next snap, louder than the first, sent me urging Eiresh into a run. He hardly needed the command. He burst into a gallop at the slightest squeeze of my legs.

The foliage was a tad thinner up ahead—sparser undergrowth with fewer places for predators to hide. A small mercy.

With no choice but to keep my head down as the forest whipped by, I focused on the sound of Eiresh's powerful stride eating up the ground. The steady beat of his hooves against the earth, like thunder rolling through our synchronized bodies, gave me something to brace my breath and racing heart against.

Just as I dared to lift my head for a look around, Eiresh dropped. I tucked, prepared to collide with the forest floor, and slammed against a downed tree. Air rushed from my lungs like a billow to a flame as sharp pain lanced through my hip.

Eiresh.

I rolled over, gritting my teeth against the stiff ache in my back, and pushed to stand. I'd be riddled with bruises, but nothing felt broken. Guess the gods hadn't forsaken me, after all.

A hot hand clamped around my mouth. My assailant pulled me down, and I whirled, blade poised to pierce between those crucial third and fourth ribs. I froze. Alarmingly green eyes below dark sweat-matted hair peered into mine, imploring me to be *quiet.*

"You," I seethed. "What the fuck are you doing here?" I scurried back from Balis. Had he been following me this whole time? "Did you hurt Eiresh?"

I didn't care how accusatory the question sounded. After scrambling to my feet, I spotted the pit he'd fallen into. With a careful eye on the druid, I stepped up to the edge. Eiresh reared, trying to gain purchase on the dirt walls. His frantic whinnying echoed through the forest.

"Get him out," I demanded.

Balis yanked me by the wrist, pulling me down again. My viscous objection faded when he snapped a finger to his lips. *Voices.* He guided me into the thicket a few paces back, to higher ground, and I crouched beside him among the brambles. His hand settled against my side and I arched a brow, but his gaze was set ahead.

Out of immediate earshot, we had a clear view of my horse. He calmed, but his ears were pressed tight and he stood still as stone, as if listening too.

A grungy, middle-aged brute stomped through the undergrowth. "Well, look what these sons-a-bitches caught in their pitfall."

Eiresh bucked his head in defiance.

"What a world of hurt you got yourself in." The man braced his hands on his knees as he peered over the edge.

His partner joined his side. "Well, fuck me sideways. You know what that is, Harlem?" He scratched the peppered scruff on his neck. "That's an Arestellian stallion, that is." He clapped his partner on the shoulder.

"One of them mag-trained beasts?"

"Exactly. Worth a fortune back home."

Balis cast me a smug smirk from the corner of his eye. My nose wrinkled. *Cocky bastard.* He tracked me all this way. Worse yet, I didn't know if I should be angry or thankful.

The taller man straightened, scanning the forest. We crouched further into the brush.

"What you lookin' for, Roe?"

"Look at the tracks there." He pointed. "Fresh. This just happened."

Harlem grunted, unconcerned. "Yeah, what of it?"

"Where's the rider?" My stomach sank.

Roe's strides crunched, slow, careful steps closer. The sound paused, and I dared a glance ahead. He knelt beside the place I collided with the tree, canvassing the ground as if inspecting fine artwork. Then his eyes lifted to our thicket and my mouth went dry.

A tracker—and a confident one at that.

Balis' hand tensed on my side as Roe stepped over the log in our direction. His touch slid away, finding the ax on his hip. I did the same, reaching for my steel. *One more step.* My eyes glued to the place on his chest where my blade would sink.

Balis shook his head in the smallest motions, a silent 'no' on his lips. He settled his hand over mine, but Roe took his last step, crossing that imaginary boundary I made. My grip tightened around my weapon, and I shrugged off his touch, prepared to lace the air with my blade—

Eiresh heaved a deep, furious sound—one I'd never heard a horse make. I stilled, arm half-drawn back, as Roe spun toward the pit. The animal beat at the dirt walls with his hind legs, threatening to cave the ground in around him.

"Good boy," Balis whispered.

I cut my eyes to him, noting a knowing look in his emerald eyes as if Eiresh had acted accordingly. I couldn't address it now. The horse thrashed, and his screams of fury and fear dredged up horrible images of my mission with Eurok, churning my stomach. An acrid, bitter taste swelled in my throat. I drew in a deep breath and shook the memory away.

I couldn't fight the adraknid, but these were men.

And I was done hiding.

I propelled forward, tucking and rolling through the brush. My fingers poised on the hilt as they had a thousand times before. I relished the light metallic *ting* in my ear as I let the blade go. It flew with the precision of a serpent's bite. Roe dropped in a heap before he registered I was there.

Startled by the commotion, Harlem jerked my way. I reached across my body, retrieving another throwing knife, when the tubby brute's attention shifted from me—to the brush behind me. A massive blur of velvet fur and dagger-sharp claws flew from the thicket, landing square on the cowering bastard's chest.

My night-black feline stalker had caught up to me.

Horror and awe warred within me as I gawked at the cat's powerful, flawless movements. The beast's teeth sank into Harlem's neck with a crunch, breaking his screams in a stifled squelch. Then it raised its massive head, crimson dripping from its maw, and turned its gaze on me.

My panic caught in my throat. Something like pride showed on its features—pride in its kill. The cat stepped off the poor bastard's chest, and squared itself on me, posture low to the ground, crouching.

I fought my way out of countless bad situations, using wit, flesh, or steel to save myself. None of those would save me here. I was entirely at this creature's mercy. If Balis hadn't already emerged, he must be dead.

My fingers wrapped tight around my dagger's hilt, determined not to go down without a fight. I reached for the second blade at my thigh, but the cat stopped. A quizzical expression narrowed in on my hand, then flicked up to my face as if it understood my intent. With slow, measured steps backward, one after another, I retreated until my body pressed against a tree.

The cat stalked closer with idle calm, the same strange demeanor as when I fled from it earlier. My eyes clenched shut, bracing for the pounce, accepting my end.

Desperate to distract myself from the despair, I scrambled for a fond remembrance, my last thought before death.

Wildflowers sway and rustle in the breeze. Me, my mother, and—no, that memory was just as painful as this beast's teeth would be on my throat.

The cat's low grumble had me tucking my chin, lips pulled in a wince. But where I expected claws and shredding flesh, a rush of air snapped at my skin. Tangled up in the gust, my hair whipped at my face. I squinted, peering through the debris and leaves. Silky black fur transformed into familiar, smooth, tawny skin.

My breath snared, and I pressed myself into the tree. Rough bark dug into my spine as the waning funnel drew closer. I snapped my eyes shut again, shielding myself from the whipping torrent.

Then it stopped.

When I peeked, I was met with Balis' crooked, sly grin.

Wicked amusement enriched his features. "Are you going to stab me with that, princess?" Eyes dropping to the blade I had poised in his direction.

"It's been you this whole time?"

"Hey, I–"

More voices cut his retort. He hauled me behind another batch of shrubbery. Eight or so men broke through the treeline, all disheveled and panting as if they'd been running. Most likely drawn in by Harlem's screaming. They sported various states of filth, though each of them had a brand new sword at their side.

We listened as the strangers found the bodies. They took no time concluding the two must have stumbled upon the horse and impeded a predator's meal.

Eiresh, still agitated but draining fast, bucked his head and snorted at the group encircling him. They were engaged in a heated discussion, debating the best approach to extract him from the pit.

Hunched behind the brush, I couldn't choke back my questions any longer. "Why didn't you just tell me it was you?"

"You wouldn't have let me follow if you knew." His answer sounded so logical for being so outrageously misguided.

"No shit. What was your first clue?" I did my best to stifle my volume. "When I said I didn't want you anywhere near me? Or when I pointed my dagger at your heart?"

"Spit venom all you want, princess. I told you I wasn't that easy to get rid of," he purred.

A fiery retort danced on my tongue, but I decided better of it when the men rigged a pulley system to haul Eiresh out.

I set my jaw and turned my sharp eyes on him. Moments ago, I felt stupid for turning away his escort. "You can help, but I'm still not going back with you."

"Fine."

"Fine."

Forcing my gaze from the infuriating druid's stupid, handsome face, I watched as the men worked. Some pulled at the reins while the others hoisted my horse up. He had the proper sense not to thrash until he had solid ground beneath him.

"What did you mean when you said, *good boy?*" My persistent irritation laced my question even as I kept my voice low.

"You have no idea how special Arestellian stallions are, do you?"

"He was a gift."

"From who?"

"Sidelle."

Balis seemed to consider this for a moment. "They're raised by the druids of the rider clan."

My eyes rolled. "So I've been told."

Apparently, it was clear by my expression that I missed the significance of this because he continued, "The rider clan's primary form of mana is spiritual attunement. They connect with these horses, train them to bond their lives to their rider. An Arestellian will do anything to protect its rider, even sacrifice itself." He nodded in Eiresh's direction. "His instinct will always be to protect you."

They secured him with enough ties to subdue his bucking. A strange, unfamiliar ache tugged in my chest as they led him away.

Calrund no longer mattered.

"Let's go," I said, moving to follow.

I expected Balis to advise against it, but he didn't. Instead, he flashed one of those mischievously wicked smiles fit for the beast form he just shifted from.

"That's my girl. Lead the way."

We tracked them as they pulled Eiresh along, their progress stifled by his steadfast resistance. As they struggled to get him under control, we laid low on an overseeing hill.

"Why didn't you just stalk me as a cat from the very beginning?" The question had picked at me since witnessing his shift from an immense beast into a stunning druid. He'd been so close—his scent, that spiced cinnamon and smooth cedar, lingered in my every breath.

The strangers moved on and we stood to follow.

"Well, to be fair, I didn't expect you to be this—prickly. Eurok wasn't exactly forthcoming with his description of you." His eyes dripped over my body like a spring shower. "In more ways than one."

I ignored the way my stomach fluttered as he paced ahead. I let him take the lead, navigating a drop in the forest floor where tree roots were torn from the ground. The solid muscle of his tanned arms flexed as he lowered himself from the small ledge, then offered his hand to help me. I took it. The warmth of his skin against mine was staggering.

Ahead, a small creek cut through a ravine, and the group stopped, arguing among themselves about how to best maneuver Eiresh across. We took refuge behind two large trees at the top of the ridge.

"Besides, Eurok didn't order me here simply to track you down. He brought me here to be your trainer."

"My what?" My face fell slack, and I didn't bother to hide the aversion on my face. "Eurok was supposed to train me himself."

Was I not worth Eurok's time, so he sent his most charming lackey to train the stupid human? One day with me, and he was ready to hand my training over. The sting of rejection gnawed at me in the pit of my stomach, but I shoved it off. It didn't matter. I left.

"He planned to work with you whenever he could, but he's the captain of the druid army," he said, tone harsh. "He needed someone to cover when he couldn't be there."

"So why give you the shit job?"

"Believe me, if Eurok ordered *me* to train you, he sees something in you."

Guilt wrenched in my gut, and I snapped my mouth shut as we continued on. The group stopped again when Eiresh seized an opportunity to wrap a few men up in some juvenile trees. The others that made it through unscathed razzed the others, telling them to get their shit together.

I hadn't missed Balis' emphasis in his statement. "You make it seem as if you're entitled to the task." I pinned the warrior with a stare, intently curious who Eurok sent after me. "Who are you exactly?"

Eiresh's energy waned again, but it was clear he drained the group of all their stamina, too. They untangled themselves from the bramble and brush, looking like battle-worn men, then moved on as we crept behind.

Beside me, Balis rolled his lips, then dipped in closer to speak low, his voice like supple leather in my ear. "Eurok has devoted a lot of time to my advancement. I guess, like you, he saw something in me. His wish is for me to assume the role of a commander and trainer, similar to his previous position. This was supposed to be a big year—my chance to make that a reality. But I think because of this, it will have to wait."

Illogical disappointment writhed in the back of my mind—I might've enjoyed spending more time with him. I ignored it, forcing my emotions into compliance.

"It looks like I'm doing you a favor by leaving then," I said.

"Yeah, guess so."

"So then, why try so hard to stop me? Why are you here?"

"The druid army fights for no king," he answered without hesitation. "We fight for honor, and much of that comes from who we choose to serve. My loyalty rests with Eurok Dramagan. I trust him, as he does me."

"Choose?" I cocked my head. "Druids have a choice under whose command they fall?"

Balis nodded. "Most often, we accept whatever assignment given to us, but if we prefer, we can decide for ourselves."

His devotion to Eurok's leadership was clear, and I respected that. Though, truthfully, I couldn't imagine living my life devoted to a cause that wasn't my own. To what end, I wondered, would he follow Eurok?

Questions crowded my thoughts. How much did the captain tell his most loyal warrior? Did he disclose they believed me to be a reincarnation of Princess Annorah? Did Balis know that just by training me, he'd be working behind the druid council's back?

"So what about this druid council I keep hearing about? Do they know where you are?"

He huffed a short laugh. "No. Eurok made it very clear that can't happen."

"But you said druids seek their honor in who they choose to serve. Where's the honor in keeping secrets?" I challenged.

"You make the mistake of believing Eurok seeks his honor in serving the council."

"What else is there? If druids pursue peace for their people, and the council is meant to hold that same standard..." I let the question drift off.

"Can you think of nothing, no one, else he might serve so selflessly?"

All expression fell from my face.

Sidelle.

CHAPTER FOURTEEN

MIRA

W e kept ourselves hidden until the men reached their camp. A large group formed around the party, hounding them to explain what happened and how they found the stallion. I stole a glance at Balis from the corner of my eye, unable to stifle a grin at the elated amusement gracing his features. Their comments on the assumed enormity of the beast that brought down both Harlem and Roe made him chuckle.

I avoided that little detail. Part of me was furious at him for having me believe I was being stalked by a wild beast. But the other part—the part that watched him take down that man in my defense—was willing to accept his explanation and move on.

Balis nudged me on the shoulder and pointed to a spot that offered a better vantage point. I nodded, and we moved around the backside of a hill that faced the northeastern edge of their camp where most of their tents were pitched. I noted every entry and exit, where they stashed their weapons, and their sleeping quarters.

It was clear these men were nomads, possibly bandits, judging by their simple setup. Their camp's center focus sat at the main square of the village they occupied, spreading through the streets and between buildings. Their presence stuck out like a sore thumb—rough, dirty, and all human. But the village, while simple, was breathtaking.

Each building, once homes perhaps, was adorned with some variation of a dragon's profile etched into the keystone. The structures' walls were constructed with small, oval-shaped stones, a beautiful array of red and brown hues. Astonishing craftsmanship. These men were an eyesore in comparison.

"Who are these people? This isn't one of the human colonies?" I whispered.

"Human colonies?" Balis' questioning glance surprised me. "There are none in Vylandria."

My immediate reaction was defensive. "Yes, there are. I read about them when I was younger. The author stayed within the small colonies while he researched various beasts and creatures in the forest." I grew frustrated by his clear, disbelieving countenance, like I was a child telling a tall tale. Still determined, I said, "The author was," I paused as my mind made the connection before my mouth finished the sentence. "human." *It was all a lie.*

Everything I believed to be true about this place was wrong. That author had probably never set foot in this province. I deceived myself into thinking I had some minuscule understanding of the threats I was exposed to here. But now, that tiny shred of comfort I clung to was gone.

Consumed by a feeling I can only describe as drowning, I swallowed hard, forcing myself to breathe and wiped the shock from my face. I cleared my throat, all too aware of the heat warming my cheeks under Balis' apologetic stare.

"So, who are they, then? What is this place?" I forced my voice to be as even as a scale.

He pursed his lips but let it go. "This is a Dogu village."

"Dogu?"

"Dragon people. They worship the Empress—a high god said to rule over the twelve gods of the variants, including Erezos and Aethier. See that?"

He gestured toward the rear of the clearing, extending beyond the thatched rooftops. The area featured a half-finished pyramid-shaped platform. I nodded.

"Every winter solstice, they perform a sacred ceremony to ask the Empress if it's time to bring them home."

"Home?"

He shrugged in a noncommittal way. "They think each variant has a purpose, and when that purpose is complete, there's a transcendence of some kind."

"These Dogu people, do they look like dragons?"

"The texture of their skin, perhaps," he said with a chuckle. "Otherwise, they're similar to druids and humans. They just don't exude mana the way we druids do."

"So, why are *they* here?" I asked, gesturing to the men.

"I'm not sure," he admitted. "Whatever the reason, it's not fucking good. This place shouldn't be empty. Humans could never overrun an entire village of Dogu, nor would they want to. They are peaceful, self-reliant. They have nothing of value to humans."

We watched in silence, surveying the men as they settled in for the evening. One tied Eiresh to a post near some tents on the outskirts of the village. Some roasted meat on a spit over a crackling fire, others took to drinking themselves to sleep, while another coaxed a partner into his tent with a suggestive whistle. I didn't have to wonder where that was going.

"So what's the plan?" Balis asked with hushed, eager focus.

He's asking me again?

"Wait for nightfall, sneak Eiresh out, then go our separate ways."

"Hmm. Yes. Yes. And... not a chance." He shifted, making sure our eyes met. "I'm curious when you'll grasp the concept—you're stuck with me."

I set my jaw. "Clearly, you don't recognize when a snake is done being toyed with."

"Venomous, are we, princess?" His voice dropped lower, thick and husky.

I raised an eyebrow, daring him to find out.

"Good," he said.

He leaned in close and—my gods, that delicious *smell*.

"I don't run from wild things—I embrace them, protect them." His gaze flicked to my lips. "Tame them."

"Is that what I am?" My heart stuttered, nearly clipping his last word. "Something to be tamed?"

With a surreptitious grin, he redirected his focus to the village.

"I know why the dear captain sent you." I plucked a few leaves from the bush nearby and tucked them under my knee to guard against the moist ground, paying no mind to his questioning expression. "You're charismatic, and Eurok thought I'd fall for that bullshit. But I won't. So you can save your breath."

He didn't say as much, but I read the *'if you say so,'* in his amused smirk. I ignored it, and we entered a long silence, waiting for the sun to fall behind the treetops, and their harbored shadows to consume the land.

"I'd like to use this last bit of light to nose around," he whispered. "Something doesn't feel right. Like I said, this village shouldn't be empty."

I regarded Eiresh with deliberation before granting my approval with a nod. If I was being honest, I wanted to know more about what was going on here, too.

"Let's follow the treeline to the southern side," he said. "See what we can find."

Again, I nodded, and he took off in a low-crouched stance. I wondered if he wasn't switching to his cat form for my sake as I followed.

This was familiar territory, prowling unnoticed through the shadows, taking care not to stumble on roots, snap twigs, or alert anyone who might be on watch. It was a practiced art, and yet, despite being twice my size, I was a bull in an apothecary compared to the ease with which Balis moved over the dense forest floor.

From what I could tell, most on this side of camp had already drank themselves into a stupor. They'd be just as oblivious to our presence if we marched, calling out cadence as we went.

We paused as we rounded the last corner before entering the village. One of them held tight to a tree on the edge of the forest, puking up his liquid dinner.

My stomach turned sour. The reek of it, the sickening squelch as his bile splattered the dirt, hurled a deluge of unpleasant memories of my father to the forefront of my mind. I forced them back as the man retrieved his bottle and returned to his tent.

"You okay?" he asked.

I was unsure if he could sense my discomfort or if he was alluding to the fact that we were about to venture beyond the safety of the treeline. I nodded.

As he faced me, he reached into the pouch on his side, then offered me something. I opened my hand, and he dropped a small vial into my palm.

"What is it?" I asked, regarding the metallic-colored liquid inside.

"Diablerie elixir," he said. "I won it a few years back. When you drink it, it's supposed to react with any effect you need most."

I raised it up, inspecting it in the dim light, and resisted the urge to question why he gave it to me instead of keeping it. "So what if someone really needs to get laid?"

"I love a woman with a wicked mind," he said, his voice low and tantalizing.

Despite my efforts to remain rational, the praise ignited a warmth within me. A devious smile crossed my face as I tucked the vial away and we emerged from the forest, stepping onto the smooth dirt path.

I tightened my grip on the jewel-encrusted handle of my dagger and appraised our surroundings. On this side of the half-pyramid structure, the village was devoid of any signs of life.

We crouched low and fled to the safety of the nearest stone wall, weaving in and out of shadow and moonlight like a pair of fireflies dancing along the edge of a field.

"Where are we going?" I asked.

"I want to check some of these buildings, see if they left in a hurry."

"Okay. I'll keep watch."

I pressed my back against the side of a building as Balis forced his way in through an open window. With a vigilant gaze, I scanned the shadows, attuned to the faintest rustle of footsteps or interruption in the cacophony of nighttime creatures.

Nothing.

When he returned, he shook his head, and we moved on to the next.

Nothing.

We combed through numerous households, making steady progress until we neared the lower section of the offering dais.

"There's no sign of anyone," he said, dropping to the ground from the last building's window.

It was impressive how focused his demeanor had become, as opposed to the quipping, smart-mouthed druid I experienced until now. And I couldn't help but notice how natural it felt to work as a team, something I never dreamt of doing with another soul before. I brushed off the thought and drew a deep breath, flustered by our lack of answers.

A vile, putrid stench assaulted my nose. My hand flew to my face, the scent unmistakable. *Death.* "Do you smell that?"

His demeanor mimicked mine, and I knew he did. "Where is it coming from?"

My attention was drawn to an opening at the base of the raised platform. Convinced that was where the odor emanated, I rushed over. Balis ran alongside me, showing no intention whatsoever of stopping or discouraging me. He simply followed.

Sure enough, the reek grew stronger the closer we got. The entrance greeted us with an oppressive darkness, accompanied by that putrid odor that threatened to coax a dry heave from my empty stomach.

"Here," Balis said, reaching toward my face.

I froze as he spread a cool liquid above my lip, his touch gentle and sure. The scent of robust coffee and cinnamon filled my nose, and the terrible redolence of death faded. I absently moved to dab at whatever substance he wiped on me.

"Don't." He swatted my hand away. "You'll wipe it off. It'll dry."

If I hadn't been so concerned with what we were about to walk into, I might have smiled at this seamless comfortability I felt around him, like I'd known him half my life.

"Thanks."

As he spread the same coffee-scented liquid under his nose, I let myself for the briefest of moments imagine what it might be like to stay. I shook my head as if to shed the distracting thoughts and refocused on the task at hand.

"I know you're not much of a fire wielder, but do you think you could keep a torch lit?" My chin jerked toward the one secured by the entrance.

An unimpressed leer flickered across his face as the torch ignited in a burst. He grabbed it as we passed, and I took a deep breath to steady my nerves as we ventured inside.

Hundreds of intricately carved pictures covered the walls of the first chamber. Their arrangement suggested they were stories, but I couldn't comprehend their meaning.

Balis caught what drew my attention and said, "I don't know how to translate all of them, but I recognize that." He pointed to one of the more elaborate scenes. "It's the story of the birth of our variant."

That word again. Variant.

I heard it multiple times since being in this province. Sidelle said it when she explained Annorah's sacrifice. *'The High Witches of the Vylandrian Covens, myself included, freed her soul from her body while allowing her mana to reside in this variant.'*

"What is a variant?" I asked.

"Humans might call them realms," he explained. "Our world exists as one of many planes." He pointed to another image, which consisted of multiple concentric circles. "A specific god oversees each plane, though they have been known to interfere with others."

Humans, druids, and now Dogu, all worshiped different deities. "Who is this variant's rightful god?" I asked.

"I'm no soothsayer or shaman, but it's said that Erezos was here from the beginning."

"Not Aethier?"

He disregarded my question and continued on. I huffed an impatient sigh and followed.

The air was balmy and stale here. Every sound bounced off the stone walls, surrounding us in the hollowed echoes of our shuffling footsteps.

I stopped to marvel at this new chamber, staggered by the immense effort put into its construction. These were not the same small, oval stones that made up the village's buildings. These were massive, rectangular, red-brown bricks that could easily crush ten men beneath them. And there were hundreds, if not thousands, of them, making up the entire structure.

At the other end of the antechamber, a large, gray boulder blocked our path to the dais' center. The flickering torchlight revealed faint drag marks, indicating it was pushed into place. I swallowed hard against the fear that laced my veins, the gravity of the horrors that may lurk beyond the doorway sinking in.

"What now?" I asked.

Balis stared at it, seeming to weigh options I didn't see. There was no way I'd be of any help moving that massive thing.

His palm settled against its smooth surface. "I can move it," he said. "But there's no telling how loud it will be."

My jaw fell slack, and I snapped it shut.

"Or I could send a tremor through it," he mused, "to break it up. It would be quieter..."

"But?" I prompted.

"It would take a lot of time and mana."

I sensed from his gaze that he was awaiting my decision.

I thought back on Eurok, the power he emitted to end the adraknid—how exhausted he was when it was over.

While druids were capable of wielding immense power, it seemed to cultivate certain side effects, physical exhaustion being one of them. I had no idea what Balis' limitations were, but if he wore himself out, and the men were alerted to our presence, we would have to fight.

"Drag it," I said.

He didn't hesitate. He braced his shoulder against the massive stone and heaved in an explosive shove. The boulder lurched into movement and scraped across the ground, just as we expected. A loud, long groan echoed through the antechamber as he opened a space wide enough to pass through. The fetor of decay hit us in a staggering wave.

The elixir above my lip was still present, but the delicate magic did little to mask this grotesquely inhibiting stench.

"Oh, gods." My hand clapped over my mouth as I fought every involuntary convulsion in my stomach.

We exchanged a wary glance, then squeezed through the space. Thick darkness consumed the torchlight, leaving me uneasy, as if we stood in the belly of a massive chamber.

Balis handed me the torch. "Don't move."

I froze. That whirlwind ensued again, whipping vulgar air against my face. He emerged, teeth and claws, wrapped in black silken fur, his emerald eyes glinting at me in the fluttering torchlight. How anyone could ever get used to this, I didn't know. He stepped into the darkness as I stood in my halo of flame and safety, waiting for him to return. The bitter bite of my inadequacy gnawed at my pride.

He was back a moment later, his transformation a burst that was faster than the last. "They're dead."

For the first time, I witnessed a display of intense anger hewn into his handsome features.

He hesitated, as if the words made him sick. "All of them."

"H-How? Illness?"

He shook his head, teeth clenched, sending a tense ripple through his jaw. His fingers dug against his scalp as he turned on his heel, pacing.

I tracked every step, waiting for our next move. We were here to save Eiresh, but when he slowed and met my gaze, tension thickened to something tangible.

We needed to end these men for what they were.

Murderers.

"How did fifty men overpower an entire village?" I whispered.

"I don't know."

"Let me see."

His brows lifted, clearly surprised. "You're sure?"

For a moment, I thought I might change my mind. Instead, I nodded.

After a pensive glance, he raised his hand toward the ceiling. In a flare of amber light, a burst of flame erupted from his palm, illuminating the massive chamber. He wouldn't sustain it for long. The shadows burned crimson as the firelight danced across the sea of bodies. My blood went cold. And everything—*everything* inside me collapsed in on itself. The world swayed beneath my feet. Males, females, *children.* Their throats had been slit and their bodies piled atop one another. Left here to rot.

I recoiled, and Balis' flames dissipated, leaving nothing but the torchlight. Unable to choke it down any longer, my stomach purged its meager contents onto the stones. I found myself thankful for the veil of darkness as Balis rushed to my side. He retrieved the torch from me as I hunched over, bracing my weight on my knees.

"Who are they?" I asked between staunched breaths.

He placed a gentle, reassuring hand on my back, moving it in small circles. "Poachers."

I wished the term was unfamiliar. But that black-market bullshit ran rampant in the cesspools of Calrund.

After a moment, he gripped my shoulder, easing me upright.

"Here." He pressed another vial into my palm. "This will help. Don't swallow it, though."

That last bit didn't sound promising, but I did as instructed. I tossed back the strange, tasteless tonic, then spit. The vile, acidic burn on my tongue and throat dissipated, and my stomach eased completely.

I composed myself and we retraced our steps, leaving the way we came.

"The druid army's been tracking these bastards for months," he said, voice echoing throughout the stone corridors. "There must be prisoners—survivors."

My lips formed a line, letting him sort his thoughts as we trudged through the final chamber.

His head shook, conveying his frustration. "Dogu villages are protected—wards, elemental defenses. They never should have been able to enter with malintent." Concern tugged his features into a frown.

We emerged into the bright silver light of the moon, and I drew in a lungful of fresh, summer air. "They have some way around your magic—that's obvious," I said. "But aside from that, these men are fucking morons."

Balis inclined his chin.

"I mean, you saw them." I gestured in the camp's direction. "Tripping over each other, hollering throughout the whole damn forest, stealing horses—these aren't professionals, Balis."

He watched me with strange intrigue. The depth of his stare had me thinking about trees and wanting to climb them. But now wasn't the time for that. These bastards had to be dealt with, and I was committed to helping deal out their punishment.

"They were hired by someone," I said. "Let me help you figure out who."

CHAPTER FIFTEEN

MIRA

I crouched behind a stack of crates beside a tent, listening for the rhythmic breathing of its occupant.

There—barely audible beneath the crickets playing their night song from the treeline.

I gripped my dagger, fingers finding their familiar grooves, and pulled the canvas flap aside. Complete darkness welcomed me, but my eyes adjusted and found the man asleep on the ground, a thin bedroll tucked beneath him. He had little to no possessions, and no papers. He didn't have what I was looking for. I slit his throat and moved on.

It was unlikely I'd find anything on their employer in these outlying tents. That information would be with men closer to the center, where they thought themselves safely guarded. But the carnage these bastards exacted on this village was fresh in my mind—the image forever burned in my brain.

I was naïve to think myself better for seeing what lay beyond the darkness of that chamber. I was no stranger to death and figured I would be prepared. But I was wrong. Nothing could prepare a person for that. And I wasn't—*we* weren't about to let any of them live.

From the next tent over, there was the soft wet sound of teeth puncturing flesh as Balis ended another. We used the shadows to sweep our way through each shelter like reapers, delivering deaths fit for their horrific crimes.

We made it past the first few rows, nearing the center. This was where I expected to find whoever was in charge—someone who knew the full span of their mission here. Balis crept into the nearest one, silent as falling snow, while I moved on.

The scuffling of feet caught my attention, and I took cover behind a few barrels of coffee stacked near the entrance, a clue that this might be the shelter I sought. The higher the rank, the more luxury goods.

Two men walked past, unaware that I lurked within striking distance. They shuffled toward a tent with a guard posted out front—a shift change of some sort. One of them entered through the canvas flap, and a fourth man exited. Was that another armory hold, or maybe where the prisoners were kept?

The soft graze of a hand touched my upper back, and I jumped.

Balis.

'Sorry,' he mouthed.

I shook my head with an exasperated, quiet sigh, then pointed in the men's direction. "Two-man teams. One posted inside, one out," I whispered as the guards took their positions.

"Do we know what's in there?"

We paused as the relieved men passed.

"Not yet." I flashed a suggestive smirk. *Gods, mana would've made bounty hunting a breeze.*

Just as I hoped he would, Balis sent a gust of wind whipping at the canvas door. The guard wrapped his arm around his head, trying to keep his hat from flying off, and gripped the hilt of his sword with the other. These lowlifes were not trained professionals, and yet, those swords were brand new, and somehow—familiar.

I squinted into the dim light to make out what lay beyond the tent's flaps. Hopefully Balis' druid eyes saw what I couldn't.

"They're in there alright," he said, focused indignation in his gaze. "Find your evidence—I've got the prisoners."

I nodded, a pitiful part of me warming at the confidence of his command.

He weaved his way between shadow and silver moonlight as effortlessly as mist through the forest. A small amount of mana radiated from him, even as he fought to suppress it for the sake of our mission. But I saw it—the barest glow accentuating the curve of strong muscles lining his back, shifting and flexing as he moved over the ground.

I forced off irrational feelings better suited for a brothel than a poacher's camp, then shifted into position to enter the tent. *Eurok is such a dick for sending him.*

I slipped inside, waiting for my eyes to make sense of the dimly lit space. So dim, in fact, that I hadn't noticed a lantern lit from the outside. *Shit.* I spun on my heel to leave, but froze at the cold sensation of steel against my throat. *Shit. Shit. Shit.*

The blade pressed in on the tender skin of my neck. Whether it was sweat or blood trickling down, I wasn't sure, but I fought to keep my breath even. My attacker's stench of ripe fruit, musk, and pipe tobacco lingered from behind. More fine goods.

The lantern sat on a stack of books atop a wooden table, illuminating an array of scrolls sprawled across it in a golden glow. The chest at the foot of the cot overflowed with clothing and books. This was indeed the man I needed to speak with.

"Who are you?" he hissed. His voice was nasally—how I imagined an angry goose would sound if it could talk.

I refused to answer. Instead, I focused on positioning my dagger, preparing to strike at the most opportune moment.

I didn't have to wait long.

A barrage of furious shouts pierced the night, startling my tense assailant. I twisted, clutching the man's bony wrist, then squeezed on that perfect point until the weapon fell from his grip. It hit the ground with a thud, and my dagger caught him in the side. His piercing howl told me I got him good.

I put a few paces between us before I faced him. Doubled-over, his features were stuck somewhere between a scowl and a wince. The dim lighting made it difficult to see him clearly, but I sensed he was no ordinary hired hand. His night clothes were dark blue silk, and he wore a long fur-trimmed robe with matching slippers. He limped over to the table to brace himself, then added more oil to the lantern, brightening the space, then dropped into the chair.

With a wheeze that hinted at surprise, he said, "You're human."

With my blade at the ready, I snatched the scrolls sprawled across the tabletop, and scanned a bright-red parchment that looked like a decree—an order to obtain samples of problematic Vylandrian specimens. *Problematic, my ass.*

I turned it over, searching for any indication of where it came from. There was nothing. No signatures, no seals telling me who'd written it. Though, its weight and elegant script suggested fine quality. I brought it closer, examining the thin gold line bordering the edge. The parchment seemed familiar, but in this light, there was no way to be sure.

I stuffed the scroll in my pocket, then turned on the man. He glowered, clutching his side as thick blood seeped between his fingers. Simple poachers wouldn't have taken out the entire village and risk drawing the druid army's attention like this. This had been an extermination.

"Who are you?" I demanded.

He didn't answer. The air between us went as taught as barbed wire.

The noise outside went from stagnant to uproarious in a matter of seconds. Boots pounded against the dirt, arrows knocked. The cold rush of desperation clawed its way up my spine.

"Who hired you to kill these people?"

The tent shuddered as a huge gust of wind ensued nearby, followed by screams and the sickening thud of bodies hitting the ground.

Balis bought me precious seconds. "Tell me who hired you, and I won't kill you."

"Seems you shoulda made that bargain before you stuck your blade in my side, girl." His head lulled as he stared at the scarlet pool growing beneath him.

Fuck me, he can't die yet.

I peeled back the tent flap to peek outside and was met with half a dozen arrows pointed at my face. I was sorely outnumbered. Someone demanded I exit with raised hands, and I reluctantly obliged. As I stepped out, I steeled my spine, preparing for a fight I might not win.

Then I saw Balis. Cool moonlight cast him in silver-gray light, hardening the lethal intent on his features as he slammed his fist into the ground. The earth trembled, then ruptured beneath the men like jaws, opening to accept them as an offering to their depths. Their screams echoed from the chasm until the sound dissipated.

When I met his gaze, I could tell he released the damper on his mana. His eyes were a brilliant jade, glinting with satisfaction, but then his radiance fluttered ever so slightly as he made a move toward me. He halted with a jerk, face contorted in terrible agony, the silver glint of a blade protruding from his chest.

Ice laced my veins. Behind him, a poacher yanked the sword free, and Balis dropped to his knees. With a roar of pain, he spun with an outstretched palm, a desperate maneuver to thrust a pulse of power. Nothing happened. Had he drained his mana completely?

The man reeled back, slamming his fist into Balis' jaw, and a gut-wrenching crack rang out over the silent camp. Blood splattered the ground as he fell forward, bracing himself on his hands. He lifted his eyes to meet mine, and something inside me soured. All that beautiful radiance I admired moments ago—gone. Snuffed out like candlelight.

My head pounded, and my chest heaved as a sob built in my throat. I swallowed it back. He never should have been here. He wouldn't have if it weren't for me. How many times did this godsforsaken province need to prove that I don't—that *humans* don't belong here?

I clenched my fists at my side, savoring the bite in my palms. That's what these people were, though. Humans. And maybe they found a way around these Vylandrians' powers—as hard as that was to believe—but I had no such weakness.

Cold, bitter rage filled every muscle, every vessel, and fiber of my being. I allowed myself, even for the briefest of moments, to enjoy another person's presence. I lowered my guard and let myself feel what it might have been like to have *someone* by my side. But I should have known better. *People like me don't get a someone.*

The world fell silent, drowned out by the thunderous pounding of blood rushing in my ears. I lunged—my *need* to have him dead exceeded my pace. I slung my dagger ahead to sink the gilded hilt into his eye socket. My seething rage darkened my vision, lapsing time and distance. Before I knew it, I was on him, fingers snaring his hair while I yanked my blade free from his head.

He dropped in a crumpled heap.

My knees sank onto the cool ground beside Balis. I tore a piece of fabric from my shirt and pressed it to the gaping wound. "You're gonna be okay."

He hissed, staring up at me with an odd expression, as if confused. "You—"

"Shh, don't speak. Save your energy."

My head whipped in frantic beats, making sure the last of them were dead or dying. The prisoner's tent was obliterated, blown apart by Balis' power. The captives, the Dogu, were huddled together, mostly unharmed.

Balis was right. They did not differ from any druids I met while in Vylandria, but as they got closer, coming to help, I noticed the clear difference in their skin. Less like an alligator, as I originally imagined, more akin to the shimmering scales of a snake's belly.

A male dropped across from me, placing his palms over my fists clutched to the fabric. "Let me see." His tone was steady despite the tremble in his hands.

I nodded, my vision blurred. I was somewhere between shock and rage and wasn't sure if I should let go, but I did.

"Is he going to be okay?" I asked, failing to withhold my panic.

His eyes darted to the dead man behind me, then removed the red-soaked fabric from the lesion. "I might be able to help him. I just hope..."

"Hope what?"

He didn't answer, attention focused on Balis.

I rocked back on my heels and stood, wiping my forehead with my wrist. Blood-spatter matted my hair, slicked my face and neck. *My neck.* I touched the place where the blade had been pressed against my skin.

"There's a man in that tent. I need him alive. Can one of you save him too?" I asked, voice trembling. I had to make sure the bastard stayed alive or all of this—Balis' death—would be for nothing.

No. I couldn't think like that. These beings had mana. They'd heal him. Hot tears spilled over the boundaries of my eyes, dripping onto his shuddering chest. I hurried to wipe them away.

The Dogu looked over his shoulder and signaled a female just behind. She nodded in return and hurried into the tent, her long, ash-colored hair swaying over her back. His attention returned to the wound, and the greenish-gold healing light of his mana cast iridescent glimmers across his dark, shimmering skin.

Balis' gaze, still alert but waning fast, tracked the girl as she ducked inside the tent, before he fixed that perplexed stare on me.

My brow furrowed. "Why are you looking at me like that?"

"You," he winced with the effort it took to speak, "you vanished."

I moved to cradle his head in my lap, not sure there was a point in arguing with a dying male. "You're going to be fine."

He didn't relent. "You did. I–" A horrendous growl cut his words, features contorted in agony. "Fuck!"

I gripped his shoulders, cringing at the horrible sound.

He bared his teeth, eyes clamped shut. "You vanished."

The Dogu interrupted my retort. "He's right," he said. "You veiled from there," he dipped his chin toward the tent, then to the dead man, "to there."

Disbelief trudged up a plethora of arguments, but I bit my tongue, dropping the subject. Someone brought a bucket of water and the male poured it over the stab wound. I pinned Balis' shoulders, trying to hold him steady as he writhed. The gash hadn't improved despite the Dogu's mana.

"What's going on? Should it take this long?" I asked through Balis' clenched-teeth screams.

"It won't work, you filthy fucking beasts," a nasally, arrogant voice seethed from behind.

I looked over my shoulder to find the man I stabbed, barely able to stand, gripped tight in the female's grasp. A dark crimson stain soaked his side.

"He won't heal either," the female said. Her rich tone shared the same elaborate accent as the male.

"It's got to be something I can't see." The Dogu shook his head, then poured more water. "It's those ruddy blades, I tell you."

"We need to keep flushing the wound," someone spoke up from behind.

He threw a dejected glare at the dead man's weapon. "Yes, water. Water is what he needs most."

More tormented, hellacious growls ripped from Balis' throat. Terror clamored up my spine as blood gushed from his wound. Making to stand, I settled his head against the ground. *Water is what he needs most.* I had to help—had to *do* something. I glanced around, ready to retrieve another bucket.

Needs most. Balis' words from earlier rang through my mind like prayer bells on worship morning, waking me from my haze of panic.

"It's supposed to react with any effect you need most."

Need most. My hand flew to the pocket lining the inside of my vest, retrieving the small vial he'd given me. I held it up between the Dogu and me.

His dark eyes sparked like stricken flint. "Diablerie elixir?"

I nodded.

"Do it," he urged without hesitation. "Now."

I used my teeth to rip out the cork, then pressed the glass to Balis' pallid lips. He struggled to swallow, but I managed to get every metallic, inky drop down his throat. Discarding the bottle, I gripped his face, his rough stubble scraping my palms. This had to work.

The asshole I stabbed refused to shut up. He spewed endless insults and threats. To my surprise, he wasn't dying as rapidly as

I thought. Motions slow and gentle, I set Balis' head down, then stormed over to the bastard.

The female held by the collar of his shirt like a misbehaving child as I drew my fist back and threw a punch straight at his jaw. A dull ache ricocheted up my arm, but nothing compared to the pain he must have felt. The Dogu released him, and he collapsed, silent at last.

By the time I turned around, Balis was already sitting up. When he faced me, the brightness of his mana chased away that death-like pallor, and he smiled.

I shook out my tender knuckles, starting toward him. "What?"

"You wasted it."

My brow pinched. Surely, he didn't believe saving his life was a *waste*.

A slow smirk formed on his stupidly perfect face. "You were supposed to use it to get laid."

The Dogu supported his weight, helping him to his feet, and I rolled my eyes, giving his arm a playful shove. *These druids will be the death of me.*

CHAPTER SIXTEEN

MIRA

Once Balis was on his feet and looking like his irritatingly handsome self again, we helped the prisoners. He and Kresh, the Dogu who attempted to heal him, searched other sections of the camp for remaining captors, while I worked my way to the north side to retrieve Eiresh.

I swore actual relief washed over the animal when I approached. The unfamiliar sting of tears welled in my eyes, and I surveyed him until I was convinced he was safe and unharmed. Full of gratitude for his safety, I held his head against my body for a moment, and he let me. I liked to think he needed it as much as I did.

Dawn's blue haze had morphed into a blanket of gold by the time I led Eiresh back to the village center. In total, we discovered three more prisoner tents scattered throughout the camp, each holding fifteen to thirty Dogu. Kresh was directing the last of the prisoners to the dais plaza for a census, and Balis was nowhere to be seen, so I leaned against the wheel of a wooden cart and took my first deep breath since waking up yesterday morning.

Kresh joined me, securing his long machete-like blade at his side. "Glad that's over," he said.

I nodded in agreement, though I wasn't quite so sure. The scroll in my pocket and the questions it raised burned through my thoughts like wildfire. I heard Eurok and Sidelle speak about poachers, of the devastation they've caused across the province. But now, having witnessed that destruction for myself, it felt imperative that it be stopped. And the vicious part of me wanted to *see* it done.

With a stray strip of canvas in hand, I wiped the blood from my dagger. "Will you stay?" I asked.

I hoped he'd say no, even when I understood they had very little choice. Where else could they go? Greggor, the man I killed for the king, smuggled mana-wielding refugees from their own kingdoms here. This was supposed to be a haven—yet they were slaughtered.

"This is home," he said. "We will make it feel that way again with the clans' help."

I nodded.

Balis appeared from behind a tent across from us, a stray gust of wind tousling his hair. It was hard to ignore my involuntary reaction at the sight of him, like every square inch of my body bristled with a need to be touched by him. I never tried to hide when I wanted someone, but this draw was different. Stronger. *No, I can't be this stupid.*

This was exactly why the captain sent him after me instead of coming himself. Eurok counted on me to fall for his maddening good looks and flirty smile. If I wasn't so guilty of using flesh as a weapon myself, I might have resented him for it.

Kresh's gaze narrowed on my hands. "Where did you get that?"

"This?" I held up my dagger as Balis reached us. "I've had it since I was young. Why?"

"It's just like theirs."

He pointed to the heap of dead poachers, and their golden-hilt swords piled beside them. The identical swirling pattern of amber, emerald, and quartz jewels on each hilt suggested they belonged as a set.

"There's something strange about them." A sense of unease laced his statement.

"How so?" Balis asked.

"When cut, mana fled our bodies—unable to wield or heal. They restrained those of us who were unharmed, but the shackles somehow interfered with our mana as well."

Balis dipped his chin. "Lead?"

Kresh shook his head. "No. Lead doesn't respond to mana, but it doesn't have an effect, either. These were almost like a lock, both on our physical bodies and our spirit." With another dejected shake of his head, he said, "I've never seen anything like it."

"What does it mean?" I asked, looking between the two.

Kresh folded his massive, dark arms over his chest. "I'm not sure."

"Well, what do you say we ask our new friend?" I raised a mischievous brow and motioned for them to follow.

We rounded the corner, and both males let out a chorus of laughter. The man hung from a tree limb by his feet like a gangly weasel caught in a snare, swinging and spinning as he bellowed and complained.

Balis chuckled dryly. "Ah, so you didn't kill him after all."

"A villager flushed the wound and stitched him up enough for me to get some questions out of him." I shrugged. "Looks to me those stitches are working loose, though." With a pointed gesture, I drew attention to the fresh red trail that trickled down his naked torso and pooled on the ground.

"Let me down, you bitch!" His complexion darkened to an impressive shade of purple.

"That's not very nice." Balis sent a pulse through the air, knocking the dangling man about.

I cut the rope at the base of the tree, and the poor bastard crumpled in a heap. When I knelt beside him, I balanced my dagger precariously on his temple. He froze.

"We've got a few questions for you. Starting with, where did you get those pretty new swords of yours?"

"Just kill me." He spat on the ground at my knee.

"You know, the thing about us humans, we're always in *such* a rush," I purred, adding pressure to my blade's edge.

Balis and Kresh snickered.

I pushed myself up, then slammed my boot to his chest, shoving him onto his back. "But I've got time for a little fun." I angled my dagger at his cock, and he went rigid.

"W-what are you doing?" he stammered.

"Who hired you?"

"I-I don't know."

My knife's tip pressed against his trousers, and he whimpered.

"I found your scroll. You know something."

"I'm telling you," his voice pitched higher, "I have no idea."

My tongue tsked against my teeth as I pushed harder. The blade pierced into his tender flesh. His terrified wail echoed off the stone buildings and sent birds fleeing from the treetops.

"Okay. Okay!"

Scum, like him, always crumpled when their manhood was threatened. It wasn't my preferred place to aim a weapon, but it had been a long night. Like I said, impatient humans and all.

I withdrew, hoisted him upright, then indicated for Balis and Kresh to position him against the tree. Crouched in front of him, I cocked my head at the terrified man, dagger poised and ready to strike.

"Start talking," I demanded.

"The guy was rich—walked with a limp. He gave the order. I just organized the crew."

"What does he want?"

"I don't know."

I whipped the blade to the side, nicking the thin skin above his cheekbone. "Why are you poaching Vylandrians?"

"You better tell her before she carves out your eye," Balis warned.

The man's whole body trembled as I gave him a wink and a wicked smile.

"He wants live mags."

"What kind?" I asked.

"Any—all. Told us to start small, work our way up. We poached lesser fairies first, then–"

"Work up to what?" A hardened edge overtook Balis' tone.

The man's watery gaze filled with terror, as if he feared his next word would be his last. "Druids."

For a moment, I entertained the thought of fulfilling his expectations. But I found, somewhere in the lines of fear on his face, the control to step away. He didn't deserve to live, but it wasn't my suffering he and this band of lowlifes caused.

He hiccupped on a sob. "That's all I know, I swear."

"Hmm." My lip curled at his pathetic state. "I believe you."

I turned and left with Balis falling into step behind me.

"You're leaving?" His cries morphed into a panicked shout. "That's it? I'm free to go?"

"Nope," I called over my shoulder. I gave Eiresh a loving scratch on his long nose, then climbed into the saddle.

"You're gonna kill me?"

"Nope. You're not mine to kill." I jerked my chin toward the village. "You're theirs."

I clicked my tongue and urged Eiresh on.

The man's frantic screams pitched higher as Kresh dragged him toward his fate. A small gust of wind tickled and tugged at my hair, and I didn't have to look back to know Balis transformed, following my retreat.

We maintained a steady pace until we broke through the treeline, finding the trade road. Eiresh's hoofbeats crunched a steady rhythm against the gravel as Balis shifted again.

"So, are you going to tell me who you really are?"

The question caught me off guard, and I arched my brow. "What's that supposed to mean?"

"Eurok claimed you're believed to be a princess, but you neither speak like one—"

"Because I'm not."

"Nor act like one. And you can wield man—"

"Don't say it."

"Mira."

"Don't!" My grip tightened on the reins. "I haven't lied to you. I'm a bounty hunter from Calrund who was mistaken for someone else. And now I'm trying to leave before I get myself or anyone else killed."

"You veiled across a twenty-yard gap in less than a second. If your goal is not to get anyone killed, you ought to stay and learn how to control that power."

"I don't have power," I said through my teeth. "Besides, you were nearly dead. You don't know what you saw."

"Except Kresh saw it too."

His insistent stare was disarming. And infuriating. How could someone so irritating be so damn attractive? If it weren't for the sturdy muscles cording his arms and the stubble on his chin, he might've looked like a child throwing a tantrum. Instead, he was a powerhouse of a male teetering on the edge of his patience.

I stopped Eiresh and tugged the reins so I could face Balis properly. "Just because you helped me get my horse back doesn't mean I owe you anything," I said. "Least of all, an explanation."

"You're running scared, Mira."

The unapologetic way he said my name, the sound of it on his lips, made me take pause. It begged me to release the damper on my emotions, to let the truth bubbling below like a geyser finally release.

"I *am* scared." My words broke through the tightness in my throat. "Since I've stepped foot in this godsforsaken province, I've heard phantom voices coming from stone men, been rendered unconscious, pinned to a tree by a demon spider—"

Balis moved a step closer.

"I've had strange dreams every night, been hunted by a hot, shape-shifting warrior—and saw the butchered bodies of an entire village of innocent dragon worshipers." I bit down on my tongue as that tightness threatened to turn into a sob.

Balis had closed the distance between us, grabbing the reins like he had that first day we met, and looked up at me. Despite my admission of fear and what I'd gone through, the determination in his deep green eyes was unwavering.

"You think I'm hot?"

I kicked at him, a quip of laughter escaping my thick throat, but he dodged it with ease.

"You're insufferable," I hissed, fighting my mirth.

He laughed along with me until his features hardened—serious again. "You've been through a lot. I get it. But if you think those are reasons you should leave, you've got it all wrong."

I rolled my eyes.

"No, really. Listen," he pressed his lips, considering, "gimme one day."

"For what?"

"To prove this place isn't all bad. If you slowed down, got to know us, and gave yourself a minute to think clearly, you might even *want* to give us a chance."

He pinned me with a gaze that robbed me of words, and my attention fixed on the treeline. The smarter choice would be to keep riding, leave just as I planned from the start. I'd been fighting an endless internal struggle since entering this province. That intuitive whisper promising Sidelle's intentions were pure, that urge to protect Eurok while he was no more than a stranger. And now, with Balis, this attraction between us was becoming impossible to ignore. Despite everything, I looked back into those jade eyes and knew. I *already* wanted to stay.

I sighed a deep, relenting breath. "Just one."

His bright, answering grin was like a sledgehammer to my already crumbling resolve.

CHAPTER SEVENTEEN
MIRA

I thought Eiresh had been fast when we fled from the black cat, before I learned it was Balis. This was closer to flying. I sat behind the druid, arms wrapped tightly around him, as the forest whipped by in melded shades of green and brown. Thank the gods Eiresh had a smooth gait, or this'd never work.

I clung to Balis' tunic 'til my fingers ached, aware of every inch of our body's pressed together. In my head, I replayed the moment he asked me to stay over and over again. All the years I spent reading people, learning those little nuances that spoke a language of truth and lies, I never came across someone so flawless and enigmatic.

There'd been no hint of deception in that line between his brow when I confessed my fear. Nor in the laugh lines near his eyes when he smiled as I kicked at him. It all seemed so characteristically genuine, which made him infuriatingly irresistible and impossible to say no to. So here I was, ass aching, and two days behind schedule.

Still, it was naïve to think the druid had any genuine interest in me beyond following orders. His charm was nothing more than a clever ruse to manipulate me into returning with him.

My growing attraction to the warrior aside, I had other reasons to be grateful for the delay. Though I held my tongue about it, I had to admit how cruel it would be to leave Eiresh behind. Especially knowing the fate he could face in the human provinces—captured and sold off to gods-knew-who.

Now, that considering look from Balis when he learned Sidelle had gifted me the horse made perfect sense. A wordless bond had settled in my bones—an intuitive connection that told me I'd protect the horse as fiercely as he would me. Maybe it'd been a part of her plan the whole time.

I tugged on Balis' shirt, and he slowed Eiresh into a walk.

"Where are you taking me?"

Hopefully, it wouldn't take all day to get there. My ass was already sore from two days of riding.

"It's a surprise."

"If this is your attempt at convincing me to stay, you're off to a terrible start. I hate surprises."

"Has anyone told you that you have a control problem?"

"No one still breathing," I quipped.

His laughter, light and contagious, danced beneath my hands. "And you call me insufferable."

I peered past the few trees that hugged the road, drawn to the wide expanse of the valley unfolding in the distance. A dusting of periwinkle and sunshine flowers dotted the grassy hills. Far beyond that on the horizon's edge were great, round forested mountains.

"The least you could do is tell me what part of the province we're in."

He heaved a loud sigh. "I believe persistent would be a word I'd use to describe you," he mumbled.

"Persistent. Insistent." I shrugged. "You decide."

He glanced at me over his shoulder, an amused spark in his eye.

"We're in Star Hewn Valley, rider clan territory. This is where I was last assigned before I met Eurok."

"How long ago was that?" I asked.

He seemed younger than Eurok, closer to my age, had I not known how deceiving their appearance could be. There was a youthful essence to him, a playful side that balanced his rigidity. Different from my sharp edges—more polished, controlled.

"About a thousand years ago," he said. "I'm two-hundred and eight, if you're wondering."

"And yet, you don't look a day over a hundred and ninety."

Another rumbled chuckle drew my attention to my hands, and I fought the urge to splay them, to feel his warmth and the hard ridges of muscle beneath my fingertips. The impulse worsened when he gave the reins a snap and his stomach tightened with the effort, tugging at the taut rubber band holding together my self-control.

Everything about him seemed to draw me in now. The low, gravel timbre of his voice when we'd toy with each other, as well as the way he fussed over making sure I was comfortable before we started our tandem ride—to the point I snipped at him to just get on the damn horse.

Just one good fuck. That's all I needed. It was reckless, foolish to be sure, but I'd gone all summer without the release that only came from completely losing myself to a mind-blurring orgasm. A dry spell—that's what this boiled down to. Then he could return, Eurok none the wiser, and leave Eiresh and I to do whatever it is I decided in the morning.

For now, though, I wanted to have some fun.

I dared to spread my fingers over the planes of his stomach. It felt as good as I imagined, like gripping sheer strength itself. My touch moved upward, resting on the sculpted muscle of his chest. His body was tense with the effort of the ride, so it surprised me how easily he stirred. I swore a shudder rolled through him, a deep carnal purr, as he slowed Eiresh again.

"Keep touching me like that, princess, and we'll never get there."

"We wouldn't want that, would we?" I smiled.

He subtly cleared his throat and adjusted himself in the saddle.

"Can I ask you something?" I asked.

He nodded.

"Will you be punished when you return without me?"

"That's assuming I'll go back without you, which I won't."

He spoke with such confidence that I almost believed him. He'd have to at some point, though. Wouldn't he? Surely a warrior in the druid army would eventually be missed.

"I'm not refusing to return out of *fear*, if that's what you mean," he said.

That *was* what I meant—another attempt to understand his true motives. If he was unafraid of punishment, then why not give up already?

"The captain can be a hardass at times, but he isn't unreasonable." He peered over his shoulder, a knowing, mischievous glint in his bright eyes. "He rarely gives me anything I can't handle."

A thrill buzzed beneath my skin and I arched a brow, lost for words. Gods, the coiling throb between my thighs was hard to ignore. In reality, that was all I seemed to want—for him to *handle* me.

"Now, can I ask you something?"

"Sure," I answered.

"What really made you become a bounty hunter?"

"That's not a *today* conversation," I said, removing my touch to lean against Eiresh's hindquarters.

"According to you, we only have today."

"Exactly."

He went quiet before starting again. "It just... It seems like something has to happen for a person to decide to kill for a living."

"Says the warrior meant to train me in combat," I jested. I wanted to keep the mood light, but I was not up for being psychoanalyzed.

"My people kill to protect." His tone wasn't confrontational, but it was obvious he wouldn't drop the subject.

Maybe it was knowing how temporary his companionship was, matched with his undeniable witty charm, that had my lips loosening. I was usually a locked vault when it came to the unpleasant details of my life. But like a moth to a flame, I couldn't seem to help myself around him. He embodied this inevitable force, a presence I craved to lay my innermost self bare to.

"That's what I do too." I ran my fingers through my hair, pulling the heavy, dark sheet off my too-warm neck. "At least try to, anyway," I mumbled.

The memory of Greggor's face grated against my mind, accompanied by a dull ache rising from the depths of my stomach.

"I'm not without regrets, though." I chewed my lip.

His ears perked. "Regrets?"

"Two actually."

"And what would those be?" he asked.

I tipped my chin toward the sky, sunlight flickering between the leaves of the canopy above, and surrendered to his prying questions. "The man I should've killed. And the man I killed and shouldn't have."

Ironic that the person I regretted laying a finger on was the exact reason for my current situation. Everything I worked for, killed for, was gone. This had to be the gods' idea of a sick joke—recompense for ending an honorable life after spending so many years dealing out such justices.

Balis was silent for a moment, as if trying to decide if he should ask the question dancing on his tongue. "Who was it you should've killed but didn't?"

Damn it all, here we go.

"My father."

He turned in the saddle to see my face. "I'm sorry," he offered, brows drawn together. "Is he still alive?"

"No clue," I said. I picked at my nails.

The air between us grew pensive. "Is he why you became a bounty—"

"Can we talk about *anything* else?" I interrupted, replacing my arms around his waist again.

I hoped my proximity would distract him. Instead, he glimpsed my arms, and I knew what drew his attention.

"Did he do *that* to you?" he asked, his voice low—measured.

Three days without it meant the tangerine oil had worn off. My scars were as visible as they'd ever been, glowing silver lines against my ivory skin.

"Not all of them." I pulled away.

Many of the silver-white marks were from the rough fibers at the end of my father's whip. But more were sustained while learning to protect myself—and others. Those I didn't mind so much.

The tick in Balis' jaw and the white-knuckle grip he held on the reins told me he had his own feelings about them.

"Besides," I ran my hand down the satin soft hair of Eiresh's flank, "I hate him for what he took from me—not the marks he left."

His abuse drove me to find the courage to leave, to become stronger. What he stole only weakened me—left an inescapable void that no amount of revenge could ever stave.

Balis inclined his head, asking the silent question.

I let out a short breath. "My sister."

He snapped around again, but I wouldn't meet his eye. If he wanted the story, he would have to excuse me from any emotional display. I refused to cry over the one thing I spent years moving on from. That vile, drunken bastard would get no more tears from me.

"Your father took your sister's life?"

My silence was all the answer needed. "I've never spoken of her."

He reached for my hand, then placed it around his waist and held it there, tracing small circles with his thumb against my skin. I pressed my cheek against his back, allowing myself to focus on the warm comfort of his touch, instead of the unpleasant memory I wished no longer had so much control over me.

"What was her name?" he asked after a while.

"Zoe," I whispered. "She was sixteen."

Her face, soft-featured and beautiful, our mother's almond-shaped blue eyes, and the same mouth and nose as my own, flashed behind my fluttering eyelids as I tried to keep the tears at bay. No more. Crying helped nothing.

Balis didn't ask any more questions about her. He either had no interest in learning more or he understood I didn't want to delve deeper.

So, I omitted how when I was eleven I arrived home to find my sister on the floor, clutching her stomach after Father tried to beat the unborn child from her belly. Nor did I talk of how that night, while he thought I slept, he gagged and bound her. Then dragged her out the door, murmuring something about extra mouths to feed.

A while later, Balis sucked in a breath, breaking the melancholy silence. "So tell me about this dagger of yours."

Thank the gods, anything else.

219

"My father was the royal foreman, and when Momma fell ill, he sometimes brought my sister and I to his job sites."

"That's where you stole it?"

I nodded, practically watching the wheels turn in his head.

"Do you know the name of the man you took it from?" he asked.

"No, I was young. Didn't really pay attention to things like that. I just knew I didn't like him."

"Don't you find it strange that your dagger looks so similar to those swords?"

"I mean, yeah. It's strange, I guess."

He scratched his jaw. "You said your father was the *royal* foreman?"

The inflection in his tone piqued my interest. "Yes. Why? What are you thinking?"

"What does it matter?" He arched his brow. "You're leaving, remember?"

"Smug bastard."

"I do believe I've heard those two words used to describe *me* once or twice. Though never from such a spectacular mouth."

I rolled my eyes, and he laughed.

"You think your dagger has the same effect as those swords back there?" he asked.

I let out an exasperated sigh, irritated that he refused to answer my one question to his thirty. "No idea. I've never stabbed a Vylandrian with it. Would you like to volunteer?" I asked, placing my chin on his shoulder.

"I've been stabbed enough for one day, thanks."

"You're no fun."

"Hmm, let's see about that."

He kicked Eiresh into a high-speed run again. I flailed, grasping for the fabric of his shirt as we took off.

The remaining bit of forest faded, and the soft, rolling hills grew into harder, jagged ledges. For the next hour, open plains stretched as far as I could see until the landscape changed once more. We rode through a narrow path carved between two solid rock faces—a ravine.

"Where are you taking me?" I demanded again.

"You'll see, we're almost there."

Further up the road, we lowered ourselves out of the saddle. Balis hitched Eiresh to a tree while I rubbed at my sore muscles. My legs felt as if they had a permanent bow to them as I started walking, but they eventually loosened as I followed Balis down an embankment through some red pine trees.

He held a finger to his lips and waved me forward to crouch with him behind a fallen tree.

"Outsiders aren't permitted here, so we have to stay out of sight until they leave."

"Until who leaves?"

I grinned at the mischievous light in his eyes as he shifted the branch blocking our view. Half a dozen druids stood in a staggered four-by-two formation on the shore of a vast lake. Waves kissed the white sand, gleaming in every color imaginable, like liquid rainbows.

The druids, clad in a mixture of leather and hide fabrics, each wore a waist piece that hung to the ground. Their elaborate headdresses were adorned with cascading braids and feathers. Black paint spread over their eyes, and their smooth, sculpted chests were bare, decorated with markings I assumed held ceremonious meaning. Awestruck, I leaned in closer as they projected a chant over the water.

Balis leaned in close to whisper in my ear. "These are the Opalis Shaman."

The caress of his breath sent welcome chills over my skin.

"They trek here once a month to perform the traditional dance of our creation and bathe in Star Hewn Lake."

I gazed over the calm waters that lapped at the druids' feet. Vibrant shades of red, sunshine-yellows, and cool hues of blue, green, and violet. I held my breath as they pounded a fast-tempo beat on their drums while the others began to move.

While we watched the creation dance from the safety of the forest, Balis explained the story of the day Erezos called on the gifts of the heavens—the rainbow and the aurora. And how they met in this place to create the Star Hewn lake, and from it the first druids were born.

He went on to explain how, afterward, the rainbow went south and the auroras north, leaving the druids to live and look after the whole of Vylandria.

As I listened to his story, the shaman moved in powerful, masculine unison—a series of short, tight movements. Their chant, like thunder echoing over the waves, was a language I'd never heard but whose meaning I could feel in my very soul. I found myself drawn in by their beauty, their dedication to the ritual, and the strength of their presence.

"Where will they go once they leave?" I whispered.

"Each clan has a set of Opalis Shaman who travel across Vylandria, offering their services. When they finish here, they'll move on to the next village."

Balis sat back, leaning against the fallen log, and stretched his arm along it. He patted the ground beside him, offering me a seat.

"Might as well settle in. We might be here for a minute."

"They're not why we're here?"

He smirked, as if it were obvious. "Oh no, they're a bonus."

"So why *are* we here?" I sat down.

He settled his large tattooed arm around my shoulder, a cunning grin decorating his cheeks. "We are going to bathe in the Star Hewn."

CHAPTER EIGHTEEN
MIRA

Just when I thought the daytime views in Vylandria were the peak of possibility, the night swept in and took me by surprise. Star Hewn Lake, in bright sunlight, cast rainbows on its shores as smooth and fluid as satin sheets, but in the moonlight it emanated a melancholic beauty that was truly remarkable.

Auroras glided in haunting iridescent mists, orchid hues of green, and rose across the water, beckoning me like a siren's song. Standing on the raised bank where the brown grass gave way to silky white sand, I stared out over the water, mesmerized, but trying to decide if its beauty was a deception as so many things were in this place.

Balis appeared beside me, placing a warm hand on my lower back. "Let's get closer."

I dug my heels in, halting myself against his nudge. "I don't want to get my boots wet."

A stall tactic, yes, but keeping these things clean *had* been a conscious effort throughout this whole endeavor. And so far, they were still pristine.

But I also couldn't ignore the echoing howl of apprehension in the back of my mind. It felt *wrong* to be here, as if I gazed upon something not meant for my eyes.

"I don't think I can do this," I said. "I shouldn't be here."

The waver in my voice drew his attention, and he tugged at the silver buckle near his chest, releasing the leather spaulder from his shoulders. He let them fall to the ground.

"You can't swim?"

It was evident I was the only one affected by this negative nervous energy. He was so casual, so confident.

I pulled a face. "Yes, I can swim."

"Dress down to whatever you're comfortable with." He knelt to unlace his boots, then lifted his head to look out over the water. "I've only ever been here once." He yanked a boot off and dropped it beside his spaulder. "It's frowned upon to come unless you have real need of it."

"What sort of need?" I asked in a hurry, not yet brave enough to follow him down the bank.

"When a druid bathes in the waters of Star Hewn, all inhibitions are washed away. His authentic wants and desires are laid bare."

My arms folded over myself as I tapped my foot, the sound lost to the soft sand. "How do you know what you're feeling is authentic?" I asked. "Sounds no different from taking a euphoria elixir." Something I knew little about, having only seen it on the shelves in Agatha's shop, but one could make the assumption.

Balis, unable to contain his amusement, walked back up the bank with a playful grin on his face. His touch settled on either side of my waist. He'd done so once before. Though, this time, I savored it—the warmth of his large, strong hands heating my skin, gripping me.

"Can't you make anything easy?"

I cocked my head. "Don't know. Never tried," I said, then pushed my way past him.

I skipped down the bank, yanked off my boots, and dropped them in the sand. If this was to be my last night with the druid, I planned to have those hands touch more than my waist.

226

I stopped just out of reach of the water's gentle licks, politely asking me to dip my toes in. The rational side of me still clawed at my thoughts like a hungry cat, howling for my attention. This was reckless, stupid, a needless setback. I drew a long breath through my nose, then released it slowly.

Rationale aside, here I was, completely unforced, a willing participant. I knew full-well I would get into that water with the druid. I only needed to decide how much of my clothing to shed.

"How deep do you have to go for it to work?" I asked.

"You have to surrender entirely." Nothing but absolute certainty in his voice as he strode past me—completely and gloriously naked.

I scolded myself for how little thought it took for me to strip bare at the sight of him and follow. I let myself unfold beneath the crisp, clean water. Its silken touch kissed my skin, and I was lost to it. As I fanned out, an unusual sense of weightlessness washed over me, and I surrendered to the soothing embrace of the cool liquid.

It was like being cast out amongst the stars, surrounded by auroras. Their colors danced against a backdrop of the luminous sky, and I closed my eyes, drifting aimlessly, freely, all sense of time and place lost to the waters.

Then, waking me from a deep sleep that probably hadn't been more than moments, gentle fingers folded between my own. Butterflies whirled, a chaotic dance, as he pulled me toward him. My pulse quickened as his jade eyes drank in the curves of my body, floating amongst the reflection of a star-drenched sky.

He reached out, slow but unhesitant, and pressed a warm hand on my stomach to steady me. A rumble of power rolled through him like a sleeping mountain's warning. Yet all I could focus on was how the roughness of his calloused palm felt against my bare skin. Goosebumps bloomed across my body.

"What is it?" I stood, letting the heavy, dark sheet of my hair settle over the curve of my breasts.

His eyes dipped, then flicked up to meet mine. "Suddenly, what the captain said makes sense now."

"It's a shame you're so honorable, then," I mused, lowering myself again.

He smirked at my sarcasm and sank beside me.

We sat on the sandy lake bed, side by side, looking out at the moonlight cascading over the water's surface.

"Does anything feel clearer to you?" he asked.

I ran my hands over my shoulders, considering. The waters invoked a noticeable vacancy in my thoughts, as if every heavy burden lifted from my mind. I took a moment to focus, allowing myself the freedom to be absent of my skepticism, my worry, and my past pressing down on my desires. *Without inhibitions.*

"I want to belong here." I whispered over the water that caressed my chest, so quiet I could hardly hear my own words.

"What makes you think you don't?"

"I don't believe I am who Sidelle claims." I hadn't needed the lake to tell me that much. "And I'm afraid of what it means if she's right."

I stole a glance in his direction. He sat still as a monolith, his features void of expression. Waves kissed at his perfectly sculpted chest as colorful mists swirled in the air between us.

"But you want to be here?"

"Yes," I said, smiling.

He spun, turning his body to mine, and I was left breathless, pinned by those striking eyes. He was so close I was forced to lean back. Water dripped from his disheveled hair, landing on my bare chest. I swallowed, knowing without a doubt that, as close as he was, I wanted him even closer.

"So then stay," he said.

My lips parted, but I closed them again, still fighting what I just openly admitted. *I want to be here.*

It was the first thing that settled on my mind when I entered these waters. I had people who risked their lives to save me, defied their careers to keep my existence a secret, and compromised their dreams to find me.

I wanted to be someone worthy of that—so I nodded.

Genuine happiness lit his gaze.

"On one condition," I said.

A flicker of confusion shifted across his handsome face as I raised up, forcing him to retreat. I crawled, urging him to his back until I straddled one of the most powerful warriors in Vylandria with unbridled confidence.

When realization set in, he flashed a devilish grin, then grabbed my hips with a firmness that heightened my desperation. "Are you sure?"

Gods, yes.

"You said these waters remove all inhibitions," I teased. "What do you think?"

He smirked. "Alright. But I have a condition of my own."

The deep, breathy rasp in his tone was already enough to make my hips arch.

"And what would that be?"

"You have to trust me."

"I trust you."

My surprise at the ease of the words must've been written on my face. He sat up, this time forcing *me* to retreat. I crawled backward. Soft sand grazed my back until he was above me. His already hard cock pressed against my stomach where his hand had been moments ago.

Earlier, I questioned the druid's intentions, whether his attraction was genuine. There was no denying it now.

I reached down, wanting to wrap my hands around the thickness of him. But he pulled away, just out of my reach.

"Ah, that's why I need you to trust me," he whispered, mischief lacing the velvet in his voice. "I can't let you touch me."

His eyes locked with mine, and that vague explanation was all it took to convince my need-addled brain to agree, but he explained anyway.

"If you do, I can't be sure I won't lose control, princess." The admission was a breathy caress across my skin. "You make it so hard."

The tantalizing warning wasn't lost on me. His mana seeped from him in dark waves, intermingling with the misty auroras surrounding us.

His lips grazed that tender spot along my jaw, and I inhaled a sharp, shaky breath as restraints, bendable like saplings, encircled my wrists at my sides.

"If this is what you want, we're doing it my way." He pulled away just far enough to meet my gaze. Wicked need burned like emerald fire in his eyes. "I've wanted to touch you, taste you on my tongue since seeing you drenched, free, and smiling up at the sky in that fucking rainstorm."

He rested his weight on his knees, then stroked himself from base to head. A muted glow emanated from his cock like veins of mana. My eyes drew to the motion, and he seemed to take pleasure in whatever it was he saw in my expression. With one last appraising look down my body, he closed the space between us, bringing his face a breath's width from mine.

I arched my hips into him, searching for some leverage to pull him into me without the use of my hands, but as soon as I did, another vine secured itself around the small of my waist.

"Impatient?" he teased.

"Very." I laughed, loving this game we played. I could think of a million words to call him right now. Masculine. Wicked.

Devastating.

Thanks to the waters, I clearly meant it when I said I trusted him. I knew if I asked him to release me, he would. But the most primal, hungry part of me had no interest in that whatsoever.

When his head dipped low, and his hot mouth pressed against my clit, my face tipped toward the sky, lips parted in a gasp. The deft swirls of his tongue had my breaths hitching as heat bloomed and radiated from my core. Gods, I could have come undone from that alone.

Then he slid two fingers inside me. My world tilted and his insatiable rhythm pulsated through my body, the sensation dragging me through the high I'd been craving. A building pressure clouded my mind, and I rocked my hips into his touch, craving *more*.

Vines ripped from the sand and seized my thighs. I gave a soft yelp of surprise as my ass was hoisted off the ground. My breath hitched at the sight of the powerful, shape-shifting warrior between my legs. That fierce enjoyment in his jade eyes—a predator that laid claim to its prey.

A crescendo of heat and bliss raked through my body, tightening every muscle around his unforgiving fingers. The wave of pleasure consumed me, intensified by my inability to move.

He nipped and kissed along the smooth, sensitive skin of my inner thighs, before his mouth found my center again. This time, faster. He hooked his arms around my legs, pulling me against him. He drove his tongue into my middle over and over while working my clit with his thumb.

The restraints forced me to relinquish all control. All focus was finite on the coil, winding tighter and tighter with every deft stroke. With little to nothing to grip on to, I clutched handfuls of heavy, wet sand. My whimpers melted into cries of blissful release as my pussy trembled against him.

He waited just long enough for the dreamy haze to clear from my body before bringing me to his hungry mouth one last time. When I was little more than a puddle in his capable hands, coming down from that final ride over the edge, the tethers released and sank into the ground at my sides.

Balis kissed a trail from my thighs to the line of my jaw. My scent intermingled with his, and I opened listless eyes to find him hovering over me, his lips soft and full from their masterful work. His gaze darted over my head to the shore, a wide smile spreading across his face.

I propped myself up on an elbow. "What is it?"

"Well, now you *have* to stay." He gave an almost imperceptible jerk of his chin, motioning behind me. "I knew you belonged here."

I turned, following his gaze, and all understanding left me. From the exact place I lay, a barrage of brilliant white flowers amidst green, winding vines splayed over the beach. They were luminous, flickering like silver, flameless light along the sand. I snapped my glare to Balis, but he shook his head, stone-faced, as if to say, 'It wasn't me.'

A delicate tingle at my fingertips drew my attention. I turned them over. Nothing was out of the ordinary, but through the space between my fingers, I glimpsed two white flowers rocking in the gentle lapping waves, right where my wrists had been tethered to the ground.

"You veiled," he said, "in the village. Mira, you're a wielder."

"No." My mouth formed a hard line. "I didn't–"

Words escaped me. I couldn't argue. Not anymore. I peered at my hands again, then back to the deluge of luminescent flowers mocking me with their brilliance.

Holy shit.

CHAPTER NINETEEN
SIDELLE

"I knew I'd see you soon," Agatha crooned, her voice as creaky as the old hinges on the wooden cabinets in her little shop. Dark flasks and glass bottles lined their tops, covered in layers of dust and webs that had no doubt been accumulating for centuries.

"I couldn't let such a gesture go without a personal thanks."

I shifted her grimoire to one arm so I could move the stack of volumes from a small chair, then shoved aside a mess of papers, herbs, and glass jars strewn over the tabletop. When I sat, I settled the large tome on my lap.

"Find what you were looking for?" she asked.

With her back to me, she reached overhead to grab a handful of lavender from the bushel that hung from the ceiling. She tore the petals from the stem, and mixed them with the various herbs and oils in her mortar, then beat the pile into submission with the pestle.

Drumming my fingers on the book's cover, I shook my head. "The more I dig, the more questions I come away with, it seems."

"Ah, sounds like you've been keeping too many of 'em to yourself then," Agatha chastised in her matronly tone. "A witch can only get so far without the council of her sisters."

Agatha had no way of knowing just how true her words were. I bartered with the empty guilt in the pit of my stomach, reassuring myself. *All in due time*. For now, I would put no one else in the king's crosshairs if I could help it.

"I am inclined to believe that," I said. "Which is why I'm here, hoping you could answer a few."

She nodded, seeming enthused to both assist and to have her advice be heard. She filtered the concoction through a straining cloth into a small vial. It wasn't until seeing the rose-colored glass and black label that I realized she was preparing the calming brew I'd been purchasing from her for the last two centuries.

Agatha hobbled across the groaning floor planks, set the vial on the table, then pointed her bony finger at me. "You know the drill," she said. "Allow it to sit on the windowsill in direct sunlight for a few days before using. I have a feeling you haven't been letting it rest long enough, and that's why you've been running out so quickly. You know as well as anyone that mana works best when unhurried. You don't force nature to do anything."

Agatha was full of advice this morning. She wiped her hands on her dingy apron and gripped the table as an anchor to lower herself into the creaky chair with a sigh.

I nodded, unwilling to tell her I had run out because my life recently took on a whole new level of stress. Without fail, her special brew was my lifeline, keeping panic attacks at bay. My supply had depleted the same day Mira left. I'd been so worried I accidentally called a rather nasty thunderstorm that lasted the entire night and maybe even spread to a greater part of the surrounding area.

"So what questions can I help you with, High Witch?"

With a polite smile, I unfolded the book, flipping to the image drawn in the top corner featuring Vitany's family name. Pointing with my long, dark-painted nail and tapping lightly, I said, "This here, written in the margin. Can you tell me about it?"

Agatha's brow furrowed with suspicion. "That's the quartz formation the Vitalis family used to commune with the gods."

"Why would their family spell be in your grimoire?" I asked.

"They were the only ones who perfected it."

Agatha pulled an old handkerchief from her pocket and plucked a dried yellow petal from its folds. After crumpling it into her pipe, she drew a long, boisterous inhale as though she could breathe properly for the first time in ages.

"Chrysanthemum." Her mouth twisted into a small smirk, as if she told a private joke, then stuffed the kerchief into her pocket.

I pasted on a patient smile, waiting for her to continue.

"Each of the four original families, mine especially, tried to replicate it. My theory is that the formation is family-specific," she said with an indifferent wave of her hand. "When Erezos last visited the earth, the Vitalis created this spell to communicate with him. Some claim with other gods as well. It's how they rose to power in those early years."

"How did they handle the emergence of soothsayers after the clans were established? They must have been bitter at having their livelihood become obsolete once Erezos blessed individuals with the gift of seeing."

"If that were the case, they never said as much. Wouldn't have been very smart of them to openly dispute Erezos himself, now, would it? Not with Vitany's great-grandfather on the druid council at the time, and eventually, your mother offering her grandmother the position of high witch."

Violet Vitalis, Vitany's grandmother, had been one of the witches who had joined us on the day Annorah sacrificed herself. She was one of my mother's dearest friends. When I tasked Saura with gathering two of her most trusted witches during our move to secede from the druids, Violet had been her first choice.

"So it was just forgotten about?"

"Seems that way. But what I've always wondered—why did Erezos feel the need to create soothsayers at all?"

I chewed on the inside of my cheek, scanning the small, dimly lit room with unseeing eyes. If I proceeded with more questions, Agatha would inevitably start interrogating me, and it was crucial nobody else found out the truth of Mira's identity. Even the old witch, as tight-lipped as she was.

I hoped she would have the answer to casting this communion spell without the need to consult Vitany. I needed to speak to the god by any means necessary, even if it meant dredging up an incantation that hadn't been used in well over nine centuries. Erezos was the only one who would truly have the answers to unlocking Mira's power, but Vitany posed a risk I didn't take lightly. She hadn't been my first choice for High Witch of Black Sand Calms, a sentiment I'm sure was read in my absence from the Honing, despite that not being the reason.

With her grandmother dead, I had no way of knowing if she shared the truth of Annorah's sacrifice with Vitany. If she had, and I asked her to help me reach Erezos, would she? Or would she go to the council? Would I be handing a potential enemy a dagger to end me with?

"Thank you, Agatha." I stood, placing the grimoire on the seat, then turned to leave.

"Take it with you, High Witch. I don't know what you're up to, but it might come in handy."

With a small, grateful smile, I retrieved it from the chair. I paused at the threshold when Agatha called out again.

"Oh, about that human girl of yours–"

My heart clenched.

"Bring her around more often. I'll teach her a thing or two. She was as lost as a fawn in a herd of night-mares when she wandered in—but she's got wit. I like her."

"Will do."

The bell on the rickety doorframe chimed its worn, lazy sound as I left.

I stormed up the front stoop and through the green wooden door, slamming it harder than I meant to. The glass sconces on the entryway walls clanged in protest. I set my calming brew on the windowsill and stalked into the sitting room, tossing the day's messages from the courier onto the writing desk, then ventured out back to the gardens.

As I passed the spot where I introduced Mira to Eiresh, painful thoughts clawed into the recesses of my mind. I forced them away and quickened my pace toward the tranquil shallow pool of blue-green water, formed from the waterfall's runoff. I had to *think*, and this was the perfect spot for it.

Lily pads large enough for me to skip across, topped with fragrant white blossoms, lined the shore. A small frog leapt from one, rippling the water, while dragonflies buzzed haphazardly in all directions. I sat on a rock near the water's edge and let my feet dangle in it as it lapped lazily against the stone. It was peaceful, beautiful, but it did little to ease the turbulence in my soul.

My eyes stung with bitter frustration at my compounding troubles. What would I do if Balis failed to return with Mira? Or if the council moved against the king before Erezos answered my pleas?

"Rough day?"

My heart almost escaped my chest at the unexpected voice. "By the mountain, Eurok."

He laughed, continuing his approach down the small hill to sit beside me. His presence effortlessly offered a sense of comfort to my clenching chest and clouding thoughts.

"When did you get back?" I asked.

"Just now. I saw you step out here while I was coming up. You looked upset."

"Yes, well–"

"I take it Mira and Balis haven't returned yet?"

My lips pressed tight as I shook my head, afraid that speaking would reveal my dissatisfaction. I assured Eurok I trusted his decision when he suggested sending the warrior after her—even dared to be hopeful after doing so. Still, the lack of communication was maddening. It'd been three days since Mira left. On Eiresh, she could've reached the border in two.

"He'll find her. You and I both know she didn't actually want to leave. She thought she was doing it *for* us."

"Yes, well, I gifted her the horse because I believed as much, so relying on that shred of hope alone seems to have only made things worse."

He moved behind me, wrapping those impossibly strong arms around my middle. I smiled, letting my head rest against his shoulder as he swayed us from side to side.

"You couldn't have known."

"I'm a seer, Eurok. I *should* have known." A sigh escaped as I shook my head. "She's such an enigma to me. Like trying to see to the bottom of a raging river. The image is always obscured, always changing."

We grew quiet for a few moments, enjoying each other's presence. I savored the sturdy warmth of him against my back, but my mind wouldn't give me a moment's peace. As soon as I forced aside one intrusive thought, another was there, like a queue of disturbances holding my sanity hostage.

Amidst everything, I'd forgotten to tell Eurok of Greggor's death, and a violent eruption of self-disgust coated my insides. Mira, the girl he swore to protect and train for me, took his best friend's life. How could I have overlooked his tie to the smuggler? I doubted he'd believe it was an accident and not a deliberate manipulation tactic.

I drew in a deep, steadying breath and stirred under his arms, praying the stillness of the moment might quell his anger. He pushed himself back, allowing me room to face him from my seat between his thick thighs.

"Eurok," I said, the tone of apology already heavy in my voice, "I'm afraid I have something to tell you."

And of course—because this male couldn't help but be absolutely perfect in every way—he placed a warm, reassuring hand against my cheek, drawing my downcast eyes to meet his.

The rustle of cicadas and songbirds stirred behind the low measure of his voice. "I think I know."

Guilt threatened to take me under like a riptide, but I forced myself to hold his gaze. "I'm so sorry."

"Shh," he hushed. "You have nothing to apologize for."

That wasn't true. I had an endless supply of regrets where Eurok was concerned.

He leaned back to brace his weight on his arms, his hands splaying in the thick grass, and I couldn't ignore the flawless picture of his muscles flexing with the movement. He was absolute perfection. Sensitive, protective, trustworthy—a calm to my wild that no being ever compared to.

"You deserved to hear it from me, though," I said. "Eurok, I'm so sorry. I–" My words faltered, part of me not wanting to mar the moment with useless excuses.

He sat in silence, waiting for me to finish tormenting myself for what he never dreamed of punishing me for. Then he pulled me into him, wrapping me in an iron-tight embrace.

I used to think that if I held out long enough, he'd move on—find a nice female, have children. That he could find the life he deserved while leaving me to my work. I thought that was what I wanted all these years.

But now, the idea laced my gut with an ill, green sensation. I didn't want to think of another female in what had come to feel like my place. My place was at the center of that admiration-filled stare of his.

Even now, when I'd fallen so far. Poachers breathed down our peoples' necks. The druid council plotted behind my back. And, with Mira gone, no future existed where Atreus wouldn't retaliate once he learned of my deception. Yet, here was Eurok. Just as he'd always been and always would be.

Each fleeting respite from this never-ending worry had been in his presence. He'd become my shelter from the storm, my unsinkable ship on turbulent seas, and I needed him in a way I never let myself admit before.

"Tell me what you're thinking, love."

My stomach fluttered, and I licked my lips, preparing to say the one thing he waited to hear for the last three centuries. "If I'd only been honest with myself from the beginning," I said, "then I wouldn't have denied us so much time."

Over and over, I played our past moments like a fluid dream. Every cool, appraising look from the sparing fields to the painful, longing glances we shared in later years when we parted. I ignored them all, alongside the cold, surging emptiness that never eased until we were together again.

A glimmer of elation creased the edges of his golden eyes, while a hint of sadness pinched his brow. He cupped my chin in his palms. "Sidelle, no. You haven't denied us anything."

His understanding nature never ceased to surprise me.

"You have been a constant embodiment of what our people need. I wouldn't have followed you, wouldn't have *loved* you any other way."

My heart *surged*.

"The Sidelle who led druid females from their subjugation and gave witches their name, the Sidelle that bore a burden so heavy no one could possibly understand—that is who you are, who I choose to love. I love you, Sidelle. No matter how long I have to wait for you, I will always love you."

Say it.

Just. Say. It.

"I love you too, Eurok." A single hot tear slipped past the weak boundaries of my eyes.

A small gasp escaped me as a flood of heat and strength consumed me. My body angled toward his as he eased me down to the soft grass. My silver hair fanned the ground as his kiss traveled the hollow of my neck, landing on my collarbone. His mouth felt so good against my skin—every press seared straight to my heart.

He pulled away too soon, a flicker of that wicked humor in his grin. "Are you saying what I think you're saying?"

The brilliance of my smile reflected in his eyes as I nodded. To my surprise, he rocked on his heels and stood, pulling me up with him. He dipped, pressing another kiss to my lips, then stepped back. His excitement was contagious—a reprieve I so desperately needed that he never failed to supply.

Then he offered me his arm

My mouth fell open, but I snapped it shut. A happy laugh escaped me as I realized what was happening. I locked eyes with the handsome warrior, *my* handsome warrior, and trailed my touch down his upturned forearm. Butterflies fluttered in my stomach as our fingertips met in the customary way. After three hundred years, we finally chose each other.

Our mana swirled around us in shimmering gold and lavender smoke. It entwined our arms as Eurok closed his hand around my wrist, pulling me into his embrace. He pressed soft kisses to my forehead, my closed eyes, my cheeks. The scent of warm, sun-kissed skin engulfed me, and I inhaled deeply, aching for this as much as he did. The shimmer of our mana dissipated on the calm breeze as the final breath of it left us with a sigh, linking us as a union. Forever bonded.

My eyes fluttered open at the brush of something unfamiliar over my body. Soothing, like being wrapped in a sun-soaked towel. It enveloped me, drew me in, offering warmth to my very soul. Eurok's energy.

A wide smile broke out across his handsome tan face in response to the elation on my own. He leaned close, ready to press that first bonded kiss to my waiting lips—

A shattering explosion fractured the air overhead.

Our eyes shot to the sky.

No. Not the sky. Our barrier spell.

It disintegrated with a crackling flare, like burning flash powder rippling through the air. The once-muted roar of the waterfalls was deafening, but it wasn't the only sound assaulting my senses.

Screams.

We were at the main gate a few hurried moments later. The bombardment of crunching wood and thundering rhythmic slams sent citizens scooping up loved ones and fleeing to the smaller western gate. The guards used various tactics to reinforce the failing wooden doors. Some braced thick beams, while others used a shield of wind to cushion each brutal blow.

"What is it?" The hellacious cacophony of noise drowned my words, but, by some miracle, Eurok heard me.

His earlier tenderness was all but tucked away beneath a druid captain's demeanor. "Drakboar."

My gut twisted.

"Get to the west gate," he said. "Make sure everyone's safe."

One more devastating ram, and the gate's center crushed inward with splintering force. A gleaming, enormous tusk penetrated through. Chunks of debris the size of wagon wheels crashed below as the guards lurched back.

"Go." He guided me back by the waist.

Nodding, I took a step to reassure him I was indeed leaving.

He turned and drew his ax, shouting orders. "Fall back! Prepare the tethers!"

I spun away, letting my paragon wolf break free for the first time in months.

Adrenaline surged as I raced toward the western gate. My four legs effortlessly outpaced the limitations of my usual two. Once there, I was relieved to see the majority of the village made it safely.

Whirling back into my druid form, I grabbed Morica's arm. "Take them west. I'll send for you when this is over."

She nodded and hurried off to spread the news. She came to Raven Ridge from a western mountain clan. Morica knew those lands. She'd keep them safe.

I glanced back at the village. The drakboar forced its tight fleshed body through, cramming itself between the jagged jaws of the gate. Splintered wood tore into its flank, soaking the dirt with blood as the druids fought to tether the foul beast with their vines. Its shrill squeals and ear-splitting grunts threatened to shatter my bones as it reared its disgusting, tusked head and thrashed.

After a few more bursts of violent rage, it severed all its binds except a tangled few that hung loosely at his back. This was by far the largest drakboar I'd ever seen, and to my horror, as it forced its way in, a mass of skittering adraknids followed it inside our tumbling wall. My mouth went dry at the sight.

A flicker of movement near the village square caught my eye. Two females exited a small shop on the corner, doing their best to hurry, if not for one's hobbling state. A frigid, chill spider-walked down my spine.

Agatha and Belle.

I phased mid-air as I leapt into action, fleeing down the cobblestone path with little regard for my safety. The massive mutant animal charged down the streets in the center of town like an enraged bull. As it surged forward, it left a trail of destruction—our shops, plaza, and homes crumbling.

With all my strength, I pushed myself to move faster until I rounded the last corner, putting the witches in my direct line of sight. Belle struggled beneath Agatha's weight, unwilling to leave her mentor. Terror painted their faces as the beast headed straight for them, nose down, lethal focus in its milky, soulless gaze. Like battering rams, its tusks destroyed everything in its path.

The pads of my feet tore across the cobblestones, and I threw myself between them and the hybrid. The ground trembled, rattling stones and shattering terracotta planters as the drakboar neared.

A shout drew my attention behind the beast.

Eurok.

He shoved an attacking adraknid back. His ax connected with the mutated animal's gnarled head, dropping it at his feet. He spun, and in that fleeting moment, our eyes met.

I rallied my mana, and the force of it pulsed through every vein in my body. My heart hammered in time with the beast's vast strides. Closer—*closer.*

As the hot moisture of the drakboar's rancid breath reached us, I pushed a massive burst of flame and wind down the hybrid's throat.

I spun and curled around the two witches, securing a shield around us as it reared backward in a frenzy, screaming and bucking. Its hind legs collided with the front of Agatha's shop, glass and stone raining into the street, spraying my shield.

It thrashed its enormous head, reeling from the scalding flames. Its squealing shrieks cut short as a spike of earth protruded from the ground, skewering the beast's middle.

My gaze snapped toward Eurok, anticipating he caused the creature's demise—

Balis. With a stony expression, he acknowledged me with a single nod before redirecting his attention to the last of the adraknids.

Long raven hair caught my eye. Mira yanked her blade free of another fallen hybrid. Balis ran to her, tapped her on the shoulder, then pointed my way. The roar of the falls and the sputtering screeches of dying demons consumed all sound as she locked eyes with me across the field of rubble—her blade dripping with fresh onyx blood.

She's back.

CHAPTER TWENTY

MIRA

Restoration efforts started immediately following the final hybrid's death. Each druid set to work with fluid ease. They gathered supplies for the injured, began repairs on the gate with their mana, while others reunited family members and took a census. There was no milling about or useless chaos. Everyone seemed to know exactly what their purpose was.

I made myself useful by taking advantage of Eiresh's speed and rode west to retrieve the townspeople that fled. Most of Raven Ridge was repaired by the time I returned. Bits of rocks and splintered wood scattered the roadway as I led the people through the smaller gate.

I passed Sidelle, busy repairing the border spell. We hadn't had a chance to speak since she noticed me earlier. Her long silver hair, gray with dust from the rubble, hung low over her back as she faced the sky, working her mana like a graceful interpretive dance.

As I headed toward the plaza to find Balis, the roar of the falls reduced to its ambient muffled sound, signaling the spell was in place. He was there, repairing the bridge that Eurok and I had spoken on the last time I'd been here. His hands were raised in front of his chest, a green glow emanating from his outward-facing palms. My jaw fell slack as the banks sprouted twisting roots, entwining like a lover's embrace. The final product revealed a stunning walkway that rivaled the original.

My stomach fluttered with an anxious combination of awe and excitement. His mana was incredible. I let go of the reins and stared at my palms, a strange inadequacy churning in my gut. It took forever for Balis to convince me the luminous flowers were my doing. He ventured so far as to return that wicked tongue between my legs. When he made me come again, the same brilliant, glowing blooms formed beneath my hands—and I ran out of excuses.

I stood in firm divergence from the idea that Annorah's soul floated around somewhere inside me. Still, I needed answers, and I wouldn't find them in Calrund.

"I'm almost done here," Balis called.

With his shirt tossed over his shoulder, he secured a wooden swing to a tree branch. Once again, I was struck by how magnificent of a sight he was—a sculpted, honed force of nature that I could easily get swept up in. I stilled that reckless tide of craving and tore my gaze away. No way was I stupid enough to fall for him, regardless of how easy it would be. I had to be smarter than that. But damn it if he wasn't incredible to look at.

"So what was that, exactly? Another demon hybrid?"

"Yeah. A drakboar." He stood back, marveling at his work, then admired the plaza as a whole. "Never seen one run with a murder of adraknids, though."

"Everyone is turning in for the day, rejoining families before the storm." I collected the reins again. "We can head up to the quarters now."

"You ready for that?"

He lifted a dark brow, then collected some scattered chunks of stone. When he tossed them into the river, the plopping splash echoed off the quiet walls of the empty plaza. Dark clouds hung heavy in the sky behind him. It wouldn't be long before they opened and released a downpour.

As much as I wished to avoid it, my time was up. "I'm not sure what to tell them."

"They won't care what you have to say, only that you're here."

He dusted his hands off, blatantly unaware of how unfamiliar that concept was to me.

"Maybe. It's just," I rolled my eyes, letting despondence take over instead of words, and shook my head, "I've been trying, but I haven't been able to make anything like those flowers happen again since we left Star Hewn. I mean, shouldn't I feel... *something?*"

His gaze fell to my waist. "I've been thinking about that too, and I might have a theory."

"What is it?"

"Let's get this over with first."

With an effortless leap, he settled behind me, scooting close. His bare chest warmed my back as I nudged Eiresh into motion.

The clouds kept their promise. We made it through the door just in time for the rain to catch up and shower Sidelle's home with large, heavy drops. The familiar scent of wood-fire, clove, and citrus permeated my senses, and I wondered what a place of my own might smell like. I wouldn't mind if it were similar to this.

Our entry interrupted a muffled conversation and was followed by hurried footsteps. Sidelle burst around the corner, a look of teary-eyed joy on her face as she pressed a soft palm to my cheek.

"Are you okay?" she asked.

I nodded, and she hugged me with surprising strength.

The males clasped forearms beside us.

"Good to see you, Captain," Balis said.

"Welcome." Sidelle offered Balis her hand.

He took it and bowed low in a show of respect. "High Witch Sidelle, thank you for receiving me in your home."

"Of course."

Her practiced tone and careful scrutiny gave me the impression they were unfamiliar with one another. He was indeed here based on Eurok's recommendation alone, and I wondered how she felt about that.

"Come. Sit. We have a lot to discuss." She motioned toward the sitting room.

I turned to follow but Eurok dropped a hand down on my shoulder.

"Welcome back, kiddo," he said with that same confident smile he had last we spoke, like he never believed for one second that I wouldn't be back.

As soon as we settled into the semicircle of chairs surrounding the fireplace, the conversation took off and moved with brevity. I sat, feet tucked beneath me, sipping on spiked cider, as Balis rehashed the details of our encounter. He supplied more detail than I expected, even admitting to stalking me in his prowling cat form. But there was a directness to his words that told me there would be no mention of how he kissed me and made me come on the beach of the Star Hewn.

When he gave them every detail of Eiresh's capture, our discovery of the poachers, and the attempted Dogu's extermination, Sidelle's face went ashen. Her dark, painted lips quivered, and I didn't have to wonder why when she excused herself moments later. My heart still ached, too.

"We learned something though," Balis said once Sidelle returned and stood behind Eurok's chair. His gaze tore free from the place on the floor where they'd been glued and swallowed the last swig of ale from his mug. "Mira questioned one of the poachers."

Their eyes flickered to me, and I took another sip of cider.

"He spoke of their employer—a rich man with a limp."

Sidelle's brows pinched. "Did he give you anything more than that?"

"No—but I should also mention the Dogu had suspicions about the poacher's weapons. Injuries inflicted by those swords weakened their mana. I experienced it myself."

The druids' expressions blanched with heady alarm. The room grew quiet, and Sidelle's hand flew to her mouth, as if realizing something. She spun, as if ready to pace, or flee—yet she froze.

"Sidelle?" I asked. "What is it?"

"The ash," she whispered.

Balis and I exchanged a glance.

Eurok pushed from his chair, moving to stand before her. His strong hands found the small of her waist as he lowered himself into her line of sight. "The ash Annorah discovered?"

She gave an almost imperceptible nod.

"You believe he's using it to make weapons?" he asked.

"It's the only thing that makes sense," she said. "My gods, I've always known this day would come."

"Hold on," my brow furrowed, "what ash?"

Sidelle faced us, hands gripping the back of the chair like it was her only hope to remain standing. "Before Annorah's sacrifice—"

My gaze flicked to Balis, wondering if he put it together yet, who they thought me to be.

"—the council granted Annorah the use of a small squad to do a reconnaissance mission. They observed a fleet that departed with unknown cargo from the royal shipyard that later returned with barrels of ash."

I set aside my cider. "Ash from what?"

"They were unable to determine its source. But when one druid came into contact with it, he could not wield his mana."

"Do you think the king is behind this?" Balis asked.

His steady calm acted as an anchor against my raging thoughts and the growing list of reasons I craved to cut out King Atreus' heart.

Sidelle swallowed hard. "I do."

Balis' jaw flexed. "That might explain something else, then."

It felt like I sat beside a different version of him than I'd seen thus far. A honed focus consumed his eyes as they fluttered unseeing over the floor, turning thoughts over in his mind.

"Mira, you mentioned your father was the royal foreman?"

I nodded.

"And your dagger? You stole it from someone at one of your father's job sites?"

Again, I nodded—that irresolute cobra inside, coiling.

"What do you remember about him?"

I dropped my chin, extracting memories better left forgotten. I remembered water, a 'summer home,' as the man called it. His face was lost to me. I avoided those hollow gray eyes at all costs. But that meant I spent a good deal of time staring at the floor.

A clear picture formed in my mind—two feet clad in shining black boots beside a mahogany silver-tipped cane. I stretched my fingers, recalling the pain of pinching them in the cupboard door where I hid. And the steady, shuffle-click, shuffle-click, shuffle-click of his footsteps as he passed by.

"He had a limp," I said in a far-off voice, still not fully broken from my thoughts.

When I looked up at Balis, I couldn't help but notice the flicker of empathy in his emerald gaze. I unfolded my legs from beneath me, feeling the sudden urge to stand and move.

"The vizor," Sidelle confirmed.

Balis continued, "Mira's mana flared on two occasions. Once when she threw her dagger to end my attacker at the poacher's camp, and the other while swimming in the Star Hewn. I can't say for sure, but," he turned his attention back to me, gesturing his chin at the weapon sheathed at my side. "I suspect that blade, its constant contact with you, has been suppressing your mana for some time."

My heart skidded to a halt.

"It makes sense," Sidelle mused. "You didn't have it on you when we visited the stone forest."

My mouth went dry. The need to move drained from me as quickly as it'd set in. I dropped back into my seat. *Holy shit.*

She pressed her lips, as if ruminating, then headed for the beverage cart.

"We have to tell the council," Eurok announced a moment later, Balis nodding his agreement.

Sidelle faced us, clutching a steaming mug in her hands. "No."

"Sidelle..." The captain started toward her.

It was hard not to notice how rarely they allowed space between them. When one walked away, the other soon followed.

"Love, we don't have to tell them about Mira. We will keep her out of this."

"That's not it," she said. "I mean, of course, I'm not ready for them to find out about her, but there's more." The room's silence urged her to go on. "My influence in the council has been waning since Broderick was sworn in. If they hear of this, it's over. They'll declare war."

"Our forces are stronger than ever," Eurok said. "We have the numbers—"

"Why do you think I haven't killed him myself?" She stared him down. "If King Atreus dies, Aethier has promised the destruction of our variant."

253

The druids paled—their auras dimmed like a cloud cast over their glow.

"What does Aethier stand to gain by insisting Atreus remain alive?" I asked. "You mentioned before that Annorah possessed a fraction of Erezos' power, so it would make sense for him to want to protect it. But aside from his long life, Atreus possesses no power, does he?"

"No. And unfortunately, Aethier's reasoning was never divulged, and it wasn't a bluff I was willing to call. But if the council finds out about this, I can't guarantee they won't order the attack I've been advising against. Not if they've already begun questioning my reasoning behind serving as liaison."

She turned away from Eurok, set her cup aside, and braced her arms against the table. At first, her eyes were unseeing, lost in endless debate, but then they registered something on her writing desk—a stack of mail.

She plucked a folded message from the pile and opened it. A blood-red envelope fell out with a soft plop. I waited with bated breath as Sidelle, glaring at the wax seal, picked it up and tore it open with her long, dark nails, a clean rip sounding through the silent room.

There was a moment when Balis turned toward me as if he wanted to reach out and touch me. I wished he would've. Instead, we sat locked in wary glances until Sidelle spoke.

"It's an invitation." She looked up, her eyes on me. "For Mira and I to attend a ball."

"What?" Eurok took a step closer to peer over her shoulder.

She relinquished the summons to him. "In four days."

He studied it as if he could find the king's motives somewhere hidden on the piece of parchment.

Was this a trick? Had he found out Sidelle lied to him? "What sort of ball?" I asked.

"It doesn't say."

Eurok held up the envelope, eyeing the seal. "Did you speak to anyone outside Raven Ridge, aside from the Dogu?"

I shook my head, sensing Balis' focus on me.

"Then the only people who know about your connection to Annorah are in this room?" Eurok dropped the thick paper on the table.

I nodded, my attention on Balis, still as stone in my peripheral. "But if you're trying to keep my existence a secret, then maybe I shouldn't attend," I gestured to the note, "whatever *that* is."

Sidelle folded her arms around herself, head cocked, almost a mirror image of myself. She wanted out of this as much as I did.

"If you don't, it would look suspicious," she said.

"We can go with you," Eurok suggested, "provide backup if you were to have need of it."

Sidelle retrieved her brew and took a long drink. "The king would never allow druid warriors into the castle."

A tense quiet fell over the room. I stared over my shoulder at the dancing flames in the hearth, feeling their warmth on my cheeks. My thoughts soured. When I finally admitted to myself how badly I preferred to be here—how fucking ironic that I might be forced to the human provinces just as I discovered my ability to wield.

I winced as though I had a vise around my stomach. It tightened every time I thought of those flowers. It was a heavy, cold feeling that wouldn't go away or give me a moment's peace. My fingertips traced along the jeweled inlay of my dagger's hilt.

Eventually, I'd have to choose. Wield the blade that saved my life more times than I could count—or wield mana and, if everything Sidelle believes is true, stand to save the entire godsdamned kingdom.

My hand brushed up against my pocket, the small sound of crinkling paper stealing my notice. I pulled out the scroll with the golden border I'd taken from the man at the camp. Unrolling it, I retrieved the invitation and lifted the two beside one another.

An identical match.

"I'm curious," I said.

Everyone's eyes were on me as a wicked plan unfolded in my mind.

"How would the king respond if he felt I shared his disdain for your kind?"

A knowing look drew the edge of Sidelle's mouth up. "I can't imagine he would expect anything less. He believes any right-minded human would feel the same."

"And if you needed protection from me?"

Her eyes fell on the stoic druids on either side of the room.

"What are you suggesting?" Eurok asked.

I dropped the pair of parchments on the table and crossed my arms, pacing as I worked out the plan in my head. "We need to find out if he is behind this ash, right?"

They nodded.

"Well, he's just delivered us the perfect excuse to get inside the castle."

"What if it's a trick, Mira?" Balis retorted.

"Sidelle already said there's no way around it. Anything else would draw suspicion. I have no interest in going, but she's right."

He wasn't pleased, but dropped the argument with a tight sigh as he leaned back in his chair. Eurok cut a glance between the two of us and locked an accusing stare on me.

Ignoring him, I went on, "He requested you train me in druid combat," I gestured toward Sidelle for her to back me up, "something of which he understands little about?"

"To him, we are as feral as a pack of wild dogs. He knows nothing of our ways," she answered.

I gave a pointed nod.

"So you want us to attend as Sidelle's personal guards as protection from you?" Balis clarified.

"Precisely."

"I could say she tried to attack me in a fit of rage," her dark gaze fixated on Eurok, "claim your presence is just a precaution."

The captain stood, arms crossed, an unreadable expression on his face.

"Exactly," I said. "I'll make myself his favorite person, build a rapport with hatred of your kind, and lead him to believe I am on his side. If he *is* behind the poaching, there's a chance he might try to pull me in."

"I don't like it." Balis was almost seething now. "What if your mana flares and he picks up on it? They won't let you in with your dagger."

I ran my fingers along the gilded hilt once more. "I have a plan for that, too."

CHAPTER
TWENTY-ONE

MIRA

The conversation eventually died off once our plans were made. The lateness of the hour was palpable in the silence of the quarters. Eurok slipped off somewhere while Sidelle reassured me once more of how glad she was to have me back, then excused herself to her den.

It was clear she wasn't pleased about the prospect of going to the castle again, especially given the uncertain circumstances. It was the last place I desired to be as well. Despite the unease, I sensed a weight had been lifted off her shoulders. A small spark of life flashed behind her eyes when Balis shared his theory about my dagger, and I'd be lying if I said my curiosity wasn't piqued, too.

I pulled off my baldric, my shoulder singing in relief, and hung it on the back of a chair. Then, I stepped out onto the balcony to test the theory for myself—but found Balis leaning against the railing, deep in thought. His brown hair was disheveled, like he ran his hands through it over and over, but he offered a gentle smile when he saw me.

"Sorry," I chewed my lip, "I didn't realize anyone was out here."

I turned to leave, but a gust of wind slammed the door with unnatural strength for the evening. I peered at him, only to see his gaze return to my face after climbing my body.

"We've barely spoken all day." He patted the railing. "Come join me, princess."

I rocked back on my heel and scoffed.

"Still don't like the name, huh?" A sardonic light glimmered across his features. "I'm sure it'll grow on you."

With a half-amused huff, I strolled closer. "That day in the forest, when you asked me who I really was, did you have any idea? Who *they* thought me to be, I mean?" I pulled my sleeves down and wrapped my arms around myself, guarding against the slight chill in the air.

"I had my suspicions once you did that veiling shit." He lifted the crystal tumbler to his lips.

"Why didn't you voice it?"

"You made it clear you didn't want to hear what I thought on the subject."

A twinge of guilt knotted at the memory of cutting him off when he tried to tell me I veiled. He was right. I hadn't been willing to hear it.

"And in the end, it wasn't my place." He shrugged.

"Oh, I see." I quirked a brow and leaned against the railing. "So it *is* your place to fill my middle with your tongue." I let the words linger between us, daring the predator in him to come out and play. "But confirming the identity of whom you're tasked to recover—that's going too far? Well, I'm glad your mission is complete, then."

He faced me, rising to meet my challenge, and all air fled my lungs under his darkening gaze.

The scent of bourbon danced off his breath as he said, "Careful, princess. Someone might mistake you for caring."

My stomach and middle quaked with conflicting interests, and I snapped my teeth in his face. He laughed a low-timbered chuckle.

It was at Star Hewn Lake when I realized there were two sides to this powerful male. One—highly logical, loyal, and *good*. But the other? Cool and dark, like an eclipse to the warm light he otherwise was. It was this side of him that I found myself craving more of.

Driven by curiosity and free of my dagger, I decided to try to witness the energy Sidelle referred to. I focused on reaching toward him with surreptitious intent, trying and failing at first. After a few more attempts, and with a bit more fervor, there was the smallest wisp of an unfamiliar sensation. It seemed to sweep by me, barely there, like ice gliding over my skin. A cold, smooth caress. When Balis' eyes lit up, I knew I'd gotten it right, even for the briefest of moments.

His tumbler clinked against the surface as he set it aside. He moved over me, pinning me between his arms, braced on either side. With the hard railing and steep drop behind, I was at his mercy. Realizing how vulnerable I was, I straightened. But he didn't retreat. He seemed to prefer me in vulnerable positions.

His touch slid to my waist, then wrapped around to settle on the small of my back. "I said nothing because I didn't care who you were."

I narrowed my eyes, not expecting those words in the slightest. He didn't care? *He followed me, helped save me... He would have to care a little, wouldn't he?* A sharp, sour sensation pooled deep in my chest.

"If I were meant to know who you were," he said, "Eurok would have told me."

"Oh, please." An irritated flush crawled across my skin as I rolled my eyes and turned my head.

He snatched my jaw and brought my gaze to his, squeezing my cheeks so that they smooshed together against my teeth. The part of me that wanted to jerk away, lost out to the part that loved it.

261

"You were my mission. Your identity was none of my business. That was between you, Eurok, and Sidelle."

He released his grip but left a finger at my jaw, tracing the soft edge. Chills exploded beneath my skin, and I had to force myself not to lean into his touch.

"But everything else about you," his voice lowered as he gripped the nape of my neck, "*that* is what I wanted to make *my* business."

My breath stuttered at the irresistible grin on his face. He knew exactly what he was doing, the effect he had on me. The rough pad of his thumb brushed against the soft flesh of my bottom lip. I fought the urge to nip at him again.

All annoyance swept away when, for the first time, I sensed those dark tendrils of his power lick at me, tasting the air. And I couldn't stop the growing ache between my thighs.

All I wanted was to mold into him, feel his mouth on mine. I tipped my chin, lips parted, tasting the sweet bourbon on his breath–

He pulled away.

Rejection boiled as he returned to his glass on the ledge. My predator morphed back into the loyal warrior just as Eurok stepped out onto the balcony.

"I thought I'd find you together," he said.

The accusation made obvious in his tone had me pursing my lips.

"What's *your* problem?" he asked outright.

I caught Balis' warning glare in the corner of my eye but didn't care. "For starters, you're a hypocrite."

Eurok's head ticked in surprise. "Excuse me?"

"You fucking heard me."

I folded my arms as he stalked toward me, his jaw ticking. He stopped close by, demanding I lift my challenging stare.

"Elaborate."

I dove in without a second thought. "You pine for Sidelle, wanted nothing more than to bed her for the last three centuries, and for what—"

"Don't you fucking dare reduce my feelings for her to simply 'bedding' her." He rose to his impossibly full height, hard anger turning the pools of gold in his eyes to solid amber. "She's not some godsdamned dog in heat—unlike some."

I clenched my jaw at the perceived jab.

"You think I haven't noticed the looks between the two of you?" he scoffed. "That I don't catch the scent of your cunt dripping when he's near you?"

A wave of heat flushed across my chest and over my cheeks, but I stood firm in my defiance. "Who gives a fuck? What difference does it make if the druid and I are interested in one another?"

"The fucking difference, Mira, is that Sidelle and I have centuries of experience setting aside our feelings for the betterment of our people. I've suffered longer than you could fathom, longing to be near her, and never having the chance, waiting for her to let me in."

My lip curled. "Some of us don't have that kind of time. Human, remember?" I pointed a petulant finger at myself.

"I don't give a fuck if you're a human or a godsdamned garden gnome. You have a purpose here, whether or not your bratty ass wants to admit it. Until you prove to me you care enough about our people to choose them over whatever the fuck this is—"

I honed in on his choice of words—*our people*.

"—then yes, I will discourage you from catching feelings for one another. Because I know how painful, how destructive, how distracting they can be."

My stubbornness raged, wanting to argue, but the small rational voice inside ensnared enough strength for me to hold my tongue.

"Whatever the fuck it is going on—it ends now." His glare darted to Balis. "You are here at *my* request. I need you for this. Her training is priority number one. I can't have you two fucking around and complicating an already precarious situation. Got it?"

"Yes, Captain." Balis gave a tight nod, his expression unreadable.

Eurok's attention refocused on me. "Sidelle thinks you may have a shot at ruling someday, overthrow that royal horse's ass on the throne and—"

"I don't want to rule. That's not why I'm here," I retorted.

"Mira," he quieted, his defensive posture eased, shoulders relaxed, "nobody is forcing you to do anything, but fate has a funny way of finding us, no matter how far we run from it. I know you don't believe that you possess Annorah's soul, but Sidelle believes you do. All I know for sure is that one way or another, the truth will be revealed to us."

He paused, then let out a deep sigh. "You've been through a lot. I'm sorry to be asking this of you., but for now, can we agree to work toward the same end?" His heavy hand found my shoulder, squeezing.

I was still caught up on his previous statement, reminding myself again that I *wanted* to be here, that I longed for those words—our people—to feel as true as it sounded coming out of the captain's mouth. So I nodded and let him pull me into his side for a hug, even leaning into it a bit, something I'm not sure I'd ever done before. He was warm and solid and smelled of the sun and earth.

"I'm glad to have you back, kid."

I forced a smile, despite it grating on my stubbornness. Then he nodded at Balis.

"Both of you."

"I'll be honest," Balis said, "I don't think I've ever seen this side of you before, Captain. As warm and cuddly as a child's teddy bear." He pressed the glass to his lips.

Eurok stepped away with a haughty smirk and sauntered over to him. "Don't get used to it, either."

He jabbed Balis in the shoulder, then grabbed a spherical decanter from the table along the back wall and poured himself a drink. Watching them, I wondered to myself how long it'd taken for them to form this seamlessness between them—a captain and his subordinate—how they maintained those boundaries and yet, still seemed to possess a comfortability with one another that resembled friendship. Did those lines ever get blurred?

"So now that we are on the same page, there's something I wanna ask you that Sidelle won't," he said, finding my stare.

My brow pinched. "Why wouldn't she?"

"She believes it's too much to burden you with."

"I'm listening." I tilted my head.

He took a long sip and loosed a satisfied sigh before topping the glass off again. "She has experienced a lot in her life, but she has never needed to survive the city streets of the human world. She underestimates the strength that it takes."

Something tugged inside of me, like the first unbinding of a tangled knot in the pit of my stomach. "You've spent time in Calrund?" I asked.

"Quite a bit, actually." He paused, staring at the amber liquid in his tumbler. "Greggor was my best friend. I'm the reason he became what he was for this province."

My chest caved as if I'd been decked in the gut. That tangled knot pulled tight again. Unsure what to do, I backed a step, my legs finding the balcony railing to brace my weight against.

"I don't blame you for anything, Mira. It was *him*." He ground the last word through his teeth, features marred with seething hatred.

I knew he meant it. But I looked away, unsure if I'd be capable of forgiving myself so easily. Or ever.

Balis stepped beside Eurok, setting his hand on the captain's shoulder. "This province has a lot of painful history with the king—almost a thousand years of it. Don't blame yourself. You were just a pawn in one of the endless games he plays."

A wave of bitter shame washed through me at the tenderness in his voice, crashing against my growing rage for the man on that throne.

"And Annorah was the first," I said, my whisper harsh.

Both druids nodded.

They gave me a moment to regain myself, but really, I was listing every way I'd like to make King Atreus pay for the things he'd done, the pain he caused. The clinking of glass as Eurok poured himself another round pulled me from my murderous thoughts.

"So what is it you want me to do?"

"Attagirl." The side of his mouth ticked as he settled himself against the edge of a tall bar chair. "We need you to find his journal."

Balis shifted apart, resuming his position near the railing.

"We should have a second approach in case he doesn't confide the details of his plan." He swirled the liquid in his glass. "Sidelle says this journal is the most likely place we'll find information about the ash and, hopefully, these poachers."

I nodded, even as I felt tension rolling off the stoic druid beside me.

"She said he keeps it with him constantly, but–"

"It's unlikely he will have it during the ball." I finished for him, showing I understood where this was going. "So where does she think it might be?"

"In his council chamber."

I folded my arms and stared at the moonlight bathing the balcony in a silver beam, remembering the room where Sidelle met with him. It was right off the great hall, where the ball would most likely take place.

"It'll be damn near impossible to sneak in unnoticed," he said.

My thought, exactly. I pushed myself off the railing, pacing a small circle. "Which means I need to get him to invite me in." I paced some more, considering, then stopped and put my hands on my hips. A sly smirk lifted my cheek, and I cocked my head. "What exactly is the king's type?"

An involuntary rumble escaped Balis' chest.

"You thinking about seducing him?" Eurok asked, seeming to weigh the option.

Balis' slow blink, gawking at the captain, told me *he* was not.

"I mean, it could work," Eurok said. "You think you could handle something like that?"

Sidelle's dress flashed to mind again—the one she wore the first time I met her. "Yeah, I can do it."

Gods, the idea of that vile man even *looking* at me had me fighting a gag. But if Sidelle could spend the last nine centuries wielding the man's wit against him where her mana couldn't—I could handle one night.

"You can't be serious." Balis scoffed. "You want her to be alone with him?"

Eurok raised a brow at the clear disapproval in his tone, and I thought back to those blurring lines between friend and soldier.

"It's her choice." The captain dipped his chin. "It is, after all, her plan."

"I'll do it."

I swore steam blew out Balis' nose.

"Welcome to the team, kid." Eurok flashed a smile and one of those stupid winks as he inclined his drink toward me.

I gave a half-amused laugh and started past them. "Good. Now, if all you big, tough druids are through with your dramatics, I'm turning in."

I snagged Balis' glass from the ledge and downed the last swig. My gaze lingered on his just long enough for me to set it down—and turn away. His stare, fraught with frustration, burned a hole in my back, and I imagined my energy blowing him a taunting kiss.

For a moment, I was unsure if I'd done it right. But before I disappeared through the glass doors, there was a cold, airy pinch on my ass. *Goodnight Balis.*

CHAPTER TWENTY-TWO

MIRA

The sound of clashing weapons woke me. I looked out my window to find a dirt paddock and fence in the area behind Sidelle's personal stables. Neither of which had been there last night. Balis wielded his ax like some fierce and beautiful form of art, and the sight stirred something warm low in my belly. I was tempted to tend to that need myself, but getting a closer look seemed to be way more fun.

I perched on the wooden crossbeams and dipped my chin. "*Someone* had a busy night."

But Balis stalked by, still pissed about our plan, and pissed at me for coming up with it. His stare was hard, jaw feathering at the temples, and the brown tips of his hair gleamed with sweat. *My gods, how could Eurok be so cruel?*

"And here I planned on giving you a gift," I called.

He stopped with an aggravated halt, then faced me. "What?"

"Testy, are we?" I taunted, then hopped from the fence. I held his glare as I flicked open the top two buttons of my black-lace tunic.

He stared, fists clenching. "We can't."

"All that loyalty, and what do you get in return? Punishment."

"I'm not the one asking to be punished here, princess."

The growl in his voice did little to deter me.

"No? You mean it doesn't feel like a punishment when you watch me do things like this?"

His chest heaved faster, as if he wanted to pounce. Whether to stop me or to replace my hands with his, I couldn't be sure. Regardless, I savored the confliction painting his features as I lifted my leather skirt. My touch traced delicate trails up my thigh, over my holster, then between my legs.

His jaw relaxed, only for his mouth to form a hard line as his emerald eyes tracked my every move. My fingers, glistening from my arousal, charted a course up my body, over the bare skin at my chest, up to my lips. Warmth coiled in my middle, watching him lose the war within himself as I slid my tongue up my finger, then motioned for him to come to me.

With the faintest hint of a smile, a breathy, dark chuckle purred from his throat. My blood roiled, and time danced at the edge of a blade as I waited for him to move.

He stalked toward me, his expression dripping with predatory intention. The fence creaked when he grabbed it, bracing an arm on either side of me. He towered over, my back pressed against the rough wooden panels, utterly consumed by him. And yet, it wasn't enough. I wanted *more*.

But his gaze tore away from mine, dropping to our feet. "We can't," he repeated.

"Can't we?"

I slipped a finger under the waistline of his pants, pulling him closer. His expression pinched, tortured, as if denying me was physically painful.

"The way I see it," I mused, "as soon as I step out onto that field, you are my trainer, my *superior*."

He clenched his jaw once more. Something about that word excited him. His cock hardened beneath his dark brown trousers.

"But there's still a little time." I flicked the next two buttons on the flimsy blouse, letting my shirt fall open.

"Fuck, Mira," he growled.

His gaze shot behind me, checking if anyone was around. But only the stillness of morning surrounded us, and I knew I won.

"Once your training begins, though, Eurok is right. We can't be distracted."

"If you say so."

I lifted onto my toes to silence him with my mouth. His fingers tangled in my hair, twisting and gripping hard enough to send shivers over my scalp. He tasted of salt and crisp wind—an intoxicating savor that I lost myself in. If this was to be the last time I had his hands on me, I wouldn't hold back.

His tongue slid along mine, taking me in like I was the air he was desperate to breathe. I raked my touch up his body, over his chest, memorizing every dip and bulge, every ridge, and valley of those honed, dangerous muscles.

He pulled away, both of us panting. That wicked need I'd been searching for flecked his jade irises.

"So what is this gift you mentioned, princess?"

The heat in his gaze was damn near tangible as I clutched onto the clasp of his belt, tearing at the materials like they were a nuisance. He grasped my wrists, staying my attempt, and my eyes flew to his face. His tongue peeked between his full, soft lips.

"I can't. No matter how badly I want to." He lowered his forehead to mine. "No matter how badly my cock aches to feel your pussy pulsing around it as you come. But if I fuck you today, I'm not sure I'll have the strength to hold back tomorrow."

He wrapped my hair around his fist and pulled, giving him easy access to my throat. He pressed soft kisses against the sensitive line of my pulse, quickening at his every touch. The contrast of his warm breath and the cool morning sent shivers skittering over my skin.

He tipped his head, finding my gaze. "But–"

The barest flicker of light flared across his gaze as two winding vines caressed my thighs, embracing my curves as gentle as a lover's touch. They lifted me, tightening around my body as he forced my skirt up, baring my middle to him.

"I'll be godsdamned if I don't taste this pussy one last time," he said. "I'm going to savor the way you tremble against my tongue." His voice was low, timbered with dark desire. He slid a finger inside of me, coaxing a soft moan from my lips.

"Well, what are you waiting for?" I managed to breathe out, arching my back, my body whining for another touch.

He grinned up at me, a sight so beautiful that I committed it to memory. Then he wrapped his arms around my thighs and tore through me like a rogue wave. My head tipped toward the sky at the first forceful lick against my clit, my body going lax under the binding vines. His tongue and his mana worked me, filling me in every place I ached for it.

My legs quivered, and I dug my fingers through his hair, urging him closer, further, deeper. To my surprise, he let me. No vines restricted my hands as I held onto those brown tendrils, fooling myself into believing I had power here. I bucked my hips, riding out the coiling pressure against his tongue and savoring the grit of his stubble scraping my soft thighs. This would never be enough.

I cascaded toward that brink. His fingers pumped into me at a punishing rate, tongue swirling to gather all the slick need pouring from me, devouring it. I struggled to keep my moans locked down with every panting breath, every nerve centered and pulsing with my building orgasm. It threatened to break past my lips.

Balis reached up in a flash, cutting off the sound at my throat. His eyes narrowed in warning. I challenged him with a mischievous smirk, and he squeezed. The sweet pressure of his fingers digging into my skin sent another torrent of pleasure. My body trembled against his tongue—just as he promised.

Dizzy from the mind-numbing wave he just coaxed from me, my chest heaved, legs shaking, as his vines eased me onto my feet. I drew a deep breath as the tide receded. Gods, I needed to make him feel this way—taste him on my own tongue. It was all I could think about.

I tore at the buckles and clasps of his gear and belt, letting them fall to the ground with muffled thuds. I sank to my knees and pulled down his pants. The length of his cock sprang free.

"It's so fucking hard," I said, peering up at him, stroking his satin skin, and running my thumb over the precum dripping from the tip.

The faint glow of his mana tracked through his veins as I dragged my thumb down the length of him, then back up.

He fell forward, bracing a hand against the fence, cupping my cheek with the other. "That's what you do to me, princess."

His touch slid to the nape of my neck, fingers gripping the hair at the base of my skull as I ran my tongue from base to head. I held his gaze, giving him something to miss on a lonely night.

"*Fuck*." A tremor rolled through him. "You're not gonna make this easy, are you?"

With my tongue still dangling at his tip, I shook my head. Then I took his cock into my mouth, forcing him down my throat.

The way he gripped the fence, like boiling madness, told me he wrestled with restraint, resisting the urge to force himself deeper. I would have let him.

I increased my efforts, sucking and licking him until he could hardly stand. A *crack* splintered behind me, the fence shattering beneath his grip—a reminder that his control was necessary after all.

I pulled away, my eyes watering from both the stretching ache in my jaw and the lack of air, but his head snapped down at me.

"Don't you dare stop, princess. I'll wreck this whole fucking arena if I want to. Put my cock back in your mouth."

That demand had me clenching my thighs, my arousal buzzing again. I laughed, opening wide and resuming to take him in.

"Good girl."

The first involuntary jerk in his movements told me he was getting close to that blissful edge. A red-hot swell of pride bloomed at the thought of bringing this powerful warrior to this point, of affecting him this way.

I dipped low and stayed there this time, working him with my tongue until the head of his cock pulsed. His whole body tightened above me, the warmth of his come coating my throat. Another splintering crack laced the air and a fence post fell beside me, rattling the earth below my knees. Unflinching, I swallowed, the motion making him pull back, unsteady.

He blew out a sharp breath, grinning at me as I stood, buttoning my shirt.

"You really will be my worst punishment yet."

Then he took me in his arms for a final kiss.

My legs were about to fall off. Balis, who seemed as if he barely worked off his breakfast, sauntered beside me. We had our first training session after our morning *discussion,* in mutual agreement that it might be the most productive practice we'd have for a while. At least until we got used to being around each other without wanting to rip the other's clothes off. It'd be difficult, considering how few shirts he seemed to own, but I figured I would do my best to respect his and Eurok's wishes. *For now.*

I fingered through the selection of daggers on the training racks. A new blade was a priority. So far, none that I currently carried nor found here at Sidelle's would make up for the loss.

"So," Balis began, "there's something I've been wanting to ask."

"Mmhmm?"

"Why didn't *you* tell me who Eurok and Sidelle thought you to be?" he asked.

I paused, lifting a brow. "That's kind of obvious, isn't it?"

"No, not really. You shared some pretty personal things, and I never felt like you were holding back. But with this, it seems like you did." His tone wasn't accusatory, rather a casual observation.

I debated the short version, telling him, 'I just didn't want to.' It was bratty, of course, but with anyone else, I wouldn't have cared. I would have thrown up those walls and waited for whomever was asking to tire and leave. But Balis? He had a way about him that made restraint difficult. He was perceptive and irritatingly persistent—enough so that he'd never buy my shallow answer, nor would drop the subject.

So I gave him the most honest answer I could think of. "Sometimes, I don't like the way she looks at me." I tried to sound more indifferent than I knew myself to be.

"Sidelle?"

I nodded.

"I saw it in her the day I left. It's like she's waiting for me to disappear—for Annorah to surface." I paused, wanting to continue, but stopped myself.

Somehow saying, 'And I didn't want to see the same look in your eyes.' felt like crossing an emotional line in the sand that would cause more harm than good at this point.

His face fell like he sensed I held back again, but then the corner of his mouth lifted in a half-smile. I almost expected him to lift a hand and place it against my cheek, but he didn't.

"We've survived nearly a thousand years without Annorah, but I'm not so sure we'll survive another thousand without you, Mira."

My heart pounded. His words flooded my mind, but the effect was immediately dimmed by the weight on my chest, like an anvil forcing the breath from my lungs. The pressure of fulfilling others' expectations was becoming more pronounced and difficult to bear.

I never wanted this—recognition, responsibility.

I lived in a world where I was better left faceless, hidden in plain sight from both targets *and* other bounty hunters. Keeping myself alive was hard enough in those first few years. I wasn't in a hurry to add others' lives to the mix.

But since my mana had shown itself, somehow, the idea of being a part of all this had rooted itself in my soul. And though I still didn't believe I was Annorah's reincarnation, Eurok's words from last night were sinking in. *Fate has a funny way of finding us, no matter how far we run from it.*

What if I *could* do some good here?

A serene wave washed through my body. I paused for a breath before realizing it was Balis' energy. Those smooth, icy tendrils from last night gave way to firm, sturdy crests. Still cool, but more like the dampness of the earth than of dry silken sand. But still, undoubtedly, Balis.

"Well," I started toward the house, unwilling to let him see how his words affected me, "I don't seem to have much of a choice in the matter."

He chuckled and fell into step beside me, gravel crunching beneath our feet as we trekked up the hill.

"Venomous even when touched by a tender hand."

I rolled my eyes, letting the jeer die between us, and rubbed at the sore muscles of my upper thighs. They complained in heavy knots as the incline grew steeper. *I bet Eurok's healing could spare me from this radiating ache.*

I was growing more accustomed to the convenience of mana, though learning to wield it myself was another story. Thank the gods, my mana flared while on Vylandrian soil. There was no end to the trouble this power could've gotten me into had I continued with my plan to leave. And I doubted I'd learn to control it, much less use it, without these druids' help. But as badly as I wanted to tell myself that was the sole reason for me being here. It wasn't.

Perhaps the water from the Star Hewn caused this shift in me. Or maybe it was sharing energy with the earth for the first time, the way it responded on that lakeshore. Whatever it was, something in me had snapped into place. When I saw those flowers, all those fleeting things that made me human seemed to take a sigh of relief. Because despite how jaded or broken I'd become on those streets, how ghastly my soul came to be—I *wanted* to belong here.

We walked the rest of the way in silence, and I reached for the door but stopped before opening it.

"I will do whatever it takes to find that journal." I leveled with him. "Whether Sidelle knows it or not, her mission is now mine, too. None of this has been easy for her, either."

"Which part?"

I thought for a moment. "If this king is as bad as he sounds, probably the last fucking nine hundred years." I pushed open the quarter's door and strolled through.

The place seemed empty as I headed to the bar cart. I poured myself some always-cold water from the pitcher. As it cascaded down my throat, coolness spread through my empty stomach. I turned, still holding the glass to my mouth, and noticed Balis' curious stare.

"What?"

"What do you mean, you'll do whatever it takes? You already mentioned your plan to seduce him into talking about the ash weapons and poachers, but how far are you willing to go? You wouldn't actually fuck him, would you?"

I wiped my mouth on the back of my hand. "I need to get into his private office *alone*. What would you recommend?"

"You would give yourself to him, just like that?"

"It's not the first banner I'll be waving, but yes, Balis. It's just sex."

I attempted to laugh off his unflinching stare, refusing to disturb these last few moments of normalcy before he strictly became my trainer. This was a side of me he hadn't seen before, and his ambivalence toward it was obvious.

While hunting, I did what I had to do, and sometimes that meant giving myself over to the most primal parts of a man for information. It wasn't something I had to do often, but the only thing that mattered was success. The idea that someone would actually care what happened to my body in some virtuous way was laughable to me. So it surprised me to see him physically darken at my words.

I made one more attempt to lighten the mood with humor. "You can't convince me you don't enjoy a random fuck here and there. Not with those skills I just experienced. And if you haven't, then I might consider that a crime to society."

Balis was having none of it. His jaw ticked. "This isn't some random fucking stableboy you use to get your rocks off, Mira. He's a snake in the grass—a dangerous one. He's our enemy."

"You think I don't know that? I saw that slaughtered village, too. I'm well aware of who the *enemy* is." My brisk stride closed the distance between us. "And maybe you don't realize this because you've never had a pussy, but I guarantee you it's the only thing a king like Atreus hasn't warded against."

There was no give in his expression. Without another word, he turned on his heel and stormed out of the quarters. He let the door slam shut, rattling the sconces and punctuating his disapproval.

CHAPTER TWENTY-THREE

MIRA

Rain-soaked, Balis climbed onto his horse ahead of me. His beige shirt clung to his skin, and his wet hair dripped over his face and onto his shoulders. When his gaze locked on mine, there was no charming smile, no wicked smirk. He was still pissed. But that broody expression only made my mind wander to the exquisite sensation of that set jaw working to perfection on my middle until I climaxed harder than ever before. I was clenching my thighs before I could snuff out those thoughts, and Eiresh's rocking saddle wasn't helping.

We'd been on the road for a day. It was Eurok's idea to forgo the carriage and ride the whole way on horseback, but I didn't mind. Despite the unsettling knowledge I acquired about the horrors of these forests, I couldn't help but find solace in it. There was a purity to the danger here, unlike the vile filth that littered Calrund's streets.

Sidelle shifted and took off into the forest. She and Balis had been taking turns all day, enjoying the chance to run freely in their four-legged forms. If I had the opportunity, I would, without a doubt, abandon my body and run in the rain. For the next few hours, I pondered over which animal I might transform into and which one I'd pick if given the choice.

Eventually, the glacier-white fur of Sidelle's wolf broke through the trees, icy-blue eyes full of momentary joy. She shifted back and climbed on her horse beside me.

"Did Annorah possess the ability to shift forms?" I asked. These flares of mana sparked an interest to know more about the princess—her identity, the extent of her abilities. Perhaps if I understood her better, I might recognize that part within myself the witch was so sure existed.

Sidelle shook her head. "No, but she could veil."

Balis' comment flitted through my thoughts. *I had my suspicions once you did that veiling shit.*

"So I've heard." I readjusted my grip on the reins. "That's what Balis called it when I killed his attacker."

"Really?" Her brows shot up, as if delighted by the news. "See, Mira, you're a natural."

I smiled but was less sure. "What is it exactly?"

"Movement from one place to another, using mana. She'd been working to perfect the skill before she died."

I considered this. Annorah had still been learning to control her power when she died, despite blooming when she was just a girl. Would I ever catch up?

I rolled my fingers over the small gilded snake dangling at the hollow of my throat. The jewels embedded along its back marked the distinct pattern of a forest adder—the most venomous snake in Calrund. It glinted in the sun every so often, casting rainbows in all directions. My beloved dagger, remade.

"Why does your wolf not have the same black eyes as your druid form? Balis' are green either way."

"We choose the form we take, but once the choice is made, it's final. I chose blue for my birth mother."

"Were you adopted?"

Her features softened, as if considering a distant memory that deserved regard. "In a sense."

"Is that common among druids?"

"No, not really. But my case was... special."

Her calm, relaxed tone suggested she didn't mind the topic, so I raised my brows, urging her to go on.

Her laughter was as light and delicate as a feather. "You want to hear the story?"

"Unless you have someplace to be," I deadpanned.

As if in answer, thunder rumbled overhead, and lightning streaked across the sky.

"Okay then." She cleared her throat.

SIDELLE

Details flitted through my thoughts as I pondered where to start. It'd been so long since I told it.

Mira waited, grabbing handfuls of her hair, picking through the ends, her hips swaying with Eiresh's leisurely pace. Her new choker accented the burgundy in her eyes, and the brightness in her cheeks gave me a sense of elation. She seemed so pallid when we left the castle—and *thin*. Despite her days on the road with Balis, she put on some healthy weight. Her presence here breathed life into her, as if she'd been reborn.

And now she was showing an interest in our history—*my* history. I couldn't help but feel hopeful again.

"The Drak War had been ongoing for nearly two centuries," I began. "During which, humans were introduced to our variant as allies against the demons."

"By the light god, Aethier."

She *was* paying attention. "Correct," I said. With the war coming to an end, there was an increasing sense of caution between druids and humans. Druids formed the council, made up of two elders from each clan, hoping to combat the growing tension. But, some time after the council's formation, whispers stirred concerning the females' waning strength."

"Only females?" Mira asked, brushing a scuff mark off her boots.

I nodded.

"So, what happened?"

"My mother, Astrid, happened." A smile lifted a corner of my mouth. "She took it upon herself to find out what was happening to the females' power by sneaking her way into a Gracing ceremony."

Her nose wrinkled. "What's that?"

I rolled my lips and drew in a deep breath, the weight of the atrocity still heavy on my heart. "The elders would bring newborns from each clan into the sacred lodge and use their direct line to the gods to ask for blessings for the child."

Mira nodded in understanding, despite the unease shaping her sharp, elegant features.

"Females were not permitted on the council. When Astrid snuck into the forbidden meeting, and witnessed what happened behind those closed doors, she understood why."

Mira's brow pinched as though she questioned her decision to request this story from me.

"As she listened to the elders that night, she learned of their betrayal. They were using their decanting gifts, which we druids use to usher nature's souls into the veil, to remove mana from female infants."

She scowled. "You mean *stealing* it!"

Mira darted a glare between the males. Both warriors, as if sensing the weight of her accusation, held up their hands in surrender.

"Don't look at me. I wasn't alive then. Good thing, too." Eurok leaned to the side and spit on the gravel road. "I'd have broken their fucking necks had I known."

"Don't you worry," I said, hoping to ease the discontent growing behind her wine-colored eyes, "they got what was coming to them."

"What were they doing with it?" she asked.

"They were containing it within another vessel to be used however they saw fit, giving them an edge on the battlefield both with the drak and," I shrugged a shoulder and shook my head, "the humans if it ever came to it."

"What sort of vessel?"

I pulled my staff loose from its place on the saddle.

Mira froze, eyes locked on the stone affixed to the top. "A moonstone?"

"Once it contains a core of mana, it becomes a manastone. But yes, the males carried staves that, unbeknownst to females, contained the mana of their very own daughters, sisters, and friends."

"What happened after your mother found out?"

"Well, part of the reason she was so compelled to uncover the cause of the female's declining mana—she was about to give birth herself."

The rain intensified, but we continued on our way, unfazed by the downpour.

"She was pregnant?"

I nodded.

"With you?"

I nodded again. "The very next day, her labor started."

Mira swallowed as if she realized this story ended in tragedy.

"We druids have a tradition surrounding the birth of our children. When a pregnant mother begins labor, she must ascend the Aupex Mountain."

An incredulous expression distorted her face. "You have to climb a fucking mountain while in labor?"

285

"It seems rather cruel, yes, but wherever that mother gives birth along the way determines how powerful her child will be."

Her expression remained sour, as if she couldn't decide how to feel about the topic.

"On the day Astrid's labor began, so did another female's. A female named Saura."

"The two of them climbed for hours. Eventually, Saura was the first to slow. She came to a stop halfway to the summit. Astrid, however, kept climbing. Her labor was long and difficult, but she fought her way up the sacred mountain, fueled by fury and determination. Finally, when her pains became so intense that she could go no further, she dropped to her knees. When she looked up, she realized she reached the summit, and that was where she delivered her child."

"You," Mira said with an air of reverence.

"She is the most powerful female druid ever born," Eurok said, riding just ahead of us. He turned to look at me over his shoulder with that same hungry stare he knew affected me so completely.

I embraced the flutter of butterflies that rose in my stomach, then turned to Mira. "Few mothers in druid history have reached the summit before giving birth, and those that did bore males. But Astrid made it, and for that, I am eternally grateful." The sting in my eyes sent a flush of warmth over my cheeks. I swiped the moisture away. "But her lifeblood drained—rather quickly. She knew she wouldn't survive the descent, and alone on the top of that mountain, she feared for her child's life.

"Astrid descended as fast as she could, carrying her newborn child. She stumbled and fell over the treacherous terrain, but kept going until she found Saura."

Mira's knuckles were white, gripping the reins as she listened.

"Saura was sobbing, hysterical, covered in blood—curled around her stillborn babe. She wailed, pleading for the gods to return her child to her. Astrid approached and replaced the lifeless infant in Saura's arms with her own daughter. Then, clutching the stillborn to her chest, Astrid lay beside the grieving mother.

"While they lay there, she told Saura everything she learned about the males' betrayal and asked for her help. It was on that mountain, Saura made a mournful but devoted vow to protect me, raise me as her own, and put a stop to the transgressions committed against females. And then Astrid took her last breath."

The road went silent—save for the crunch of shifting gravel, hoofbeats, and thunder. Mira stared off into the forest, her expression somber, and I wondered if she regretted asking the story of my birth.

After a long moment, her soft smoky voice asked, "So did she? Stop them?"

"My mother, Saura, and I did it together," I answered with a triumphant smile. "She became a voice for the females, speaking against the atrocity, sharing Astrid's story, effectively ending the cruelty that took place by demanding the blessing ceremonies be done publicly. She tried to convince them to allow females on the council, but they refused. Still, Saura raised me to recognize the power we females were meant to have, both of mana and spirit.

"When the conditions aligned, we came together with others who shared our conviction, adamant that a shift was necessary. We seceded from the males, formed the four covens, and the witches were born.

"Over the first century, a synergistic alliance took root. Annorah was a large part of that. She represented hope for all the wielders of Vylandria, that with someone capable of such power on the throne, we could achieve peace with humans. But, unfortunately, that never came to fruition."

She paused a melancholy moment, then asked, "Did all the females leave with the covens?"

"No. We never expected them to. Some females chose to stay with the clans, with their bonded. And some bonded couples came to us together. Our goal was never to keep the genders separated. We aimed only to offer a place where, should something like that arise again, females could go. Someplace where they were appreciated—someplace they belonged."

CHAPTER TWENTY-FOUR

MIRA

D ressed and ready to get this evening over with, I opened my chamber doors. The displeased look dropped from Balis' face as soon as he saw me. He looked viciously handsome, wearing a simple dark brown leather vest over a forest green tunic that made his eyes stand out in a way that felt dangerous to our situation. *How am I supposed to pretend to not be attracted to that?*

My gaze climbed his body like ivy climbs stone, and I silently wished I could wrap myself around him in the same way. It was one of the few times I'd seen him fully clothed, and I hated how my heart stuttered in response.

He pushed himself from his leaning position against the wall across from me and crossed his arms over his strong chest.

"You don't have to do this," he said.

"Worried I'll get caught?"

His head lowered, and he peered at me from under pinched brows. "I'm worried about you being alone with that deplorable asshole. He—he's not known to be gentle."

I stepped over the threshold and let the heavy wooden door slam shut behind me. "I get that it isn't ideal," I snipped. "We have to be here, though, so why not learn something?"

My strappy black heels clicked against the stone floors as I walked away from him. His long stride easily caught up, and the symphony of our echoing footsteps bounced along the empty corridor.

He grabbed the crook of my arm, pulling me to a halt. "Will you just listen?"

His gaze fanned over me, but instead of the heat I'd grown accustomed to, apprehension grayed the vibrant hue.

"There are other ways," he said, resting his palm against my cheek. "You don't have to dive headfirst into the serpent's den. Don't leave yourself vulnerable to him."

"Stop it." I took a step back. "I'm not yours to worry about." It felt harsh even coming out of my mouth, causing me to inwardly wince. I drew a breath, bracing myself for the words about to leave my mouth. "We decided to keep this professional," I said in a steady tone, less edged for argument. I hated the words, but I refused to be held back by emotions we weren't even supposed to be feeling.

If he and Eurok were going to dictate our physical relationship, then I would dictate our emotional one. A much easier wall for me to man, anyway.

"I need you to treat me like you did in the Dogu village. Like a partner—someone you trust to make decisions. Not this. Not like I'm something fragile for you to protect."

This had been exactly what Eurok meant by 'distractions.' And by the look in Balis' eyes, he knew it too.

He swallowed hard. "You're right. I never want to be the person who tells you that you cannot do something. Just—"

He took a step forward. The hint of cinnamon on his breath quickened my pulse as he raised his hand, as if to place it against my cheek again, but he hesitated, and let it drop.

"Just—be careful."

Then he turned, resuming his role as escort, and stayed a few paces ahead.

I fought off the sting in my eyes as we walked. My mind stalled on the moment of recognition in Balis' gaze, confirming that he understood the truth of my words. He was concerned about me. A concept I would have found laughable weeks ago.

Now, though, it felt like one of many gradual moments that eroded the protective wall I built around myself. But its looming height still towered over me, and I knew it was safer to stay in its shadow. This was the most suitable option for our mission—the right decision for everyone.

So I blinked back tears, committed to stand by my decision, and focused on the task at hand. Get close to the king, get invited into his council chamber, and find the journal. Everything else, even this, came second.

SIDELLE

The great hall felt nothing like the cold, hollow room it normally was. Vibrant ivy with leaves the color of ripe cherries wound its way up every other alabaster pillar, accenting the painted historical murals that wrapped around the others. The night sky was a blanket of silver-glowing stars above, visible through the glass ceiling. Upbeat instrumentals played over the delighted crowd of various nobles, businessmen, and their families. Atreus had spared no expense, which only heightened my suspicion. *What is he up to?*

I spotted Mira across the room. Her meandering exuded an air of elegance, and periodically her gaze flicked upward toward the balcony where Balis lingered. It was clear the choker fastened at her slender neck was doing its job, leaving her unable to sense exactly where he was.

I wasn't a fool of the attraction they shared. An oily snake of guilt slithered in my gut at having agreed with Eurok's disapproval of their intimacy. Mira, as rough around the edges as she might be, was still a young woman, and I was no stranger to the effects a handsome male warrior could have.

The object, to my own effect, sauntered over, looking devastating as ever in a pair of brown slacks, a white button-down, and suspenders. His sleeves were rolled to the elbows, and a bored expression painted his handsome face. This was the last place he wanted to be, but he hid it well behind that mask of indifference. He pulled a drink from a server's tray, threw it back, and replaced the empty glass before the server even noticed. Then he grabbed two more, passing one to me when he reached my side.

"You are in danger of your dress tearing, love," he purred, admiring the way the bright orange gown hugged my hips. The fabric splayed out into a gauzy pool that trailed behind me.

I played coy. "Oh, really? How so?"

"Hmm, if I can talk you into a dark corner, I'll show you."

I giggled and shoved off his arm that was sneaking around my waist. "Behave yourself," I said, heat rising to my cheeks. "We have work to do."

"I haven't seen the royal swine since we arrived. Are we sure he's even here?"

"If I know Atreus, he's going to make an entrance."

I finished my drink, then refilled it with water from the community pitchers placed at each of the glass standing tables around the room. Surreptitiously, I heated it with a small, steady stream of mana until steam rose from the top. I reached up the draping sleeves of my dress and retrieved a narrow, cylindrical sieve from the pouch secured at my forearm. Without hesitation, I dropped it into the flute. My calming brew steeped in the liquid, emitting a heavenly floral scent.

I checked on Mira again. With unwavering confidence, she strolled along, her attention captured by the opulent feast adorning the far wall, ignoring the three young men following her hips as she passed.

Eurok dipped his chin, watching me closely. "Are you okay?"

"I'm fine." A slow sigh flowed with my first sip. "Just ready to get this evening over with."

"So now might not be the best time?" he drawled.

"Might? That usually means it's absolutely not the right time, but go on." I took a longer drink, savoring the hot tea.

His brows rose at the bite of my tone. "I told Mira about the journal."

My teeth clenched, and I drew in a deep, slow breath. "Why would you do that—and why choose *now* to tell me?"

I forced a smile as a familiar courtesan accidentally met my eye. Her gaze flicked to Eurok and her cheeks flushed.

"Because I know she can handle it, and I didn't want you putting a stop to it," he quipped as if it were obvious. Which it was.

"I hardly find this funny," I said, making to leave "And the joke's on you because I'm still putting a stop to it." I stormed off, not bothering to glance back. His mask of indifference would only piss me off further.

I found Mira standing at the edge of the crowd, her slender arms adorned in black silk gloves that left her fingers bare. They were delicately wrapped around a flute of champagne. A pattern of lace roses climbed the length of both her sides but was otherwise sheer, and her dark hair hung in a long, silky sheet against her ivory back. She was devastating—a siren on the hunt. When she caught sight of me, her face turned into a repulsed scowl, a part of her carefully planned persona.

"I haven't seen any sign of him yet," I said as quietly as I could manage over the room's idle chatter. "Eurok told me he informed you of the journal."

"Doesn't surprise me. Figured he wouldn't keep that from you for long." She never dropped the displeased facade, giving the impression she would rather be speaking with anyone else, playing her part beautifully.

"Yes, well, he has a sick sense of humor. Which is why he is only telling me now while I have such limited time to talk you out of it."

"I like him more and more every day." She smirked into her flute as she took a sip. Her dark plum lips left a kiss of color on the rim. "Look, I promise I won't put myself in any situation I can't handle, but I need you to trust me, too." She locked eyes with me for the first time. "I'm well practiced in this, so please just let me work."

My face faltered, losing a bit of the stone-calm exterior I adopted this evening. "I–"

"Well, well, well, what a pleasant surprise this is," said a voice possessing all the charming deception of an opium flower.

A tight knot wound in my stomach as I faced the bright sea-blue eyes of Vitany Vitalis. Poised intrigue enveloped her narrow, sharp-featured face. Her gaze shifted to Mira, then back again. *What is she doing here?*

I pressed my cheek to hers in a polite greeting, forcing my voice to sound as pleasant as possible. "Vitany–"

"Rumor has it you brought some warrior eye candy to the party. You wouldn't mind if I said hello to Eurok, would you?" She lifted onto her toes as if trying to spot him.

I quirked a brow, a sharp green sensation in my chest. It was no secret she wanted to bed Eurok. And I wanted to tear her perfect teal curls out of her head when she spoke of it. Her bright eyes, accented by her dark skin and thick lashes, fluttered between Mira's skeptical sneer and my tight grin.

More people trickled in, causing the room's heat to reach near-stifling degrees. The lush, bitter scent of alcohol permeated the air.

"Vitany, might I introduce you to my girl, Mira?" I said, eager to change the subject.

A veil of astonishment widened her venomous smile. "Sidelle, are you altaring a human?"

"Is that a problem?" Mira sniped, indignant.

I flashed her a glance of warning, despite the swell of reassurance at the way she was unintimidated by the high witch's remarks. She would do well in this echelon once we got that temper of hers under control.

Vitany's eyes flared, like she was searching for Mira's energy. I held my breath. I hadn't planned on another druid being here, let alone another high witch. Why would Atreus invite her? Or, better yet, how did he even know her?

I stepped between them. "Mira is a special case," I said, smiling sweetly, but sending the message over my energy that this was not the place to discuss this.

Vitany inclined her head, receiving the message but ignoring it. "Indeed, she must be to acquire such an opportunity." She peered over my shoulder, addressing Mira with a quizzical glint in her sea-blue eyes. "If I may, do you possess a mana core within you?"

This little bitch.

Inwardly, I recoiled at the brush off, but kept all signs of my contempt from my face and waited for Mira's answer. Jumping in on her behalf would seem too suspicious, and Vitany was not someone I wanted to upset. She may still hold the key to contacting Erezos. Her grandfather still sat on the druid council, and with my standing already precarious where the druid council was concerned, I may need her help someday soon.

Mira regarded Vitany with indifference, and I had to ask myself for the first time if she was still playing a part. It was astounding how flawlessly she carried this mask of hers.

"I believe you are capable of answering that yourself, are you not?" The sharp edge of her words sliced the air between them.

Vitany's gaze narrowed, but she kept that fine smirk on her lips. "Your girl seems to have quite a bark, Sidelle." She turned to me and leaned in close. "Do try to keep your pet on a leash."

As she spun on her heel and left, the dangling silver gems adorning her mint gown swayed, accenting her every step.

"Bitch," Mira spat once she was out of earshot.

I took a long breath. "Be nice."

"She's a vulture." Her mouth twisted into a scowl. "You heard what she said about Eurok?"

"Yes, well, that's their business, not mine." I waved the idea off as if it didn't matter to me in the least.

"So you're saying you wouldn't care?"

"Care about what?" I asked, ignoring the hard way she eyed me. *Not here, not now.*

Mira scoffed and spun away.

I grabbed her arm, trying not to call attention to us. "Where are you going? We're not finished."

Her jaw worked as she faced me. I lifted my gaze to her deep, wine-colored eyes and saw true anger behind them. Anger at me.

"I'm supposed to trust you with my life. He trusts you with his," she said, shaking her head. "And yet, you can't even admit that you care about him?"

The emotion in her words struck me like an unexpected swell.

"You don't deserve him." She pulled free of my hold and carved through the crowd.

I stared after her, watching the mass of shifting bodies swallow her whole. Heat rose to my cheeks as a few nearby patrons eyed me with faux concern.

The music stopped, and the royal horns blared, announcing the king's arrival.

CHAPTER
TWENTY-FIVE
MIRA

I tore through the heart of the crowd, determined to put distance between me and Sidelle. I couldn't stand to listen to her any longer. Warning me off the journal as if I were an inexperienced novice. Then, to top it off, she practically purred at that little blue-eyed high-bitch and acted as if I were clueless about her and Eurok's relationship.

Something told me she played it off as an effort not to seem hypocritical. But for fuck's sake, Eurok was in love with her. He spent the last two centuries pining for her, selflessly serving her every whim, and she couldn't even admit that she cared for him beyond their friendship. I meant what I said. She really didn't deserve him. So why did I feel bad for saying it?

I found the edge of the crowd closest to the dais, where it would be easy for the king to spot me. Two women stood ahead of me. One with long straight blonde hair, the other with dark chocolate waves. Something struck me as oddly familiar about the brown-haired girl—then it hit me. *My dream.*

I reached forward, unsure what I was doing even as I did it. "Excuse me," I said, tapping her shoulder.

She spun around in a startled whirl, her eyes narrowing in question—her very unfamiliar eyes.

"Sorry, I thought you were someone else."

They leaned in, whispering to one another like hens, then shuffled a few steps away.

I brushed off the odd encounter, and a pair of thin men clad in royal suits of crimson and gold stepped onto the dais. They raised brass trumpets to their lips, announcing the king's arrival, and I winced at the horrendous, seagull-like squelching. The two women preened and hoisted their elevated breasts even higher, each of them flitting a glance at me as if in comparison. They likely hoped to garner a glimpse from the king.

Sorry ladies, unfortunately, he's spoken for tonight.

That familiar scent of cinnamon and cedar filled my senses, and Balis' warm mouth pressed close to my ear. Goosebumps peppered my skin, and I forgot where I was. Steeling myself against my quickening pulse, I squared my shoulders, fixated on the dais.

"If anyone can bring a king to his knees," he purred, "it's you in that dress."

My heart skipped a beat, and the king sauntered onto the stage, his arms raised in an enthusiastic, charismatic welcome.

"I promise I'll stay out of your way," Balis whispered, "but you're not leaving my sight."

Gods, the tenor of his voice, the warmth of his breath on my neck, knotted and coiled low in my belly.

King Atreus stopped at the center, appraising the crowd of partygoers as an impossibly warm hand wrapped around the small of my waist. My lips formed a hard line, trying not to let his scent and proximity unhinge me.

"And if he harms you, princess," a razor-sharp edge darkened his tone, "I'll make him beg his light god for death."

Then he was gone.

That distracting heat grew within my core. The urge to abandon my task consumed me with a vast desire to find those emerald eyes and admit I didn't mean what I said earlier. Fuck, maybe even tell him to take me right here in this crowd. But I didn't. I stood there, feigning disinterest. If the king looked this way, hopefully, my face conveyed that indifference and not the conflicting geyser of emotions blaring through my chest. In an effort to maintain composure, I forced my breath into a steady, calm pace.

King Atreus scanned the faces nearby. When his dark gaze landed on mine—it locked. My heart lurched into my throat, but I clenched my teeth and smiled at him, determined to stay in character.

"Ladies and gentlemen," he said, "I extend my sincerest gratitude for your esteemed company." A dizzying amount of awe and adoration buzzed across the crowd. "As many of you are aware, I have exciting news I wish to share tonight."

The two women shared a glance with small, excited squeals.

"It is my honor to announce we have discovered the cause of our declining populations."

Cheers erupted in a deafening wave, threatening to shatter the glass ceiling.

"Due to the unfortunate decline in the health of our beloved river, it has been determined that the Ebbonharrow will not tolerate our human presence on these shores much longer."

A few heads nodded while others whispered and murmured, as if hearing this for the first time. I thought back, certain I'd never heard of such a thing, even during my travels around Calrund. No one ever spoke of issues with their water. Declining populations and an increase of infertility, now that was a constant topic among humans.

"After much deliberation with my council," he went on, "I have decided to initiate a commission for the construction of a new castle."

The way he commanded the room was like watching the moon command the sea—effortless, confident. Despite my distaste, I could see what so many humans found attractive about him.

"In solidarity with our druid companions," he said, "construction will begin within the Black Sand Calms territory of Vylandria, where land and river meet the Dead Calms Sea. A stronger port, a better city, will be born, ushering in a new era of prosperity, unity, and peace between our people." Another uproar of cheers. "And what else should such a monumental leap be called but Port Carlisle?"

A great number seemed eager, but there was the occasional taken-aback, stilted smile. I searched for my companions, but none were within my line of sight.

The king clapped along with them, growing more excited by the moment, as if he were a bard entrancing them with his charm alone. "All of this was made possible by the newest High Witch of Vylandria," he said. "Vitany Vitalis."

He extended his hand toward her. She stood near center stage, and partygoers nearby stepped aside, clapping politely. She dipped into a small bow, her long, curly, teal hair tumbled over her sharp shoulders as she did. When she straightened, she wiggled her fingers in a bashful wave. I couldn't help but want to gouge out those pretty little sapphire eyes. *Snake.*

My heart pounded against my ribs like a caged animal. Poachers, ash weapons, a new castle, and now he works with another high witch other than Sidelle? Something was definitely going on, and that journal could be the answer.

For a moment, I thought about how easy it would be if I had my dagger. I could burst onto that stage and slit the king's throat in front of everyone. The metallic tang of blood teased my senses, as I imagined the spatter that would coat my face, the opulent room, and the elegant attire of everyone present, including Vitany. I could almost hear the screams, the rustle of silks and acrid panic–

As pleasing as the thought was, this wasn't a problem a dagger could solve. *I* was the weapon tonight.

I learned over the years that a woman could serve as both a man's salvation and his undoing. And tonight, I intended to embody the latter. I'd find that surreptitious thread and *tug* until every one of his malicious dealings unraveled. I may not be Annorah, but I could still be someone of importance.

This sudden onslaught of purpose still felt strange to me, foreign. But I was done denying I wanted to be here, determined to make a difference. I wanted to end the pain and violence the Dogu suffered—that Eurok suffered at *my* hands when I killed his best friend.

And then there was Balis.

A tightness grew in my throat. He relinquished his greatest chance at becoming a commander, just to be here to train *me*.

We survived nearly a thousand years without Annorah, but I'm not so sure we'll survive another thousand without you.

The King clapped his vizor on the shoulder, another man whose throat I'd like to slit, then directed him toward me. I said a silent prayer to any god willing to listen. *Erezos, Empress, whoever, bless me.*

Sidelle materialized beside me, a rigid force as she positioned herself between me and King Atreus. Her face was a stone carving of contempt.

"Are you okay?" I asked in a clipped, wary tone.

"The outrageous nerve it takes to name a new city after the man whose life you watched slip away as you ordered his daughter's head at your feet—whose kingdom you ravage under an undeserved title."

Her words weren't meant for me, but they stirred something in me, nonetheless. While she ranted, I maintained a deadpan expression, my gaze fixed beyond her, fully aware of the king's watchful leer.

"That's the vizor?" I asked.

Despite the man's limping gait, he followed the king with an air of confidence. I scanned the vizor's pointed, unkind features for any sense of recognition, but found none.

Sidelle peered over her shoulder, then back at me. "Yes. We'll deal with him later. This changes nothing," she said, as if she could read my mind. "Find the journal if you can, but please, Mira, be safe."

The trepidation in her voice rippled like waves beneath a rowboat. Her concern was another blow to that sturdy wall I hid behind. My jaw set as I drew in a long, deep breath. I tucked my hatred for the men walking toward us away in a neat little compartment, forcing it back into the catacombs of my mind. I locked eyes with the king.

"Sidelle, I'm so glad you made it." The king took her hand and kissed it in a surprisingly warm greeting. A few haphazard dark curls fell forward to rest on his forehead when he stood straight again, and he flicked his head to cast them back in place.

Something about him felt younger, less encumbered, than when we first met, and I wondered how much of this was the real Atreus. Or was he still riding the high of his adoring crowd?

"You remember my vizor, Marcus? He will be overseeing the project in Vylandria."

"Yes, Marcus," her polite grin was potent, "I am pleased to meet the man willing to take on such a daunting task."

Marcus looked down his nose at her, and bile rose in my throat like venom. I wanted to spew it into his eyes. He gave her a tight nod, then turned to the king and excused himself from the conversation.

"Always the talker, Marcus," the king jested. His attention pulled over Sidelle's head, sampling the crowd. He waved at someone and mouthed a greeting.

"Indeed."

She cleared her throat and straightened herself, shaking off the disrespect with an air of poise and grace I would be hard-pressed to mimic.

"Speaking of," he said, "I hear you're having difficulties of your own with this one." A placating smile lifted the corners of his full lips as his wandering gaze settled on me. "It's nice to see you again, Mira. You've been giving Sidelle a bit of trouble?"

I steadied my breath and plastered a confident grin on my face. "What can I say, Your Majesty? I don't suffer fools lightly."

I put on a show of contempt, pasting on a mocking sneer. The witch played along, releasing an exasperated sigh with arms crossed tight.

The king laughed. "My, my, aren't we feisty?"

She stepped closer to converse privately with him. His eyes flickered to her chest for a fraction of a second before checking those nearby, as if making sure no one witnessed his proximity to her.

"If you don't mind, Atreus," she whispered, "I think hearing from you as to why it is so important she receives our training—"

"I'm right here, witch," I snarled.

"I understand perfectly." King Atreus took his time running his sleazy stare down my body, unapologetically pausing at my cleavage. He rolled his lips, straightened from Sidelle at his ear, and moved closer, placing a hand on the small of my back, leading me away.

Our slow pace led us along the outline of the ball beneath the balcony. The time passed with idle chatter about things like our travels from Raven Ridge and what I missed about Calrund while living in Vylandria. It was a short list.

When we approached the door to his council chamber, my heart pounded against my ribs despite my better mind asserting it wouldn't be that easy. Sure enough, we walked by. I fought the temptation to look at it and kept my eyes drifting between his face, the floor, and the patrons waltzing on the dancefloor.

"I'm surprised you accepted my invitation," he said in a conversational tone.

"Forgive me, but I didn't want to at first."

"Oh?"

His brows rose, but he seemed neither offended nor angered by this. Instead, he appeared to be intrigued by my honesty. Ironic, because it was about the only honest thing he would hear from me tonight.

"I was worried you still suspected me to be connected to your sister." I took my first steps out onto that thin ice, waiting to hear if I should tread lightly forward or retreat to safer ground.

"Sidelle told you." It wasn't a question.

I nodded. "The witch also divulged the true crimes of the man I hunted down for you."

A tedious question sat unsaid behind his eyes. I paused, hoping he would ask something that I could use, something from which I could give a like-minded answer while allowing him to steer the conversation. That was one way I convinced many enemies I was on their side. People were more willing to trust if they believed they were in control, that they pulled the answers from you. But he said nothing.

In fact, he'd been choosing his words carefully so far. I assumed it was his attempt to feel me out to see where my allegiances lie. Which meant he may be pulling the same shit on me as I was him, using my own trick against me. Rather than fight against it, I'd do better to use it to my advantage.

"After hearing that, I was eager to meet you again, under... better circumstances." I braved a wry smile.

To my relief, he returned it. I dropped my eyes, feigning self-consciousness, giving him another false sense of control. He was smart, so I would have to be smarter.

The skepticism didn't entirely leave his face, but he warmed. "Am I to believe you are not a fan of your druid companions?"

Good, a question I can work with. I scoffed, shaking my head as I feigned a sip of champagne. "*Companions.* I've never been more proud to be human."

His laughter was genuine, and his shoulders relaxed a fraction.

"These druids, the way they live, are so... primitive." My nose wrinkled. "They rely so heavily on their magic that they lack vision."

His dark brow quirked. "Vision?"

"Yes, vision. Those people are afraid of change. They've been doing the same thing for centuries, blind to any other possibilities."

My intent to appeal to one of the most human of all instincts, progress, piqued his interest. His appreciation for my indignance toward the druids was evident. His gaze canvassed my curves with a hunger akin to a vulture scouting its next meal, and I knew we were getting somewhere.

I dropped my eyes and dredged up a coy flush to my cheeks. "You, though—you realize the potential for improvement. Hence this castle you've commissioned. I can't wait to see it." My gods, I was going to make myself puke.

As I spoke, the distance between us shrank. He stood so close that bystanders were beginning to stare.

"Come," he lifted his head, "I'd like for you to accompany me this evening."

"Your Majesty, as flattering as that is, my feet are killing me. Perhaps there is someplace private we can continue our conversation."

That might've been too bold. He stopped and eyed me, looking first at my heels, hidden beneath a pool of black silk and lace, then to my cleavage, covered in the same sheer fabric that ran down my sides. I made my seamstress cry this afternoon, insisting on absolute perfection during alterations, but it was worth it. I looked incredible.

A silent war waged in his head, stuck between getting me alone and showing me off—the latter unfortunately winning. "I can't disappear this early into my arrival, but," he scanned the party, "Sidelle!" he called.

Moments later, she wove her way through the dense crowd. He made no move to meet her halfway, so neither did I.

She inclined her head in the smallest show of respect. "My Lord?"

"Be a dear and heal poor Mira's feet. I'd like her to join me for the rest of the evening."

"Your Majesty, please. I don't want help from magic," I said. A complete lie. My feet ached as if I'd been navigating a rocky shoreline barefoot. I'd sooner cut them off than spend the rest of the night walking around on them.

The king leaned close. "Dislike them all you want—you might as well reap the benefits while you can."

A chill spider-walked across my skin as his words breezed against my neck. *While you can?*

I smiled in surrender, despite my stomach turning to stone. Sidelle, to her credit, masked her contempt with expert precision. None of the razor-sharp fury I knew sliced at her from within was detectable. She did as she was asked and lifted her hands in a silent, beckoning motion. The discomfort in the balls of my feet vanished, making it seem as though I were walking on air. I gave her a tepid nod, and the king grasped my hand.

"Come, let's mingle." A suggestive smile curved his mouth. "Then we can get to know one another a bit better."

The party's constant chatter grated against my ears. And as the night went on, the more nauseating the reek of alcohol became on everyone's breath.

King Atreus, though, hardly drank a sip. It was a minor disappointment considering how much easier it was to wear a drunk man down than a sober one, but I was pleased with how quickly he took to my company, regardless. He did, however, continue feeding *me* drink after drink, which meant pretending to be as drunk as a cock-hungry lush, hugging up on his arm, and feigning a stumble here and there in my tall heels. In reality, I enjoyed the first two flutes he placed in my hand. By the third, I requested he show me through the gardens, then dumped them into the bushes.

A young servant wandered into the plaza with a tray of neatly prepared finger foods. I chose one that resembled raw fish topped with a creamy dollop and a dill garnish, all on a dark-grained cracker. After my first bite, I had to refrain from asking the boy to leave the tray.

"So why try to kill Sidelle?" the king asked.

"Killing her wasn't my intent," I stated matter-of-factly, dusting my hands off after finishing the finger food. "I was simply proving a point that blades, when wielded skillfully, are just as lethal as any druid's ax. The last thing I wanted was those brutish cock-stains teaching me anything."

He let out an amused chuckle.

"I, uh, I apologize for my colorful language, Your Majesty." I feigned a blush.

"Nonsense," he said. "You're an impressive woman—and call me Atreus."

I averted my gaze, not finding pleasure in the captivating effect of his attractive smile. "No, I couldn't do that."

"Yes, you can."

He placed a hand on my knee. A slight shock of discomfort spread through my body, and I had to remind myself that this was good. *At least he's buying it.* I cleared my throat, sensing his intention to move closer, but for a flicker of a moment, I thought I heard a low guttural growl from the bushes.

After I sighed a deep breath, I pushed the worry away, unwilling to let a possessive, hypocritical druid impede on my work. I settled my palm on top of his touch. *Okay, that was definitely a growl.*

"So you were saying?" Atreus asked. His thumb traced slow circles against my skin.

I took a real sip of champagne this time.

"Right—having worked with these feral beasts," *pun intended,* "I see now why you wanted me trained in their combat. While their ways are... primitive, their fighting skills are of an elite caliber."

The words tasted like literal acid as they left my mouth. Speaking this way about *my friends* to this man felt as if I rotted from the inside out. I feared the disparity between my voice and my genuine emotions would be as glaring as an oil slick on a watery surface.

A group wandered into the plaza and politely, if not a little sloppily, greeted the king with raised glasses—a jovial thanks for their pleasant evening. Atreus pushed to stand, bidding his farewells to the guests. I stood beside him, swiping the wrinkles out of the flawless fabric of my gown. He pressed his hand to the lowest part of my waist and waved a final goodbye. Then he turned to me, the last remnants of a grin on his cheeks.

What if this *was* the real Atreus? Here, at this very moment? A man capable of reason if he had someone to help him discover it. He seemed almost boyish, the outline of his face illuminated by the light reaching out from the castle windows. He looked young, like me. Nowhere near the nine hundred years I knew him to be. I searched for a glimpse of age in his oaken eyes, but found nothing. Not the way I could when appraising Sidelle. He felt so... human.

The faint chatter of people filing out of the great hall drifted across the plaza. Our lingering gaze broke, snapping me back to my senses. His only interest lay within the hatred he believed we shared for the Vylandrians. Males, females, children—their bodies piled on top of one another flashed to mind, left to rot because of this man's hatred. There was no good there. Only a deceptive monster in need of slaying.

I slipped my hand into his, a bold move, but the ball was ending sooner than I thought. My window was closing. Balis' quiet warning, an irritated chuff from the bushes, had me straining against tight cheeks to keep the smile from my face. *Easy boy. I've got this.*

"Is the party over?" I asked, sure to dust the words with the perfect amount of disappointment.

His eyes dropped to our hands, and doubt chilled my gut, but he didn't pull away. Instead, his fingers laced with mine.

"Not if you don't want it to be," he said. Another deceptive, albeit attractive, smirk graced his lips.

I flashed him a dazzling smile of my own. "I'm not ready for this night to end *just* yet."

He squared himself on me, lifting a hand to trail the back of his finger along my jaw. "I'd like to kiss you," a conflicted crease settled between his brows, "but I worry you might find it too forward of me."

"Would it be too forward of *me* if I said I want you to?"

His smile reached his eyes, and in a blink, his lips were on mine—soft and surprisingly gentle. As his tongue traced that delicate spot beneath my ear, he took my ass in his hands. Balis' glare bore into the back of my head. His rage was palpable, hidden behind that thin shield of brown and green hedging.

More partygoers filtered into the gardens, and I thought Atreus might pull away, but he didn't. He settled one hand firmly at the nape of my neck, while the other roved between the curve of my hips, down to my ass again, gripping a handful tight. I moved with him, matching his intensity, and kept a solid foot in reality, firmly expecting Balis to snap at any moment. But our kiss wasn't severed by the maw of a black, predatory beast. It was the bright streaks of familiar blue-white lightning that filled the sky overhead. *Sidelle.*

Atreus started at the loud crack and tipped his face toward the darkness above. "Seems like there's a storm blowing in," he said.

"Maybe we should move inside?" My breathy words had the perfect amount of desperation. "Take me someplace we can be alone."

His eyes heated, and he didn't hesitate. How easily his judgment was clouded. He led me toward the castle's entrance. A burst of success flooded my veins, but was short-lived. Instead of taking me inside, he tucked us into a covered alcove just off the main path, out of sight. *Damn it.*

He pressed my back against the stone wall. His hands moved over the tight fabric of my dress in great sweeping strokes, down my waist, over my breasts, and up to cup the sides of my neck.

My mind wandered to Balis. Could he still see us? Truthfully, I hoped he couldn't. Nausea curdled my gut at the thought of him watching from the shadows. Seeing my body molded to the king's like plaster casting to a sculpture, my dress inching up my legs with every broad stroke of his hands. The force of his cock pressed against my middle through his trousers.

As if an answer to my prayers, a gust of wind hurled itself around us like a monsoon, drowning out all sound with its wailing howl. It echoed off the alcove walls, kicking up dust and whipping my hair over our faces in stinging angry bites. Atreus pulled me away from the wall to shield me from the gales. Something told me this wasn't some rogue gust of wind. It felt intentional, familiar, not unlike the winds that dried me on the first night I left Raven Ridge.

Balis.

"What the fuck?" Atreus ground out. His fingers enclosed around my wrist, leading us inside, his eyes wild, like he couldn't get me alone fast enough.

I eagerly waited for him to make a decision and prayed to whatever god was on my side tonight that he'd choose his council chamber.

He didn't.

CHAPTER TWENTY-SIX

SIDELLE

I tapped an impatient rhythm on the table beside me. "If I'd known they'd be gone this long, I would have searched the damn council chamber myself."

"Be calm, love."

Eurok placed a reassuring hand on mine with a gentle, teasing smile, as if I were behaving like an overbearing mother.

"I'm calm when I put my mind to something," I said with a bite.

His unbothered demeanor, his unwavering confidence that everything would work out, bothered me to no end. But then again, Eurok had always been more comfortable with delegation. I, on the other hand, preferred doing things myself, and sitting here hour after hour was as enjoyable as wearing a crown of thorns.

"I need some air."

With an abrupt turn, I beelined toward the door to the gardens. If I got eyes on them, perhaps I could gauge whether there was enough time to search the council chamber myself.

Eurok fell in beside me. "We should let her be, Sidelle. Let her work—she's got this."

I gritted my teeth to keep from snapping at him. A wasted effort. "She's not a trained warrior, Eurok. She's a twenty-three-year-old woman and the reincarnation of the rightful leader of this kingdom. We have to protect her. I can't sit here and wait to find out he's..." My words died in the air, unable to bring myself to admit the fear that plagued me.

"You underestimate her."

I scoffed. "That's ridiculous. Yes, she's skilled—it's just... You know how these humans are with Atreus. They adore him."

"You don't trust her to stay aligned with our plan?"

"No, that's not it." I stopped near the large, bone-white stone archway leading to the gardens. "I don't want her falling for his charm."

"His charm."

Eurok's deadpan expression told me I'd done nothing to convince him of my faith in Mira. I was confident she was capable of this, especially after our interactions earlier. But still, a nagging, rearing ache jerked in my stomach. Had I failed to prepare her for what to expect from Atreus—the enigmatic, captivating man most of these humans experienced? Convincing the king that she didn't possess mana meant opening her up to that version of him. And even more problematic were his, by human standards, charming good looks.

"Never mind," I said, starting for the door.

"They're not out there," Balis called from behind Eurok.

His disheveled appearance suggested he also had a challenging night, evident from his untidy vest and tousled hair. His flushed face and sweat-beaded brow suggested the heat was getting to him, too.

"Where did they go?" I asked.

"I lost them when they ducked inside while I shifted," he said, frowning. "Their scent leads to the second floor, but the guards won't let me through."

He slid his hands into his pockets and stared at the gray stone floors, purposefully avoiding eye contact. It was clear he was cautious about revealing too much, especially his deep concern for her, which was almost palpable.

"It seems he has no intention of bringing her to his council chamber," I said. "So I'll go."

Eurok's attention snapped to me. "Let me do it."

"No." I shook my head, casting a glance toward the shadows beneath the balcony. "I'm familiar with the room. If I'm caught, it will be easier to explain."

His face fell, but he nodded.

"And you're sure it's in there?" Balis folded his arms over his lean, muscular chest.

"It will be in one of two places," I said.

"And the other?" Eurok asked.

"Where I suspect he's taken Mira." I didn't intend to, but I caught myself gazing at Balis. "His bedchamber."

His face blanched and his fists clenched. For a moment, I thought the thin veil of control he had would shred into tattered ribbons. But he somehow gathered enough composure to straighten his shoulders and address his superior.

"Captain, I'd like to request you stay here in case Mira returns. I want to attempt getting past the guards in case she needs help."

Eurok deflected to me with a raised brow. I nodded.

I crept behind the pillar just outside the council chamber, hiding within the heavy gold fabric that draped over it.

The mural on this column had been acid-washed to erase its shared history, yet I recalled it vividly. Two towering figures were depicted. The first figure was shapeless—the artist's attempt to capture Erezos' ever-changing forms throughout history, always embodying darkness and power. The other was a beacon of light. Aethier.

Each god was the backdrop to the two smaller focal points, infants bundled in blankets, each a mirror image of the other. Both bore the crest that adorned each guards' armor and every flag that waved over the castle towers—one any Westryellian recognized. The only difference depicted was the material of the infant's blankets.

One glittered like gold, reflecting Aethier's brilliant light. The other resembled the winding black and burgundy branches of the Diablerie tree, which stood in the place Erezos first emerged in this variant. The same tree Atreus had burned soon after ordering Annorah's head at his feet.

Further down the concealed pillar, where the acid failed to remove the pigment, an image showed a king kneeling in the foreground. His face, painted with artful joy, and arms raised in victory. I could still remember the uplift in the streets. Everyone within the kingdom rejoiced when the news spread that King Carlisle's prayers for children had been answered. But now the memory was a wound that refused to heal—a dull ache where unrestrained joy once lived.

Atreus was a disease, a cancer to this land. One that, if left to fester, would surely be the death of us all.

I concealed myself in a veil of shadow. If not for the dim light beneath the balcony, it would have looked oddly out of place, but it did the trick to conceal me as I tip-toed to the door–

Secured with a lead lock.

Atreus had guarded against mana being used to enter. *Of course.*

I searched for something—anything to help me gain entry. Just beyond the balcony's shadow, a magnificent spread ran the length of the room. Two guards stood posted on either side of the table, their view of the immense feast blocked by enormous potted flowers wilting in this hellish heat.

To avoid arousing suspicion, I straightened my shoulders and lifted my chin before approaching. No one seemed interested as I scanned the silver platters of various foods—stews, braised beef, and elaborate pasta dishes with fine cheeses—all still hot from the constantly revolving door of servers from the kitchen.

There, leaning on the edge of a half-eaten platter of braised beef, a carving fork. I checked for any stray glances, then grabbed it, sliding it up my sleeve. A heavily inebriated gentleman stumbled back. Tremors of rattling china echoed across the hall, drawing unwanted attention. The nearest guard rushed over, helping him to stand as onlookers gawked. I took quick advantage of the distraction and stepped into the shadows, concealing myself in a dark haze once more.

Over the centuries, I learned that honing my skill in a specific element allowed me to bend its effects to my advantage. This smoke, for example, could be called to my aid when needed. A young wielder like Mira would only have mastery over flame. While they could burn, they lacked the finesse to manipulate its smoke or heat as isolated constituents without extensive training or divine intervention, such as challengers received in the Aupex Proving Games.

I pulled the fork from my sleeve and, using the small crack between the door and the stone frame, snapped it in two. I jammed the broken end into the keyhole, fidgeting and prying on the lock.

After every botched attempt, I reined in my nerves. This had to work. I was out of options. If I failed, whatever Atreus was subjecting Mira to in his bedchamber would be for nothing. Balis' pained expression upon learning her whereabouts shattered any resistance I had to their attraction. Perhaps I made the mistake of imposing my beliefs on them—the same that led me to deny my feelings for Eurok even after I bound my fate to his. I said the words, made the commitment, yet I stonewalled my first opportunity to be proud of it and lied to Mira.

I should have told Vitany to go fuck herself.

Mira was right—I didn't deserve him.

Another fail, and I slammed my hand against the door with an audible grunt of frustration. A rhythmic pulse of footsteps and shifting metal sounded from around the corner. I threw a glance over my shoulder and jiggled the mangled carving fork at the pins and springs. From the sound, I could make out two guards, most likely on rounds, caught in a tired, wary conversation.

For now, the drapery and a massive vase filled with blood-red and white flowers obscured my position. But as soon as they rounded the corner, they'd have a full view. I tried again.

Click. Snap. Nothing.

Click. Snap. Click. Snap. I had time for one last attempt before...

Click.

The lock fell slack. I tossed it into the vase and darted inside. Bracing my weight against the weathered door, I held my breath as the echo of leather boots sounded off the stone walls outside. A few thunderous heartbeats later, once I was sure the guards moved on, I drew in a lungful and released my nails from the woodgrain, then opened my eyes.

Candelabras were lit, casting the space in an ambiance similar to what I enjoyed in my own study. It felt strange here at night, though. At the center, the large stone table with its carved map of Westryelle gave off a menacing vibe. The arches and divots of its landscape and movable figurines stretched long shadows over the polished surface.

I tried not to dwell on the nefarious dealings Atreus conducted from here. Perhaps it was my bitter penchant for always assuming everything about him had a darker side. In this light, the room felt distinctly different from my previous experiences—as though the walls held secrets, and the shadows longed to whisper them in my ear just to scare me. Unable to take it any longer, I funneled a small bit of moonlight to brighten the space.

Something glinted in the corner, drawing my eye to the towering bookcases along the back wall. I moved closer to inspect it, angling the light with my hand to aid my venture.

Another glint, half-obstructed by a large book I pulled out the thick leather-bound tome—then it slipped from my grasp. It slammed against the stone floor in a thud that ricocheted through the room.

There—it was small, no bigger than the palm of my hand—a moonstone.

No. A manastone.

I kept one foot of consciousness on the door, holding it closed with a steady pulse of my mana. It would provide a moment's warning if someone tried to enter, not much, but it'd have to do.

The stone's pulsating, familiar energy called out to me. I reached closer out of instinct rather than curiosity. I recognized it even before my touch slid against its hard, smoothly carved surface. My fingers grazed the stone's coolness—I jerked back. It felt like the cold expanse of eternity. Power, unimaginable power.

Just as I thought.

Erezos.

My knees threatened to buckle, as if the floor beneath me was ripped away. How? How did the human king, a direct creation of his light god, possess a minute fraction of my god's power?

My skin lit up with crackling spiderwebs of lightning. World spinning, I lowered my gaze, trying to compose myself. *Mira.*

This changed nothing. *Gods berate me, of course it did*. But not tonight. Not when Mira was up there with him. I had no idea how it was possible, but if Atreus was using Erezos' power, there's no telling what he planned to do with it.

She was in the lion's den now. We all were.

MIRA

Atreus led me through the upper level's long winding halls while my plans seemed to slip through my fingers like sand from a tight fist. I couldn't fight it. Doing so would only make things worse and raise suspicion. I kept playing along, hoping by some miracle I'd get another shot at that journal in the future.

But tonight had gone to complete shit. I pushed Balis away, told him to let me work, that he shouldn't care. Then I failed, anyway. I had nothing to report back to Sidelle. Atreus hadn't so much as mentioned a word of ash weapons or poachers, regardless of how well I convinced him I was of a similar mindset concerning the Vylandrians. And now he only had one thing on his mind.

Fair enough.

I had no idea where my companions were, and I was sure Balis couldn't have followed us up here. A small part of me was glad about that. At least he wouldn't have to watch the king try to fuck a failure.

"Where are you taking me?" Skepticism tied knots in my stomach, though I tried to keep it out of my voice.

His answer was a sultry smile.

We turned down what seemed to be a private hall, and at the end was a tall set of thick, sturdy wood doors. Atreus opened them, and I must've appeared awestruck because he gave a pleased chuckle, then pulled me inside. When he pushed the way shut again, to my relief, he didn't lock it.

As if he read my mind, he held up his hands in surrender. "You're not trapped here. You can leave whenever you like."

The gesture improved my mood a bit, but the precariousness of the situation wasn't lost on me. I was still alone in an isolated room with a dangerous man. And, save for a small dagger I stowed between my breasts, I was unarmed.

He sauntered toward the elaborate bar cart near the hearth and poured a drink. When he offered it to me, I grinned up at him in thanks.

"You seem nervous," he said, tucking my hair behind my ear.

"Forgive me, Your Majesty–"

"Atreus." His brows raised in a gentle yet imploring look.

"Atreus." I smiled meekly. "I guess I'm so used to being the hunter that I've forgotten what it feels like to be the prey."

With an attractive roll of his lips, he smirked. "And what a beautiful prize you would be."

I swallowed hard, my body tensing as if I *were* prey, locked in a silent duel with my pursuer, waiting for his next move. His gaze dropped to my mouth and his touch cupped the side of my neck. His warm hands were surprisingly rough. Perhaps he was a skilled swordsman. He had the body of one—tall, lean waist and broad, strong shoulders. Did he train with his guards?

"But," his tongue clicked against his teeth, "I have other plans for you."

My chin dipped, my narrowed eyes conveying my silent question.

"Would you like to see something?" he asked.

A dash of excitement lifted the corners of his lips. I nodded, and he grabbed my hand, pulling me to his bookshelf. Again, that boyish human quality emanated from him.

Monster, I reminded myself.

We paused before what appeared to be sturdy shelves laden with books. However, with a gentle tug, he guided me *through*. An optical illusion. What I perceived as thick oak and endless tomes was actually the rear wall of a passageway veering right behind the fireplace. With my hand clutched tight in his grasp, he led me around another corner to the left, unveiling a hidden room nestled within his chambers.

A breathy gasp drew from my lungs. It was an enormous solarium filled with the most beautiful, lush, leafy plants, all cascaded in spectacular silver-blue moonlight. Above was a masterful illusion of deep blues, purples, and black. Starlight broke the dark hues in dancing, twinkling displays of light.

"There's nothing like a desert night sky." Atreus spoke with a sense of reverence.

When I faced him, I found his heady stare already taking me in. This time, when he grabbed my hand, my heart stuttered in a way that felt... wrong. Like *I* could be wrong about him.

I pushed the thought away. *I'm not, and I can do this.*

"Why do you have all of these?" My fingers traced the smooth, waxy surface of an enormous green leaf speckled with yellow dots.

"I've collected them from all over the world." His posture straightened, conveying a sense of pride as he eyed his extensive assortment. "Plants have always fascinated me."

He tipped his head, urging me along to the other side of the room. We stopped before a low-lying shrub, his excitement palpable. Something inside warmed when he pointed at the small, unimpressive foliage with its spiky leaves and pink pompom flower.

"This is a shameflower," he said.

I snickered a faint laugh. "Why on earth would it be called that? Is it ashamed of its size?" I teased, then furrowed my brow in a dramatic pout. "Do the other plants pick on him?"

Atreus playfully flicked my bottom lip, smirking. The glint in his eyes stalled my mirth.

"I'm not sure why it's named that," he said, "but it is a powerful fever reducer."

"You study them? These aren't all just pretty little collections?" I hoped I didn't sound as shocked as I was.

"No, not at all."

My perceived interest elated him. But in reality, those knots were returning to my stomach. He collected plants and studied them for their uses—*the ash*.

"Do you use them?" I shot out the question a bit faster than I intended and did my best to backtrack, to cover my eagerness. "I—I mean, do all plants have uses?"

"Not all, but many do. I only use them when necessary."

He was still lost in the excitement of sharing it all, that he didn't notice my slight lapse in attention as he led me along.

"I've traveled all over the world studying them and how their properties are applied in different kingdoms."

"What are they used for?"

I wasn't completely oblivious to the employment of plants for medicinal purposes, but I was far from knowing if something grew that nullified mana.

"All sorts of things—medicine, sleep, poison." He stopped and moved in my path, resting his palms on my waist. "They're fascinating, aren't they?"

"Very," I said.

My captivation wasn't entirely feigned. When he touched another delicate stem, his sturdy hands guided it toward the sky to avoid it tangling with the plant beside it. Something tugged at my resolve. The reverence with which he cared for them felt like a contradiction to my reasons for being here. It made my heart sink a little.

Again, I shook the sensation away. "What's your favorite?" I asked. An innocent enough inquiry.

"Well," he said, "that one there, behind you, is a powerful aphrodisiac."

I turned, spotting the plant in question. Tiny curling vines peeked between its waxy leaves. When I faced him again, I found his roguish grin settled on my face.

"Come on, let's get you back to the druids."

A jolt of relief surged through my body, followed by a wave of confusion. The emotion must've made its way to my expression because his features pinched.

"Are you disappointed?" he asked.

"No," I said, realizing the flaw in my mask. "You're just–"

"Different than you expected."

I stared at my hands, attempting to summon the confident, spiteful, awestruck girl I was supposed to portray. However, with the plan's evident failure, embodying that character no longer felt as urgent or necessary. I peered up at his face, framed by melding shades of night and stars, and it struck me just how at ease I felt.

Not smitten. I wasn't attracted to him in the way I'd been pretending, unlike most humans. Yet, I started to question if there could be some truth to this Annorah thing. If I was truly her reincarnation, what if my purpose wasn't to end the king's reign but to enhance it? What if I was destined to foster harmony among Westryelle's warring races, to serve as a bridge across the divide that even Sidelle struggled to uphold?

A reverberating blast shook the room, rattling the floors. I started, and Atreus stumbled, but regained his footing quickly.

A deep, riotous voice added to the ground's turbulence. "Where is she?!"

Balis.

CHAPTER
TWENTY-SEVEN

MIRA

Atreus' previous ease was replaced with the stern, commanding air of a king once more. A fierce and angry ruler. He stormed out of the solarium with me close on his heels.

"What is the meaning of this?"

I rounded the corner just as Balis squared himself on the king. He was disheveled, that forest green tunic untucked and open at the chest, and sleeves pushed past his tattooed forearms. His fists were secured to his sides as if it took everything in him not to come undone.

Atreus looked from Balis, then over his shoulder to me, noting the relief that softened the druid's hard lines when he saw me.

"I couldn't find you," he said, as if the king weren't even in the room.

My gaze flitted behind him. Those enormous wooden doors were shattered, smashed in. Splintered wood hung from its frame. A cacophony of armor clanged down the hall, mixed with the hurried voices of guards racing up the spiral staircase.

Balis, what the fuck have you done?

Heavy storm clouds hung over the easy green of his eyes as realization settled over his features. I was neither in danger nor missing, and he just made a perceivable attack on the king.

Atreus seethed. "What gives you the right to force your way into *my fucking chambers!?*"

His bellow echoed through my chest, punctuated by the entrance of half a dozen royal guards. Without hesitation or order, they moved on Balis, securing his arms behind him. He didn't fight, didn't take his eyes off me.

My jaw clenched as I forced a slow, tight breath between my teeth. I told these fucking druids to leave me alone, let me do my job. Finally, I made some semblance of progress with the king, and now... I tore through the confines of my mind, scrambling for a way to de-escalate this.

Atreus looked at me for an explanation. "Can you speak for this insolent fool's actions?" The tone he used with me was a stark contrast to how he'd spoken to Balis.

Stone-faced, I tightened my fists until the bite of my nails threatened blood. For a moment, I thought about dropping the facade and going to his side. His actions, however infuriating, were out of concern. *Concern for me.* But dropping the ruse would only make things worse at this point. If I stood any chance of getting us out of this, it wouldn't be with the pitiful dagger stuffed between my breasts.

"I'm afraid not," I said, forcing my voice to remain even.

Everyone's attention pulled to the clicking of heels as Vitany stepped into the room, her hands folded neatly behind her back as she surveyed the scene.

My heart quickened.

"Vitany," Atreus greeted, "I'm glad you're here. It seems one of our guests has found himself a bit taken with my new assassin."

Her blue-green brows perked at this revelation and eyed me with suspicious intrigue.

Atreus sauntered over, pace slow and deliberate, his steps a muffled thud on the ornate carpet I feared Balis' blood might soon stain. He stopped nose-to-nose with the druid, a breath's width away from a male capable of killing him with a pulse of energy so quick he could never stop it.

"You like our women, do you?" he asked, mocking the warrior.

Balis refused to meet his eyes. They remained locked on my face.

"See that he takes a visit to the shaft, will you?"

My heart became a thunderous roar in my ears as the guards pulled Balis toward the shattered remains of the door.

"Your Majesty?" Fear drowned out reason, and the words were out before I knew what would come next. I had the good sense to keep my eyes off the Balis, focused only on the king. "I hope you will forgive me, but I ask that you reconsider this, Atreus."

A disdainful look distorted Vitany's expression at the use of the king's name, but ignored it.

"This druid," I said, turning my back to Balis and lowering my voice. "is one of the druid army's most talented warriors. Killing him may not be in the best interest of your endeavors within the Vylandrian borders."

The king looked up at Balis as if sizing him to the achievement I paraded.

"I also believe he is to take part in my training soon, and I would hate for this to impact things on a much larger scale." I peered at him through my long, dark lashes, goading him with a soft smirk.

"Gorgeous *and* brilliant," he purred and pinched my chin between his thumb and finger.

I fought the urge to bite them off and forced my eyes to sparkle at his approving grin.

He turned back to Balis. "You should consider yourself lucky that my new assassin thinks so highly of you. I won't kill you, but I assure you. You won't leave this castle without learning a lesson."

The druid dared his first look at Atreus. "And what would that be?" Balis asked.

Something inside me stirred at the low-timbered tone he used to speak to the king, dark disdain lacing each word like reinforced steel.

"You will lay no claim to anything that is *mine.*" With a wave of his hand, the guards pulled Balis from the room.

After spending the evening painstakingly behaving as if there was nothing wrong, it was becoming difficult to force my smile. I drained every avenue, aside from fucking him or sucking his cock, to lower his guard enough to speak of poachers or ash weapons. Not a word on either topic left that silver tongue of his.

It was clear I made an impression on him, and once I witnessed him have a laugh at Balis' expense when he was dragged out, I decided I would beat him at that same serpent's game.

He wove a tapestry with his talk of the lavish lifestyle we could have, a king and an assassin. *A brilliant future,* he called it. But all I saw when he spoke was druid blood running through the streets of Port Carlisle. His faux charm didn't fool me a second time, not like it did in the solarium. I craved his death now more than ever.

I was grateful when he concluded the evening with nothing more than a kiss and an invitation to see him again. With my energy drained, both mental and physical, all I wanted was to go home—to Vylandria.

All of us, safe.

I descended the stairs ahead of Atreus toward Eurok, who waited at the bottom step. I locked my severe stare on his and mouthed, *'Balis. Dungeons.'*

He peeled his gaze to the king. "It seems I'm a male short, Your Majesty. You wouldn't happen to know anything about that?" Eurok cleverly edged his tone in a way that melded his carefree energy with that no-bullshit flare. By now, it was easy for me to hear the, *'Fuck you, give him back.'* he layered within the words.

As if on cue, a door opened with an echoing bang. The unhurried click of heels filled the foyer as Vitany approached with two guards in tow, dragging a bloody, broken Balis. His legs moved listlessly, shuffling beneath him, until they gave out and dropped. I jolted as if to catch him, but steadied myself, realizing my mistake as Eurok swooped in.

Beads of red splashed against the gray stone behind him from what I assumed were injuries to his back, and I fought to conceal my searing pang of guilt. This was the second time he bled for me.

I couldn't take my eyes off his bruised face. Dark splotches marred his skin, his lips were split and bleeding. He was unrecognizable—a swollen mass of flesh. My own lips trembled, and I tightened them against my teeth, fighting an impulse to reach for a dagger that was no longer there. They beat him beyond his mana's ability to heal himself. My gods, how much would that have taken?

Eurok started at the sight of him. "What the fuck is this?"

There was a familiar tremor of power beneath my feet, and I wished he'd unleash it on them all. I wanted him to kill every last one of them, even if it meant getting caught in the crossfire. I refrained from glaring at the bastard king by trying to find Sidelle, but saw no sign of her.

"Calm yourself, Captain," Atreus said. Resistance flickered over Eurok's face. "It seems your soldier needed a lesson in manners while he is a guest in my home."

He descended the rest of the stairs and approached Balis. I stood idly on the last step, gripping the banister, until my knuckles blanched.

"I have no patience for riddles, King. What is the meaning of this?" Eurok demanded.

He shoved off the other guard, bracing Balis' full weight. Balis let out a hiss of pain, and it took everything in me not to run to his side.

"Your soldier attacked my chambers for reasons unknown. Though, it seems to me that he believes he has some claim on our lovely Mira, here," Atreus mused. "Either way, it deserved correction." He inclined his head, speaking as if Balis were nothing more than a misbehaving canine.

"And what does *our lovely Mira* have to say about this?" Eurok asked.

I knew what he was doing, using me as a springboard to gauge how we should proceed.

"It was a rather unnecessary display of unrequited feelings." My voice was cold, guided only by my exhaustion. "But if you don't mind, I'm quite tired, and ready to leave."

"Oh well, by all fucking means, let us not hold you any longer." Eurok's sarcasm was laced with the perfect amount of venom to sell it.

"It's been a pleasure, Your Majesty, truly." I lifted onto my toes, placing a kiss on his cheek.

He gave a tight nod, eyes locked with the captain in a challenging glare, as I strode away. I fought hard to focus on the hollow echo of my heels and not the blood of my friend pooling in the hall.

They'd pay for that later.

SIDELLE

Erezos, a god of immense influence, embodied both good and evil. He manifested in various forms, each tailored to specific roles and realms. In alternate dimensions, he played the role of a visitor or a constituent, while in our realm, he was revered as our creator. The native beings of Westryelle, predating human arrival during the Drak War, were his first creations. This realm was Erezos' home, and we were his people.

I shook my head, unable to keep from curling and uncurling my fists, trying to stifle the rage building in my chest. Gods never allowed a single fraction of their capacity to be contained, and for good reason. Doing so meant enabling a vessel from which others could wield that power. Once someone had that, what would they need a god for?

That's what made Annorah so special. She was the first manifestation of our god's abilities outside of himself. I suspected that was why Atreus possessed no inherent gifts beyond his eternal life. Aethier had denied him such power. *Well, he can't have this power either.*

I had to get this out of here. My mind whirled, plotting how I might smuggle it out of the castle. I'd figure out what to do with it back in Raven Ridge.

Boom. Boom. Boom. Boom.

Someone pounded on the door. My heart launched into a frenzy and I ducked beneath the stone table, heaving in air like there suddenly wasn't enough.

Boom. Boom. Boom.

Whoever it was, they didn't try to enter. Perhaps they searched for the king, which meant Mira was still with him in his bedchamber.

I waited another few breaths. The knocking stopped, and irritated footsteps stalked away.

I crawled out, my attention falling on the book I dropped. Splayed open, its faded, browning pages were brittle like autumn leaves, hardly readable. Still, something seemed off about the way they sat. I flipped the odd-looking cluster of paper over.

Beneath them, a journal lay weathered and worn. The leather binding bore marks of age, as though it basked in the sun for centuries. As I reached for it from the hidden compartment within the second half of the book, my fingers brushed against the black numbers stamped on the cover. They were faded, nearly illegible, inviting a closer examination.

Atreus

Year of the Light God: 1023

It was one of Atreus' journals, though not the one I was looking for. I traced the words again, making sure I read them right. The year of Annorah's sacrifice. My breath left my lungs in a surreal, elated exhale.

This was everything I could have ever dreamed of finding. Within this journal, we could uncover every answer we sought for centuries. Running my fingers over the words one more time, making sure I read them right, I flipped it open and savored the faint scent of aged paper.

A warm caress against my mana at the door said it was time to go. *Eurok.* My gaze snapped to the manastone, and a seed of contempt took root. Atreus, using my god's power in any capacity, soured and pained me to my very core.

I removed a ribbon from my hair, letting it fall around my shoulders. My scalp thanked me for the release of tension as I fastened the journal to my thigh. It wasn't perfect, but it would do. As I returned the large tome onto the shelf, I hesitated, eyes locked on the manastone.

Twenty-three years since I last heard his voice, and I couldn't shake this feeling. Erezos had always been a reclusive god, one that rarely tolerated questioning. This whole time I believed this was some sort of test—

But could this have been the reason he went quiet?

The idea of leaving it behind created a void where the joy of discovering the journal should have been. *If he discovers it's missing, then we'll figure something out.* Even in my own mind, the thought lacked conviction. My decision wavered. Pausing mid-grasp, my hand hovered over it, as if preparing to swat a fly, struggling to reach a conclusion.

Another brush against that mana at the door brought me back to the present. I swallowed hard.

I shouldn't be doing this—Atreus will surely notice. But this might be the reason for his silence. Though, with the stone gone, he'd be more likely to search for the journal. But what if Erezos is truly trapped? This could be the key to bringing him back.

'Leave, Sidelle.'

The last words weren't of my own mind. They were... a command. *Erezos.*

My instinct to obey that dark, steel voice flooded every inch of my body. I cloaked myself in smoke, slipped through the door, and replaced the lead lock. I hurried along, dispersing the shadows in a natural manner to avoid drawing attention from any observers. As I approached Eurok, who stood at the room's center, I ensured my movements were inconspicuous.

"We have to leave—*now*," he said, his hand resting on my lower back as he moved me along.

His energy entwined with mine in a hard, protectively sturdy way, and I knew something was wrong.

"What is it? Where is—"

"Mira's fine. She's at the Market Square Inn. We're rendezvousing there."

As we crossed the foyer, I peered over my shoulder, trying to figure out what had him so riled. At the staircase to the second floor, blood smeared the tiles like paint on a canvas. Two servants, on hands and knees, scrubbed at the shining crimson pools. He tugged me along, his pace strained and far from natural.

"Who–"

"Balis."

My stomach sank like a heavy stone to a river's bottom.

CHAPTER
TWENTY-EIGHT
MIRA

After healing Balis a fraction, Eurok departed to fetch Sidelle, leaving us to find our own path to the inn.

Every step I took dismantled and chipped away at the remaining shreds of my composure. But I kept my back straight, maintained my utterly bored expression, and walked ahead of my injured druid guard, determined to appear indifferent—apathetic to the trickles of precious crimson, to his pain as he hissed through his teeth. While I wanted to rush through these streets, it would've revealed too much. The king probably had spies all over the city.

The few individuals we passed on the lamp-lit cobblestone streets glanced between me and the trailing druid. Their curiosity was piqued by the sight of a Vylandrian guard accompanying a human. They seemed more preoccupied with this unusual pairing than the blood they carefully sidestepped.

How Balis ever made it, I'd never know.

I sat on a stool beside his bed, watching his ragged breaths. With every passing minute, my mood oscillated between uncontrollable rage and paralyzing concern. I thumbed through a stack of rags with shaky hands, grabbed a small piece of cotton fabric, then blotted at the blood oozing from the shallow gashes across his skin. The deeper ones that covered his back were nothing but muscle and fascia peeking beneath strips of bruised, swollen flesh.

Eurok and Sidelle took turns healing the worst sections, but the process was incredibly painful, and the stubborn bastard refused to pass out. He hissed another sharp breath as Sidelle lifted one of the garlic-soaked cloths to peek beneath.

"He won't be able to handle much more healing tonight," she said, reading the question on my face. "Looks like he's in for a long night."

My lip curled in a snarl as I dabbed at the trail of blood dripping down his side. "You're so fucking stupid."

"And your bedside manner is shit, so I guess we're even," he rasped, attempting a bit of levity.

It didn't work. All I thought about was how labored the words were as they escaped his barely parted, dry lips.

I tossed the blotchy rag into the pan of rust-colored water, sending splashes over the sides and onto the floor. I braced my elbows on my knees and let my head drop into my hands, staring at the single droplet that landed on my foot.

Sidelle and Eurok had all but tied me to a chair to stop me from leaving. Their cool tendrils of power had only just released their heavy weight on me. Once I saw reason, they convinced me to stay by reminding me that the high-bitch was valuable. Killing a high witch and granddaughter of a druid council member would end badly for all of us. War was, after all, what we were trying to avoid.

"Mira," he breathed, "look at me."

I shook my head, unable to meet his eyes or unravel the tangled web of rational and irrational thoughts plaguing my mind. How could I express how *angry* I was while he lay there, wounded and bloody, for attempting to protect me?

Protect. Me.

My throat tightened, and I strained to keep in the sob threatening to escape. I was furious with the king, yes. But Vitany? I ground my teeth. She shredded his back to ribbons, stained those halls with the blood of her own kind—and I wanted her head for it. I wanted to watch her life fade from those glittery, deceitful eyes.

"Why couldn't you just let it be?" My resolve snapped, fire lacing each word. "None of this would've happened if you stayed out of the way like you promised."

The wooden chair scraped against the floorboards as I shoved to my feet. I paced in a tight circle, unwilling to leave his side but unable to suppress my fury any longer.

"I know." He winced as he lifted his head, angling his neck to see me better. "I don't deny that."

Concern wracked my chest, putting a pause on my rage as I helped him adjust his pillow.

"But I also said I wouldn't let you out of my sight. And that if he harmed you," he grimaced, "I had no plans to hold back. I would've torn through every door, dismantled every brick of that castle to find you. When your scent ended outside his bedchamber and I couldn't sense your energy, I—"

His full lips pursed as he glanced at Eurok, who leaned against the small desk in the far corner. Something in the captain's expression cut his words short, and I hated him for it.

Sidelle walked over and stood beside me with crossed arms. "What do you mean you couldn't sense her energy, Balis?" she asked, then looked at me for the answer.

I took a deep sigh, trying to match my focus with the shift in the conversation, even though I still wanted more from Balis. "The king has a secret solarium," I said, facing her. "It's hidden behind the fireplace in his chambers."

Sidelle's onyx eyes widened. "Really? And he showed you this?"

I nodded. "I was thinking about the ash weapons—perhaps they're connected to a plant."

Eurok took up a place beside Sidelle, his shoulder slumped in concern. "Have you come across anything like that?"

She shook her head, her long silver hair brushing her arms. "No, but it's safe to say I'm no expert. I can ask Agatha. She's an herbalist. Or maybe Saura."

"Would either of them have knowledge about plants from other kingdoms?" I asked.

"They might be less familiar, but it's possible."

Eurok rubbed his jaw. "There are thousands, tens of thousands—"

"If only we could pinpoint it somehow," Balis said in a drowsy drawl.

Sidelle shook her head in pure dejection. Then, with quick strides, she paced to the desk and returned with something in hand.

A journal.

"You found it?" I stepped forward, retrieving the supple leather book, then flipped through it.

My face dropped. The pages.

They were blank.

"What is this?" I asked.

Her expression was crestfallen. "It's written in a Heliac script," she answered. "An ancient text deciphered only by the light of the day it was penned."

She held out her hand in a silent request. I passed it to her, and as she flipped through, the faint scent of old paper wafted up. At a quarter of the way in, she tipped it, providing a clear view.

Today's date was written on the top in delicate script. Except the year, which was dated almost a millennium ago. There was a brief journal entry below it.

Father left for Vylandria today in hopes of furthering magical trade relations with the druid council. I shall prepare for his return by ensuring Annorah and I have concluded this ridiculous disagreement. She has yet to leave her room.

I read the words out loud for Balis to hear. His furrowed brow was an exact match to mine.

"I don't understand."

"Heliac script is used by the light god. Many of his devout priests learn it well," Sidelle said.

"It means," Eurok cut in, "that even though this journal likely contains the answers to everything from the ash to Annorah's sacrifice, we can't read any further ahead than one day at a time. It will take us a year for us to study it in its entirety."

Fuck.

We commissioned a carriage to transport Balis back to Vylandria. Sidelle and Eurok insisted I ride with him while they continued on horseback. Whether they thought it was where I preferred to be, or because Sidelle worried I'd run off and sever Vitany's head, I wasn't sure.

Before we left, Balis drank a potent mixture of poppy milk and lavender to ease him into a dreamless sleep. The ride was mostly silent, and I spent every few hours changing the garlic coverings over his wounds. His injuries improved since that first night, but every time I exposed his back and discovered a new lash I hadn't seen before, rage surged like a serpent beneath sea waves.

He never should've come looking. So what if the king killed me? I wasn't worth *this*. I wasn't a damsel in distress who needed a hero. Balis was more valuable to Vylandria's plight than I ever would be. His people needed him, and he put his life on the line for me.

Pain leached into my bones at the thought of shutting him out. He'd been something of a safe harbor since I met him, a still force to brace myself against while chaos raged. To be honest, I looked forward to spending more time with him during our training sessions, finding solace in the ease between us amidst the madness.

But Eurok and Sidelle had been right to dissuade our... attraction, I guess. Whatever one could call it, it was best kept out of the equation. It was a distraction, a dangerous one Vylandria couldn't afford. My life wasn't worth the risk, powers or not. If I wanted to make a difference, this absurdity had to stop, no matter how much it hurt.

Balis took a ragged breath, drawing my attention. His eyes fluttered open and searched haphazardly, then locked on me. A weak smile found the corner of that perfect mouth. The easy relief in his expression almost capsized all the resolve I spent the last twelve hours reinforcing. A cold, ill feeling churned in my stomach.

"Where are we?" he asked.

"Half a day from Raven Ridge."

"Have you been here the whole time?"

I nodded. "Sidelle and Eurok made me. I think they're worried I'll run off again."

Something like disappointment dampened his expression, and the first fissure of pain spiderwebbed across the brittle surface of my heart. He licked his dry lips, and I reached for the waterskin lying at my feet, lifting it to his mouth for him to drink. His eyes didn't leave my face as he did.

When he finished, he said, "Talk to me, princess. There's something on your mind."

Replacing the top on the waterskin, I laid it down and sat back against the plush cushions. With my arms crossed tight, my pensive stare focused out the window on the world passing by.

"Mira, what is it?"

I took a deep breath, then released it slow and smooth, steadying myself for the inevitable conversation. "What you did—almost cost your people everything."

His brows pinched, and I swallowed against the urge to take it back, to lean forward and run my thumb along that furrowed brow, smooth it, maybe even kiss it away. These were the thoughts I had to eliminate, the part of me I now had to battle while rebuilding the barrier within me that he chipped away at. His forest-hued eyes stayed steady, focused on me.

"That night on the balcony? Eurok told you he needs you."

"The captain and I will work it out," he said. "I'm sure he knows exactly why I did what I did. He's the one that sent me after you, remember?"

"He also told us to keep our feelings out of it."

"And now you agree?"

"I agree that it's unfair to put *this*," I gestured between us, "ahead of everything."

"Mira," my name on his lips was breathy, airy, as if he sensed my intention, "don't. Don't push me away."

"Eurok *was* acting like a hypocrite—but he's right. Whatever this is, it's a distraction from what matters. You're catching feelings that you're willing to act irrationally on." My hands trembled, my heart stalling, but I kept my voice steady. This was how it had to be.

"Are you saying you have no feelings for me whatsoever?"

My breath grew shallow, my throat tight. "No, I'm saying that it's because of my feelings that I think you should leave. Once you're healed, I want you to leave, Balis."

The pain etched into the perfection of his face was a mallet to my brittle, cracking heart.

"You can't get rid of me that easily, prin–"

"I mean it, Balis." My words sharpened, cutting his off.

"Mira." My name again, a whisper, a plea.

It broke me.

Unable to speak, fearing the sting in my eyes would give me away, I stood and left the carriage.

CHAPTER
TWENTY-NINE
SIDELLE

The muffled thud of the front door closing stirred me from my sleep. I lifted my head from the crook of Eurok's shoulder, careful not to wake him, and made my way to the window. The first cool light of morning sighed in through the curtains, carrying a slight chill. Winter had been unusually mild, a small blessing given Mira's frequent visits to the forest. I caught the last glimpse of her slipping off, her foraging pack swaying with her stride.

After returning to Raven Ridge, she kept herself busy in every way imaginable, determined to keep thoughts of Balis and the guilt of sending him away at bay. Mornings and early evenings, she foraged herbs and ingredients for Agatha's shop. During the day, she filled her time with endless training, even when Eurok couldn't be here to instruct her. When she wasn't honing her skills with the dual blades she now wielded, she combed through the library with me, searching for clues to the many questions still plaguing us.

I let the curtain drop, then retrieved the king's journal resting on my bedside table. Thus far, it proved useless. With no indication as to why it was written in the sacred heliac script, it contained nothing beyond the mundane details of the young king's life. Aside from his growing frustration with Annorah's lack of control over her powers, there'd been little mention of her. In fact, most often he spoke of his admiration for a woman whose name he had yet to reveal.

I peeled back the worn cover. The dried purple aster Eurok had picked for me last summer marked my place, and I flipped through the brittle pages.

Blank.

He'd written nothing on this day all those years ago. I dropped it closed, forgetting in my irritation that Eurok was asleep. He stirred at the low thud.

"Good morning," he said, his voice heavy with sleepy grit.

"Morning, I'm sorry to wake you."

He pulled back the covers from my side of the bed, a silent beckon to join him again. I curled myself into him, savoring his warmth.

"By the mountain, Sidelle."

I giggled as my chilled fingers trailed over his chest. He tucked me in close and pressed a kiss to my forehead. This was a rare, quiet morning—the kind I craved during the long weeks that took him away from Raven Ridge. A melancholy realization settled in my bones, souring the moment. This was our last chance of peace before another prolonged absence. I pushed the ache aside and tried to remain present, unwilling to let the future disappointment spoil things.

After a while of soaking in the morning from the comfort of Eurok's arms, I made my way downstairs and prepared my brew. A timid pecking clicked against the window, drawing my attention. A raven carting a familiar brown envelope perched on the sill. I pulled open the latch to let the large onyx bird inside and offered a chicken egg so he could regain his strength. He dropped the letter, retrieved the egg from my hand, and promptly turned and exited.

I turned the envelope over, ignoring the knot in my gut, and added it to the tipping stack on the counter.

"Another one?" Mira asked.

I hadn't heard her come in. She stared at the pile, lips pressed in a sullen grimace, mucky boots, and a tight grip around the strap of her bag.

"It is."

My palms encircled my cup, drawing in its heat to guard against the bite in her eyes. For three long months, Balis sent weekly letters. She refused every single one. I could never bring myself to toss them, hoping that one day the barrier she secured around the emotions weighing her down would soften and she'd read them.

She said nothing. Instead, she spun on a heel and stomped up the stairs. The rush of running water echoed down moments later.

I loosed a throaty sigh, set my cup aside and braced my elbows on the countertop, dropping my head in my hands. Vylandria had become her home. She said as much on multiple occasions, and for that I was grateful. We grew close over these last few months, but whenever Balis was mentioned, I sensed the weight of her despair. It was heavy, and what's worse, I didn't know how to ease her pain.

Mira was resolute. She couldn't be pushed or influenced to go against her wishes. So when Eurok revealed Balis recently threatened to show up and demand to speak with her, I forbade it. If distance was what she desired, the least I could do was ensure it was respected. For now, at least.

"Day's just started, love."

Eurok's broad hand stroked comforting circles on my back, and I lifted my head to bask in that charming smile.

He cast a knowing look upstairs. "I take it another letter came?"

I gave a defeated nod.

He shrugged. "She'll have to talk to him, eventually."

"I'm not so sure."

"She'll come around. Balis is patient. He'll make sure she knows he's not going anywhere."

I eyed the pile of letters with dejection. "I think that might be the problem."

"You plan on working with her today?"

"I prefer our time be spent in the library. I need to find a means for her mana to bloom consistently, instead of these random spurts she gets."

"Too bad you can't just give her some."

My eyes shot his way. "What?"

"Your mana—it would be nice if you could hand it over, so she could practice."

I gasped a sharp inhale, a spark like flint to kindling flaring in my mind.

"What is it?" he asked.

"How do you suppose the druids used the mana they stole from the females?"

His brows lifted in understanding. "I don't know. To my knowledge, it was never investigated. The staves were destroyed, and the mana returned to the earth."

"They must have found a way, though, right? Why else would they store it in the staves?"

His brow furrowed as I hurried into the den. He followed, tight on my heels.

"What if–" I snatched the light-weight wooden staff from its place beside the bookshelf, determination settling into every fiber of my being. "What if we can not only extract mana from one core, but also transfer it to another wielder?"

He remained quiet, letting me sort out my thoughts.

I paced a tight circle. Why hadn't this crossed my mind earlier? I'd been so focused on trying to force Mira into her blooming that I never considered other options. This could be it. I lifted hopeful eyes and leapt at him. My arms encircled his neck as I pressed my lips to his.

He responded with an intrigued grin. "You're positive about this?"

"This is it," I said, elation fueling my racing heart. "This is it, Eurok. I can feel it. This is the answer we've been waiting for."

MIRA

Sidelle and I stood on the edge of a massive lake north of Raven Ridge.

My nose wrinkled as I peered below. "Are you sure there's even a shipwreck down there?"

"I'm positive. It was stranded here when the river changed course hundreds of years ago. Now focus."

"How did it sink?"

"Do you want a history lesson, or do you want to wield?"

I sighed a temperamental huff and let my eyes flutter shut.

"Good. Imagine your power reaching beneath the water's surface. Sense your target, visualize it. Wielding is all—"

"All about intention, I know."

I pictured her displeased, pursed lips without needing to look. We trained nearly every day for the last two seasons, and I heard those words a thousand times.

Nine months passed since I sent Balis away, since I melted under his mischievous grin, embraced the cool touch of his energy sweep against mine.

"This feels like a lot for half a core of mana. Are you sure we shouldn't have refilled today?"

I still lacked the ability to call on my own mana from the earth. But Sidelle had found a way to ration Annorah's power from her staff for me to draw into myself. At first, it felt strange, heavy. But as the weeks passed, adding little by little, I found relaxation in its fullness, even grew accustomed to its personality.

The witch warned me it would develop an animalistic identity, and she wasn't wrong. As I grew acquainted with its behavior, it formed a distinct shape in my awareness, something similar to a large cat. Maybe it was just my subconscious missing Balis, but I found comfort in it nonetheless. I even let it take shape and walk beside me or lay at my feet by the fire on calm evenings.

"No. Half is plenty for this. Besides, I need your core empty today."

"Empty? Why?"

Cold worry accompanied my disapproving tone. Having an empty core bothered me now. It caused a gnawing hunger-like pain in my chest, leaving me vulnerable despite the physical strength and skill I gained from training with Eurok.

"Because Eurok returns tonight to accompany me west to Cedar Shield for the games. We'd like for you to join us."

"The Aupex Proving Games?" My focus snapped away from searching the waters for this elusive ship. I squared myself on the witch, wary of where this was headed.

"Yes." Her shoulders stiffened, as if bracing herself. "Balis is competing and–"

"No," I interrupted. "I'm not going."

"Mira–"

"No."

Sidelle's mouth snapped shut with a subtle click, her brows furrowing as if she were mentally crafting how best to re-approach the subject. "He cares about you, Mira. He asks Eurok about you every time he sees him. Please. Come with us. Just talk to the boy."

"You and Eurok insisted on keeping emotions out of this. Now, you're asking me to consider those emotions before he—what? Dies in a meaningless competition?"

When Balis mentioned his chance to become commander might be at risk due to his assignment to find me, I later found out he was referring to the Aupex Proving Games. I also learned the games were a display of the most fearless and ferocious battle-ready warriors the druid army had to offer. It was an all-out, ruthless arena battle against their own comrades, many of whom died at the hands of brothers they trained beside for decades.

Druids believed that by pitting their strongest warriors against one another, their true leaders, their commanders, would be revealed. Those who didn't survive these trials would ascend to take their place within Erezos' ranks.

The prospect made me sick.

"Can we just finish up here and go home?" I asked.

Sidelle crossed her arms in defiance, unwilling to move on. "Fine, how about a bet?" I mimicked her stance. "You bring that shipwreck to the surface, and I'll drop the subject. You can stay. But fail, and you come to Cedar Shield with us. Deal?"

I rolled my eyes, weighing the options. In our last session, I used a funnel cloud to lift a boulder to the top of the waterfall. How much harder could this be?

"Deal."

CHAPTER THIRTY

MIRA

After hours of riding through a wide expanse of rocky terrain and ancient cedarwood forests, the Aupex came into view on the horizon. The lush green mountain dwarfed its white-capped and hard-edged neighbors. There was no denying the power that resided in this place.

My skin tingled as mana searched around me, bouncing off my body like mosquitoes trying to gain purchase instead of flowing through me as Sidelle explained it would after my blooming. The crease between her brows when she said it, though, made me wonder how sure she was.

As we reached the massive wooden gate wedged between two enormous rock cliffs, it creaked and groaned, opening for us to enter. I expected to be met with a city, but instead it was a vast grassy valley with a single gravel road running through its center, lined with hundreds of vendors, pavilions, and ongoing shows.

I read the flags blowing on the light breeze from poles lining the road, the Festival of Night.

Sidelle rode beside me as we followed Eurok through the crowded roadway. Endless spectators set up tents and meandered through stands, while others cheered on champions as they made their way through the gates.

Beings of all kinds—humans, druids, dwarves, greater fairies, and even some I didn't recognize—waved and raised beverages in Eurok's honor. A brightly dressed halfling bard on a wagon stage played a strangely shaped stringed instrument while he sang about Eurok's victories.

'Oh, Eurok of West Haven, known far and wide,
With might of the forest, and moon as his guide.
Through ages he battled, heart steadfast and true,
In woodland's embrace, where ladies he wooed.'

The captain laughed, waving him off, then cupped his mouth to project over the bystanders. "Hey, I told you that in confidence, Bartov."

I stifled my laughter when he looked over his shoulder to Sidelle. He shook his head as if the song were ridiculous, then yelped as her mana gave him a quick shock to the ass.

"Where are we going?" I asked as we wound through the masses. I saw Cedar Shield's village near the valley's end, but not much else.

"Balis will be formally announced as a contestant during the commencement ceremony," Eurok answered. "We're headed to the city's counsel lodge."

A cold sweat coated my palms at the thought of seeing Balis, and I forced the butterflies flailing in my stomach to die.

A druid warrior to the left of our party hollered in our direction, "Captain, show us Landslide!"

Sidelle sighed good-naturedly, "As if his ego needs any of this."

"Some other time, friend." Eurok smirked. "We have a champion to see."

As we rode away, drums pounded, setting a demanding tempo. The crowd thinned as we passed through another set of stone and wood gates, entering the mountain village of Cedar Shield.

"So what is Landslide?" I asked.

He rolled his lips, then retrieved an ax from his saddlebag that seemed too large to have fit. As he held it up, I marveled at the rivers of emerald running through the blade, catching the light in mesmerizing patterns.

"This is Landslide," he said, "my gift from the gods."

"Why have I never seen you with it before?"

"Because I don't use it."

I drenched my tone in a heavy dose of sarcasm. "You were gifted a weapon from the gods, and it's not good enough for you?" I raised a brow and gave a mocking shake of the head. "Just when I think your ego can't get any bigger."

He let out a loud, boisterous laugh. "Ah, I don't need deities to tell me I'm magnificent."

My eyes rolled. "So, what's the real reason?"

"Easy. I've never been a fan of the divine." He shrugged a disinterested shoulder. "It never felt right wielding something clearly designed to coax me into ardent admiration."

I couldn't help but laugh at the irony of his nonchalance for the gods, especially as we rode through a festival dedicated to one.

"How do they deliver such a gift? Did you meet one?"

"Fuck no. They're way too smug for that. No, I believe it's different for everyone. I found my sword in the belly of a mule deer I took down before my journey home after our victory in a seven-year battle. We won under my command, and I guess it was their way of saying 'good job.'"

My brows pinched as my mouth twisted into a grimace.

"What?" he asked.

"Did you still eat the deer?"

Amusement danced on his lips. "Yeah, why?"

"I don't know—just seems... weird."

Eurok glanced at me sideways, as if the idea hadn't crossed his mind. I shot him a similar look, and we burst into a fit of laughter. It was invigorating, like a lungful of fresh air after a deep plunge.

As we ventured deeper into the city, the throng grew denser, yet this gathering appeared to consist mostly of members of the druid army. The slate streets still bustled with dancers, merchants, food stands, and leisure tents, filling the air with the vibrant ambiance of the festival.

At the crest of a tall hill, we dismounted and huddled together, making our way toward a massive stage attached to a beautiful log building, presumably the council lodge. A row of imposing men stood across it, facing the multitude, with Balis positioned near the right end.

I expected hesitance to course through my veins. I prepared myself for guilt to surge at having rejected his every attempt to contact me. What caught me off guard was the sudden urge to throw caution to the wind at the mere sight of his confident smile. He looked so fucking good up there. His eyes trained on me as if I were the absolute center of his focus during this pivotal moment. I drew a shaky breath.

"It's just the opening ceremony, Mira. Nothing is happening today." Eurok's voice was soothing, as if he could hear my heart pounding.

"I know."

My retort held a defensive edge I hadn't intended. He laughed and squeezed my shoulder.

Balis' expression turned fierce, matching the males' in formation to his right, as an elderly male hobbled onto the stage. The old druid was frail. It seemed as though the only thing keeping him from being swept away by the mountain breeze was his immense, elaborate headdress and long maroon robe, which bore a large wolf skull on one shoulder.

"That's the shaman," Eurok explained. "After praying over the ceremony, he'll bless each contestant with a boon."

"What's that?" I asked.

"Free mana to be used once during the games with no cost to the competitor's reserves."

The fragile-looking male stepped before the twelve massive warriors, all clad in their finest leather armor. "The gods again have blessed us with another fine array of champions for this year's proving games," he called over the crowd. "It will be my honor to pray over each of these fine young males—"

Young. I snickered to myself.

"—and bestow on each of them a boon to use as they see fit."

He grabbed a small wooden bowl from a nearby table and approached the leftmost warrior. The male dipped low, letting the shaman apply a single streak of black, oily liquid across his brow. He then swept downward over the competitor's eyes, giving him a menacing appearance.

"Blessed by the Aupex." He swept again. "Blessed by the Twelve." Another sweep. "Blessed by the Empress." He angled himself toward the crowd, projecting his voice. "Airynn of the rider clan, you have been gifted the boon of healing."

The lean, muscled druid nodded in thanks and straightened. The audience gave a respectful applause before falling silent as the shaman stepped in front of the next male and began the process again.

"Cyan of the rider clan, you have been gifted with the boon of smoke."

"Ah, tricky, but a good one." Eurok nodded approvingly. "You don't want to disorient yourself, but when used correctly, you gain the upper hand in a fight. You can blind, confuse, or buy you time to outmaneuver your opponent."

The shaman stepped away from the third male, also from the rider clan, who had been gifted ice wind as his boon.

"Next will be the border clan," Eurok said.

These males were very similar in looks. They all had the same long, straight curtain of black hair with dark gray skin and eyes of scorching white fire.

"All three of the border clan contestants this year are cousins. Mallak, Anvil, and Salve."

"Mallak of the border clan, you have been bestowed the boon of invisibility."

I sucked in a sharp inhale. That seemed like a pretty unfair advantage compared to others given so far.

He continued on to Anvil and Salve. Anvil was gifted burning touch, and Salve, something called quake. The shaman moved on to the next three contestants from the dark clan.

My knowledge of that clan came from snippets of conversations between Eurok and Sidelle. They were known as vicious cave-dwelling druids and were considered the most ruthless among the four clans. Their city, Ebbonrock, was situated in a cave near the rocky shores of western Vylandria, where they spent most of their lives in the dark. Their skin was nearly translucent, a milky white, while their eyes were large and black, devoid of color, like an abyss of nothingness. Where Sidelle's onyx irises reflected light and possessed obvious life behind them, theirs were cruel and endless, as if they consumed it.

I shuddered at the sight of them. The shaman, though, seemed unbothered as he swept that inky substance across their brow and continued on. The dark clan contestants consisted of Phaegen, Jacolb, and Deacon. They were gifted boons of blinding touch, loop, and shield.

"What's loop?" I asked Eurok.

"It allows the bearer to jump back in time a few seconds," he answered.

I didn't wonder why that would come in handy—another seemingly overpowered gift.

My chest tightened the closer the old shaman got to Balis. After dealing out the boon of waterbody and immobilize to the two mountain clan warriors, it was his turn.

Balis bent at the waist so he might perform the prayer before announcing his boon. My stomach felt as slick and oily as that strange substance the shaman spread over his forehead. My mouth went dry, my palms sweaty.

"Balis Gailstrong of the mountain clan, you are bestowed the boon of focus."

Focus? It seemed like a rip-off compared to invisibility and burning touch. But Balis nodded with a pleased smile as he straightened, leaving the shaman to say a closing statement before the ceremony commenced. Once over, the crowd erupted into a chaotic mass of cheering bodies. Balis, foregoing the stairs, hopped off the stage and beelined toward me.

I dove deep to wrestle the last dregs of my resolve to the surface, reminding myself why I asked him to leave in the first place. This wasn't safe. This magnetic pull was a disaster waiting to happen. The stakes were too high to risk it. But seeing him now, bedecked in armor, staring as if he craved to find a dark corner and kiss every inch of my body—none of that seemed to matter as it had before. *Gods, help me.*

"So you do own a shirt," I quipped when he reached me.

"You came," he said, completely ignoring the comment.

"I did."

His quiet smile weakened me as he offered his arm. "Would you do me the honor of allowing me to escort you to the festival, princess?"

I peered over my shoulder to Eurok and Sidelle, caught up in a conversation with a group of decorated warriors. They waved us on, causing me to stifle a groan. *Of course. They probably planned this.*

At a leisurely pace, we followed the flow of the crowd down the hill and out to the festival.

"So what'd you think?" he asked. "About the ceremony?"

"I think some are more favored than others."

He gave an acknowledging nod, but his face said he disagreed. "The boons are meant to play off our strengths and sometimes aid our weaknesses."

"So a boon of healing means that Airynn guy is a great healer?"

"Or a terrible one."

I caught the familiar decadent scent of cinnamon and sugar. I released his arm and darted through the crowd, Balis rushing after me. He halted with a laugh when he found me paying a vendor for a large bag of assorted roasted nuts. I threw back a handful.

"These are my favorite," I said around a mouthful.

I licked my fingers, then offered him some. He popped a few into his mouth, nodding with raised brows as he chewed.

The atmosphere buzzed with life throughout the festival, like the mountains surveyed and echoed the joyful honoring of the warriors who would give their lives tomorrow.

Despite my distaste for the games themselves, a large part of me wanted to join in on the celebration. But I couldn't help the doubt that slithered its way into my thoughts, reminding me only one survived. Would it be him? Or would he be just another pool of blood in the arena's sand?

Nausea rocked me, reminded again that this was the whole reason I demanded space between us. This constant fucking worrying for his life and how easily he was willing to throw it away. For me. For his people. For his god. How could I let myself have feelings for someone when it was damn near inevitable that we'd lose each other? I forced it all into the depths of my mind, resigning to the fact that I could change nothing.

Ahead, a large circle of druids and humans laughed and chatted, and it occurred to me that I'd never seen so many humans and Vylandrians side by side, wildly enjoying each other's company.

Following my attention, Balis lowered his mouth to my ear as we passed, causing familiar shivers to spider-walk up my spine. "Many humans here live in the smaller outlying villages of Calrund. We don't face as much tension out there compared to the royal city. In numerous places, humans and wielders coexist, depending on each other for trade and various necessities. It's a more synergistic environment than the royal city would have you believe."

"Do you spend a lot of time there?" I asked, noting the conviction in his tone when he spoke of them.

"I grew up in one," he said.

"You grew up in a village with humans?"

"More than that. I *am* half-human."

My head snapped to him, mouth agape.

"Why so surprised?" He laughed. "What? Did you believe we were the first human and druid to have chemistry?"

I snapped my mouth shut and fought against tight cheeks. His brazen words stoked those still-hot coals between us—a heat that, no matter how hard I stomped on it, always caught at the first sign of kindling. It was simple to tell myself that distance was the wise choice when we had no interactions, but in this captivating environment where the possibilities felt endless, it threatened to ignite a wildfire.

"No," I shook my head, "it's just..." My words caught, unsure how to say it without sounding like an unfair expectation, that he was somehow weaker because of his half-human blood. That couldn't be further from the truth. "I've only met a few half-mags before, but..."

"But?"

"You just seem so... different," I said.

"What is it? Am I stronger? Smarter? Better look—"

"Cockier." I cut him short.

As we neared another group encircling a fire, that familiar ease between us returned. They were engaged in intimate conversations and warm smiles. I watched, curious, as they passed around a long pipe. Each of them took a drag of the pungent, earthy smoke before passing it onto the next person.

A pretty, dark-haired woman eyed us as we approached. "Would you and your friend like to join, warrior?" she asked, holding up the pipe. "There's plenty to go around."

Balis peered at me, mischief in his opulent emerald eyes. I shrugged, willing to seize just about any opportunity I could with him—*just* for tonight.

We joined the circle, sitting in the spots where people moved aside for us. I studied the process of smoking the pungent plant before it made it to me. When I inhaled for the first time, though, my lungs wretched in agony. The smoke billowed from my nose and mouth like a sputtering fire as I coughed and gasped for a lungful of clean air.

The aged dwarf beside me gingerly patted me on the back, murmuring words of encouragement. "Attagirl, get it out. It'll do ya some good. Out with the old, in with the new."

Balis inhaled a long, deep pull, and it occurred to me that he'd done this before. He held his breath a moment and then released a smooth, thick stream of white smoke toward the fire. By the time it rounded to me again, my head was already feeling light. I passed it to Balis, who took another drag. After thanking them, we continued on our way.

We paused again to observe a ritualistic dance performed by the Serandari people. Balis explained they were an immigrant culture who fled their sinking island more than two thousand years ago, who now resided in the rolling hills of southwestern

Vylandria. Their beautifully colored ensembles and serpentine dancing were an homage to their dragon god, whom they called the Yellow Dragon.

Their last piece took place just as the sun started its descent, another homage to their dragon god. It began with an elegance that was almost ethereal, moving with grace and fluidity. Then, as they lit their twirling rings of fire and swirled them overhead and along their bodies, the tempo picked up. The beat became heavier, the movements more rapid and feral. Still, a beautiful, ancient story unfolding.

After the Serandari performers finished their act, another group took the stage. They played a wordless melody of chords that began slow and rhythmic before evolving into a sensually captivating vibe. The music drew me in as if I were lured by its spell. Balis followed, and the beat grew louder the closer we got. The drums reverberated in my chest and resonated beneath my feet, yet my focus remained on the comforting touch of Balis' hand in mine.

We reached the open patch of grass that acted as a dance floor in front of the stage. Amidst the swirling multitude, Balis tucked me under his arm to avoid getting separated.

Whether it was the pipe or the music leaving my mind unencumbered, I wasn't sure, but I embraced the moment and danced, pulling him deeper into the crowd until we were lost to it. I secured his arms around me as I pressed against him, swaying my hips in reckless circles. Before long, my fingers found the nape of his neck, craving the firmness of his muscles beneath my touch.

He leaned in close, his warm breath brushing against my skin as his hands explored my body. They felt just as I remembered—rough calluses, battle-honed, and strong. They brushed over the curve of my waist, casting away the last of my willpower to stop it. World be damned.

"My gods, you feel so good, princess," he said in my ear. "I've missed you."

I turned to look up at him, my attention shifting from the heat between our bodies to the fever in his eyes. "Let's just make the most of tonight."

A small chuckle lifted the bow of his lips. "You mean because I might be dead tomorrow?"

I didn't balk at the words. "Yes."

The heady atmosphere and lightness of my thoughts alleviated my fear. Nothing mattered anymore but this moment.

I studied him through my long lashes as the glow of dozens of fires and fairy lights cascaded above. His heavy-lidded smile drew me in like a moth to a flame. I wrapped another hand behind his neck, relishing the feel of his earthen brown hair between my fingers. The scent of cinnamon, cedar, and smoke on his breath enraptured my senses as the music came to a close.

"I know this is difficult for you," he began, voice husky, "but thank you for coming."

"Truth be told, it was against my will."

He gave a light chuckle at my snarky comment. "Somehow, I doubt that. Nobody is more willful than you." He pressed his lips to my ear. "You wouldn't be here," he purred, gripping my waist with strong hands, "if you didn't want to be."

Sweeping a stray hair from my face, I fought the smile that forced its way to my cheeks.

"When Eurok first assigned me to train you, I was angry." He paused, letting the words hang between us as his thumbs traced little circles on my hips. "I couldn't imagine what could ever be worth giving up my dream of becoming a commander. But, after meeting you and after witnessing your determination, your instinct to protect, your fight—I get it now."

I wanted to pry, ask for him to elaborate, but I let the question die on my tongue. His answer wouldn't matter. If he lived tomorrow, I'd save my question for then. However, if he didn't, tonight's answer would only deepen the pain of losing him, which I could hardly handle to begin with.

I tried to recall a moment when I felt that anger he mentioned, but I couldn't pinpoint one. He could have abandoned me that day—let me face the dangers of drak hybrids, forest beasts, or poachers alone. But he never hesitated—never gave up the mission he was tasked with. It all made sense now; why Eurok sent him. It wasn't in hopes of me falling for this druid—it was his unyielding faith in who he was as a warrior, and who he served. And yet, somehow, I shifted that faith on its axis when I entered that room with the king. And that was why this was dangerous. I dropped my hands from his shoulders and took a step back.

A conflicted look crossed his features, torn between drawing me closer or giving me space. He never got the chance to decide. The moment was lost to an approaching figure weaving through the crowd—one of the challengers.

The black pools of his eyes seemed impossibly deep, oozing lethal malice. His mouthful of sharp, narrow, pointed teeth made my blood run cold as he stopped a threateningly short distance away, looking down his nose at us. His lips curled over those razor-like teeth, and I almost expected a snake tongue to slither between them. But Balis didn't flinch. Instead, he seemed to welcome the challenge, as if he predicted it.

"If it isn't Captain Dramagan's little bitch," the stranger sneered in a low, challenging hiss.

"Deacon, how wonderful to see you," Balis said. "Listen, I know those eyes mess with your depth perception, but do you mind backing the *fuck* up?"

"Where have you been?" he snarled.

"On assignment."

"Assignment my ass. You've been gone for months."

My gaze flicked to Balis, wondering where he'd been since I refused his training. *Maybe I should have read his letters.*

"Nothing is more important than what we face now," Deacon went on. "So I ask again. Where have you been while your brethren have been fighting this scorn?"

"I don't answer to you."

He dared another step. "You don't belong in these games."

Balis angled his body, shielding mine. His energy pulsated with anticipation, as if ready to take on the dark druid at the first sign of danger.

"The council seems to think differently," he said.

"You're going to die tomorrow, mountain druid."

My knees quaked at the warning, and my fingers itched to slide my blade between that vile druid's ribs. If I killed him now, it would be one less opponent for Balis.

"Well, I suppose we'll find out soon enough, won't we?" Balis stood firm against that hard glare.

Deacon's gaze shifted to me. His cold, analyzing stare scanned me with a chilling intensity that penetrated my bones.

"Does getting your cock wet in this human child's pussy have anything to do with your *special assignment,* mountain druid?"

A rumble of earth-shattering power resonated, and Balis was nose-to-nose with the bastard, his blade aimed at the tender flesh of his throat. Deacon, to his credit, hardly acknowledged it.

A slow, calculated grin spread across his ferocious face. "If you think you have even the slightest chance of winning tomorrow, you'd best be prepared to answer for your whereabouts. Your absence hasn't gone unnoticed."

Then he shoved off Balis' arm and stalked away.

CHAPTER THIRTY-ONE

SIDELLE

These festivals were never my idea of fun. They were noisy, crowded affairs, filled with a variety of altered states that made everything too unpredictable for my liking. Especially now that night had fallen.

As I stalked toward the only vendor I had any interest in seeing tonight, the dark corners outlined silhouettes of bobbing heads, legs resting on shoulders, accompanied by the hiss of panting moans.

"Oh, my girl!"

Saura leapt off the stool just outside her wagon door. Her cascading blond curls bounced as she jaunted over, arms outstretched in welcome. She beamed that bright, beautiful smile I'd missed so much and cupped my cheeks in her heavily ringed hands. Her blue eyes glittered in the gold light that poured from the wagon's interior.

As we embraced, I glanced over her shoulder and noticed the shelves lined with hanging herbs and crystals. Saura, a renowned scryer, attended the Festival of Night annually to offer her services. I was here both as a visiting daughter and a paying customer.

"It's good to see you, Mother."

"Come in. Come in." She waved me on ahead to climb the stairs that hung off the back of the wagon and enter the cozy warmth waiting within.

"I apologize—I don't have much time. I've brought you something, and—Oh, I'm sorry."

My steps halted as a pretty woman with auburn hair stood from the mussed bed across the way. I fixed my mother with an inquisitive gaze, though I was far from curious.

"Go on and fetch us some drinks, will you, D'nita? Let me visit with my daughter," Saura said.

Without more than a meek glance, the woman finished buttoning her shirt and swooped out the heavy wooden door. It groaned, then clicked shut. Mother didn't so much as blush.

I cleared my throat. "As I was saying, I've brought something for you to look at."

"Is this about that human you've been hauling around the province?"

I hadn't seen her since Mira entered my life. Given the great lengths I'd gone to over the last nine months to keep it that way, I expected her to grow suspicious and wonder why. But what surprised me was her knowledge of Mira.

"How did you know about—"

"Sidelle, we're seers. Does anything actually happen without us knowing about it?"

Not entirely satisfied with that explanation but unwilling to push the matter, I moved past it. "Normally, I would be inclined to agree with you, but unfortunately, I've been experiencing quite the learning curve over these last few months."

"Oh?" Her light brows raised high.

I reached into the pocket of my long cloak and handed her the journal. Warm candlelight glinted off the large silver ring adorning her thumb as she grasped it. I waited, half-expecting the effects of her power to be immediate. But she only opened it and flipped through its blank pages.

"Heliac script," she said.

I nodded.

"And what do you wish to know?"

"Can you read it?"

"Not in the context of scribed text. No." She turned the book over in her hands, brows furrowed as she studied it closely. "But there is something here."

"What is it?"

"Tell me why it's important."

I released a deep sigh and plopped into a chair beside a round table covered in crystals, crow feathers, and various books. Her beady-eyed crow, Guntram, perched on a rafter overhead. He squawked, preening his feathers, causing another to drift down, landing on the table beside the others.

With a groan, I pressed the heels of my palms against my eyes. I bore this burden for so long that the thought of unloading any of it onto my mother's shoulders felt wrong, but if I could trust anyone's guidance, it was hers.

"I stole it from Atreus. It's from the year Annorah sacrificed herself," I said, frustrated with the lack of help it supplied thus far. Only the ramblings of insignificant daily occurrences. We needed to be able to look ahead.

"I'm not blind, child. I can read that much here on the cover. Now what is it you're *not* telling me?"

I slowly inhaled what felt like my last breath before the entire world changed. "When I took that from Atreus' council chamber, I also found a manastone."

Saura paled, and I hadn't even gotten to the worst part.

I swallowed hard. "He has a manastone containing, at least some, of Erezos' power. I wasn't able to get it out of the castle."

Her hand covered her wine-colored lips. "Have you gone to the council?"

"No."

"Sidelle, why not?"

"Because I fear that it will ensue a war. Already, it seems the mysterious ash that Annorah and the druids had discovered on the king's ships has resurfaced. He's making weapons."

She stood and walked to a small counter, her long lilac cloak brushing along the dusty floor. She picked up the pestle from the grinding stone and worked out her frustrations on the small pile of herbs within—a habit I learned from here. I always seemed to think better when my hands were busy.

"I'm sorry, I don't see how this correlates to you *not* telling the council. It seems like an inevitability that our people deserve time to prepare for, does it not?" I didn't answer.

"You're smarter than this, Sidelle. You know you can't take this on alone."

"I don't need a lecture. I have a plan. If I can just stall them longer, I might have a solution to save everyone."

"Which is?"

"Annorah's reincarnation walks the earth. She's here. With me."

Saura dropped the pestle. It clattered and rolled off the grinding stone as she braced herself against the tabletop. "The girl?"

I nodded.

"Who else knows?"

"Eurok."

She surprised me by chuckling. She straightened, wiping her hands on her crisp, white apron.

"What?" I demanded.

"I should've known you'd call him the moment you sensed trouble. I bet you he came running, didn't he?"

"It wasn't like that. He just so happened to be assigned as council liaison."

"Mmhmm." She crossed her arms in a show of disbelief. "Are you two a union yet?"

"As if that makes any difference."

She quirked a brow.

"Yes, okay." I waved her off. "We have claimed our union with one another, but we can worry about that later."

"It seems like you have little time left, child."

I winced at her stoic words.

She came to stand in front of me, cupping my cheek. Her touch was gentle, a gesture of reassurance. The aroma of cedar, rosemary, and mugwort wafted toward me, and I drew a deep breath, savoring the scent of her sacred smoke bombs—her best sellers at these festivals.

I pressed her palm against my cheek. She always hoped Eurok and I would give our relationship a shot, but as usual, her timing was terrible.

"You deserve some happiness, Sidelle. *He* deserves some happiness."

I tightened my lips together and forced a smile.

Dropping the matter, she loosed a sigh and put her hands on her narrow hips, returning to her work. "The gods? What do they have to say about this?"

My mother's ability as a seer didn't function like mine. Her abilities lay within the energy of objects—the residual essence left behind by the life or experiences of the item.

"I fear Erezos can't answer. That, or he's being watched." At least that would account for his silence. "The Empress has suffered an immense loss of her own recently, and I stole that journal from Atreus, Aethier's gift to humanity, so I don't think I should go crawling to him for help."

My mother pursed her lips. Then a loud, musical knock cut her train of thought short. "Come in, Eurok," she called.

The way opened, and he squeezed through the small opening. He occupied nearly half of the space and had to bend his neck to avoid hitting his head.

"Sit down before you knock over the lavender." She clicked her tongue against her teeth. "It's good to see you, son."

He gave me a soft kiss in greeting. The essence of campfire and salt lingered on his plush lips. He dropped beside me and draped an arm over the back of my chair.

Saura pecked him on the cheek and placed a cup of tea in front of him. "We were just talking about you."

"All good things, I hope," he said with a chuckle.

I sat back, letting them chat with each other a bit, and let myself ease at the flow of their natural conversation—a lift in the mood Eurok seemed to bring when he entered. Maybe a residual effect from the festival, but still, I needed the distraction. Tomorrow would be the culmination of everything he and Balis worked for. He deserved a night to relax.

I spent the last months tied up in never-ending concern—a constant parade of pros, cons, and effects weighing on me. Then there was the endless research. Finding ways to push Mira's mana to bloom, all while scouring herbology records for a plant that mimics the effect of these ash weapons. Most days, I felt like an overloaded ship capsizing under the weight. But today, I looked at Eurok, ankle crossed over his knee, an easy smile on his face. Today had been... nice.

Once their chatter slowed, I placed my hand in Eurok's. Saura was right. The idea of our limited time hurt, but he had always been my rock. He deserved to receive that kind of devotion from me as well. He squeezed my fingers. It was comforting to turn to him when I needed support, knowing he would be there for me. I could handle anything with him by my side. Even the end.

"So, Mother, what can you tell me about the journal?"

She picked it up off the counter and brought it over to the table. She sat across from Eurok and me, turning it over in her hands. As she flipped through the pages, she closed her eyes. "There's something here, a shift of some kind."

"A shift?"

"Almost—two different writers. It's strange. I sense Atreus all over this journal, but there's something else there. It feels... ancient."

"Like a god? Is it Erezos?"

She opened one of her bright blue eyes to glare at me, as if to chastise for my interruption.

"Sorry." I leaned back, taking a sip of tea as I waited for her to continue.

"Where do you notice this shift, Saura?" Eurok asked.

"Right about at the halfway point."

I thrummed a finger against the tabletop. "So summer?"

"Most likely."

He glanced between us. "What time of year was it when you performed Annorah's sacrifice?"

My mother quirked another sly brow in my direction, surprised by how much I told him. I ignored her.

"Late June," I answered in a whisper. "What else do you sense?"

"Not much. It seems to almost be split in half. The first bit is purely Atreus—I sense his humanity. The other exudes a heavy, brooding energy."

Her eyes became distant, focused on something beyond the present moment, yet they shimmered like sapphires in the candlelight. This ancient, beautiful witch guided me through countless tribulations, from teaching me to take my first steps to aiding in dismantling an odious system meant to stifle us. When she broke that unseeing gaze and met my own, I knew I'd been unbearably foolish for not telling her sooner.

"That's all I can see," she said, quiet and regretful.

Eurok and I exchanged wary glances. He uncoiled his energy and wrapped it around me in a shield of warmth and protection, like an impenetrable wall of sunlight and safety.

I caressed it with my own in surreptitious thanks, sensing the rippling shiver against my touch. A smile spread across my face, and a glow crept throughout my soul. I truly did love him. My stomach leapt. Saura was right. Let us enjoy this small taste of happiness, even just for tonight. It was, after all, what we were fighting for.

CHAPTER THIRTY-TWO

MIRA

G ravel crunched beneath my boots, the sound echoing through the deserted festival as the sun crested the eastern mountains. Soft snores whispered from the dew-covered canvas tents as I passed by, heading to the city. More specifically, the sparring yards where Balis said he and Eurok would be.

The village was just beginning to stir as merchants and tradesmen set up their carts and stands, readying for the morning rush of servants making their sunrise grocery runs. They'd close again for the games this afternoon. Eurok said everyone in the city would attend. It was hard to fathom so many congregating in one place, but then again, I hadn't seen the arena yet. It had to be massive.

Metal clanged from the training yards. I approached, unsure which area Balis was assigned. But as I grew closer, unfamiliar voices rang from within. I should've turned and left. But something in their sharp tones had me pressing against the hard granite brick instead, straining to hear what they said.

"Nobody's seen the fucking pussyfoot shifter since the first recon mission. Back then, it was just the lesser fairies getting snatched."

I peered around the corner to lay eyes on the speaker, finding Mallack, the largest of the border clan contestants. A shiver rocked my spine. He was gargantuan, a mountain of a male with boulders for muscles that rivaled even Eurok's.

"Shit, it's only gotten worse since then." It was Salve who spoke as he swung a large sword overhead and brought it down, effortlessly cleaving a wedge into the training dummy's wooden head.

"Exactly." Mallack ripped his ax from his dummy's chest. "And what's this shit about him clearing out that camp of Dogu poachers last summer?" He whirled another devastating blow, sending splinters in all directions.

My mouth went dry. There was no doubt that it was Balis they spoke of.

With the swagger of a killer, Mallack stalked away from his dummy, which lay crumpled in an unrecognizable heap.

"What of it?" Salve asked.

"You believe it?"

"Fuck, yeah. I was assigned to the cleanup detail. They kept saying it was Balis and some human woman who saved them." Salve was perched precariously atop the shoulders of another training dummy, practicing his balance as he swung his battle sword in an array of various blocking maneuvers.

Mallack snarled. "Well, I don't believe it. Why does he get the notoriety and the chance to compete when we've worked our asses off?"

Deacon's words from last night rang through my mind. *You'd best be prepared to answer for your whereabouts. Your absence hasn't gone unnoticed.*

This is what he warned us about. My questions regarding Balis' actual whereabouts faded. It didn't matter. I told him to leave. It wasn't my business where he went afterwards.

"You better watch who you say that around," Salve said. "Don't underestimate him, Mallack. He's the captain's pet for a reason."

"I don't give a fuck who hears me. B'sides, the way I hear it, the lot of us will be gunning for him today." He spun a pole between his hands and took a shot at a new training dummy, severing it at the neck with a single blow.

"I guess it'd be foolish not to take him out while he's got such a large target on his back," Salve said, his smirk darkening with cruelty.

My stomach did a sickening flip, and I took off, sprinting from my place along the wall toward the only other training yard with sound spilling from it. Without hesitation, I stormed in, my focus gazing past Balis to Eurok's sweaty brow. I cut between them. A gust of air blew back my hair as Eurok redirected mid-swing, just missing my face. I didn't flinch.

"Are you crazy?" Balis yelled, pulling his weapon from a strike.

I paid him no mind and raised my chin to the captain, letting him know I was there to confront him.

"What do you want, Mira?" he asked, expression deadpanned.

I stared him down, despite needing to crane my neck a ridiculous amount. "Why did you ask him to train me?"

"What?" He jerked back, surprised.

"Why would you assign your *finest* to mentor a human girl while we're on the brink of war?"

"You mean the poaching?" he asked.

"Yes, the fucking poaching." My words echoed across the stone walls. "How is it so bad that every druid warrior here today has been fighting against it, yet you assigned your *best* to run an errand to go find *me?*" My final word ground out through my teeth.

Eurok's jaw clenched.

"Mira, what is this about?" Balis asked, cautiously placing a hand on my shoulder.

"Every contestant on that field today will be gunning for you," I answered without removing my icy glare from the captain.

His expression remained undisturbed, making me wonder if he even heard me.

"Mira, we know," Balis said, gently urging me away from Eurok.

I let him, half-stunned by the revelation. "What do you mean, you know?"

"I know I have a target on my back."

I studied the fine lines of his handsome face for the slightest hesitation. There was none. "Then why are you doing this? It won't be a fair fight." My words were as hot as the fire coursing through my veins.

Why would anyone put themselves in that situation? Even with *his* ego, he had to realize he couldn't overcome those odds.

"I'm a warrior, Mira. We train for battle, not fair fights."

Everything in me told me to stand my ground, to unload my fury, my pleas, my...fear. But I fought off the urge and forced the swell of rage to subside. The stone in their faces conveyed unyielding cliffs. I shoved Balis, seething, and stormed out before I said something I'd regret.

How could he be so stupid?

Why would Eurok expose his top fighter to such blatant targeting? And for what? A human that can hardly wield?

Unbridled fear and rage fueled my every step to the village. I hardly knew where I headed until I reached the lodge we stayed in last night. I climbed the spiral stairs to Sidelle's room, but she was nowhere to be found. Frustrated and unsure of my next move, I turned away—but paused when I saw her staff leaning against the shelf by the small desk in the corner.

I approached with cautious steps, my gaze drawn to the intricate, swirling designs adorning its sides, and the radiant, uncut manastone crowning its peak.

Sidelle'd been granting me small bits of power for training, but there was still an enormous amount left within. I sensed it luring me like that initial encounter in the stone forest. The only difference being how accustomed I'd grown to it.

If I had any chance of saving Balis, I had to replenish my core and absorb as much as I could withstand. My healing mana had been developing nicely. Maybe, if I could heal him from a distance, I could keep him alive, save him.

It was a ludicrous plan. I'd never done it before, and surely they had rules against this sort of thing. Still, it was the only one I had and no less reckless than sending the best warrior to a certain death. This was my only chance—his only chance.

My touch encircled the manastone, and I focused on the warmth that radiated against my hand, asking the mana to wind around that cold, hollow core within me.

"Just enough to protect my friend in that arena today," I said, assuring myself.

My palms stung as the heat intensified, but I refused to pull away, rushing the power to flood my veins and find my core. My heart leapt at the sudden slam of a door and the echoing footsteps ascending the stairs, catching me off guard. Whoever it was, if they reached the top, they'd have a full view of what I was doing. I concentrated harder, willing the mana to come to me faster.

Faster.

Pulling with all my might, ice laced through my power-filled veins as a nearly imperceptible crack sounded from between my hands. Sharp panic swept over. Trembling, I got to my feet, replacing the staff against the bookshelf.

The molten heat of mana swelled in my chest, satisfying proof that it worked. But it did little to stave off the cold sweat on my brow at having cracked the stone. I brushed aside those concerns—there was no time to dwell on them now. My best option was to ignore it, or my whole plan would be derailed.

Rushing, I pulled my choker from the lead-lined bag Agatha had made me on Sidelle's request and wrapped its silk ribbon low around my neck, tucking it under my tunic.

"Mira?" Audible surprise tinged Sidelle's tone when she reached the landing. "I didn't know you were here. I thought you'd be at the training arenas with Eurok and Balis."

"Oh, I am—I mean, I was. Forgot my blades."

A curious flicker crossed her expression. Shame churned in my gut as she nodded, seeming to accept my bullshit excuse.

"But I'm good." I patted them at my side. "Got them right here."

I attempted to rush past her, making for the stairs, but she stopped me with a gentle hand on my shoulder.

"Are you okay?"

My guilt surged as her soft, concerned eyes scanned over my face.

"Yeah, fine. I'm... worried, I guess." At least that part was true.

Sidelle nodded in understanding and released her hold. "Did everything go alright between you and Balis last night?"

"Yeah, it did." My strained smile wavered. "But look, I gotta go. I'll meet you there later, okay?"

"Oh, good. Well, okay. See you there."

She nodded, and I sped down the stairs and out the door.

The city streets thickened with excited patrons waiting to enter the arena. I remembered Eurok mentioning friends and family of the contestants had reserved seating, so I followed the long line, using alleyways to cut ahead. I slipped into what seemed like the midpoint of the line, veering into an alley that appeared to ascend toward the next hill, likely leading me closer to the front.

At the edge of the corner, shifting gravel at my back stole my attention. Cold, large hands wrapped around my waist, tugging me against a dark doorframe. Like the swipe of a cobra, I unsheathed my dagger and spun, the sleek point of my blade making contact with the tender skin of my attacker's throat.

"Whoa, now," a familiar voice cooed. "You'll want to be careful with that."

Deep, oaken eyes peered down at me over a black cloth mask. His hood covered his hair, but I knew beneath it lay short, sandy brown locks.

I nearly choked on my gasp. "Atreus?"

He pulled down his mask, revealing a wickedly delighted smile that made my breakfast curdle in my stomach. *Fuck. What kind of day am I having?*

"What are you doing here?" I asked, reeling to dredge up that false and vile side of me I used at the castle. I flashed an intrigued smile. "Did you sneak away?"

"I had to see you," he said.

It was obvious he meant for this to be some grand gesture—one a more foolish woman may have swooned at his feet over. I craved to sever each of those loathsome fingers clutching my waist and sprint to Balis.

"Don't worry," he smirked, "no one will notice I'm gone."

"But, how? Do you have guards with you? This feels so dangerous," I said, feigning concern. Truthfully, I was interested in how many were in his company.

"No need for guards."

My brows pinched. Noticing my confusion, he reached into his cloak and withdrew a smooth white stone, very much like the one I just cracked.

"I don't understand," I said, dancing between my fake elation and true terror. "What is that?"

"This allows me to travel from place to place at will. It's a manastone that possesses the power of these druids' god."

My eyes grew round. *He's using Erezos' mana to veil from province to province.* "Is it safe?"

"I've been practicing." He dipped his chin, drawing my attention away from the stone, to his face. "Meet me here after the games. I'll show you a much better time than these animals ever could."

Words left me. I gave a stunned nod, and he replaced his mask, none the wiser to the trepidation wracking through my body. Then he ducked down the alley and was gone. *Fuck.*

Fuck. Fuck. FUCK.

CHAPTER
THIRTY-THREE

MIRA

I somehow managed to make it to the edge of the arena. Bracing myself against the chilly, unyielding stone, I let go of all thoughts except for the sensation of its rough texture against my forehead. *My gods. Atreus is here.*

Grateful for the fact I thought to wear the ash choker, my hands lifted to my neck. The stolen mana raged in my veins like a trapped stallion bucking for release, but the dangling serpent charm, thankfully, kept it tethered. Bile rose in my throat, acrid and burning as I struggled to decide what to do next. How would I use this power to save Balis if Atreus watched my every move?

I retched onto the ground once, twice, then rested my forehead against the cool stone, waiting for my senses to steady.

When the strength finally found me, I made my way through the massive iron and wood doors and took my first shocked look around at the arena. It was a colosseum. A colosseum built into the center of an open mountain. Sunlight poured from above as the crowd gathered in the stands. Eurok's words rang true. The entire city seemed to have converged upon this place.

An attendant pointed me in the direction I needed to go, and I spotted Eurok and Sidelle near the front. With her hand wrapped around the staff, the witch scanned the crowd. When she found me, it wasn't anger in that onyx gaze, but tenderness. *She must not have noticed the crack.*

"I'm glad you made it. We saved you a seat," she said, gesturing with her elegant fingers to the place beside her.

I flashed Eurok a hard glare, which he blatantly ignored. *Arrogance.* So much fucking arrogance. My nerves writhed like a coiled ball of snakes as I sat.

We sat in the front row, directly across the arena from a set of metal doors. We were dead center for the events that would unfold below.

Beneath me, the seat was smooth, meticulously carved rock, each row chiseled further and further back into the mountain as they rose. Balconies had been carved into the shaft above, rising until the mountain reached its peak where the sun's golden morning glow illuminated the sandy arena where The Aupex Proving Games would take place.

I chewed on my bottom lip, nerves jittery as I debated whether to reveal Atreus' presence. But I couldn't risk their reaction. The last thing I wanted was to leave, and it's possible they'd try to make me. My heart raced with determination as I clenched my fists, eyes locked on the arena ahead. *Balis needs me.*

I mulled over the possibility that this was a mistake, yet the boiling mana coursing through my veins served as a stark reminder of the rationale behind my decision. If my power truly benefited the kingdom, I couldn't stand by while Balis died because I was too afraid to use it. I had to try. *Mana is all about intention.*

My mind fixated on Balis' impending doom, overshadowing all other thoughts. War drums began to thunder from opposite ends of the arena. The reverberations echoed through my body and the mountain, their ominous rhythm setting the stage for the looming conflict. The crowd came alive at the sound, and Sidelle placed a gentle hand on my knee. I glanced at her delicate lilac hands before meeting her gaze.

"Everything that happens today unfolds according to divine will, without exception. We have to trust it to end as the gods see fit."

She spoke as if she read my intentions. That couldn't be true, though, or she'd have never let me stay.

The two massive doors swung open across from us, revealing the first druids poised to enter. My heart quickened, its rhythm rivaling the pulse of drums.

The tempo grew more intense as the warriors filed forward, entering the open sandy arena in two lines side by side. Once the front pair, whom I recognized as Phaegen and Jacolb of the dark clan, reached the center of the arena, they made sharp turns away from one another, pacing in opposite directions. Each of the druids replicated the action in perfect unison, halting at different points to form a wide, v-shaped pattern. And standing at that apex, looking me straight in the eye, was Balis.

My breath caught, and my throat stung. I held his stare, refusing to give in to the emotions attempting to claw their way to the surface.

The thundering drums ceased. Sidelle's hand still sat on my knee, and I shifted under the touch, remembering that Atreus might be watching.

Movement from above caught my eye as a falcon flew from the mountain shaft and perched on the lowest of the balcony railings as if arriving for the show.

I found Balis' eyes again and gave a single slow nod—the only acknowledgment I could manage without my emotions breaching. He flashed a charming grin, showcasing the dimple in his chin, though I was too far to see it. My heart fluttered and my stomach sank.

A lean druid, with skin similar to my fair complexion, spoke from a platform above. The contestants pivoted to direct their attention toward him, their backs now to us.

The games were about to begin.

CHAPTER
THIRTY-FOUR

SIDELLE

B rodrick, the high council speaker, stood before the eleven seated council members. All of whom were adorned in various colors of ceremonious robes similar to the one worn by the shaman during yesterday's ceremony. His nasally voice echoed through the arena and I winced. Why they chose him as the speaker was beyond me.

I tightened my grip on Eurok's hand, hoping to dispel the lingering sense of unease that plagued me all morning. The deafening noise of the audience pounded in my head, causing an ache to form. I struggled to focus. Mira's anxious, darting eyes scanned our surroundings with nervous intensity, then repeatedly returned to Balis. *What is she looking for?*

"Champions, take your positions," Brodrick said with a gesture of outspread arms.

Drums pulsed like a singular, excited heartbeat as the crowd stomped in thunderous unison. The competitors moved in to form a large circle, and all stood facing away from one another. The beat of the drums ceased, and the arena was plunged into an eerie calm.

"At my signal, the games will begin. They will not end until a single victor stands among you. Mana, boons, and weapons are permitted. All fighting must be within the borders of the arena. No shifting forms or interference from the crowd will be permitted. Do you agree to these terms?"

The warriors nodded.

"May the gods lay blessings on all of your souls."

Then Brodrick lifted his hand. Mira tensed at my side as a flame grew from the size of a single lent into a ball that engulfed his palm and he thrust the flame into the sky. It soared above the competitors, erupting into a shower of sparks that scattered in every direction.

The ground shook as all twelve of the contestants erupted into action, racing toward the center, and were met by a cloud of smoke engulfing the entire group. The audience, unable to see through the haze, was left in blind suspense, waiting to find out what unfolded within.

Four stood at the fringe of the vast gray veil, their figures mere silhouettes in the blur. The three mountain druids and Cyan of the rider clan.

Balis looked over at the druid, puzzled and at the ready. Cyan, who I realized was the one to have used his smoke boon, made no move to attack him. Instead, he raised his ax to rest on his shoulder. My sensitive sight and hearing could just make out what they called to each other over the crowd.

"Don't take this for excusing your absence, Balis," he drawled, "but you're too fine of a warrior not to be given a fair shot."

Balis offered the rider an amused nod and twirled a dagger between his fingers. Cyan gave a tight nod in return and ran around the side of the dissipating smoke without another word. As the thick haze faded, the carnage that ensued revealed itself. A small gasp escaped Mira's lips, her eyes wide.

We knew Balis would be a target, but it seemed with all other warriors consumed in the cloud, plans to descend in unison were cast aside, resulting in an all-out war within.

Airynn, another member of the rider clan, dodged incessant swings aimed in his direction by Phaegen, a dark clan druid. Phaegen swung his great sword with ease as Airynn stayed on the defensive, dipping and diving, just clearing Phaegen's devastating blows. To put space between them, Airynn thrust his sword into the ground and used the weapon as an anchoring point to flip his body through the air.

Once he was safely on his feet and out of Phaegen's range, he let two daggers loose. They whizzed through the air like hornets with expert precision. But Phaegen was quick. He knocked them away and ran toward Airynn, heading up with a killing blow. Airynn's lean stature came through, though, and in a whirl of evasive maneuvers, each more impressive than the last, Phaegen's efforts missed their mark. Airynn's final evasion left him kneeling, and he thrust his dagger through the taut muscle of Phaegen's passing leg.

The dark clan member howled, sharp and shrill. In a desperate move, he lunged forward, grabbing Airynn's shoulder in a vise-like grip. With a surge of power, he unleashed his boon, blinding touch, onto the unsuspecting rider. Airynn's sense of sight was lost, and the druid's hands flew to his eyes. Phaegen used the advantage to position himself behind the kneeling druid, his injured leg leaving a trail of crimson in the sand, then plunged his sword into Airynn's back. A thick gurgle slipped from the rider's lips as his unseeing eyes lifted skyward. Phaegen shoved his foot against Airynn's listless body, freeing his weapon.

The reek of blood, sweat, and metal was heavy. Lifeblood leaked from the corner of the dying druid's mouth just as his clanmate, Cyan, leapt over his fallen brother and sliced the Phaegen's shoulder. Upon landing, he whirled, ready to rain another flurry of attacks. But before Cyan could close the gap, Phaegen, with a wave of his hand, raised a large, twisting funnel of air and sand, enveloping the rider. The force lifted him off his feet. He flailed and thrashed before crashing hard onto the ground. Phaegen stalked to Cyan's side and sank his twisted blade between his ribs.

Twelve were now ten.

Phaegen prowled away from the fallen riders, his gait predatory as he returned to the group of battling men. With a deft flick of his wrist, he rid his blade of Cyan's blood, already seeking his next challenger. The crowd reached near deafening levels as people pounded their fists and screamed their cheers.

As I spotted Balis amid the warring druids, he was engaged in a duel against Anvil, a detestable cousin from the border clan. A concussive rattling of metal sent sparks flying off Balis' ax as he parried a lethal blow. Anvil spun and lifted his leg to deliver a sharp kick to Balis' back. As he stumbled, Anvil took the opportunity to conjure a thick web of vines, ensnaring Balis' wrists and ankles.

Mira's knuckles whitened as she clenched the stone bench beneath her, eyes pinned on Balis as he unleashed an enormous burst of wind that threw Anvil off-balance. Seizing the momentary distraction, Balis wrestled his arms free and freed his ankles with a deft stroke of his ax.

He conserved his mana well thus far, only using it as a last defense. If a druid were to exhaust his reserves too quickly, it would leave him vulnerable to physical attack.

His use proved necessary as Anvil regained his footing. He raced toward Balis, a blur of lethal fury poised to strike. But Balis was ready. He rolled, avoiding Anvil's thrust. The border clan druid pressed on, his blows coming in rapid succession. With every thrash, the air crackled with tension, stilling the breath in my lungs.

I closed my eyes for a reprieve from the gruesome scene and searched for some relief from this growing headache. My empathetic senses were a bit haywire amidst the overwhelming chaos. With so many heightened emotions, it was difficult to block them all out.

When I looked again, Anvil's muscles bulged with brute strength as he forced Balis to the ground, overpowering his defenses with sheer force. I glanced at Mira—her face etched with horror.

A stalagmite erupted from the sand, blocking our view and impaling a contestant just a few paces away. The lax body atop the enormous earthen spike rained blood toward the crowd. Quickly, I spelled an ethereal shield over the audience to protect against the red spray. With a wave of my hand, I transfigured the splatter into flower petals of the same vibrant color, casting them away on the breeze, then dropped the shield. Following the path of the petals as they floated up and out of the mountain's open expanse, my gaze caught sight of a falcon eyeing the scene from a balcony overhead.

Strange.

The stalagmite shattered, raining bits of crumbled rock and the druid's lifeless body to the ground. The arena was visible again, a chaotic display of scarlet-soaked sand and intense combat. Shards of steel from broken weapons and scraps of leather armor littered the battleground alongside the fallen bodies of contestants. The air was heavy with the mingling scents of sweat, blood, and dust.

Mira, her complexion pale with fury, scanned the crowd, absorbing their adrenaline, pride-filled faces. I could only imagine the thoughts racing through her mind. She, on more than one occasion, made it clear how disgusted she was by the idea of wasting good warriors' blood to the sand. And though I respected this ritual for what it meant to the druids and to Erezos, I understood. She spent her whole life training to survive, while these males, it seemed, trained all of theirs to die.

I spotted Balis again, still in a blow-for-blow with Anvil. Both tirelessly evading and deflecting strikes.

I searched the arena for the other border clan contestants. Where one vicious cousin was, another was surely not far off. I found Salve in a similar battle for the upper hand with Klaus, a clanmate of Balis.

Salve seemed more willing than most to push his boundaries by using his mana. He pooled a pit of thick mud beneath Klaus' feet, plunging the mountain druid waist-deep into the viscous substance. Klaus, unable to move, did his best to block the onslaught of strikes that Salve rained down before snapping his fingers to release his boon, waterbody. Klaus' solid form morphed into crystal clear water, and, maintaining his shape, he launched himself from the muck. With the force of a great rapid, he plunged himself down his opponent's throat.

The crowd roared. Salve clutched and scratched at his throat, eyes bulging, desperation and fear lacing his reddening expression. A rush of red-tinged water gushed from the druid's nose and mouth as Klaus reformed, regaining his solid state. Salve buckled under the relief of air that now passed through his lungs, gasping for more and more as Klaus stalked up to him. He reeled back, ready to deliver a final, lethal blow. In that same moment, Salve grabbed Klaus' leg, snapped his fingers, and unleashed his boon of quake.

A bone-rattling shudder spread throughout the arena. The audience held fast. Screams echoed from somewhere behind, while others gasped, horrified by the devastating effect the force had on the druid's body.

The crunch of bones and the squelch of innards liquefying resonated through the shuddering earth. Blood seeped like tears from Klaus's eyes. The druid was dead before the quaking subsided. He crumpled in a heap of mangled flesh and fragmented limbs.

I fought back the urge to purge my stomach, averting my gaze.

Despite the intense tremors, the others had not halted their fighting. Balis, at some point amidst the chaos, defeated Anvil, but the relief was short-lived. Mallack's gigantic form charged across the arena, away from Deacon's limp body, straight for Balis.

Mira stood, gripping the banister. While I realized the significance of her presence for Balis, my concern heightened at the thought of her violent reaction should he fail to emerge victorious. I gripped Eurok's hand tight, bracing myself against his steel composure and watched on.

Mallack's and Balis' weapons met in a deluge of sparks and ferocious growls.

The pain in my head surged as the crowd roared louder, utterly overwhelming my senses like a gale-force wind against a tattered mast. For a seer, navigating through a multitude of diverse emotions in a crowded space was always a challenge. This was by far the worst I ever experienced. Even as I coiled my mana tightly into myself, it pulsed with discomfort, as if trying to warn me. *These damned games. I'll be glad when they're over.*

Balis' impeccable reflexes saved him from certain death, sensing a blow from behind as a second contestant, Hunter, took advantage of the moment to gang up on him. Balis harnessed his mana, causing the ground beneath Hunter to buckle. The final rider clan druid plummeted into the jagged depths. Then Balis swung, blocking Mallack's ax with a concussive burst of air as it flew toward his skull.

"Focus, Balis," Eurok said through his teeth, gripping my hand a little tighter than was comfortable. He was right. Now wasn't the time for Balis to get careless with his mana. If he continued to use it at this rate, he would falter.

A male's mana was incredibly strong, but their downfall was in the short, brilliant bursts in which it came. Balis had thus far demonstrated cautious use of his mana, a skill honed through Eurok's training. However, under the relentless barrage of attacks, fatigue set in, forcing him to tap into his reserves.

As the number of contestants dwindled, the initial strategy to eliminate Balis gained momentum again, evolving into a three-on-one. He held out against their attacks with expert evasion, even making a few well-placed and effective strikes of his own, but Mallack was proving to be his greatest opponent. While Balis retreated to put some space between himself and the others, Mallack used the opportunity to set off his boon—invisibility.

A shuddering breath escaped Mira's lips as he disappeared, but Balis wasted no time and released his own boon of focus.

A subtle sense of calm washed over him, his face relaxed where it'd been taut, and his eyes closed as if allowing his other senses to take charge where his sight would be of no help. His movements became even more precise, impactful, and intentional.

He effortlessly blocked two blows from the others, then reeled with such force that it was a wonder he hadn't used his mana to do so. He flipped mid-air and wrapped his arms around the necks of the last two dark clan druids, Phaegen, and Jacolb. Upon landing, he whipped their heads to the side with a ruinous snap. The crowd erupted in triumphant cheers, but Mira stood tense and unblinking. She didn't even crack a smile. Though it was now a one-on-one battle, she knew as well as I that the greatest of threats was still out there.

Balis, also aware of the imminent danger, dropped to a knee. His hair rustled, and it occurred to me that the movement had been to evade an unseen blow from above. Then he dove and rolled a few paces to the side, over and over again. The burst of sandy footprints was the only indication of the onslaught coming at him.

Then Balis screamed.

His face pinched in agony as a deep red slash was gouged across the back of his thigh. He scrambled to get out of the way of another anticipated swing as Mallack flickered into view.

An icy panic bloomed beneath my skin as I fought to keep my eyes on the awful scene, when a horrendous shudder emanated from my staff, wracking through my body. It trembled, and I gripped it with both hands. Then the manastone emitted a loud *crack*. Mira heard it too but clearly struggled to decide where to focus her attention—my staff or the unfolding carnage. Her face lost all color.

"Mira?" My head pounded in another violent swell caused by what I thought was the uproarious crowd. But then I felt it. The familiar, insistent pull of my consciousness to the corner of my mind. *No.*

No. Please. Not now.

Mira didn't answer. She stood, mouth agape, unable to speak as the stone cracked again. A fissure spread across its surface, and a small purple tendril escaped, sailing through the air.

"What's happening?" Eurok asked. His gaze darted back and forth, alternating between his struggling, injured warrior and the shattering stone atop my staff.

"Eurok, we have to leave." Desperation laced my voice.

He looked at me, then to Mira.

"I'm not leaving," she insisted.

Another yank on my mind made the world sway, and though I didn't know why, my eyes found that falcon. It sat as still as a statue on the balcony railing, its sharp eyes focused on us and the escaping mana encircling Mira. Then it flew away.

"What's happening, Sidelle?" Eurok asked again.

"I don't know," was all I managed to get out.

Then the whole world seemed to pause as a sickening squelch of tearing flesh erupted from the arena.

Mallack towered over Balis, ax raised high, ready to land a final killing blow. Balis' face was a stoic, lionhearted expression of peace, a warrior prepared to accept his death. But when the anticipated blow failed to strike, he opened his eyes, his battle-worn features contorted with pure bewilderment. Mallack faltered, his ax dropping to the sand with a thud. His knees quaked, and he stumbled.

Balis scrambled to his feet, backing away as crimson spread across Mallack's back. He took another ragged step, turning toward the crowd to reveal a gaping void in his chest cavity. Blood gushed from the vacant space where his heart should be, staining the sand black beneath him.

Mira peered up at me, her features haggard and pale. There in her shaking palms, she held something concealed in a dark, dispersing haze. The remnants of a beating heart. I looked to Mallack, then back to Mira, sickening realization setting in.

"What did you do?" I whispered.

Without thought, I grabbed the heart and transfigured it into a pile of black coals, then let them fall. I stomped them into dust as I checked if anyone nearby bore witness.

Her pallid face lifted to mine and her lips parted to speak, but I heard no words as my head surged in one last violent storm of pain. A raw chill tore me from my consciousness and thrust me into the all-consuming darkness of my mind.

CHAPTER THIRTY-FIVE

MIRA

The look on Sidelle's face before she lost consciousness made my chest go cold, like I fell through thin ice, far beyond anyone's reach. The crowd roared their applause, and I thought finding Balis' gaze would make me feel better. It didn't. It was worse. Those brilliant emerald eyes demanded the same question as Sidelle. *What did you do?*

My hands tucked to my sides as I held his stare. I wasn't sorry for saving him. Whatever the consequences—allowing him to die was never an option.

Eurok lifted the witch into his arms. "Stay here," he demanded.

As if I had any volition to do anything but. I wasn't letting Balis out of my sight.

I vaguely registered the announcement declaring him the victor of the Aupex Proving Games. Admittedly, I was lost in my own thoughts until Balis darted toward me. He grabbed my hand, urging me to stand, and hurried us out of the arena, our steps swift and purposeful. We slowed to a standstill down a dark alley in a part of the village entirely unfamiliar to me.

"You gonna tell me what the *fuck* that was?"

"He was going to kill you."

"Damn it, Mira! He was *supposed* to kill me. He defeated me."

Some small part of me hated how he used my name. The teasing nickname he taunted me with felt like the only

397

acceptable thing for him to call me. I especially despised the way he said it while angry.

"You defied the gods." His shoulders squared as he straightened to his full height. "You defied *my* wishes, and you robbed the druid army of their rightful commander."

"You will be commander now."

His voice pitched louder. "You really think I can face them after this?"

"No one saw, Balis. Nobody knows except–"

"I know, Mira." He jabbed at his chest with an insistent finger. "*I. Know.*"

My frustration boiled over. "I'm so sick of this self-righteous bullshit, Balis. I've had it. You dying in that arena would be nothing but a tragic waste."

"That's not your choice to make."

"I did this for you," I said.

"No. You did this for *you*." His words were devoid of any refined tones or gentle cadence, delivered with raw, bitter sincerity. And I despised how small my own seemed in comparison. His eyes bore into mine with a furious indignation I never witnessed before. "I was ready to die today alongside my brothers," he said. "Instead, you made a mockery of our ways, our beliefs."

His words sliced like a razor, a pain I tried to deflect by reminding myself he was still alive, still here.

"You didn't do this for me. This was about you. Just like how you sent me away—*for you*." Bitterness tinged the words.

A pregnant pause hung between us, the tension palpable as I struggled to hold back the sting of tears. I steadied my breath before speaking.

"Fine, you're right. I did it for me. I did it because I couldn't *stand* there and watch you waste your life—not when I've fought the entirety of mine scraping by to survive. That game in there," I threw my arm toward the arena, "that, to me, is a mockery."

His expression softened, a fleeting moment of vulnerability crossing his features before he turned his back on me.

"My whole life, Balis, I've never felt like I belonged anywhere, to anyone. And then you come along and..." My words faltered. "Yes, I sent you away for myself, too. That night, when you burst into the king's chambers, I realized what you meant to me."

The lingering memory of his expression when he laid eyes on me and saw I was safe confirmed what I meant to him, too. *I couldn't find you.*

"How could I allow that?" The words ached, forced out through my tight throat. "How could I let myself fall for you when you're so willing to throw it all away, to risk your life, risk everything?" I blew out a shaky breath, trying to steel my emotions and force some conviction into my words. "Balis, you left me with an impossible choice."

"What choice?"

"To ask you to leave, or to accept this reckless attraction growing between us and fall for you despite it."

He turned back, pain etched into the bloodstained lines of his handsome face. "And what's so wrong with falling for me, Mira?"

The pleading in his voice threatened to destroy me.

"This!" I gestured to the arena. "This, Balis. What we're willing to do for each other—what we're willing to risk." After a breath, I took a tenuous step closer. "I can't imagine a world without you in it. I asked you to leave, knowing it was better to live my life without you than survive in a world where you don't exist."

His expression softened, but his head dipped. "When the council finds out I didn't win fairly, that future might still be your reality."

"What do you mean, 'when'?" Disbelief colored my tone. "You're not telling them?"

His head jerked back, dejected. "I refuse to carry a title I haven't earned."

"You did earn it," I said, my voice finding strength again. "Do you honestly believe Mallack would be here having this conversation? You are the commander this army needs. If I am who you all claim, then it's not Mallack I want to stand beside when we confront Atreus. It's you. Despite whatever this is between us, it has always been you."

"Mira, I can't," he turned away from me again.

"You won't tell them," I challenged.

"I can't—"

"You won't tell them!" Tears blurred my vision, the alley punctuating my words, echoing them back to us. "For gods' sake, Balis, for once in your fucking life, take what you want for yourself, what you deserve, instead of whatever the druid army gives you. Take what's yours."

My sanity hung by a precarious thread as I waited for him to say something. And for a moment, with his back to me and fists clenched at his sides, I thought he might walk away. My gaze slid to the cobblestones, expecting the rejection of his retreating footsteps—

In a flash of breath and heat, he closed the space between us, his mouth on mine. The force of his kiss propelled me back against the hard stone wall, his mouth moving at a quick tempo against my own. The scent of blood and sand clung to his skin, mingling with the saltiness of battle on his lips.

We broke away, and I peered up at him, breathless. "What are you doing?"

"Taking what's mine," he said, his voice low like distant thunder. "You think you've got it all figured out—but you're wrong. Being apart is far from the best choice for us." His green eyes burned beneath heavy brows. Pain still lingered there, muted by renewed, determined hunger. "You want me to choose for myself? Then you listen to me, princess. I choose *you*."

My breath caught in my throat. A rush of anticipation and nerves buzzed beneath my skin, causing my heart to race.

"And if you opt for the kingdom over me, great. This kingdom deserves you," he paused, holding my gaze steady, "but I'm not going anywhere. Do you hear me? Never. Again."

I marveled at the conviction drenched in his tone, and secured my arms around his neck. "I hear you, Balis," I whispered. "Never again."

He pressed his lips to mine, repeating the words against my kiss. "Never again."

I savored the way his desperate hands clung to me, pulled me into him. I gripped his hair in my hands, noting the ferocity within every swipe of his tongue along mine, the essence of his mana as it enveloped us in those silken tendrils of power.

He lifted me from the ground by my ass, and my back hit the wall again. I held his face between my hands, loving the way the grit of his stubble felt against my palms. *Gods, I've missed this.*

My legs wrapped around him like an inescapable vise. In one smooth motion, Balis reached between us and yanked the chocker free from my neck, releasing my mana from its caged existence. I smiled against his kiss as it swept through my veins with a sigh, delighted to intertwine itself with his once again.

He pulled back, still holding my body against the wall with his. His viridescent gaze fluttered over my face with a mixture of admiration and pride, a stark contrast to moments ago.

"What?" I asked, breathless, panting.

"You ripped a warrior's heart out in front of a packed arena without detection."

My brows pinched.

Then that irresistible smirk flashed over his handsome face. "I knew you'd be incredible."

401

My thumb traced over the soft pillow of his lips and everything else ceased to exist. This—this was what home must feel like.

Clicking heels against the cobblestone street pulled our attention from our momentary haven. *Why does everyone here have the worst timing?*

Balis set me on my feet and positioned himself between me and whoever approached. His stance eased as a stunning, blonde-haired druid appeared around the corner.

"High Witch Saura," he breathed.

My ears perked. "Saura, Sidelle's mother?" I asked.

He nodded over his shoulder.

"Normally I would never deign to interrupt such a joyous union. Congratulations on your victory, Balis," she inclined her chin his way, "but I'm afraid we have a problem."

His jaw rippled as he clenched his teeth. "A problem?"

"Sidelle and Eurok are gone."

Frigid panic swept in as I moved to his side. "What do you mean, gone?"

"You must be Mira." She studied me with a knowing gaze and a faint, sorrowful smile. "You really are her spitting image."

"So I've heard."

"Come, we should speak more privately. Follow me."

The witch led us through the festival, where crowds congratulated Balis on his victory. He did his best to ignore them. He dashed inside the witch's wagon as soon as we arrived, and I followed suit. With a swift motion, he pulled the door shut.

The wagon was small, but somehow larger than I expected after seeing the exterior. Lavender hung from the ceiling. A rustic wood stove stood against the wall, its surface gleaming under the warm glow. Atop it rested a matching cauldron, bubbling with a fragrant concoction of spices and herbs, filling the space with an enticing aroma. It was cozy and carried all the charm I came to expect in these druid homes. I settled in, waiting for an explanation of the witch's proclamation.

Saura dropped the hood of her lilac cloak, allowing the full length of her blonde waves to cascade over her shoulders. "I happened to step outside for a pipe before the games ended, when I spotted Eurok on his way down the hill, carrying Sidelle."

"She fainted," I explained.

"That was no faint. She was seeing—of that, I'm certain."

I glanced at Balis, and he nodded.

"Someone stopped them," Saura said. "I didn't get a good look, but one second all three of them were there, and the next they were gone."

Worry knotted my stomach. "It was Atreus," I blurted. "He's using a manastone to travel from place to place. Before the games, he found me, asked me to meet him. He must've—" I paused, unsure how much truth to divulge. This was Sidelle's mother, the incredible witch who raised a child as her own, who taught Sidelle to be such a force. I could trust her. "He must have seen me wield."

"It seems he means to lure you to him," she offered.

I nodded in agreement. "Can you help us find them?"

"Few possess the ability to walk the veil, child. There's no way to tell where he took them." Her eyes trailed over me as if sizing me up. "Only the veil can show you."

"I can't do that."

Balis arched a brow. "You've done it before."

"Yeah, once. I don't know *how* I did it, though."

"Twice," he said.

My irritated bemusement was likely written all over my face.

He lowered to my ear. "I think veiling is exactly what you did in there." He jerked his chin in the arena's direction.

I swallowed hard, trying to recall the process of what I did to save Balis. All I remembered was an eruption of chest-caving fear and my urge to stop Mallack from harming him. My vision had snapped like a rubber band, then I stood there, holding Mallack's dripping heart in my hands. Just the same as the night I killed the poacher.

"It's all about intention, girl," Saura mused, "all mana is."

"So what am I supposed to do? I don't trust myself to veil on purpose and not fuck it up."

"That I *can* help with," she said, an eerie smile on her red-painted lips.

CHAPTER THIRTY-SIX

BALIS

S aura gifted two small vials of Diablerie elixir to Mira, the same concoction used to save my life in the Dogu village. She gripped them in her delicate ivory hands, her nose wrinkling in the way it always did when she was unsure.

"So, what? I just drink it?" she asked.

"Traditionally, yes," Saura purred. "But if you'd like, you could take it rect—"

"No—drinking's fine." She cut the sarcastic remark short.

A smile tugged at my lips, unable to contain my amusement. Mira caught the subtle curve of my smirk and fixed me with her sharp ruby gaze. That's all it took—I longed to touch her, to bridge the gap between us. Her fierce, resilient spirit drew me in like a song—an intoxicating melody I couldn't free myself of.

"What exactly am I supposed to do when I get there?" she asked.

"The elixir will only ensure that your mana does not fail in conjuring the veil. It will do nothing in aiding your pursuit," Saura warned.

"Right." Mira counted off on her fingers. "Get there. Find Sidelle and Eurok. Don't get killed."

My mana reared in response, despite its heavy use today. *Never.*

"Once you find them," Saura continued, "drink the second vial and veil the three of you to Oakrend."

"Four." I stepped to her side. "I'm going with you."

The witch pursed her lips and flicked her sapphire eyes to me with one of those knowing expressions these witches seemed to have.

"Don't you have to be here?" Mira asked. "You've only just won the games. Won't someone notice your absence?"

Most likely, they already have.

"Never again, remember?" I was resolute, unwavering in my stance, and nothing would sway me from it.

When she nodded, a subtle relaxation eased the stiffness in her shoulders. My venomous little princess wanted me there, even if she wouldn't admit it. She preferred solitude 'til she met me—alone was how she survived. Despite my anger at her stealing my warrior's death and thwarting the gods' plans, I understood the fear that drove her reaction.

She popped the top off the vial and placed it against the perfect bow of her lips, but instead of drinking, she pulled it away and replaced the cork.

"Can we talk first?" she asked.

The smoky rasp of her tone was almost enough to bring me to my knees. I was still reeling from having her back in my arms after missing her for so long.

Saura leveled us with an impatient glance, then clicked her tongue against her teeth. "I'll give you two a moment." She stepped outside.

I turned to her and placed my hands on her arms, gently tracing my thumbs over her smooth satin skin. "What is it?"

"I don't know, I just..."

It was no secret she struggled with expressing emotions other than anger. Seeing her try to find the words now was like watching someone attempt to keep the silken sands of the black calms from escaping a tight fist. The more frustrated she became, the quicker her words slipped away.

She loosed a sigh, starting again. "Last night, after we danced, you said you couldn't understand what was worth giving up your chance to be commander before, but that you get it now. I realize you care for me but–"

"You wanna know what I meant?" A gentle smile danced on my lips.

She nodded.

I took a deep, slow breath, recalling the hours before I met her. "Eurok shared some intriguing advice with me before I set off to find you. He said, 'If I'm right about this, your whole world is about to change.' At the time, I didn't recognize what he meant. I assumed he was referring to the war. After meeting you, though, after our night at the Star Hewn—I started to see things from a different perspective."

That was a half-truth. I realized she'd be my undoing the moment she pointed that dagger between my ribs, and my cock hardened for her for the first time. Gods, how I wanted to take her right then and there. But later, when her flawless body floated in those star-flecked waters, I *knew* she was mine—and I hers.

"What did he mean, if not that?" Her deep, quizzical eyes asked me to lay it all bare for her.

"I believe, somehow, he sensed you'd be *my* Sidelle."

Her breath hitched. "How could he know that?"

I dropped my voice. "His exact words were, 'Balis, don't fuck her. If you end up falling for that girl, you'll never be a warrior for the druid army—you'll be hers alone.'"

Her pouty lips parted, and I traced the soft skin along her jaw with the back of my finger. My eyes tracked the touch as I swept it down her exquisite neck to her collarbone. Her body was a portrait of every one of my temptations—as if she were made to drive me mad. My own personal hell both near her and away from her.

I dropped my forehead to hers. "Little did he realize, it required far less than that."

The corner of her mouth twitched, and I craved to lean down and taste it.

"You, princess, have been my undoing every one of my convictions from the very start. I would give up everything for you. Every dream I've ever had, every aspiration of who I thought I'd become, pales in comparison to who I want to be for you—who you make me want to be."

A shallow breath escaped her lungs, and the intoxicating scent of jasmine and tangerine washed over me.

"You are venomous, strong, and protective. From now on, I will forever be the one to protect *you*. That is my promise."

She paused, steeling herself under my gaze. She cared for me. Maybe not love, but something stirred in her at my words. I saw it, felt it through the brushing of our powers. Still, my declaration hadn't shaken all the fight from her.

"And if I object?"

I chuckled. "You won't get rid of me that easily, princess."

Her rare, bright smile beamed up at me, and she lifted herself on her toes to claim my mouth.

CHAPTER THIRTY-SEVEN

SIDELLE

Deep nothingness expanded before me. I peered at my gown, billowing in periwinkle waves within a shallow pool of water at my bare feet. Had I been barefooted this whole time?

No.

No—the games. Mira. She used her mana somehow. I was sure she emptied her core before we left. But the memory of her trembling hands clutching Mallack's still-beating heart said differently. And that crack in Annorah's manastone—I hadn't imagined that, just like I wasn't imagining this.

I absorbed the vast expanse of darkness, where my presence served as the sole source of light, as if a spotlight cast upon me from above. This realm was a creation of my own, a sanctuary I once frequented to commune with my god. A place between the veil from which he spoke, and my mind.

But why? Why would he do this now? No. I can't be here.

"Erezos?" I walked on precarious ground with my tone. "Erezos, I have to get back."

I spun as if I'd find an exit somewhere behind me, but the same endless nothing mocked me from every direction.

"Show yourself to me. What do you want?" I called up, waiting for a response.

Overlapping chatter filled my ears, and my reality flickered. I stood before an unfamiliar smiling family sitting around a dining table. Mira caught my eye, sitting on the far end. My lips parted to call to her, but I stopped. *No.* That wasn't her.

Realization hit me like a charging drakboar. This was the woman Mira spoke of from her dreams. Over the past nine months, we delved into multiple discussions about these recurring visions that haunted her since childhood, pondering their significance.

I surmised they held more significance than mere night-musings, yet I never fully comprehended their meaning. My world swiveled on its axis as the pieces fell together. While similar to Mira, she was completely identical to Annorah, right down to that familiar tender warmth that radiated from her. Mira couldn't possibly dream of that without having any prior knowledge of her, which meant this was no ordinary dream. This was another variant—one where humans exist. *Aethier's realm.*

Fear, sharp and cold, consumed me, and my breath quickened like there wasn't enough air reaching my lungs. Panic loomed over me, and I had the overwhelming urge to sit. Was my heart in a vise?

"Get me out of here! I need to get back!"

"Calm yourself, little one." A disembodied voice emanated from the ether.

Or at least I thought it was. I tucked my head into my arms and clenched my eyes shut. An ease pressed against my mind, and I relaxed into it, letting it soothe me like a cool breeze over flushed cheeks. *Erezos.* Relief cascaded through my being.

"We haven't got much time." His ancient tone held an edge of urgency.

"Erezos, we have *no* time. You need to let me go. Mira, she needs me." My anxiety flared again, like brittle kindling.

"We only have now. Calm yourself."

While my heart threatened to beat out of my chest, his essence demanded obedience. I was used to Erezos pulling me to the edges of my mind to speak. Though I'd always been met with any number of comforts. Warm fires, beautiful scenery, or even fine dining—which was as strange of an experience as it sounds—to enjoy food you hadn't physically eaten.

To experience his power in this manner was overwhelming. He plunged me into a void of endless darkness within my mind, leaving me without escape, only to thrust me into an unfamiliar realm with no explanation. Yet, I sensed a purpose in his energy, a necessity that drove his actions.

"Why did you show me that?"

"You saw where your girl must go."

His voice changed, became corporeal, and a cool hand brushed along my back. I raised my head and beheld our surroundings—a vast expanse of nothingness. Above me, the piercing gaze of my deity locked onto me with ecliptic intensity.

I took his outstretched palm and let him help me stand. His skin was smooth, cool—dark gray, like thick smoke. His face was handsome with sharp, hard features, and I could feel him all around me even as my eyes were pinned on the form in front of me. However, the contours of his druid form appeared to waver like fluttering leaves in a breeze, a testament to his dwindling strength as he fought to maintain his foothold in my mind's limited space.

"Did Atreus do this to you? Where are you? How can I help you?"

"Limit your questions, little one, and listen."

My jaw snapped shut.

"Your girl is not who you think she is. But she is so very important."

My instinct was to insist he was wrong. I witnessed Mira wield mana. She looked like Annorah. I could draw on any number of the facts I'd been so sure of only minutes ago, but I let them lie languidly on my tongue. In the presence of my god, his words held undeniable authority. He was my creator, and what he said was infallible fact. Despite my unwavering faith, the weight of his revelation struck me. *I'd been wrong all along.*

His dark voice, like obsidian and crisp nights, swept through me. "We twelve were bestowed with a variant to safeguard and govern in reverence to the Empress."

I nodded, showing him I knew the history.

"When the Drak breached the veil and invaded, we were still in our infancy as a variant. We needed help to defend it from the scourge. So I sent for Aethier's aid."

"And the first humans crossed into this variant," I offered.

"He came to my aid, but in doing so, caused irreparable damage to the veil between our variants. It grew thin, weak. It's only a matter of time before it ceases to exist and they merge into one."

My hand flew to my mouth, but I remained silent.

"I created Annorah, a human capable of wielding my power, as an effort to foster peace between our kinds in preparation for that merge, and offered her to the human king as an answer to his prayers. But Aethier took my gift to humanity, my version of his creation, as an insult. He created Atreus and gave him eternal life to mock me. Then he left, leaving his precious humans behind. Or so I thought."

"I don't understand. What does any of this have to do with Mira if she isn't Annorah's reincarnation?"

"She is the key to bringing me and Annorah home."

My brows pinched, and my mouth dried, as if full of sand. *Bring Annorah home?* I stared, more questions swarming than we had time to answer.

"Twenty-three years ago, Aethier tricked me," he went on. "He stole my power, locked it away in a manastone—but not before I created one last thing."

"Mira."

He nodded.

"But then, where are you now?" I asked.

"Nature has its ways of restoring balance." A triumphant gleam emitted from his swirling gaze. "A reincarnation can only be born where I exist."

"The mystery woman—she's the reincarnation?" The pieces came crashing together. "You're in Aethier's variant?"

Erezos nodded.

My legs weakened, and I had the sudden urge to sit again. "If you've been there for the last two decades, what's changed? Why are you able to speak to me now?"

"I was hoping you could answer that for me."

I chewed on my lip, thinking as quickly as I could, fearful of his form dissipating before my eyes. But I shook my head, struggling to make it make sense. But something else came to mind. "Erezos, nine hundred and twenty-three years ago, you warned us that Atreus was plotting against Annorah, but we found out he was also hoarding–"

"The ash. I took care of it. You need not worry about that."

My mouth fell open to speak, but no words came.

He sensed my hesitation. "What is it? Speak Sidelle."

"The ash still exists. Atreus is making weapons with it."

The dark complexion of my god's skin blanched. "Then things are much worse than I feared."

"What is it?" I asked. "Maybe I could figure out how to combat it if–"

"Forget that for now. My only hope of returning to my full strength lies in ensuring your girl makes it into Aethier's variant unnoticed. She must find the true reincarnation, and together, free me from my prison. Do you understand?"

I nodded. Then a thought came to life like a lit candle. "Erezos, Aethier gave your manastone to Atreus. Most likely for safekeeping, but what if he's started to use it without Aethier's knowledge?"

"He would be very foolish to do so." Erezos' eyes swirled with the color of starlight, and a knowing smile spread across his dark features. "The released mana would find its way back to me, even from across variants. It would explain why I'm able to generate enough focus for this small feat."

"But that means if we gain control of that manastone, then we can release you. You could return, regain your control."

His features were a fragmented mess of wisps as parts of him floated free from this space. But I could still read the hesitancy in his ancient, handsome face.

"I'm afraid that's not how it works, little one."

My hope shattered. "What do you mean?"

"When Aethier forced my essence into that manastone, he sealed my weakened self away. My only certainty is that I reside somewhere within his variant and that my prison was secured using mana stolen long before the creation of the manastone."

My eyes widened. *By the mountain.* "The missing chest. Are you saying all this time Aethier has been in possession of Annorah's power?"

"It seems that way. Ironic, isn't it? Shut away with my own gifted's mana." He shook his head. "Which is why only the reincarnated can free me. For now, leave the foolish human king to his mistakes. Let him continue to use my power. Focus on sending the girl through the veil.

His haunting tone sent a chill through me, filling my heart with apprehension at the idea of sending Mira into the unknown variants alone.

"I'll go with her."

"No." His voice grew distant, his energy fading quickly. "Only human blood can pass through the veil into Aethier's variant. A being such as yourself will call too much unwanted attention. I created Annorah in the image of my brother's humans to encourage peace between our people and avoid war." A wry smile lifted a corner of the last visible remains of his face. "But I created Mira to end one."

My eyes shot open. The cool stone floor was clammy against my face. I pushed myself upright, pressing my palm to my aching head, and hissed in pain. It came away covered in warm, sticky blood. Confusion and dizzy memories addled my brain, and I struggled to make sense of my surroundings. *The royal castle's great hall?*

Wait. No—this wasn't Bronne. This was... new. *The Vylandrian castle?*

Metal shackles clanged behind me, and I turned toward the sound. An aching terror enveloped every inch of me. Eurok, shackled to the floor, beaten into a massive, bruised bloody heap, surrounded by guards. Fury surged in my chest, and I flew to my feet.

"Eurok!" My voice cracked, breaking with my panic.

"Ah, you're awake."

That deep, familiar tenor sent a cold shiver down my spine. *Atreus.* I spun on my heel, facing him.

"You lied to me, Sidelle."

415

He clicked his tongue, shaking his finger like I was nothing more than a petulant child.

I reached inside myself to brace my power—it was gone. "What did you do?" I seethed through my teeth.

"I'm guessing you've noticed your mana's missing."

My answering glare only coaxed a dreadful smile from his lips.

"Thanks to some clever masonry work," he mused, "I've been able to secure my new home from your kind."

The ash?

I surveyed the chamber's smooth polished walls. We *were* in Vylandria. He found a way to infuse it into the very stones used to construct his fortress. A flicker of amusement danced in his cold brown eyes as he observed the dawning comprehension on my face.

"I know this must be difficult for you, but your kind's treachery knows no bounds, pet. I had to take precautions."

My skin crawled at his calm, placating tone.

"What are you talking about?"

"Don't play stupid with me," he snapped, then stormed up to me, stopping a breath's width away. "The girl," he whispered.

"I don't—"

Atreus' hand collided with my face, the sting spreading like fire along my cheek. I tasted blood as my lip split, the metallic tang of copper flooding my mouth.

"Where is she?"

"I don't know." The words ground through my clenched teeth. "Why don't you use your precious manastone to find her yourself?"

His eyes narrowed, and his head quirked. "Come again?"

I reeled, then spat in the king's face. Blood and saliva spattered his tan skin. "You heard me."

In utter disgust, he wiped my defiance from his cheek and reared his arm back, preparing to strike. *Let him try to break me.* I was done playing as his precious pet.

"Stop. Don't fucking touch her." The words rasped from Eurok's lips, etched with fury that mirrored my own.

I edged away from Atreus, pivoting to join Eurok, but the guards shifted, warning me to stay put. If I possessed my full strength, I would have gutted each of them without thought.

The king snared my wrist, wrenching my arm behind my back. His painful hold locked me in place, forcing me to watch my bonded, bleeding, and crumpled on the floor. My mate. The male I devoted myself to but starved of true companionship. Tears stung my eyes, and I pressed my lips together, fighting to remain composed.

"Please," I whispered. Gut-wrenching guilt wracked me to my very core. "Please, just let him go."

Atreus' ears perked at my whimper. "It didn't have to be this way, you know. You lied to me. You told me the girl possessed no mana. I welcomed her into my chambers." He jerked my shoulder, spinning me to face him. "You tried to make a fool out of me."

"Why are you doing this, Atreus?" Tears stung my eyes as I begged him, my agony evident in every word. "Annorah? The poaching? This castle? *Why?* What is it you want?"

"You stupid, foolish witch. It's not what Atreus wants that's important."

My brows pinched in confusion as his hard, rough hand snatched my chin, forcing my stare to his. A ring of gold encircled the oaken shade of his irises. I paled—then shoved him back, freeing myself from his grip. My steps fumbled as I backed away, gaze pinned to those eyes as shock coursed through my veins, iced and acidic.

It all made sense. The other energy Saura sensed in the journal. Atreus' sudden indignance for Annorah all those years ago. And the—the falcon.

"Aethier."

"Ah, now we're getting somewhere," he chided with feigned approval. "I thought you'd never catch on."

My knees wobbled as if the earth trembled beneath my feet. "This whole time?"

"Well, not the whole time." He waved off my question in a flippant gesture of mocking indifference. "The details aren't that important. Let's just say, ol' Atreus here has proved to be quite the gracious host when I have need of him."

"You won't get away with this."

"Lies, lies, lies." He loosed a wicked fit of laughter. "You wielders can't help yourselves, can you? Where is the girl, Sidelle?"

"I don't know where she is." Gratitude flooded me for that fleeting respite, a sliver of solace. He didn't have her yet.

"She sat beside you during the games, yet when I found you and your prized beast here, she was absent." He came close, towering over me with a glint of lethal intent simmering across his features, breath hot on my face. "*Where is she?*"

A wavering, shaky smile tore the tender skin on my bleeding lip. "You can't trace her energy, can you? That's how she's gone unnoticed for so long."

His jaw clenched as I breathed an airy indignant laugh.

"Well, I can't help you. And even if I could—you can go fuck yourself."

"Hmm." He straightened, pacing away from me. "Pity. I suppose, since *you* have nothing more to offer me."

He gestured to the guards encircling Eurok. One stooped down, snaring a fistful of his hair, yanking him to his feet. Atreus—*Aethier*—stepped before him.

"What say you? Hmm?"

Eurok's mouth formed a hard line, refusing to drop his glare as he fought against the guard's hold in a feral burst of ferocity. I cringed at the sight of his wounds, so deep they stained his light sage shirt a dark, oozing black. Soon, his strength waned, chest heaving in large, furious breaths through his nose.

"Do you think yourself a worthy opponent, even without your mana, Captain Dramagan?"

The way he spat Eurok's name enraged me.

"Hand me a sword, and we'll see who's worthy," Eurok seethed through his teeth, blood, and spit spattering the floor.

I stood there, fists clenched at my sides, completely useless.

"Gods do not *battle* filthy vermin," Aethier hissed. "We exterminate it."

My knees collided with hard stone, my legs giving out as the hiss of metal echoed off the walls. I watched the god, promenading as a king, shove his blade through Eurok's heaving chest—then yank it free in a single, smooth motion. The guards let go, and Eurok dropped to Aethier's feet.

My screams tore from my throat, but I heard nothing. Hot tears burned streaks down my face as rough hands dug into my flesh, dragging me from Eurok's lifeless body as I kicked and clawed for release.

Every ounce of my strength strained, desperate to break free. With a final, violent twist, I ripped from their grasp. Something tore in my shoulder, but I didn't care. I scrambled to his side, a frantic sob choking my throat. With trembling hands, I clutched his wide shoulders to heal him—nothing. My mana was locked within like a sealed sarcophagus.

"Eurok!" My voice shattered in a discordant chorus of sobs and screams. A deluge of tears blurred my vision as the room swayed. "Eurok, please! *Please!*"

I crawled around his limp body and pulled his listless head into my lap, stroking his cheeks with my thumbs. "Please, come back." My heart shattered as his once vibrant golden gaze grew distant, hollow—unseeing. "I'm so sorry. Gods, I'm so, so sorry."

I wished I could undo all of it. Every belief, every mistake—I wanted to trade my fate for his. He believed in me, risked everything for me, and in return, I shut him out, withheld what he deserved.

I led him to his death.

CHAPTER THIRTY-EIGHT

SIDELLE

Aethier left me kneeling in Eurok's blood, weeping over his chest. I prayed to the gods to trade places with him. He didn't deserve this. He deserved none of the pain I caused him.

Now all I had was a gaping vacancy in my chest, as cold as his skin beneath my fingertips. All of that sweet, tender warmth that I spent too long craving from afar leached from his body. How could things have gone so wrong? What was left untouched of the world I loved?

Raising my gaze, dismay and fury consumed me. A fervent impulse drowned every thought—grab a weapon, eliminate as many wretched humans as I could. But the corridor was silent. Aethier abandoned me to my despair, voiding all hope of escape. What horrors awaited me if I tried to run?

A faint commotion echoed from somewhere below the hall. I didn't care. There was nothing left. I couldn't leave Eurok's side, leave him in this horrible place.

My groggy, aching thoughts drifted to the moments before I woke, when Erezos held me in that inner recess of mind to convey his message. His words were lost now—their significance diminished.

A clamor of metal and shrieks echoed from the corridors, followed by the slicing squelch of flesh and steel. Body trembling, I stood and pulled my blood-soaked gown away from my legs. I waited with bated breath as the voices dwindled, one by one.

A pause of silence stretched—and the oak doors blasted open. Mira stepped inside with Balis tight on her heels. Both bore the marks of battle, their breaths labored. Their gazes fixed on the captain's lifeless body.

"No!"

Mira's scream shattered the quiet. She sprinted toward him, reigniting the sinking despair that enveloped me.

"Heal him!" she demanded. "Sidelle!"

My throat bobbled as I swallowed against the tightness and shook my head. "I can't."

Balis dropped beside his captain. His agonizing pain matched my own as his palm settled on Eurok's still chest.

"Aethier–" A tight sob cut me short.

Their deploring stares found my face, drawn and pale in silent question.

I forced the words, every syllable foreign and strained. "Aethier has assumed control over Atreus."

Mira wiped large tears from her eyes with the heel of her palm and grasped my wrist to pull me from the room. "There's no time. We need to get out of here."

Balis didn't move, kneeling in his silent grief.

"I can't leave him." I sank to my knees again. "And I can't help you fight our way out."

A reluctant tug snared my chest to stay, to remain by his side for eternity. *My gods, how far I've fallen.* The sole person I trusted, my safety net, was dead. Because of *me.*

The clang of shifting metal echoed as reinforcements rushed down the hall. They'd kill us all. Erezos' message came too late.

She dropped beside me, hands settled on my shoulders. "We don't have to fight. I can veil."

She nodded to Balis, who returned the gesture and lifted Eurok's large body into his arms.

Mira retrieved a small vial from her pocket and held it out. "See? Saura gave me this. It's how we got here."

I gawked at the shimmering tincture within. Diablerie elixir—distilled from the ash of the Diablerie tree. One of maybe half a dozen left in the entire world. My mother, who guarded this sacred liquid for centuries, ensured Mira would find us.

I stood in a flash, Erezos' words filling my mind. *You saw where your girl must go.* I stared at the vial as she pressed it to her lips. "Stop!"

She did, brows furrowed tight with concern.

"Listen to me. You have to leave us."

"What?" Her eyes narrowed, searching mine with incredulous disbelief, her voice a sharp hiss. "We can all get home."

"Balis, leave Eurok." Despite the anguish it caused me, it was our only chance.

The warrior's hesitant, heartbroken gaze fell upon his captain's lifeless form braced in his arms.

"Sidelle!"

Mira's fingers dug into my shoulders, giving a firm shake. I ignored her, my hard stare fixed on Balis until he relented. He lowered his lifelong mentor to the floor, features twisted with depthless grief, tears wetting his cheeks.

"Sidelle!" Mira demanded my attention again. "We have to go. Now, before Atreus gets back."

"No, you have to find her." My shaking, bloody hand settled on her cheek. "Erezos found his way to me. He gave me a message."

She stared, a rebuttal on the edge of her tongue.

"Mira—I was wrong. You are not Annorah. You have never been anything other than you. A fierce, strong, radiant young woman capable of incredible things. I'm so very sorry if I ever made you feel like that wasn't enough."

Tears spilled from those garnet eyes. "Sidelle, it's okay."

I shook my head. "It's not. My girl, you have everything you've ever needed inside of you. You can do this. You are all that stands in his way."

She straightened herself from my grasp and swiped at the wet streaks staining her cheeks. "What are you saying?"

"You must go. Use the elixir to cross the veil and find the girl from your dreams. She's the answer."

Mira and Balis shared a long, silent look before she returned her gaze to me. She was resilient, admirable, and determined. She could do this.

I gave a firm nod. "The girl will lead you to where Aethier hid Erezos and Annorah's power. You'll need to find your own way back, but I'll do everything I can from here to–"

"I'll go with her," Balis said.

"You can't. She has to cross alone or risk drawing too much attention."

His panicked stare flew between me and Mira, knowing exactly what held her back any longer. His hold found my wrist. "I'll get her out."

"I'm so sorry," she whispered to him, voice tight.

He wrapped a hand around the nape of her neck, pulling her toward him. "This kingdom deserves you, remember? You can do this. But you come back to me. Do you hear me?"

She nodded, the motion jerky and frantic.

He pressed one long kiss to her forehead. "I love you."

Then he stood, pulling me with him while he drew his ax.

A small sob escaped her throat, but she reined it in and wiped her eyes again.

"The elixir won't let you fail," I said.

I wished I had more time to prepare her for whatever lay ahead. Eurok was right all along. I underestimated her, held her hostage to a comparison she was never meant for. She wasn't

Annorah—but she was strong, a fighter. I could see it in her eyes, even through the despair gripping her like a vise.

She acknowledged my easement with another quick nod, stronger than before. A rumble stirred the castle, rattling the floors beneath our feet. A storm of armed soldiers charged in, weapons drawn.

Balis pushed me behind his large frame, putting himself between me and their threat. Two men made a hasty dash for Mira, and my heart leapt to my throat. Before they reached her, she swallowed the shimmering liquid in one gulp, lifted a veil with a smooth sweep of her wrist, and stepped through.

ACKNOWLEDGEMENTS

I, honestly, can't believe I'm sitting here writing the acknowledgments for my very first novel. I, also, can think of no one better to start with than Ashton. Ashton, thank you so much for reaching out to me that day at our kid's soccer practice. I truly don't know that I would have ever had the courage to strike out on this adventure without you by my side every step of the way. You have given this book more love and attention than I ever could have expected and you are an incredible friend.

I would like to thank my PA and friend April, you have been an endless support system and I am glad that we found each other. You have the capability and know-how of a true professional and you deserve all the credit for any misconception there might be that I have my shit together. Thank you.

To the Yappers, you have helped me on this journey in inexplicable ways. Your support means everything to me and I'm so happy to have found you all. Katie, not only did you provide a safe place for so many, but it was, truly, fate that you decided to take a chance and sign up to beta read for me. Whether or not you ever pick up another beta read again, it's been a privilege and you're stuck with me for good. Thank you to my entire team of Beta readers and ARC readers, your time and dedication is priceless to me.

To Nicole, for being such a huge support for not only me but many indie authors. Thank you for introducing me to Erynn.

This novel would not have been as strong as it is without you looking out like you did. To my editor Erynn, I am endlessly grateful that you stepped in and put so much love and attention into this book, regardless of the tight deadline we were working within. You are such a talented force, a joy to work with, and I can't wait to work with you again on book two.

Finally, Nick, thank you for being the most patient and supportive husband you could be throughout this process. Thank you for all the hours you allowed me to pour into this book, for keeping me fed when I'd forget to feed myself, and for keeping the house afloat during writing and editing. Thank you for listening to all my wild ramblings while I was plotting, even when you had absolutely no idea what I was talking about or where it was going. You are my rock and a little piece of you is in each of these characters I created and have come to love. I love you more than any number of words could explain.

About the Author

When Kacie Ross isn't writing about fantasy worlds and bantering characters, she can be found basking in the sun with a book in her hand or taking part in one of her many other interests, such as playing video games, camping, crocheting, or gardening.

Kacie grew up in small-town Michigan and now lives in middle Tennessee with her husband of fifteen years, their two sons, and their spoiled cats.

Born to Rule is Kacie's debut novel and she hopes this will be the start of a wonderful career as a novelist where she can read, write, and share all the wonderful books with her book besties. Kacie can be found on Tiktok and Instagram @kacieross_author

https://linktr.ee/kaciemross
https://www.authorkacieross.com/

ABOUT THE AUTHOR

When Katie Rose isn't writing about fantasy worlds and balancing characters, she can be found basking in the sun with a book in her hand or taking part in one of her many other interests, such as playing video games, camping, crocheting, or gardening.

Katie grew up in small-town Michigan and now lives in mid-... Tennessee with her husband of fifteen years, their two sons and their spoiled cats.

Born to Rule IS Katie's debut novel and she hopes this will be the start of a wonderful career as a novelist where she can read, write, and share all the wonderful books with her book besties. Katie can be found on TikTok and Instagram @katierose.author.

https://linktr.ee/katierose...
https://www.authorkatierose.com/

Milton Keynes UK
Ingram Content Group UK Ltd.
UKHW041304050624
443376UK00003BA/4/J